D0427512

PRAISE FOR

The Year of Endless Sorrows

"A terrifically zany and grim page-turner by a storyteller whose senses are wide open to the lurid glory of the city. Rapp . . . shows a keen eye for satirical detail and a strong ear for bohemian banter."

—**DAVID COTE,** *Time Out New York*

"A novel that should be read . . . Rapp's writing . . . is wickedly funny and ordinary scenes are infused with the surreal . . . He is a very powerful writer." —**SUSAN MELINDE DUNLAP,** *Feminist Review*

"Rapp . . . has been compared to Douglas Coupland and Rick Moody, but the writer he most resembles is Nick Hornby, though with more linguistic inventiveness . . . [His] prose is energetic."

—**MICHAEL LEONE,** *The Plain Dealer* (Cleveland)

"This new novel is a testament to Rapp's ability to write in any genre with the same lucid talent. His sentences are long, detailed, and strangely poetic. The prose is clever, funny, and homesick-sad, often in alternating sentences. It is as if Garrison Keillor's Wobegon Boy, John Tollefson, finds himself in the real New York City, with all its misfortune and melancholy but without the silly sentiment—because when this book is emotional, it is heartbreakingly true."

—**STEPHEN MORROW,** *Library Journal*

"An ultra-vivid, excruciatingly precise bildungsroman, a time capsule of a young man's evolution—a young man not entirely unlike Rapp himself. It is a story of roommates and family and desire and the quest for meaning and definition while all the time bumping up against the ennui that is perhaps just the sensation of being alive and the daily absurd irony that is city life." —**A. M. HOMES**

ADAM RAPP

The Year of Endless Sorrows

ADAM RAPP is an award-winning playwright and novelist. Most recently, his young adult novel *Under the Wolf, Under the Dog* was a Finalist for the Los Angeles Times Book Prize and received the Schneider Award from the American Library Association. His play *Red Light Winter*, which he directed at Steppenwolf Theater, garnered Chicago's Joseph Jefferson Award for Best New Work and a Citation from the American Theatre Critics Association, later transferred to New York for a commercial Off-Broadway run, and was named a finalist for the Pulitzer Prize. He is also the writer and director of the films *Winter Passing*, an Official Selection of the 2005 Toronto Film Festival, and *Blackbird*, which he adapted from his stage play. He lives in New York City.

The
Year of
Endless
Sorrows

The Year of Endless Sorrows

ADAM RAPP

FARRAR, STRAUS AND GIROUX • NEW YORK

FARRAR, STRAUS AND GIROUX
18 West 18th Street, New York 10011

Printed in the United States of America
First edition, 2007

Library of Congress Cataloging-in-Publication Data
Rapp, Adam.
  The year of endless sorrows / Adam Rapp. —1st ed.
  p. cm.
  ISBN-13: 978-0-374-29343-7 (pbk. : alk. paper)
  ISBN-10: 0-374-29343-0 (pbk. : alk. paper)
  1. Fiction—Authorship—Fiction. I. Title.

  PS3568.A6278Y43   2007
  813'.54—dc22

                                    2006015879

Designed by Gretchen Achilles

www.fsgbooks.com

P1

FOR WALT

Part One

Towns

WE'RE FROM THE MIDWEST MOSTLY. We're from Lawrence and Davenport and Dubuque. We're from Kankakee and Oswego. We're from Griffith and Joliet and Mechanicsville. Platteville and Green Bay. And Altoona and DeKalb and Clinton.

We're from Joplin.

The words of the cities themselves conjure certain smells and songs. Eddie Rabbitt's "I Love a Rainy Night" and lightly buttered yams. Thirty-Eight Special's "Hold On Loosely" and the Fourth of July gunpowder drifting below the exploding purple girandoles at the speedway. Anything by Joan Jett and the sulfuric fetor of the steel mill. Stevie Nicks and the rancid, spoiled-fruit stench of the oil refinery.

Or they simply evoke the feeling of a rotisserie fork turning hotly in our stomachs.

Most of us grew up in well-heated, well-lit homes. Gabled houses with garages cleaner than grocery stores. Flagstone-laid, pineconespotted paths leading to the front porches. The black spruce bending toward the neighbor's Tudor like it's keeping a secret. A licorice-red swing set in the backyard. A small ceramic man with a Scottish hunting cap protecting the mailbox—stoic yet somehow noble.

Our towns have water towers. Great steel orbs and graffiti-smeared globes and flying saucers on stilts. An enormous iron aspirin tablet next to the high school. The Tin Man's inverted head with MAQUOKETA SUCKS in running spray paint.

ELKHART in all of its unscathed, civic propriety.

ELVON looming over several acres of unharvested wheat.

Some of us were raised on farms. We can talk about silos and combines and grain elevators and detasseling corn. We can talk about counting the beans and the fever itch of hay and how it can drive you to rinsing your arms with gasoline. We can talk about cow tipping and crop blight. We can talk about the pig doctor and how he swallows the viscous, worm-like, bluish membrane after castrating the hogs—how he plucks it out of the mutilated genitals with a pair of homemade forceps.

We can talk about highway driving and the solemn, solitary beauty of a fodder-filled silo receding in the distance; how it's there for miles and then suddenly disappears as if the horizon imagined it and then reclaimed the thought with a god-like whimsy.

We can talk about fishing.

A few of us grew up in trailer parks, and our rooms had lots of paneling. Infinite, impeccably grooved, pecky-pecan paneling. Long sheets of synthetic wood that we could drive a thumbtack through. Paneling that splinters and warps and chafes with a kind of sinister eczema. Paneling that is made to be unmade.

We are long-boned because we were well fed. We ate potatoes and barbecued beef. We drank milk by the gallon—two percent, with the royal blue cap. Some drank it whole.

Most of us have skin the color of a paper towel lightly dabbed in Wesson Oil.

In the winter, with the aluminum taste of frigid air in our lungs, we can look out over tractor-scarred fields of frozen mud and know exactly who we are.

We were raised with tornado culture and good dental histories.

When we came to New York we left behind pets. We left behind coaches and priests. We left behind friends who went to work for insurance companies. We left behind half-dead cars and VCRs and laminated baseball-card collections. We left behind two-lane, mercilessly straight, never-ending highways.

We didn't say goodbye to everybody. We couldn't possibly have said goodbye to everybody.

Some of us had never eaten garlic. To most of us, basil sounded like a prison town in southern Illinois. Ginger was that girl on *Gilligan's Island*. Some of us thought cappuccino was a *cup of chino*.

Most of us have some variation of blond in our hair. We're spaniel blonds. Rhubarb blonds. Cottonbox blonds. Peach blonds. We're soda-cracker blonds and bloodhoney blonds. We're Formica blonds.

We generally look like the people walking through the Indianapolis Metropolitan Airport on any given day.

We are Catholics and Protestants and Lutherans and Presbyterians and Episcopalians and we can recite the prayers by rote. Even though most of us have vehemently denounced our faith and want to be (or pretend that we want to be) Atheists and Marxists and Anarchists, we can still recite the prayers.

And at a pretty good clip, too.

The sofas back in our Midwestern homes smell like beef Wellington and forest rain and something not unlike the woodchip mulch used to bed gerbil terrariums.

We smell things on the street that remind us of the old pullout back in Manteno. The love seat back there in Fond du Lac. A vinyl record on the Second Avenue sidewalk between Fifth and Sixth can do it to us. A feather duster from the vintage shop on First between Ninth and Tenth can do it to us. The inside of an old bowler hat—something from an altogether different time—even that can do it to us.

Certain things always seem to send us back.

We have strong middle names like David and Matthew and Esther. Biblical names that followed us from the fishfly fogs of the Mississippi and the broken-bottle shores of Lake Michigan and the muddy, mosquito-misted banks of the Des Plaines River; middle names that quietly pursue us like private, invisible birds.

We have snapshots of our dogs. That's Waldo with a ten-gallon hat. This one here in the hand-knitted sweater is King, and look at the subtle pattern change there, see?

We keep our driver's licenses hidden from each other. We seal them in boxes and stash them in breast pockets. We slide them into old books and deny our late-eighties hairdos. That wasn't my hair. That wasn't my Ogilvie Home Perm.

Vocations

MOST OF US WORK in book publishing. We work with lots of older white men who roll up their sleeves and wear seamless khakis. Jacks and Bobs and Todds. And Blakes and Steves. Men who find a kind of sacred nonchalance in the way they wear their ties.

And we work with lots of white women, too. Maryannes and Kathies and Pamelas.

We make sixteen or seventeen thousand dollars a year, but we tell each other eighteen or nineteen. If we make twenty, that's way too much. We survive on slices of pizza and ramen noodles. We eat a lot of flaccid hot dogs straight off the wagon.

We walk to work or, rather, we bound there like power hikers, in great vaulting astronaut strides. We voom to work. We alakazzam to the office in half-ruined shoes.

A few of us walk through the precarnival hours of St. Mark's, bank across Astor Place, and cut diagonally through Washington Square Park, where as early as eight-thirty a.m. the Rastas are out whispering smoke into your ear.

Smoke and sess.

It's good, Mon.

The pigeons have schizophrenia.

The office is fluorescently lit and the carpet incredibly gray and each employee has a cubicle that smells not unlike the inside of a bowling shoe. At some point, they (the folks from human resources) employed the term *workstation* as a replacement for *cubicle*. We call the big ones bull pens and the little ones Skinner boxes.

The housekeepers shellac the Skinner boxes to the point of a high, almost vinyl gloss. The sad chemical smell of lemon cleaning fluids creeps into our clothes and settles in our hair and a hint of it can be detected if we inhale deeply into the center of our pillows.

The iteration of Skinner boxes has a museum-like quality.

We are exhibits.

Earnest Midwesterner Comes to New York.

Will work for anything.

He's in publicity. She's in editorial. He tracks the bellwether titles and circulates an in-house report. She collates book briefs and talks to agents on the phone. He's in mass market promotion but wants her job in telephone sales. She's in production and walks around with these cardboard-pizza-box-bottom-type things called "mechanicals."

Co-op advertising and *review easels* are terms we use. *Back order* and *print run* and *flap copy* are terms we use.

Tenth Between
First and A

IT WAS THE SUMMER OF REVOLT. Tompkins Square Park was a tattered, monster-movie militia of homeless men, crack whores, wild dogs, and dirty children wielding, throwing, and clinging to broomsticks, wainscoting, particleboard, refrigerator boxes, and other nameless excavated objects that constituted the hides, spines, and native totems of their beleaguered, waterlogged shantytown.

The fringes of the park were abundant with leather-wrapped rockers, tattooed superfreaks, wispy-headed, heavy-eyed heroin addicts, cops in riot gear, and articulate white kids from Connecticut with prolific facial hair and pierced eyelids, huddling Indian-style in ass-to-cement Kumbaya clusters and feigning poverty with their fashionably distressed Army fatigues and well-fed, thoroughly inoculated dogs.

After all, everyone had to revolt against something.

Feick and I lucked into a fourth-floor, four-bedroom walk-up in a prewar tenement on the south side of East Tenth Street between First Avenue and Avenue A. The apartment had been abandoned by Tokyo Stunt Pussy, a late-eighties speed-metal band whose big selling point was their penchant for gastrointestinal pyrotechnics. According to a fellow tenant who had been to one of their shows, at some sacred flashpoint during their set each member of the band would push his pants down to his ankles, waddle over to an infernal-looking blowtorch, and fart with exceptional volume into the blue eye of the flame while hammering power chords.

Before I arrived in New York, Feick lived in the apartment directly below. Unit three was a funhouse-floored one-bedroom, complete with an elfin, nook-style kitchen and a bathroom so small and cramped we nearly performed inadvertent auto-fellatio each time our hams met the porcelain.

Feick paid $900 a month, which he could surprisingly afford, as he was cast in a play at Lincoln Center that had been running for twenty-seven consecutive months. His solvency amazed me because Feick is almost four years my junior and at the time he was an eighteen-year-old NYU dropout who couldn't even grow a beard and was prone to letting his laundry proliferate in the corner of his closet like some autogenous science-fiction monster.

In the play he spoke only four lines and his stage time barely totaled six minutes, but after taxes he still cleared over seven hundred bucks a week. That comes out to roughly $875 an hour.

His greatest moment came midway through the second act. It was a rant at his mother that was punctuated by the line "You're just a pathetic extension of my eighth-grade personality festival!"

I saw the show from the booth four times, and that line always brought the house down. Feick could somehow get underneath the words. He could unlock their hidden meanings and release the purple demon music. With that phrase he became a five-and-a-half-second avatar of parental hatred, an exploding prep-school brat stomping on the Tiffany sofa. The words came out in a slathering, tomato-faced lava. They seemed to erupt straight from his gums and incisors, volleying off the walls of the Vivian Beaumont Theater. The rant had audience members wiggling out of their seats with glee.

People would stop Feick on the street and beg him to do the line. They'd say, "Oh, man, you gotta do the line!" and he would heartily oblige, sending them across the avenue in chortling hysterics, limbs a-jiggle.

At the time, my best friend from college, Glenwood Ledbetter, was teaching English in Yamato, a small town in Kyushu on the southernmost island of Japan. He was bopping smartass seventh-graders on the head (apparently an Eastern scholastic custom wholeheartedly supported by the faculty), taking biweekly judo classes, and expending an inordinate amount of energy blocking his penis from the view of his colleagues while urinating in the men's bathroom.

And he was singing a lot of karaoke in the evenings.

Prior to going to Japan, he had held E.S.L. teaching posts in Kromeriz, a small agricultural hamlet in Czechoslovakia where they drink stout for breakfast; the north of Italy; Morocco; a fishing town in the former U.S.S.R.; and Las Vegas, New Mexico.

I had received a letter from him while I was completing my last semester of school at a small, vaguely accredited liberal-arts institution in Dubuque, Iowa. Glenwood said he was moving to New York to pursue a job in publishing and wanted to know if there was any room in Feick's apartment.

After the show at Lincoln Center finally closed, despite the one-line myth he had developed and farmed in the streets, Feick couldn't get another acting gig for a while and money was tight. He started collecting unemployment, and I was making almost nothing at my publishing job. I was making zilch, in fact.

And I had the wardrobe to prove it.

Upon his arrival in New York, Glenwood immediately landed a job in the art department of a prominent children's book publisher, and both Feick and I badly needed the economics of the three-way rent split.

It worked out fine. Feick got the bedroom and Glenwood and I shared the common area. I slept on a green canvas Marine cot I purchased at an Army/Navy wholesaler on Canal Street. Glenwood spent his nights on a small, corrugated camping pad that rolled up for convenient storage.

We got used to the close quarters. There was the perpetual, unpleasant odor of our breath communally filling the room; the random, slightly yellowed pair of underwear emerging here and there; the treble clefs, ampersands, and other strange cursive-like multitudes of pubic hair lining the rim of the toilet; and the sporadic, percussive score of our farts trumpeting out in the four a.m. gloom.

We needed a bigger space.

We had heard rumors about our building being run by fraudulent management, smoky, voice-filled rumors that hung in the sodium light of our stairwell.

We basically heard that the tenants in the other five units were rent striking, so we followed suit. Our building organized.

We held meetings. A girl who often wore welding goggles took notes (unit two). A fiftyish woman with orange hair and her thumbless husband (a fishing accident) made coffee (unit one). A guy with a beard that was so vast it seemed to be a continuation of his eyebrows, and who purportedly landed a book contract to write the unauthorized biography of Jack Kerouac's lost lover—that guy—brought doughnuts (unit three). Feick, Glenwood and I brought paper plates (unit five).

Which no one used.

Ever.

So we just kept bringing them.

Whoever lived in unit four never showed up. Once I pressed my ear to the door of unit four and heard what I imagined to be the sound of someone playing a ukulele.

The meetings lasted anywhere from four minutes to three hours, depending on how things were going between the fiftyish woman with orange hair and her thumbless husband. Basically, if they were tanked the meeting would turn into a public performance of domestic brutality and the other tenants would sit around, voyeuristically watching, waving away the vodka vapors. If they were sober they could be expected to be well-behaved, pristinely mannered, articulate, hand-holding cohabitants. That usually meant we would get out early.

We met Sundays, on the roof. If it rained we'd call it off.

The meetings started out productively. We talked about city tenant support and squatter's rights and keeping rent money in escrow. We discussed changing the locks on the front door and opening an account with Con Ed to pay for the electricity in the common area. We talked about getting a lawyer.

The guy with the beard talked about a cricket bat he kept above his door that had human hair embedded in the grain.

On average, the girl with the welding goggles drank nine or ten cups of coffee per meeting and tried to be subtle about it.

Nothing happened. Ever. No lawyer. No escrow account. No new locks on the front door. Eventually, Con Ed shut off the electricity in the common area, so coming home at any hour of the evening turned into a kind of silent horror film. We anticipated rapists and stranglers and giant kidnappers on every landing. Our blood pressure skyrocketed to dangerous levels upon rounding each corner. Stepping safely into the apartment carried with it a historical, emotional weight. The light in our own units became wistfully precious.

Because of increasing frustration with regard to our lack of space (Glenwood eventually threw his back out going to the bathroom), when the apartment above us opened up (unit five; unit four was next door to us) we made our move.

We spent four hundred bucks changing the locks.

Besides my Marine cot and Glenwood's camping pad, we didn't have much to haul except for a few suitcases, a table, two chairs, a small desk, some dishes, a futon mattress, my three boxes of books, and Feick's color TV.

The abandoned apartment had a third-world quality about it. Tokyo Stunt Pussy promotional posters had been shellacked to the walls. Their choice of logo art was the crust edge of a ham sandwich on Wonder bread standing on end in all of its vertical, overtly vaginal simplicity, the ham particularly wilted and accompanied by a slim and equally wilted lettuce leaf.

**Tokyo Stunt Pussy
CBGB's
June 15th**

The band obviously believed in mold.

And sludge.

And sump.

Left behind was a vast assortment of decaying liquor bottles and beer cans and juice jars whose contents were a septic swamp of ashes and urine, the nameless gobs of things that form when organic matter is left to rot and fester. Enormous toupees of dust clusters floated about omnipotently, as if marshaling some lost and barren landscape where only things toxic and foul-smelling are allowed to exist.

A can of axle grease stuffed with cigarette butts and candy wrappers and voided lighters.

Blackened banana peels contorting with rigor mortis.

Strange, arcane graffiti wending evilly over the walls in demonic, vinelike hieroglyphics.

There were Swedish porno magazines plastered to the floor and guitar picks glued to the ceiling. Homemade aluminum-foil marijuana pipes glinted in the smoke-stained corners like forlorn Christmas ornaments. On the brick façade, smears of what appeared to be some kind of frightening, excremental paste. Resting in the fireplace was a fire-engine red, family-size Igloo cooler. When Glenwood pried it open he was greeted by a small lump of human feces.

And, of course, there were roaches.

These roaches were athletically endowed and exoskeletally gifted. These were roaches out of a comic book.

Glenwood thought he saw one actually fly, roughly four feet off the floor. Or maybe it just jumped that high.

We crushed the roaches with books and stomped on them with shoes. We sprinted at them and kicked them across the room. We used fire and water. We employed Glenwood's Windmere blow dryer with its accompanying Conair Euro Style Diffuser (to maximize the circumference of the roasting area; why he owned this beauty aid is anybody's guess). We tried to intimidate them with hard-core bully tactics. We shouted at them. Glenwood punched one; he literally boxed a roach. After a while, we even got down on our hands and knees and tried to *talk* them out of our apartment.

We tried to bargain with roaches.

After we swept and mopped and disinfected and scrubbed, Glenwood and I bought two cans of primer and two cans of flat white paint. We double-primed the walls and added the two coats of flat paint, and we could *still* see the graffiti coming through, like radioactive ghosts trying to escape.

At the end of the day Glenwood went down to the hardware store on First Avenue and bought a jumbo-size container of boric acid, with which we sprinkled the corners of the rooms and lined the baseboards. Then he shouted at the roaches as if they were truant children hiding under porches.

"You will not get away with this!" he announced.

It took a while, but the roaches eventually retreated.

Tokyo Stunt Pussy
Roaches in the Turds
In stores now

The Loach

THERE WERE FOUR OF US living there at first: me; Glenwood; my brother, Feick; and a very thin, half-Jewish, half-Italian guy from Queens: Burton Loach.

Who asked us to refer to him as "the Loach."

Perhaps he knew then that his tenure in the apartment would be the stuff of legends, that his self-imposed third person title was a harbinger, or omen, of things to come. He must have known from the moment he entered our lives that he would be the subject of vitriolic backbiting, roommate conspiracy, and domestic anathema.

About twelve minutes after we'd lined the baseboards with boric acid, the Loach walked—or rather *capered*—into the apartment and bravely announced that he had already staked his squatter's claim, but that he would be interested in "talking to us" about "sharing the space." We didn't say anything and just sort of stood there with the dregs of a thousand Tokyo Stunt Pussy nights tainting our arms. The Loach stood there as well, in a shiny, dolphin-colored windbreaker reminiscent of those worn by the Oak Ridge Boys. He was much smaller than Glenwood and I. He was even smaller than Feick. I think after a moment he finally realized the Darwinist implications of this and broke the silence by offering to go halves on the paint and saying he knew a thing or two about gardening (which would turn out to be a gross personal fiction).

Feick, Glenwood, and I exchanged suspicious glances, glances so suspicious they had a kind of architecture: our brows sprained into crumpled furrows, our mouths open just enough for a penny to slip through, our eyes pop-pop-popping white, our lips involuntarily curling, eventually receding into our gums with geriatric palsy.

And then we nodded.

Naively.

Dumbfounded.

Almost completely in sync, as though choreographed.

The Loach claimed to be a stand-up comedian and was constantly handing out harsh neon flyers to anyone and everyone who blew through the door. "Call me the Loach," he'd say (or command), and he'd hand them a flyer.

"Call me the Loach and come see my show!"

If they didn't accept immediately, he would slap the flyers into their chests in the manner of the bargain barkers on lower Broadway.

The Loach was perpetually unemployed, except during the one holiday season he spent with us, when he could be found dressed as a grim-looking toy soldier standing at rest in front of the entrance to FAO Schwarz. I think he actually spent a day working at a trade show in the Jacob Javits Center, too, this time clad as one of the Keebler Elves.

Outside of his carnival barker entreaties, his vocabulary was at first rigorously limited to the words *Yo, Hey, Huh, You, Uh-huh, No, Yeah*, and the two-word, tri-syllable expression *Forget it.*

The first full sentence the Loach used in the apartment came in the form of a question, which he asked rather aggressively. I was in the living room turpentining the brick façade framing the fireplace.

It went something like this:

He said, "Hey."

I responded, ". . . *Hey?*"

"You."

"*You?*"

"Yeah."

"*Hey you?*"

"Uh-huh."

"What?"

"Was Wolfman Jack ever on *CHiPS?*"

"Who?"

"Wolfman Jack."

"What about him?"

"Was he ever on *CHiPS*?"

"What?"

"Forget it."

On separate occasions the Loach also posed the same question to Feick and Glenwood, and eventually to everyone who walked through the door. Over time he would shape the query, adding an inflection here, removing one there, vocally eliminating the question mark, varying the punctuation, miming quotation marks with bunny-eared fingers, shading in elements of irony now and then, and even going for high melodrama.

The Loach never attended a single tenants' meeting. He always said he was too busy working on his material.

Too steeped in the honing and crafting.

Too swamped with his comic genius.

In reality he was too busy sleeping and farting and eating our food.

The Loach lived on the sofa, which was a navy blue swaybacked East Village warhorse that Glenwood and I had found on Twelfth Street. We carried/dropped/fumbled it three blocks, dragged it up the four flights of crooked, entirely too steep—not to mention slippery—stairs, and collapsed on top of it in the center of the living room as if we had portaged a ruined canoe through a Canadian ice storm.

That very same evening, while we were out, the Loach pushed it up against the far wall of the living room and made it his own.

The Loach lived on the sofa the way one might live in a van or a refrigerator box. He never left it. Or if he did, we still thought he was there, his wizened, entirely too hairy body flaring on the retina like some prehistoric mosquito floating in a lump of amber. We couldn't conjure the image of the sofa without the Loach. There was a life-raft quality to his occupancy, a sense that one could throw stones at him and he wouldn't dodge them for fear of falling off the cushions and mysteriously drowning. His system of nourishment had to have been somehow autotrophic, as we rarely saw him actually ingest anything, although various random items excavated from between the couch cushions could occasionally be seen dangling from his mouth. These objects included, but were not limited to, toothpicks, loose change, wadded Kleenex, triple-A batteries, magazine blow-in cards, an unbreakable comb, a small order form for Sea-Monkeys, and a shoelace.

Once in a while we would see him walk down the hallway and enter the bathroom, which was one of those everyday miracles, a thing one might witness in hospital parking lots—like watching someone who is confined to a wheelchair sliding into a car on a plywood board, pulling the wheelchair into the backseat, and then driving away, unaided.

It was like watching a cocker spaniel ice-skating.

The Loach and the sofa and his tattered *Wolverine* comic book and his jar of gefilte fish, funereally preserved in a viscous, medicinal-smelling gelatin like pickled, sun-bleached dog turds. This was the portrait of the Loach. This became an image we could depend on, like a red sun at the end of the day or the glassy surface of a lake in summer. He usually sat in some variation of the lotus position, with his genitals either partly or fully exposed (depending on his choice or lack of underwear); his crotch a necrotic, scorched, perennial zoysia of pubic confusion; his spindly legs evoking thoughts of plutonium-colored flies, aphids, lice, fleas, and various other nocturnal vermin crawling in and out of anatomical crevices.

And his hair was all over the place. Great tufts of at once thinning and prolific black-brown hair. The hair of a veteran fishmonger. The kind of putrescent, steely clusterclumps that are exhumed from the bathtub drain after the family dog's been bathed.

And the Loach's personal hygiene can be summed up by citing the fact that he carried his soap and shampoo to the shower in a tattered and wrinkled brown paper bag.

We suspected that he dried himself with the bag.

Was he some itinerant urban preacher who had graced our lives in the guise of an idiotic, unsanitary, anorectic con man? A Shakespearean fool whose reversal of identity would eventually bestow joy or great democratic wisdom, or even Krugerrands of gold?

No.

Not in the least bit.

He was simply the Loach.

And outside of a homicide, very little could be done to change this constant in our lives.

The Loach had a running argument with his sister over the phone that the word *when* was a verb.

One day, out of curiosity, Glenwood looked up *loach* in the dictionary and found that it is a real word of unknown origin, that it is actually a small, edible freshwater fish of the family Cobitidae.

Golden Gophers

ON MAY 17, 1991, I was hired by a guy named Van Von Donnelly at a world-renowned book publishing company in a building with smoked windows on the corner of Hudson and Houston.

The sky was an endless chromium blue. My hair was gelled and sculpted, my face thrice shaved and burning with menthol, my fingernails trimmed.

It was my first interview in New York and I approached it the way college freshmen approach the registrar's office after the drop-a-class deadline: with humiliating, lurching desperation.

I was willing to beg. I was willing to talk about god. I was willing to cry or sing or read aloud from the side of a cereal box.

I had $400 rent to come up with. The only money I had brought with me to New York was the $250 I'd won in a short-story contest (I submitted a strange, vaguely science-fiction piece about a horse with a human arm, luminously titled "The Horse with the Human Arm").

I had already spent $25 on gas to get to New York (I bummed a ride off a guy I barely knew from my college, a drama major who, in order to stay awake, sang the entire song list from *Brigadoon* in a booming tenor; he also wore a treacherous-looking pair of fireproof jackboots stolen from an experimental production of *Equus*, in which he'd played the title role), and another $20 on a ridiculous red tie that had what appeared to be sea urchins exploding across the lower cravat. I purchased the neckwear at a men's clothing store on Eighth Street. The guy who sold it to me called it a "power tie."

"For your price range, this is my best power tie," he said. "It's a powerful tie, my friend."

I was empowered.

So I was down to about $200 and rent was due in less than two weeks—not to mention my need to eat.

As a graduation gift my mom gave me a black leather portfolio. Other college friends got cars with vanity plates or Brooks Brothers suits or trips to Europe. Some got thousands of dollars in cash. One of my fellow English majors received a complete leather-bound collection of Shakespeare's plays, a fifteenth-century matchlock harquebus gun, and cows.

He actually got two hundred head of cattle.

I got a black leather portfolio from my mother, my Uncle Brad's restored No. 3 Underwood typewriter, and a cheap electroplated gold watch from my father that was evidently a gift he'd received from his bank for opening a savings account. Stenciled in cursive on the watch face was "Electrolux"—literally with quotation marks around it, which I assumed meant that the watch was somehow theoretical.

I had gone to college on a basketball scholarship. These were the kinds of graduation gifts one got, if one got any at all, when attending college on scholarship.

Inside the portfolio I neatly arranged the few short stories and poems I'd published while in school, mostly in unknown, suspicious-looking journals, two of which were pressed by my college. I also included a feature article I'd written while serving as a student stringer for the *Des Moines Register*. The portfolio wasn't too spectacular but it looked mildly professional (despite altogether clashing with my bad slacks and ridiculous, squeezed-into wingtips), and I liked the feel of the leather handle in my grasp, that feeling of having something to show. It also added interview dimension. It somehow made things more "dynamic." Most of all, I liked its size, which was roughly that of the menu placard at your local hamburger stand.

It was entirely too large.

Van Von Donnelly hardly looked me in the eye when he came to gather me from the sofa in human resources. Instead, he chose my left shoulder as his focal point. Maybe I'd trapped him with my power tie? Lured him in to the point where he couldn't pull himself from the hypnotic force field that my exploding sea urchins were generating?

We shook hands awkwardly. I'm about six-three and have a pretty big hand, so with larger men there's always the potential for one of those gladiator-like clamp battles—let's see who can crush whose bones, who can turn whose hand to jelly. There was no need to get things off to a competitive start. Van was pretty short and tubby, and his hand was soft and small, so I tried to go easy.

After the lukewarm, slightly rubbery greeting—my first official New York handshake (the guy from human resources had dislocated his shoulder in a bowling accident and was wearing an enormous torso sling; he offered his elbow as consolation)—I noticed that my right hand was too wet. Soggy, even. I had fishbowl hand. I had Mississippi Madness hand. Shaking my hand was probably like holding a dead trout.

I wiped my palm on my bad slacks and followed Van back to his office.

The thrum of corporate machinery. The surf of Freon-cooled air sliding through hidden ducts. The light that reminded me of science class. The way people watched me as I went by, their eyes crawling on my clothes like invisible beetles. The blue-green computer screens throbbing on otherwise colorless faces. Thumbtacked jokes pinned to the hides of cubicles. Celebrity headshots with Magic Markered mustaches. Liberace with a black tooth. Barry Manilow with an Afro and Terminator sunglasses.

When Van walked he waddled, and one of his shoes squeaked like two balloons humping. He didn't appear to have a neck and his ass was roughly the size and shape of a large library clock.

For some reason, I imagined him wearing body-length Winnie the Pooh pajamas (the kind with the little vinyl footies). He had a toddler's body. He was a forty-year-old Pooh-bear. I imagined him curled under the Christmas tree, loving the paint off of a fire engine.

When we reached his office he directed me to the chair across from his desk and closed the door behind him. I sat with my portfolio on my lap. Then I put the portfolio on the floor. Then I set it back on my lap and steepled my hands.

His desk was a vast and cluttered survey of American office culture. There were clips and pens and fasteners. Mechanical pencils and grease markers. "In" boxes and "Out" boxes and "To-do" boxes and slatted trays for multisize, multicolor file folders. There were disposable coffee cups and VAN vanity mugs. There were pinwheels and pipe cleaners. There was a Swiss Army knife, with the scissors extracted. There was a terrific, spaghetti-like blob of rubber bands exploding from a cigar box. There were a small hotpot and a rotary clock and an automatic flip calendar. There were doodads and thingamajigs. There was a mini atomizer, droning like faint moth wings. There were Post-its and peel-downs and message twisties. There was a silver sleeve of Pop-Tarts on top of a half-eaten apple. There were toys: a box of crayons, a Rubik's cube, a little rubber porcupine ball that looked like one of the sea urchins exploding on my tie.

There was a portrait of his wife, who was the spitting image of Mrs. Shoom, my fourth-grade language arts teacher.

Under his desk was a pair of what appeared to be sealskin mukluks. In a flash I pictured him wearing them, the laces tied up to his calves—Van Von Donnelly scooting around his office like an inebriated, hypothermic Eskimo.

Mounted on the wall and looming over the desk like a serrated thought frozen in three-dimensional hyperrealism was an enormous circular saw on which were painted a dozen or so stoic-looking mallards flying in a perfect arrowhead over a black wall of arthritic trees. The saw gave the office the air of the Big Ten Conference; it was all northern Wisconsin or Michigan bear country. There were ancient, petrified elk hiding in those trees. It was almost Canadian, this saw.

Van sat down rather explosively and went right to work. He grabbed my résumé off the top of an altogether anonymous pile and started scoring it with a pencil—literally scoring it, like a sheet of music or a baseball program. He scrawled and doodled. He scribbled and glyphed.

He flimflammed. He sketched arrows and circled text. He graphed asymptotes and calculated derivatives. At one point I thought I saw him actually drawing a pie chart.

The atomizer whirred.

Mrs. Shoom stared back at me.

The Sheetrocked walls took on a vinyl quality.

When Van was finished he set down the pencil and kind of squirmed a bit, as if those Pooh-bear pajamas were getting a little itchy.

"So you played basketball in college?" he asked.

I answered, "Yes, sir."

He had a Midwestern accent and I liked that. College was "callidge."

"What position?"

"Um. Guard."

"Point guard or shooting guard?"

"Kind of a three, actually."

"A three, what's a three?"

"Well, I played guard mostly, but I usually guarded a forward on defense. And I jumped center. But sometimes I, like, guarded their point guard, too. I was kind of a sort of a, well, swingman. It all depended."

"A swingman."

"Yes." I replied. "I swung."

"Huh."

My answer had obviously been entirely too long. And was *swung* the correct participle?

"Dunk?" he asked.

I said, "Excuse me?"

I thought he was referring to his Pop-Tart; perhaps he was offering a bite after it had been bathed in one of his twelve coffee mugs.

"Canya *dunk*?" he asked again. "Are you a rim rattler?"

I replied, "Oh. Um. Yeah."

"What are you, six-four, six-five?"

"They listed me at six-three."

"Lanky Franky."

For some reason I felt the need to say, "My foot's still growing."

He rocked in his chair. "What size you got?" he asked with genuine curiosity.

"Fourteen," I answered.

"Wowzers," he responded. "Here come the U-boats."

Yes, he said "Wowzers."

"Draw the shutters," he added. "Somebody blow the battle horn."

I had no idea what he was talking about. It took everything in my power to not look at Mrs. Shoom.

Then there was a brief pause that reminded me of reactions to the haircut I'd received on my twelfth birthday, the morning before I left for a summer camp in Burlington, Wisconsin. After dismounting from the barber's throne, I'd opened my eyes and looked in the mirror to discover what could have been a malnourished spider monkey.

It was the circular saw that brought me back to Van Von Donnelly's office. For the slightest moment I was afraid it would come spinning off the wall and attack me.

Van Von Donnelly broke the silence, saying, "Vertical?"

I said, "Excuse me?"

"How high do you jump?" he asked, clearing things up.

"Oh, vertical leap. Well, It's been measured at around forty. Depends on the day. Depends on the floor."

"Jeezus Christmas," he marveled.

"You can jump higher off a wood floor," I explained.

Then he said, "That's like black."

"Like black?"

"Yeah, like a black guy."

I thought this was a test, some sort of corporate sleight of hand he'd sneaked in to assess racism in the interviewee. A booby trap for the college boy. A little flyby P.I. So I didn't respond. I just sat there, still trying not to look at Mrs. Shoom.

"Where you living?" he asked, shifting in his chair again.

I mirrored his shift and said, "Tenth Street."

"East side?"

"Between First and A."

"I used to live on Tenth between First and Second, closer to Second. Right next to the Jew Deli. You know the Jew Deli?" he asked.

This was clearly another test.

I replied with "Um, no."

"Where I met my wife," he explained. "Seventy-four and seventy-five," he offered, rather bemused by his own history. "Days of hogbacks and dandelions. You shoulda seen *my* hair."

I was suddenly seized with waves of paranoia about my hair. The way he stressed *my*. The inflection. Waves and swells and breakers of paranoia. My hair was too long. It was too short. By virtue of some acute neurological schism I had affected a cowlick. I had dandruff. I was suddenly that shiny guy in the infomercial.

Then there was a lull. I could hear the clock. Or it could hear me. The things on his desk were gaining omnipotence.

"You like the Gophers?" he finally asked.

I replied, "The Gophers?"

"Minnesota Golden Gophers. You a Gopher Guy?"

"Oh, *the Gophers*. Sure, I like them."

"They struggle these days."

"Yeah."

"It's like watching housewives churning butter on the prairie."

I wasn't sure what this meant, either.

He added, "They slouch on D. Can't find the ball."

"Boy, I know it," I said, agreeing with his fifties TV lingo.

"They need a back court," he continued. "Got some New York kid coming in, though. Black kid from the Bronx. Dooji or Fuji somethin' or other. Blacker than a leather sofa. Blue-black, they call it, don't they?"

I thought for a moment. Blue-black. Hmmm.

I answered, "Sure."

"They need some darker ballplayers," he said, offering more alumni solutions. "The darker the better."

"They'll turn it around," I said. It was all I could come up with.

Then there was another lull. This one was historical; I could hear the lights buzzing and the rubber bands rubber banding and the tips of Van's shoelaces ticking underneath the desk.

I was waiting for the English-major questions, questions about the twentieth-century American novel (post 1950s, preferably) and why I wanted to work in book publishing. I was waiting for him to ask me to open my portfolio.

He started rocking back and forth in his chair and said, "So, you can really dunk?"

"I can, yes," I answered.

Van rocked for a full minute and then he came to a dead rest, sat there for a moment, and picked (or excavated) something from the unseen regions of his tongue—a hair or a piece of lint. Something vaguely corduroy. He made a face like heavy dental work was being performed on him and rolled the item he'd extracted between his fingers. After a quick, myopic study he flicked the tongue fluff over his shoulder and put both palms on his cluttered desk, slapping them down like a poker player might.

"You got anything to say? Any questions or suchlike?" he asked.

I thought.

"'Cause you can ask them now. That's the general poop here in the hole."

There was a word you could hang on to: *Poop*. And *in the hole*. You could take the last half of that sentence with you just about anywhere.

"Well," I said, "I really really really really want this job, Mr. Van Donnelly. I'll work hard. I'll work really really hard. I really will."

I really said all of that. I used *really* four times in a row, and then added three more just to drive it home. *They'll turn it around* twice, and *really* four times. Not to mention the double use of *work* in consecutive third-grade-level sentences.

And I had a portfolio of poems in my lap.

"Von Donnelly," he said suddenly. "It's Von."

"Mr. *Von* Donnelly," I corrected myself. "Sorry."

"No sweat. Anything else?"

"Um, what would I, like, be, like, doing here?"

"Hardcover sales. Forecasts. Call reports. Bellwether stats. NCR maintenance. Biweekly mailings. Star summaries and point-of-sale logs. Lots of phone calls to the reps. Heavy loads of voicemail trenching and tag-faxing. Mostly numbers and glory stories. Think you can handle that?" he asked.

Of course I could. "Yes, sir."

"Plus," he added, "you gotta help violate the storage room."

"Violate?"

"I mean ventilate. You interested?"

Was I interested? I sure was. "Absolutely!"

"That's it, then."

That's how he said, it, too; like he was an insurance agent who'd just finished appraising the accordioned grill on my Buick.

That's.

It.

Then.

Van got up. I got up. He waddled out and down the hall. I followed him like a dopey younger brother. Then he stopped suddenly and turned around.

"You can find your way out okay, can't ya?" he asked.

I said, "Oh, sure."

"Coffee finally caught up with me," he explained conspiratorially, almost whispering. "Gotta hit the can."

Then he turned—just like that—and waddled in the opposite direction; amid the din of fax machines and computer whir; between a pair of stranded mail gurneys; down the gleaming hall soaked with that fluorescent science light, until he rounded a corner, fully awaddle now, almost preternaturally so, and disappeared.

I found my way out.

It took me twelve or thirteen minutes, but I found my way out.

I walked north on Varick instead of east on Houston. I ambled aimlessly, like a toy that is wound up and abandoned. I strolled past restaurants and delis and check-cashing places, by locksmiths and electronics stores and bakeries and wig shops.

Somehow Varick turned into Seventh Avenue.

I tried to not-look at the tops of buildings and not-stare at the flyby faces that seemed to morph into the same concrete-hard, smileless urban countenance. It was dizzying. After twenty minutes or so I felt like I had goldfish swimming in my head.

I sat in a small park and fell dead asleep.

I had a dream about the interview. It was an almost exact replica of what had happened in Van Von Donelly's office: the same handshake at the sofa in human resources; the same cluttered desk; that circular saw with the migrating mallards; the Eskimo boots. It was a virtual prototype, except for the fact that the only word that kept flying out of my mouth was *poop*. Nothing else. Only *poop*.

When I woke up, my geographical confusion snowballed to a kind of postnap, early summer hypothermia. I grew even more disoriented and wound up in a Greek diner in the west Thirties.

I called the apartment and Feick answered the phone.

I said, "Feick."

He said, "Hey, bro."

"I'm lost."

"Where are you?"

"Thirty-fourth and Ninth," I answered.

"Damn."

"Feick, I'm wearing a power tie."

Feick told me how to catch the N and the R at Broadway and Thirty-fourth.

"Oh, yeah," Feick said, "some dude called."

"What dude?" I asked.

"I don't know. He said he was from human recesses."

"Human recesses?"

"I mean -sources."

"Human resources, like from a *job* human resources?" I asked.

"Yeah," Feick explained, his voice dull and lifeless. "He said you got it?"

"It?" I asked. "*What* it?"

"The job, man. You gotta call him back. He said something about wanting to make an offer."

Feick gave me the number and I felt a small explosion of luck flowering somewhere in my intestines.

I hung up and called human resources. I caught the man with the torso sling just as he was heading out the door.

He made an offer of $16,800.

I accepted immediately, right there on the phone.

I accepted, foolishly.

A little goofily, even.

There were things flying around inside me I couldn't name, and that made any salary sound okay. Give him a shovel and pay him in lumps of coal and laundry tokens—he don't care! Pay him with food stamps.

Slap him in the face and kick him in the slacks!

I would start the following morning in hardcover sales, reporting directly to Van Von Donnelly on the third floor. Nine o'clock sharp. Then there would be an hour-long orientation, when I would fill out tax forms and learn about health insurance and the 401(k) plan.

Back at the apartment I called my mother to share the news.

"I got a job," I told her.

"Well, that was fast," she replied, more surprised than pleased, perhaps even slightly annoyed. "Doing what exactly?"

I explained what little I knew about my new position as Van Von Donnelly's assistant. I told her about being a liaison to the sales reps and coordinating mailings and things like that.

"Is that a real name?" she asked of my new boss.

"What—Van? Of course. I mean, it's not like *Larry*, but it's a name."

"Is he a Negro or something?"

"No, mother, he's not a Negro. And by the way, using the word *Negro* nowadays is basically an egregious social pejorative."

"What are they planning on paying you? I hope it's at least twenty-five thousand dollars."

"It's not," I said. "But it's publishing. I'll be around books."

"Oh, you and your books."

Most mothers would be delighted for their son to be an avid reader. My mom just saw it as a romantic distraction from the pursuit of life's most important goals: a respectable house and a spouse (she loves the rhyming music of *house* and *spouse*) from good Roman Catholic stock, three or four kids, a two-car garage, and a front yard with quality landscaping.

"Are you getting benefits?" she asked.

"Medical, dental, the whole works. I'll even qualify for the four-oh-one-kay plan after six months."

"So tell me how much they're paying you."

"Sixteen-eight."

"Sixteen thousand eight hundred dollars?"

"No, sixteen thousand eight hundred rubles. Of course dollars."

"Well, that's paltry."

She pronounced *paltry* like *poultry*, which was a curious choice, as she spent her entire life in the northeastern sector of Iowa, where *paltry* is usually pronounced just as it should be.

"But I also get a gym membership," I lied. Oh, how my mother's disdain for poverty could elicit shame in her children.

"You're not going to make it for very long on a salary like that."

I said, "Thanks for the vote of confidence. Your faith in me is a life raft in croc-infested waters."

"Well, this whole notion of living out there is harebrained if you ask me."

"Haven't we done this enough?" I said.

And indeed we had. Round after round of the "New York Is Evil" game. From pimps to pushers to AIDS-infested crack warlocks, my mom's vision of the city was like *The Rocky Horror Picture Show* meets *The French Connection*, scored by the Village People. The night before I left she begged me to stay exactly nine times, all over the house. While I was in the shower. During my final WGN Cubs telecast (they were playing the Reds and getting killed, as usual). She shouted at me through closed doors and followed me up and down stairs. If I ran, she ran after me. If I faked left and went right she was on me like an all-pro cornerback. While I was packing the last of my socks and underwear she even went outside to plead with me through the screen of my bedroom window. And she cried in nine different ways, too—and very convincingly, I might add. It was the first time I saw where Feick got his acting talent.

Things got a little ugly when she tried to hide my Underwood typewriter, knowing I wouldn't leave without it. I eventually found it in a corner of the garage with one of my dad's dove-hunting coats folded over it.

"I won't be surprised if you're back home by Christmas," my mom added.

I almost hung up, but I didn't.

"Is Dad around?" I asked.

"He's down in the basement."

"Well, can you get him? I'd like to maybe share my news with someone who might actually give a damn."

"Don't you dare use that kind of language with me, mister."

I could almost see her pupils contracting down to little needlepoints.

"Just get him, will you?"

"He doesn't want to be disturbed."

"What's he doing?"

"He's doing what he always does down there. It's none of my business."

In the background I could hear the TV from the living room. *Wheel of Fortune* was playing. Pat Sajak was introducing the contestants and the audience was applauding. I imagined the sound of his voice sluicing by all the tidy, well-positioned, vaguely utilitarian items of the living room I grew up in: the beige carpeting and the brown leather hassock and the plaid reupholstered armchair in which my father smokes his Pall Malls and drinks his three fingers of Jim Beam every night and the ocher sofa with its plastic covering. I imagined Pat Sajak's voice reaching my mother's ear like a desperate song from a lover stranded at sea, because that's who Pat Sajak was to my mother—her lost, unattainable paramour whose compressed television voice was a kind of trumpeting analgesic to life's small disappointments. I think at some point my mom even started dressing and doing her hair for Pat. I could just imagine her honey-brown dye job, coiffed like a cinnamon roll on her head, and a new blouse from the Ann Taylor at the mall and her maroon stretch pants that matched just a hint of eye shadow.

"Look, honey," she said, finally breaking the silence, "I don't mean to be crass. I'm just concerned for you. Maybe there's a position at your new company that pays a little better."

"I have to start somewhere, Mom. It's one of the best publishing companies in the world."

"It's just that the idea of you and your brother being out there in that enormous city . . . Well, frankly it terrifies me."

"Mom, New York's not like some violent, low-budget rap video."

And then she was crying. Maybe it was the rap-music reference. Rappers terrified her. When my mom cries she sobs. I'm sure that this time it was equal parts the shame of being small and cruel and the genuine void that existed now that both Feick and I were gone. To be left alone in that house with a man who rarely spoke would be hard on anyone.

"Mom," I said. "Don't cry. Please . . ."

She was practically wailing.

"Nothing bad is going to happen."

"Just be careful, okay?"

"I promise I'll be careful."

"And take care of your little brother?"

"I will."

"I worry about him, too. He's so fair."

What his complexion had to do with anything is anyone's guess.

"Feick's doing great, Mom. He's in a hit play and he like walks around all by himself."

"Oh, that city's so dirty!"

"So is the parking lot at the Econo Foods."

"Oh, you . . ." she said.

She eventually calmed down, after I promised her that I would check the human resources job board on a daily basis for higher-paying positions. She sniffled and moaned and blew her nose several times.

We hung up a few minutes later.

Toward the end of our conversation I'm almost positive I could hear my father coming up from the basement. Besides his Pall Malls and nightly three fingers of Jim Beam, the one thing about him that was unmistakable was the sound of his footfalls slowly tromping across the living room after he'd been hiding from us in the basement for hours.

Names

WE WANTED TO UNNAME OURSELVES, to shed our Midwestern epithets and appellations. We longed for urban folklore, the jangle and jump-back of concrete street legend. We wanted Chilly Bonze and Two-Tone Phone. We wanted Terminator and Predator and Helicopter Herm. We wanted Jellyroll Joe. We wanted the names we read in Iceberg Slim novels and heard shouted out over the public address at the West Fourth Street summer Pro-Am.

We started with Feick, who requested a lot of animal names. He wanted Cooter, but Glenwood explained to him that it was too close to "Cootie," the infamous adolescent body louse. Then he wanted Jack Russell, but Glenwood and I agreed that it sounded too much like a regular name and wouldn't carry any distinction. He wanted Bull and Viper and Lemur.

He wanted Lungfish. He actually wanted to be called Lungfish.

Feick, while not being genetically albino, is probably the palest non-albino I know. In certain lights he is so supernaturally white that he looks almost un-white. When he's onstage, under the gels, his skin takes on a lunar quality. In the harsh fluorescence of the corner deli it acquires a slightly greenish, plant-like, solar hue. Under the single burning ninety-watt bulb hanging in the bathroom his pallor is a kind of bloodless, sandblasted bone. He can be a cadaver or a powdered hermit. He can be medical white, a listless geriatric in search of his wheelchair. He can be a walking biology lab, a dissection experiment thick with formaldehyde. On any given day he is a spook emanating from the argon nimbus of the thrift-store sign on First Avenue. He is both rubber and cement. Vinyl and bleached leather. Photosynthesis personified. He is white hot, blistering foxfire. At times it is something altogether blinding. He can be sun-blasted alabaster or fired limestone. He can be Alpine snow. There are long winter days when he is achingly vanilla. He is white at its highest saturation point of whiteness. He is a human reflector. If he were to lie next to you on the beach *you* would get tan. He is a science project gone horribly and irreversibly wrong.

And his hair, although technically blond, is basically white too, and lacks any recognizable texture, so it's often difficult to distinguish where his forehead stops and his slightly fish-hooked widow's peak begins. The camouflaged hairline gives him the illusion of bareheaded infancy. Feick is the only human being I know who is at once bald and bushy-headed.

At first we called him Milk.

But milk is a dairy product, and dairy wasn't cutting it for Feick, who skulked around the apartment with genuinely hurt feelings. So we tried Whitey for a while, but that was entirely too obvious and he argued that it was somehow racist, so we were back to Feick, which is his real, baptized name.

Glenwood started calling me Homunculus because, despite my being six-three and rather wiry, he insisted that my muscles were so symmetrically structured that if I were shrunk to the size of a doll I would suffer no bad proportional effects—that I would resemble some sort of well-adjusted, athletically endowed Lilliputian.

It was too strange and awkward an observation to argue with, and the name stuck.

It was later shortened to Homon.

Glenwood spoke openly about how he envied the geometrical arrangement of my stomach muscles. I explained to him that it was from years of playing basketball, that the sport demands more from one's center of gravity than perhaps any other. He called it my "eight-pack" and said it with equal parts admiration and flouting bitterness. He started referring to it as altogether separate from the rest of me, at times asking me how it was doing.

"How's the eight-pack?" he would inquire on his way to the bathroom.

Once he referred to each muscle independently. I came home from work and from the depths of his room he proclaimed, "Tell one, two, three, five, and seven that there's a bunch of office-party lemon squares on the kitchen counter. Four, six, and eight better steer clear, though."

It goes without saying that Glenwood secretly pined for his own eight-pack, so he began a rigorous abdominal conditioning program. From a yoga workshop on Second Avenue he procured a small polystyrene mat (not unlike the corrugated camping pad he slept on). He bought several pairs of shorts, and wrist- and headbands. He invested in myriad gut busters and fat blasters and tummy trimmers. From the back of a men's magazine he ordered a motorized, suction-cupped, ultrasound device that reverberated through the apartment like an electric train set being thermonuclearly destroyed.

For a while he kept the eight-pack program a secret, but I eventually caught on, when I started to hear the explosive grunts coming from behind his bedroom door—grunts that one might otherwise associate with multiple stab wounds or the onset of an acute hernia.

One day, after completing one of his woofing eight-pack workouts, he was walking around the kitchen with his shirt off and I could see that, with what appeared to be a grease pencil, he'd *drawn* an outline of his future eight-pack on his stomach.

I pretended not to notice it, instead feigning interest in one of Feick's music magazines.

A few days later Glenwood appeared shirtless in the kitchen yet again, huffing, pacing, guzzling water, and I could see that he'd added little diagonal shadings to the interior walls of each individual eight-pack cell.

He eventually abandoned his eight-pack program, complaining of general futility and a strange recurring butt pain. The grease pencil took several weeks to wear off, though, so he continued to sport his fantasy abs for some time.

When it came to his nickname, Glenwood felt that "Glen" was

somehow limiting, that it was better suited to a math teacher from Overland Park, Kansas. (His father, also Glenwood Ledbetter, was a math teacher from Overland Park, Kansas.)

He wanted at least two syllables, but preferred three. He wanted music in his name. He wanted jazz in his life.

Glenwood possessed a kind of big-boned, American-pioneer, frontier quality. There were times when I'd walk into a room and see him and immediately think of Conestoga wagons and panning for gold.

We tried Lightfoot for a while, but he ultimately declared it "too reservation-y."

So we moved on to Chuck Brown, because his head is enormous and globular and kind of perfectly round like Charlie Brown's. But after a few weeks he started to resent the name because it reminded him that he could never wear hats as a child.

"What about Lem?" I asked him one day after I got home from work.

He said, "Too limp."

I offered "Suds."

"No."

"Mr. Flood."

"Too gangster."

"Scooter."

"I see a Chihuahua."

"Klumfky."

"Can't say it."

"Frisco."

"Too swishy."

"Too *swishy*?"

"Yeah, man, and I'm not tan enough."

"What about Gorp?" I asked.

He said, "Gorp?"

I said, "Yeah, Gorp."

"You wanna call me fucking *Gorp*?"

"It's strong," I explained. "It pops, man. Like a flag snapping in the wind."

"I don't think so."

"How about Gorp*ler*?" I offered.

He simply said, "No."

"The Gorpler. It's sort of Creature Feature, monster movie–like."

I tried to see Glenwood in new ways. I imagined him in contexts that bordered on the ridiculous: driving a bus up First Avenue; chopping meat at the butcher's; delivering mail on Tenth Street. I saw him doing hair at the salon between Twelfth and Thirteenth. I pictured him as a delightfully elastic circus clown twisting balloons into French poodles for a roomful of bawling children.

"Bubbles," I offered.

"No way, dude."

"Dellwood."

"That's a milk company."

"Raven."

"Too literary."

I said, "Too literary? How too literary?"

"Graham Greene: *A Gun for Sale*."

"Come on, Glenwood."

"Don't call me that."

I thought for a moment. I said, "Wise Sleeping Monster."

He answered, "I like the tone, but it's too long."

"*Sleeping* Monster."

"Too spooky. Gotta keep the wise part."

"*Wise* Monster."

"Just doesn't do it for me."

"The Corduroy Falcon."

He made a face like he was farting.

I was getting closer.

One day he was looking out the window, and the way the light played on his head made the fleshy ensemble look like one hulking, twisting network of cartilage.

Basically, Glenwood Ledbetter is all head and shoulders. Completely Cro-Magnon, Paleolithic genes straight through to the core; there's no way of getting around it. If you imaginatively feathered this image you could start to see the nocturnal bird of prey so often stoically featured in the margins of grammar-school textbooks and wildlife TV shows, its head spinning an effortless one-eighty on the axis of its lazy-Susan shoulders, the hooked beak twisting to the camera, the solemn flash of its enormous photostatic black-velvet eyes, the pupils silvering for a half-second.

Glenwood Ledbetter resembled an incredibly large owl. Perhaps it was some kind of strange, prehistoric dinosaur owl, but it was an owl nonetheless.

It seemed perfect, not only because of Glenwood's physical endowment, but also because when it comes to pure, trivial knowledge, the Owl was and perhaps still is the wisest person I know. He is a walking encyclopedia of names and statistics. He is a one-man general survey on all things living and dead, an almanac of lore and superstition, a running footnote on anything and everything. He can speak seven languages and play Grieg's Nocturne on the piano by ear. He knows ancient Asian history and the titles of old silent movies. He can recite batting averages of second-string infielders and the win-loss record of almost every American League pitcher, year by year, without error. He knows the full names—first, middle, and last—of every president of the United States, in order, and he can disassemble, clean, and reassemble a manual 35-millimeter camera in nineteen minutes.

He can cook, too.

I said: "The Owl."

He said: "That's good."

After a few months working in the art department for the distinguished children's book publisher in the Flatiron Building, the Owl applied, got accepted to, and enrolled in the Columbia Business School for New Media.

He did it all swiftly, and with a kind of graceful detachment.

No one—including the Owl himself—knew exactly why the Owl was getting an MBA, what exactly constituted "new media," or why he was taking out a $60,000 loan to afford the schooling. But he went. He was the only grad-school student in the apartment, which made the nickname work on a slightly similar but equally important level: as a symbol of higher learning.

It worked for us.

In addition, the Owl was slightly older than the rest of us, which also seemed to deepen the meaning of his nickname. He was the old wise one, perched on a branch in the tree of knowledge, ever so slightly higher than Feick, the Loach, and me.

The Owl was from Kansas City, and he had a display-box clock that was a map of the world with little cutouts featuring the local times for major cities on every continent.

Glenwood Ledbetter was pleased that his new name was like a title. "The Owl." It was a poem or a short story or a Günter Grass novel. He thought it made him sound stately. You could sense him privately searching out his own "Owlness," going deeper inside to find the layers and subtleties.

He embraced the beginnings of a great myth. He walked a little taller. He strutted around with his chest puffed up, and his shoulders seemed to broaden.

It was perhaps the greatest unnaming of all.

Ball

AFTER WORK I PLAYED BASKETBALL in Tompkins Square Park, where the game was more like warfare than sport. Cops played. Junkies played. Ex-cons who smelled like Boone's Farm played. A cabdriver played in his Kangol cap. A West Indian guy named Trouble Free played while smoking a Newport. A Rasta with enormous, proliferating dreadlocks played in hemp sandals. A Scandinavian sculptor who wore a burlap halter top played. They played in jeans and construction boots. They played while their adolescent children smoked weed on the sidelines. White guys with bad hair. Black guys with bad hair. Yellow guys with fantastic hair. Pimps and smack dealers. Superfreaks with spotted faces. Marlboro men in sealskin spandex. A man who lived out of a guitar case. A surprisingly fleet-footed fat guy who rode a unicycle. A man with skin like dried tobacco leaves played in a turban and amber-tinted sunglasses—and he could dunk. A six-foot-ten ectomorph with horrible shoulder acne would arrive at the courts wearing a welding mask, like a postindustrial human pterodactyl. A kid from Pakistan played in parachute pants and called people "Sucka." He tried to say it the way the kids smoking weed on the sidelines said it, but it always came out like his mouth was full of silverware.

There were elbows that I'd never felt before, genetically informed elbows from the Avenue D projects and elbows from the Pitt Street Playground and elbows from Fourteenth Street between First and A. These elbows were passed down from father to son. They elbowed me on my jump shot. They elbowed me taking the ball out of bounds. They elbowed me cutting across the lane. They elbowed me when I was just standing there, waiting to play.

They elbowed my elbows.

And they gave everyone who was any good a nickname.

Once I sliced straight down the middle of the lane and caught a tip-dunk over four guys and the whole park exploded in what was perhaps the greatest chorus of my life. A homeless black man called Pops who provided a running commentary on the game in a voice not unlike Marv Albert's asked me if I was Puerto Rican.

Someone said, "He's white, Pops. White dudes can jump, too."

That's when they started calling me Opie.

That evening, while walking home from the park, I felt a small, almost soundless explosion behind my right kneecap. I heard it the way I'd sometimes hear something hitting the pavement on a distant street.

Despite the noise I walked all the way home and up the four flights of stairs, with very little pain. But the dull sound echoed in my head for the rest of the night. For some reason, I kept imagining farm-fresh eggs falling from countertops and hitting a vast sea of linoleum with little *pip*s, the yolks running out in a viscous miasma.

When I woke up the following morning, there was a blue-green corona around my right kneecap, and the surrounding tissue was so swollen that the whole joint looked waterlogged. The skin on the discolored area was hot to the touch. I iced it for a while and then, while standing on one leg, took a very lumpish and ineffective shower, after which I got dressed with the dexterity of a mule attempting a card trick and convinced myself that I would go to work and not to the hospital. Needless to say, I couldn't walk very well, so I opted for the subway.

Despite the relatively short crosstown distance, the trip from the First Avenue L-train stop to the downtown One/Nine is as convoluted as a symphony of scavenged accordions directed by an orangutan. In transferring to the downtown One/Nine train I had to get off at the Sixth Avenue stop and walk through a long, industrial-tiled, underground corridor whose humid perfume is equal parts shampoo, cheap gin, feces, and bleach.

I one-leggedly bobbed and weaved through the throngs of my fellow nine a.m. ladder climbers with the histrionic flailings of an off-balanced, lava-hopping lunatic. After reaching the One/Nine, I had to take the train two stops south, to Houston Street.

By the time I'd arrived at the One/Nine platform the arch of my left foot was fighting off seizures and I was damp with a cold, gluey sweat that did not seem to burn through my pores, but rather felt as though it had alighted on my skin like some kind of urban flopjuice ejaculated from an unseen subterranean slobber plant.

This commute lasted for many weeks. When the trains were running on time I could get to the office in fifteen or twenty minutes. When they were backed up it would sometimes take longer than walking would.

But Van Von Donnelly was sympathetic. He would often urge me to get my knee looked at by his orthopedic guy, a mysterious Middle Eastern man who worked out of his home upstate in Nyack.

The limping would eventually cause ankle problems, the overdevelopment of my right quadricep muscle, and a brief but nasty bout with sciatica that would render me completely inert and melodramatically bedridden for a very long week and a half.

Sales Assistant

THE JUNE RAINS CAME and turned the East Village streets to glycerin. The downpours would rage for twelve minutes or so and then suddenly stop, as though the weather gods were suffering from narcolepsy. The shrinking shantytown in Tompkins Square Park was aswamp with rotted cardboard, mishmash lumber, and bobbing Styrofoam. The homeless wrapped themselves in Hefty bags and hurricane fencing and the vinyl hides of awnings ripped from the storefronts of Avenue A and the lettered streets farther east.

Some shrieked at the sky.

Others cursed at puddles.

One man, wearing a diaper on his head, attacked a tree with his bare fists. He punched it as if it were an enemy who owed him money.

While waiting in a Laundromat for one storm to subside I watched a bald woman with yellowish impetigo crusts permeating her scalp bend over in the middle of Avenue A, pull her pants down, squat, and reach behind herself to draw aside a single, very elastic-looking labium between thumb and forefinger and discharge an incredible tributary of urine onto the grille of a honking taxi.

During these typhoon-like outbursts, running from storefront to storefront, arms loaded with laundry or groceries or books found on the street, was like a newly devised urban track-and-field event.

Unlike the cleansing storms of Iowa and Illinois, the rains of the East Village seemed to make things filthier. The rains would ruin umbrellas and pool sulfurously in the depressions of crosswalks.

They would destroy waterproof shoes.

And drown pigeons.

And it stunk.

For my birthday, the Owl and I bought a six-pack of Budweiser and sat on the fire escape and watched people walk east toward Avenue A.

"No westbound buses," the Owl said. "We make a pact right here and now. We do not get on any buses heading west."

"Like to the West Village?"

"No, like west as in heading back to the Midwest. You board a westbound bus and you lose. Port Authority Bus Terminal is not part of our vocabulary."

"What about north- or southbound buses?"

"We'll accept that under certain conditions, and we'll deal with that if and when those conditions present themselves. I will not return to Kansas, Homon. And you will not return to Iowa."

"Okay."

"I'll say it first. I will not return to Kansas. Now you."

"I will not return to Iowa."

"And no westbound buses. Say it."

"No westbound buses."

"Port Authority Bus Terminal is not part of my vocabulary."

"Port Authority Bus Terminal is not part of my vocabulary."

"I solemnly swear on the eyes of my periwinkle soul."

"I solemnly swear on the eyes of my periwinkle soul."

I imagined myself on a Greyhound heading west. The mocking lights of the Lincoln Tunnel streaking by my darkened window. The smell of urine wafting mysteriously. New York City rejects fidgeting and clucking their teeth and clawing their cold, reptilian flesh. The insanity of a double-A battery rolling back and forth under the seats. A dirty child with matted hair roaming the aisle. An old woman wearing a Mets cap suddenly screaming a name in her sleep. The damp film of loss and poverty coating the vinyl headrests.

I could feel my insides shrinking.

"The women here are unbelievable," the Owl mused after a silence, thankfully changing the subject.

"Yeah, they're pretty amazing."

"The things they wear."

"And don't wear."

"Yesterday I saw this chick with a boa constrictor around her neck. It was like she knew way more than the rest of us."

"Chicks and snakes," I said.

"Chicks and snakes," he echoed.

"I think I need an animal."

"Really. Why?"

"I don't know. It might help somehow," I said.

"What kind of animal?"

"Maybe like a fox. Or an iguana."

"You'd probably have to declaw the fox. And I think iguanas are just sort of boring," the Owl mused. "By the way, happy birthday. Twenty-three. That's a prime number—only divisible without a remainder by itself and one."

"It is indeed."

We clinked our aluminum beer cans and watched people with whom we liked to believe we shared a kinship pass by on the street below.

At work I spent most of my time talking to sales reps on the phone. I was the sales assistant. I was the personal aide to Van Von Donnelly, national hardcover sales manager. According to Van, I was the "point man."

I was basically the guy everybody told what to do.

Often, even people from other departments would tell me what to do, just to see if they could get in on the fun.

I was new and callow.

I was willing and able.

And I was definitely dumber than a box of sticks.

Sometimes Van would inject basketball jargon into our work vocabulary. It started out slowly, and then grew to absurd levels of stupidity. "Point man" turned into "point *guard*." I was the point guard of hardcover sales.

At first our new administrative discourse was simply a collusive, smiling intimacy, but later it would snowball into an embarrassing, shoulder-hunching obligation.

His in-box turned into the "offense" box. The out-box, of course, became the "defense" box.

Van would ask me to "jump shoot" the Western region numbers to him from the star report binder. "Jump shoot the All-Stars to me," he'd say, barely able to stand it, nearly bursting into hysterics with every syllable.

From my post at the laser printer, I would "rebound" a Van Von Donnelly memo and "bounce pass" it to the divisional sales managers through the twin admin-athletic miracles of the Xerox and fax machines.

Van and I would "huddle" in the morning and come up with a "game plan." Lunch was "halftime," and when four-thirty hit it was the "fourth quarter." A "head fake" was employed when Van would skip a marketing meeting. A "layup" was a trip to the Coke machine. A "time-out" or "T-O" (rigid hands forming the letter T) was a bathroom break. "Overtime" was simply, well, overtime.

For which I didn't get paid.

It was locker-room mania.

Sometimes he would say, "Hey, point guard!" and I would come back with, "Hey, Coach!"

At first this sporty, corporate jingoism was annoying and somewhat depressing. Here I was, an aspiring writer, working in a world-renowned publishing company in New York City, and my boss was pretending we were prepubescent jocks enacting athletic-hero fantasies with about the same level of complexity and intelligence that might be found in a game of Nerf football.

But after a while it grew on me. In fact, I started to love the simplicity of our working relationship. The roles were clear. There was a lot of smiling. And Van appreciated the team play. He rarely asked personal questions, and he closed his door a lot, which allowed me to work on my novel.

Through a combination of function keys on my computer, after a week or two of practice I had perfected the use of the split-screen fea-ture. On one document I could transcribe the sales reps' call reports and then hit a function key and—*blip*—there was my novel, and then, if necessary—*blip*—back to the call reports. If I was in a groove I could sneak in a few hours of writing every day. But I always had to be on the lookout.

My ears became incredibly sensitive to footfalls, to the plant of the approaching shoe, to the carpet-hushed fulcrum of the whirling, I-forgot-something pivot, to the drags and shuffles of poorly pronated strides. I grew to intimately know the inner-thigh swish of slacks rub-bing and the clicks and pops of arthritic knees. I could tell the differ-ence between corduroy and wool, twill and linen, silk and rayon, based on sound alone.

I knew all the higher-ups' voices: there was the red-alert, high-nasal, public-service announcement delivery of Lou Landau (president of sales); the slightly boyish, phlegm-filled snarl of Darla Nordtgard (vice president of marketing); the wistful, melancholic, child's clarinet of Besserman Staley (director of publishing operations); and the gurgling walrus grumble of Frannie Fryhoffen (executive managing editor).

And most important, I knew the rumblings of Van's office. The low, metallic thunder of ball bearings rolling in the drawer channels and the slow, angular wending of his ballpoint pen, signing the reps' expense re-ports.

Sometimes I imagined Van busying himself with his Rubik's cube or taking out some memo paper and drawing a fire truck with his Crayolas.

I knew that he was coming when I heard the springs of his chair creak three times: first for the desk push-away; a second time for the Van Von Donnelly patented lean-back-wobbletotter dismount; and fi-nally for the always deliberate but consistently well-executed lurch-gather-fishwiggle slacks check.

At first I felt a little guilty writing on the job, but the more I thought about the quality of the work I was doing for Van (which happened to be top-notch, All Conference–caliber work) versus my peasant's salary, the more the guilt faded, quickly and without pain, like so many smoke rings in a well-ventilated room.

I would write as much as possible, in a freefall of obtuse and swollen inspiration. I would *compose* nonsensically, and with great velocity. At times I would write in a kind of coded baby talk, great toddler-level sentences filled with *goos* and *gahs* and *uh-ohs* and *yumyums*.

I would write the literary equivalent of Sea-Monkeys.

And at the end of the day, with the efficiency and sleight of hand of a great international jewel thief, I would swiftly and clandestinely print out my puerile ramblings—looking left, looking right—quickly fold my new pages, and stuff them into my back pocket. Upon returning to my Skinner box I would delete the document from my computer's hard drive.

No evidence. No harm done.

I was sure to always complete my job-related work first, including the call reports. I tried to work as quickly and accurately as possible in the hope of scoring extra writing time.

Writing my novel in the office also afforded the added advantage of my *appearing* to work. Those who walked by always saw me in a state of deeply felt, brow-furrowed concentration.

Other assistants played video games and talked on the phone. I rambled on my keyboard.

My only interruptions were incoming calls from the sales reps, who telephoned the office often and irregularly, like wayward sheep bleating for their shepherd. They needed stuff and they needed it desperately.

As if their bonuses depended on it.

They needed sell sheets. They needed catalogs and book jackets. They needed the eight-by-ten acetate glossies with the marketing bullets, and the postcards containing co-op advertising price points. They needed bound galleys and star reports and display easels. They needed NCR forms FedExed to their hotels in Denver. They needed their sales kit two-dayed to their sisters' houses in Omaha. They needed expense report forms and BESTSELLING AUTHOR bumper stickers and extra cat calendars. They needed the new bellwether titles faxed to them at the Kinko's in Highland Park. They needed spinner-rack placards and complimentary lead-title posters. They wanted four more of the promotional tie-dyed T-shirts for their twin nieces, Annie and Frannie, and for their nephews Jack and Boomer.

They buttered me up. They told me I had a nice voice. They said they heard good things about me. They called me Kid and offered to buy me dinner if I was ever in Indianapolis. They thanked me profusely and with entirely too much volume.

I had a lot more power than my shoe-store-clerk salary let on.

I was their pimp daddy.

I was their pusherman.

I was Kid, the favor guy.

They had a wide range of accents and attitudes, ranging from a Civil War, southern-gothic whiskey song (Chauncey Barberhouse from Utah, Alabama) to an incredibly laconic Transylvanian tenor (Zjelco "Bump" Csernovics, calling four or five times a day from his prewar cold-water, former button-making shop on Delancey Street).

There was also Katie Todd Villanova from Albany, who never got her book briefs on time, and Rollie Goldfarb from Dallas, who loved the early nineties Mavericks with a kind of crushing tenderness despite their woeful, almost biblical failure year in and year out.

Sue Tapani from Chicago would burst into hysterical laughter if I said the word *blad*. There is really no other word for blad, a five-by-seven, six-to-twelve-page excerpt from an upcoming title with a shiny four-color cover. It's an important selling tool, and the buyers for bookstores love them. They sometimes give them away to their customers like taffy apples. A blad is simply and irrevocably a blad. And for Sue it was a powerful, Pavlovian zip word that somehow reminded her of her toddler son, Roy, opening the refrigerator and pooping on the Thanksgiving turkey.

So my conversations with Sue Tapani from Chicago about blads always involved a long spell of her shrieking in a whooping falsetto—a kind of Las Vegas jackpot laughter that kept topping itself as though she were being continuously and lovingly goosed with a pencil by a good pal.

Once, the rep from Denver, Howard Slume (who had a vague hint of Jimmy Stewart in his voice), actually had to get off the phone because his house was burning down. He said "Oh, gald." Or maybe it was "Oh, god." And then he very politely told me that I would have to excuse him, that he had to get off the phone because the flames were licking up the paneled walls of his sunporch. I hung up, briefly flirted with the notion of calling the Denver fire department, and then told Van instead. Van just sort of giggled brightly, shook his head, and said, "Good old Slumey."

There were two Beth Altmans: one from Seattle who told me she was allergic to everything except hamburger buns; and the other from Columbus, Ohio, who broke down crying on the phone on a Friday at four-thirty because the gas cap from her company car had been stolen while she was calling on her account.

The voices began to take on a shape, a physical form in my head of how I imagined the reps. Height and weight came first, then hair color and dental quality. Then came stranger things like moles and flesh burns and chronic facial ticks.

Sometimes I saw them in sexual attitudes: postcoitally lounging in their unmentionables on the terrace of the Marriott in Dallas or applying a little mascara on the skyway just after fellating a buyer in Phoenix.

The Underwood

THE INTERIOR OF THE REFRIGERATOR we'd inherited from Tokyo Stunt Pussy had been spray-painted black and possessed an ominous quality that prompted us to avoid storing food in it for fear of contracting some kind of deadly disease. In fact, we kept very few perishables in the apartment. What we did have on hand (the occasional orange or hard-boiled egg) seemed to mysteriously disappear the way sea vessels disappear in the Bermuda Triangle.

Instead of banishing the refrigerator to the Tenth Street curb, we decided to use it for storage.

Feick stacked scripts in the crisper. The Owl kept his contact-lens solution in the butter cubby. The Loach claimed the refrigerator's top tier (the latticed chamber of which was as lopsided as a stepped-on cigar box) to store his enormous, kaleidoscopic, neon scattering of comedy-troupe flyers. These featured a black-and-white rendering of the Loach himself, arm-in-arm with what appeared to be a shaggy, uninspired-looking sheepdog, standing on its hind legs and wearing a seersucker suit. Below the picture, in block letters, it read, GET LOACHED! which is how we would ultimately describe the phenomenon of our disappearing food—as in, Dude, my Oreos got Loached again.

I kept my slowly growing untitled novel in the freezer. I had been working on it for months. I liked the idea of putting a day's work in a sealed compartment designed for preserving food; it somehow married the ideas of nutritional and intellectual subsistence. There was also the ritual of opening the door, setting the new pages under the old, patting the edges even, taking one last fatherly glance at my growing baby, and closing the door—the kiss of the airtight seal.

When I was not furtively typing on company equipment, I used a 1942 No. 3 Underwood manual typewriter, a collector's item that had been restored and handed down to me as a graduation gift from my Uncle Brad. It was beautifully black, the way horses are black, and it gleamed radioactively. It was enormous and had the harsh geometrical severity of an ancient pipe organ discovered in some lost medieval belfry. Despite its overall size, the keys were surprisingly small for me and the rake was a little steep for my hands. But that didn't stop me.

Before each writing session I would mentally shrink my hands. Through yoga certain people can meditate and then fold themselves up into little human slipknots. I'd close my eyes and similarly find my center. Then I'd let go of the day; let the noise fade away; let the garbage trucks and the car alarms and the fury-laden invocations of the homeless in Tompkins Square Park and the barking cops with their clanking riot gear and the general barbarian roar of First Avenue transform into little buttercupped anemones of deep-sea silence.

After finding that underwater quiet I would clear the big billboard in my mind and psychically project the image of the hands I had as a child (trying to coop a butterfly with a Dixie cup; shuffling through my baseball-card collection; reaching through the grill of the heating vent for my dropped chewing gum).

After this I would chant, "Smaller . . . smaller . . . smaller . . . smaller," even adding a "please" now and then.

I willed the metacarpals and the tendons and all those little pinioned bones to shrink, to somehow reengineer their DNA so I could be ergonomically compatible, so the Underwood and I could have the manual romance that was no doubt experienced by the Kerouacs and the Hemingways and all those other novelists of the century's first ninety years.

The usual result was that I bunched up my shoulders and typed like an angry Transylvanian harpsichordist.

At the time everyone was buying laptops and lifedecks and dynobooks and flipdowns, things you could carry around in your book bag with twelve other items. But I wasn't embarrassed. I was proud of my machine. It was a dinosaur. It was clunky. It had a kind of iron war history, like a Sherman tank or a pull-pin hand grenade. When I advanced the manual return it sounded like a great fatal slingshot. There was no whirring. There was no dog-whistling hard drive subliminally threading through my brain. It was all pop and jangle.

Writing on the Underwood became an event. I loved it the way I might love a woman and a puppy and an old catcher's mitt all rolled into one. I loved the sounds it made, the keys like little amulets hammering against the cylinder, protecting me from the evils of writer's block and epidemics of dangling prepositions and black holes of lost, forgotten words. The space bar snare-drumming, the whole thing thrumming along with a military, parade-like percussion.

I loved its concentrated weight and its girth. It was a weapon. It would survive a nuclear disaster. If it fell off the desk it would crush the bones in my foot.

Sometimes I just looked at it. I would rest my hand on its side. At times I thought that it could feel me handling it, that it developed a sensory perception of its own, that it knew the scent or touch of my hands like a lover.

I prayed to it.

I waited for it to tell me things.

I would eventually sell it to the vintage shop on First Avenue between Ninth and Tenth for fifty bucks so our phone wouldn't be disconnected.

An acute depression ensued that would underscore many months to follow.

Loach Catatonia

ONE DAY IN LATE JULY I came home after work to find the Loach frozen in front of the TV in what appeared to be a kind of waking dream state. The temperature in the apartment was beyond domestic heat. It was so infernal I could feel the living room humidity doing things to the jellies of my eyes.

After four grim flights of stairs (book bag in tow, feet throbbing from being squeezed into my wingtips, still-cinched necktie mildly throttling major arteries), the sight of the Loach on the slowly darkening sofa wasn't exactly what I would call Happy Hour Nirvana.

As usual, I gazed upon a lack of clothing and an abundance of thinning-yet-always-resilient tufts of simian hair and the imitation topaz toenails and the bullet-hole eyes and smelled the general noisome odor of liverwurst and scalp sebum.

His mouth was hanging so far open I could see a vague uvular projection that was either esophageal tissue or Doritos phlegm. His teeth were a disaster, his tongue a gray, lifeless oyster.

And to push the envelope of reality a bit, he had barbered what appeared to be a monk's tonsure on the crown of his head. "Loach," I said, "what happened to your hair?"

But he just stared at the TV. The sound had been muted. Only street noise and the Loach's respiration.

In the frame of the Trinitron there was a man sitting at what appeared to be a hulking Formica banker's desk. He had very few distinguishing qualities. He wore a white T-shirt and was slightly balding, thirtyish, and Caucasian. Like the Loach, his mouth was also open, and his eyes neither blinked nor shifted (though he lacked the Loach's tonsured head).

Based on the poor picture quality, I gathered that the Loach was watching some sort of arty public access show.

"Loach," I said once more, but still there was no response.

I noted his odor again, which at closer proximity was all damp socks and cheese. The sofa was starting to smell like an abandoned dairy farm festering with salmonella.

"Loach, I'm talking to you," I said, raising the volume of my voice a little, my book bag nagging at my shoulder.

But he just continued staring ahead, catatonic.

"You have a room," I offered.

His nostrils were polluted with mucoidal gum and other unnameable respiratory secretions.

"Your very own room."

With the Doritos-stained remote I turned off the TV, but nothing changed. The Loach's image was now reflected in the blackened screen, as if through some sort of microwave miracle he and the public access man had become one.

"It's begging to be lived in."

His fingernails were so black around the edges he might have been mistaken for a coal miner.

"It wants a friend," I pleaded. "The Owl even put a futon in there for you."

The whites of his eyes were somehow gray.

"Friendship. Warmth. Camaraderie."

An inhale. An exhale. The rustle of nostril hair.

"A boy and his room."

A small, barely audible snore was now catching at the back of his throat.

"Your own personal space, man."

Was he sleeping?

Was he on some sort of new drug manufactured in a basement on Avenue D? Some time-release downer designed to tap into the bliss of domestic inertia and foul hygiene?

"It's ten-by-ten. There's a window overlooking the courtyard. The smell of eucalyptus drifting in from the bathhouse. It has a door, man. Go check it out."

Not a single blink.

"You can still come out here whenever you want."

Not a fiber stirred.

"You can even *have* the sofa."

I stayed there for another minute and when I realized that he was not going to respond I turned the TV back on. The man at the desk was in the same position, his mouth still open, his eyes dull and blank and enormous.

Later that night, when I came out of the bathroom, I could see the Loach wrapped in a threadbare cotton blanket (Feick's discarded childhood thumb-sucking "bankyboo"; he had thrown it in the trash earlier that same day). The light from the TV was casting lunar shades of blue on his face.

Just before I turned and headed into my room he said, "Nobody ever laughs at me."

This was not uttered as a plea for pity, but as a sad, solemn fact.

I stood there for a moment and the Loach's eyes slowly met mine. In the TV's light they looked like the eyes of a stuffed porcupine.

"But they will," he added, and then his eyes slowly found the TV again.

Church of Christ

THE WINDOW OF MY TEN-BY-TWELVE ROOM faced the north side of Tenth Street, where a small storefront spiritual meeting place called the Church of Christ willed itself out of the pavement in an almost colorless brown, truncated rectangle of concrete, cinder block, and generic mortar. There was a solitary black fire escape hardly ten feet off the ground that seemed arbitrarily arranged on the building and barely cleared the four penitentiary-style doors.

I have no idea if this was indeed a place of worship, as I never saw anyone enter or exit (although the locked metal display box housed next to the westernmost door often featured a menu of events that would mysteriously change on a weekly basis).

Directly to the west of the church, and sharing the same platoon of rubber garbage receptacles, was a seven-story, redbrick tenement whose imperfect, chipped masonry was so overly grouted that the building appeared to suffer from the construction equivalent of acute respiratory congestion.

There were four windows spanning each story. The third story featured a prolific fire-escape garden boasting twin cascades of wisteria replete with purple and white flower clusters. On the windows' four cement ledges, complementing the falls of wisteria, were clay pots filled with pink and purple geraniums and manicured flower boxes of multicolored tulips. It was an explosion of life on an otherwise drab-looking façade, an optical Tenth Street oasis.

The windows of the story directly above featured four large black X's spray-painted over the glass. Those below were dressed with what appeared to be soiled institutional linens whose holes and edges radiated a sickly pink light.

The keeper of the fire-escape garden was an incredibly tall Mediterranean-looking man who spent hours on the terrace talking on his cordless phone while primping, trimming, and watering his beloved flora.

I attributed a novella's worth of mystery and foul play to this urban horticulturalist's existence. The garden was a front for illegal (most likely narcotic-related) activity. He was the lord of the current club drug, the active substance of which was farmed from the leaves of other artificially grown, scientifically lit, domestically harbored opium poppies. Or perhaps he was a pedophile who would lure East Village children to his poisonous garden with chewing gum, Sega Genesis, and Disney action figures.

One day a few months after we settled into the upstairs apartment (ironically, it was the night after I had a dream in which this same man was painted a rich latex blue and chased me across an unharvested wheat field brandishing a volume of the Yellow Pages), I was walking home from work when I noticed the gardener sitting on the stoop next to my building. As I got closer, I realized that he was much shorter than I had thought. He was also shirtless and he possessed (because, as with all great anatomical gifts, one "possesses" such things instead of merely "having" them) a chest that was not dissimilar to that of the crucifix-festooned, thorny-browed Christ looming over the altar of my hometown parish (St. Rose of Lima). He was wearing cutoffs and flip-flops and sitting between his thonged feet was a small potted plant with reddish-orange, bloody-looking flowers.

When we made that inevitable mammalian eye contact so often featured on Nature Channel predator-prey safari programs, he said, "Hey there."

I said, "Hey."

He leaned forward a little and wiped the humidity from his brow.

"You live next door, don't you?" he asked.

"Yeah," I said. "I do."

I was surprised to discover that his accent was neither Mediterranean nor the least bit ethnic. I couldn't detect the slightest musical regionalism. It was almost completely neutral.

"Fourth floor," he added. "Window faces the street."

"That's me," I said.

"You're a writer?"

"I'm trying to be," I said.

"I see you working away on your typewriter."

Then he smiled slightly, revealing extraordinarily white incisors, and said, "You're a poet, I'll bet."

"Um," I said. "I'm actually dabbling in fiction at the moment. I guess I'm sort of a novelist."

"That's great," he said, nodding a little.

I nodded a little, too, and then my head came to a dead rest and I stood there with my bag of books and my bad slacks and my white button-down shirt, soaking up my body's foul secretions.

"What's your novel about?" he asked.

"Well," I said, "it's sort of still in the embryotic stage. It has to do with acute knee pain and the end of the world."

"Embryonic," he said, his widening smile revealing more porcelain-like teeth.

I vacuously replied, "Huh?"

"You said 'embryotic,' " he clarified. "The correct adjective is *embryonic*, I believe. Existing in embryo."

"Oh," I said. "Thanks."

Suddenly there was a swell of shouting from Tompkins Square Park. It was the indiscernible, wordless rush of man-made choral fury, like carnivores roaring. My newfound friend and I turned toward the noise momentarily and then the paroxysm subsided and was seemingly digested by the First Avenue traffic and tree breeze.

"Well," he said, "I just wanted to welcome you to the neighborhood."

Then, from between his tan, naked ankles, he proffered the potted plant.

"For you," he said.

"Hey," I said. "A plant."

I took it in my free hand. It had an odor that reminded me of Number 2 lead pencils and cat urine.

"It's a puccoon," he explained.

"A puccoon," I echoed.

"A North American plant of the genus Lithospermum. It bleeds."

"A bleeding plant," I said. "Interesting."

"And my name is Luis."

"Hi, Luis," I said, and introduced myself.

"I was going to give you a lantana, but I thought the puccoon somehow suited you. A lantana is a bit noisy, and you don't seem noisy. And that's a good thing."

I didn't know what to say so I simply floated there, like some anonymous glue-and-macaroni ornament hanging from a Christmas tree.

No, I am not noisy, I thought.

Not noisy is a good thing.

After we shook hands Luis stood and said, "Very pleased to meet you." Then he punctuated our exchange, saying, "Be safe."

He then descended the stoop and crossed over to the north side of Tenth Street with the insouciant elegance one usually ascribes to the languorous, alcoholic heroines of Tennessee Williams plays.

Minutes later I would take the plant upstairs and, after shedding my gym bag, necktie, and squeezed-into wingtips, I would set it on my work desk and stare at it for several thoughtless, blank-brained minutes, its fused corollas more fragile than an infant's eyelids. The traffic rumble of Tenth Street scored my first true plant moment. There was my puccoon, my orange plant—my friend, even—in all of its simple, solitary beauty.

Flowers.

Stem.

Pistil.

Stamen.

It was at that moment that I came to the conclusion that there is some link between plants and loneliness.

This puccoon would become the acolyte of my solitude and the sole witness to such intimate behaviors as nose-picking, conversations with myself (including a variety of accents and accompanying spontaneous folk songs), bedridden depression, general inertia (all chair positions and spinal postures), and several hundred hours of masturbation (classic style, cock in fist, nonlubricated).

After I peeled away my clothes and arranged small piles of personal detritus (books, underwear, candy wrappers, etc.), I opened my Oxford American paperback dictionary and looked up *embryonic*, which was indeed the correct adjective and yielded the definition "existing in embryo."

Starting that evening I would water my puccoon twice a day and rotate it toward the light every morning and study its leaning habits.

In a matter of weeks I would discover that its petals, if squeezed gently between thumb and forefinger, would leak a pungent, reddish-orange dye that would become a faint, bloody stain streaking the margins of my unformed novel.

The Heat

WE BRAVED THE HEAT of early August with a fan bought from a third-world sheet on Second Avenue for two dollars. Despite its massive size, it was incredibly lightweight and provided about as much relief as being licked by a cow in a warm Iowa pasture.

The putrefying smell of the East Village wafted constantly through Feick's bedroom window. The odor was like a strange mixture of congested litter box and lavender potpourri. The Owl, who also lived in one of the three back rooms, was convinced that the odor's source was some tree in the courtyard. We came to accept this theory and, like the stable boy who has to shovel horseshit all day, ceased to notice the smell within weeks.

The Owl was spending an inordinate number of hours at his publishing company in the Flatiron Building. His enormous head seemed to gather mass under the strain.

Feick, somehow unfazed by the heat, was collecting unemployment and talking of plans to direct an all-nude production of *The Bald Soprano* at Alice's Fourth Floor on West Forty-second Street.

The Loach was seemingly ossifying on the sofa, his face as lifeless as that of a stunned mackerel. When he wasn't transfixed by the television, he was engaged in a brow-furrowed study of the gnats, mosquitoes, moths, fleas, and rugged members of the Muscidae family, including all variations of the caddis, house, horse, black, and bottle-backed flies that peppered the amber ribbons of Tat Fly Paper tacked to the living room ceiling.

We would change the flypaper every three days or so, and each clean ribbon replaced a new phantasmagoric laboratory for the Loach's acorn-size imagination. Certain people take on such hobbies as topiary or origami. While the Loach's nonactive relationship with the flypaper didn't warrant hobby status, his almost holy state of observance (obovoid mouth, drool almost audibly pooling) was the closest he ever came to participating in the world of arts and crafts.

I came home once and found the Owl, who grew to hate the flies with a kind of seething bitterness, positioned under the swarm with a large can of hair spray and a lighter. Every few seconds he would engage the aerosol push-button, flick the lighter, and send a three-foot flame toward the center of the cyclone. The Owl managed to roast a few flies, whose wingless husks he would collect and, in an act of mock supplication, offer to their still centrifuging brothers.

"Don't you see?!" he would shout at them, thrusting heavenward his can of Aqua Net.

The truth is, we should have bought adjustable window screens from the hardware store on Seventh Street, but through some combination of laziness, arsonist's lust, and flypaper fascination, we instead let the bugs join us for the summer.

In the solitude of my room—the available floor area of which, with the increase in books, junk mail, and laundry, seemed to be shrinking into Lilliputian stature—I worked on my novel about acute knee pain and the end of the world. Although I kept my window wide open I would sweat so much that my clothes started hanging off me from the weight loss.

In the living room the new fan was louder than a speedboat and the dust clusters would travel down the hall with a lilting choreography. The Owl would scoop them away from his door and flush them down the toilet as if they were the powdery leavings of strange, weightless giraffes. Despite the fan's noise, the breeze it produced seemed weak and almost hotter, as though the blades somehow cooked the air before sending it punitively out into the common area.

The late-summer air was so warm and thick it acted like a kind of epidermal upholstery, wrapping around me like some boiled cloak designed to humiliate or discipline.

And the smells of the East Village seemed to fluctuate with the humidity: the drifting, peppery marijuana of St. Mark's Place; the fish-like, venereal sludge of Avenue A; the sour, garbage-truck reek of First Avenue; the uric pockets near the Fourteenth Street Post Office; the sweet, fecal waves emanating from the doorways of the crackhouses on Ninth Street between First and Second avenues.

With the fan turned off, the air slid and slouched. The vacuum of pressure created by opening a door would cause a fever to skid through the room. It folded down the hallway like something physical, like so much laundry tumbling fresh out of the dryer. If there was no draft, the heat rose through the floorboards and lurched conspiratorially. There were times when every window would be wide open and the only air moving through the apartment was the infinitesimal breeze generated by the ever-present cloud of flying insects.

It wasn't uncommon to see Feick, the Owl, the Loach, and me all clad in only our underwear as though we were some sweltering theatre ensemble rehearsing an apartment musical about sweat.

Feick donned boxers so large they seemed a preamble to a great clowning act. Repeatedly and without shame, the Loach modeled a pair of yellow-gray briefs with a striped waistband, briefs so old they looked as though they'd elementally oxidized into a sulfuric paste that, if touched, would spontaneously combust.

The Owl sported several pairs of rice-colored butt-huggers that he'd purchased during his teaching stint in Japan. They made his legs look long and womanish, and his testicles often teetered on the verge of falling out, like two balding, fearful woodchucks. He called these sleek undergarments "boxer-slicks." I think he came up with that on his own.

I wore old-fashioned, bone-white briefs, and I wore them with locker room pride.

It was a summer of heat and underwear, punctuated by the smell of unwashed men in their skivvies.

We periodically took turns in front of the fan. We'd each take a ten-minute shift, sitting Indian-style, drunk on the smell of armpits.

The Loach refused to cooperate with the shift allotment. His would often go on for twelve to fifteen minutes, and sometimes required physical deportation.

Once, the Owl had to employ a Greco-Roman-style headlock and drag the Loach vigorously down the hall, where he could be heard thrashing and cursing behind the door of the room he never lived in.

Bestsellers

ON AUGUST 24—A WEDNESDAY—there was a celebration at the world-renowned publishing company with the mirror-smoked windows on the corner of Hudson and Houston. One of our larger hardcover imprints was blessed with the great fortune of landing two new titles on the *New York Times* bestseller list.

This good news was treated like a prophecy rained down from a holy, invisible mountain.

An austere, three-line memo circulated through the editorial, marketing, publicity, and sales departments, inviting those fortunate souls who'd had something to do with the now legendary books to a champagne toast being held in the quadrant of cubicles outside Executive Editor Harlan Niederlander's office.

Van Von Donnelly intercommed and informed me that as the new kid on the block I would be the one responsible for opening the champagne, that the guys from the mailroom were unloading a dozen or so magnums of Korbel and I should go on down the hall to editorial and start uncorking.

"Go get 'em," Van said. "Give 'em hell."

When I got to the reception area, three black men from the mailroom were covering twin file cabinets with white party linens and arranging the bottles of Korbel. There was a large mail gurney boasting three silver platters. The first contained a multicolored hummock of geometrically sculpted carrots, radishes, and celery; a few tubs of mayonnaise-smelling dip (with chives sprinkled about to camouflage the no-doubt industrial-size Hellmann's frugality); and bursting sprigs of parsley. The second platter was choked with cookies and brownies and hearty lemon squares the size of our edgier trade paperbacks, the whole heart attack–inducing load heaped on an enormous false doily that could have doubled as a homestead apron in *Oklahoma!*

The final platter was a kind of garish fruit opera containing melon balls, kiwi medallions, a small forest of multicolored grapes, apple wedges, several whole copper pears, and what appeared to be a genetically fattened cluster of strawberries dipped in German chocolate.

Some deeply predatory instinct gets triggered when I am confronted with large amounts of catered office food, and my first impulse is to grab whatever I can and start eating.

I had to stop my left hand from reaching out on its own.

No, left hand! I practically shouted.

Bad hand!

When I got myself under control I focused on the symmetrical arrangement of the Korbel.

One of the mailroom guys must have sensed my appreciation, and of Harlan Niederlander he said, "Homeboy likes things tight."

I nodded with idiotic, liberal arts–induced African American sympathy, grabbed a magnum of Korbel, and proceeded to peel the golden foil from its neck. Prior to this point in my life, I had never uncorked much of anything. I had no idea what I was doing, but I was too embarrassed to ask for help.

After the three mailroom guys hoisted the platters onto the file cabinets (which were now so thoroughly costumed for celebration they resembled office furniture in drag), they returned themselves and their beloved multitasking gurney to the cinder-block splendor of the basement mailroom.

Moments later I was joined by Ford McGowan, Stafford Davidson's star editorial assistant, with his Ivy League hair and teeth so white you'd have thought they must be stolen.

I rarely spoke to Ford, largely because I was intimidated by his assured, ironic disposition: the baggy chinos, the wrinkled oxford, the eight-dollar, cleverly purchased, canary yellow ersatz jazz tie patterned with red playing-card diamonds. Ford was one of those vaguely privileged, overly educated guys, all too aware that he was vaguely privileged and overly educated, yet somehow he came off as being at once charmingly self-effacing and infinitely bored. I always envisioned him standing on a portico of some impossibly expensive Ivy League school, a snifter of brandy cradled in his hand.

"Libations," he said to me, half-smiling and drawing his blond bangs away from his eyes.

"Yeah" was all I could muster in response, as I was still busy wrestling with the Korbel. I had managed to untwist the cap wiring and was now trying to excavate the cork. Its bulbous head looked too artistic to be fouled by a corkscrew. I had been staring at it for a full ten seconds when, with the assured nonchalance of one who can rattle off Shakespearean sonnets or recite the beginning of *Beowulf* in period-perfect Old English, Ford finally said, "Allow me."

He seized the Korbel by the throat, anchored its pregnant end between his knees, and twisted the cork out. It made a startling pop and then a lazy, sweet-smelling smoke undulated from its perfect little orifice.

"Voilà," Ford said, offering the Korbel. I took it and placed it beside the other bottles.

I thanked him and began work on the next one.

While I peeled away the foil, Ford leaned against the file cabinets, popped a chocolate-covered strawberry in his mouth, and said, "So, I hear you're a scribe."

"Who told you that?" I asked, suddenly paranoid that Van Von Donnelly was aware of my writing on the job.

"Oh, let's just say word gets around. It's okay," he assured me. "Practically every assistant on this floor has a slowly growing manuscript hidden somewhere."

"Well," I said, picturing my novel in the refrigerator across town on Tenth Street, "I guess I can't deny it."

"What kind of stuff do you write?" Ford asked.

"Fiction."

"Short stories?"

"I'm writing a novel, actually."

"He chooses long-distance. Very cool. What's it about?"

"Uh," I said, the Korbel between my thighs now like some kind of strange, schooner-shaped prosthetic erection, "it's sort of about acute knee pain and the end of the world."

Ford's eyebrows danced a bit, and he said, "Like orthopedic knee pain?"

"Yeah," I said. "Medically unsolvable knee pain. There's sort of a mystical, science-fiction element."

"Wow."

"It's still pretty unformed," I explained, popping the cork.

"I admire your panache," he said.

"Panache?" I asked, not sure of the implication.

Ford said, "It's tough times for fiction right now. The climate's sort of brutal."

"How so?" I asked, arranging the open bottle with the others and going to work on another.

"We're in the middle of a recession," Ford explained. "Returns are alarmingly high. When Old Mother Economy gets her panties in a knot all the little boys and girls who normally haunt the superstores are too busy watching NASDAQ and buying canned goods to journey down literary rabbit holes. It's not a good purchasing time. Most people would rather check books out of their local libraries."

I tried to imagine Old Mother Economy in a literary rabbit hole. I came up with an enormous, bovine-looking woman (grotesquely bearded) stomping through an alfalfa-choked meadow with several of the bunnies from *Watership Down* trailing behind her, pink noses aflutter, desperately in search of the entrance to their burrowed lair.

"The recession's sapping our ability to dream," Ford continued professorially. "Bottom-line economics and imaginative empathy just don't seem to mix. How can I save my home? How will I afford to send little Tina to my alma mater? How am I ever going to finish building that woodshop in the garage? People out there in Consumerville want financial security, not purple prose and freaky, Joycean landscapes."

For a moment I considered the color of my own prose. Was it fuchsia, or lavender, or a hue likened to the skin of some unattractive species of river fish?

"How is the recession affecting things here?" I asked, going to work on bottle number three.

"Well," Ford said, practically fellating another strawberry, "all of our truly interesting, more *midlist* authors are getting cut in favor of those noble scribes of crime fiction and cookbooks. Take Donald Amblin. The fact that *Elect Mr. Rouge* was a nineteen-ninety *San Francisco Chronicle* Bay Area Best Book and got some of the most hyperbolic reviews of anything on the fall list doesn't mean diddly now because he didn't even sell through his print run."

"He didn't?"

"He barely earned out his advance."

"What was his print run?"

"Ten thousand copies."

"What was his advance?" I asked.

"I'm not at liberty to divulge that kind of info. Let's just say that you could do better working the grill at Burger King. You don't earn out, you're suddenly a bottom-line liability. That's just the stink-hole climate right now. Thus, celebrity cookbooks and novels about serial killers who eat brains in Kennebunk. It's amazing how cannibalism can ride out even the toughest times."

"I love *Elect Mr. Rouge.* I've read it three times. "

"It was an editorial darling. Stafford was pressured to let his favorite author go."

"So what's going on with Donald Amblin?" I asked. "Are we doing *Elect Mr. Rouge* in paperback?"

"Oh, we'll excerpt the reviews and slap a sexy, slightly expressionistic cover on it and print a few thousand copies and let the embers die out gracefully."

"What about his next book?"

Ford said, "Unfortunately, no one's doing his next book."

"What's it about?"

"Acute stomach pain and the end of democracy . . . Just kidding. It's actually about a boy from Indiana who mysteriously starts to look like Abraham Lincoln. Sort of Kafkaesque." Ford swept his bangs away again and added, "He's taking a teaching job at some junior college in the middle of Illinois."

"Whoa."

"Yeah, whoa."

"That really sucks."

"Indeed it does," Ford agreed. "He's a semi-celebrated author without a house. It's an ugly time. Yet, check this out," Ford said conspiratorially, swallowing several whole grapes. "Just today Stafford signed up a novel about an alligator that mysteriously shows up at the county seat of a small, unincorporated town in Nebraska with a million unmarked American dollars slung around its neck in an Adidas duffel bag. It's being made into a movie. Big studio fare. The writer-director is a twenty-year-old former skateboard champion from Venice, California. Johnny Sonic. The movie—*Wrestling the Alligator*—is scheduled to be made and released in three years. The quote-unquote *novel* was bought based on fifty pages of a screenplay and a twenty-minute conversation with a thirty-year-old Hollywood executive on the West Coast."

I had uncorked my fifth magnum of Korbel, and I set it on the file cabinet.

"Is the novel gonna be called *Wrestling the Alligator*?" I asked, genuinely intrigued by the title.

"Either that or *Alligator Wrestling*. Stafford likes *Alligator Soufflé*, but I doubt the reps will be able to sell that."

I said, "I always thought books turned into movies, not the other way around."

"Well, right now the movie tie-in thing is a powerful little marketing engine, and frankly we need all the help we can get. Maybe if the novel about the alligator movie sells well we'll be able to re-sign some of those authors like Donald Amblin. I think it's a means to an end. That's why getting these two bad boys on the bestseller list is such reason to celebrate."

"Did you read them?"

"I had to. I wrote the flap copy."

"Are they good?"

"Not in the least, but that's not the point."

"What's the point?"

"The point is 'Do they sell?' Or, more specifically, 'Will the housewives of middle America buy them, read them, and testify to their greatness to all the gals at the Bettendorf, Iowa, District Quilting Tournament?' And the answer to that question is yes. *Wawatosa Sisters* is about menopause and a small entrepreneurial chocolate business. *Drowning All the Gardeners* follows a middle-aged woman who has rabid affairs with the four most powerful horticulturalists in Joplin, Missouri. These are the books that women over forty are buying in the Great Plains right now. Ingram prints its list. We get buzzed from the numbers and go back to press with gleeful abandon. Then the *Times* prints *its* sacred little list in the Sunday *Book Review*, and all those housewives and their friends go out and buy multiple copies. Sometimes they buy it just for the anecdotal capital it generates. The spines of the books alone become little totems of intellectual commerce. The flurries of sales transform into a full-fledged snowstorm. My boss starts getting invited to more important parties. He contemplates starting his own imprint. Thus, congratulatory strawberries and a case of champagne."

Ford piled three kiwi medallions on a cracker, forced the spaceship of fruit into his mouth, chewed, and swallowed.

"So do you write, too?" I asked. "Other than flap copy?"

"I screwed around in an MFA program for a while," he replied, wiping crumbs from the impeccably shaved corners of his mouth. "But after a fair amount of useless months in front of my laptop I wound up buying several ounces of hydroponic cannabis and a secondhand guitar and taught myself Dead covers in a small cold-water apartment in Portland, Oregon. I couldn't keep my hands on the keyboard. Never had the patience. What do you think of that temp in mass market? Have you seen her?"

"No," I said. "What's she like?"

"Great tits. Olympic ass. Kind of this Ayn Rand meets Winona Ryder sexiness about her. I think she's from Utah, which means she's probably Mormon. No doubt plenty of defiling to be done. I invited her to our little celebration."

"Cool," I said, on my eighth Korbel now.

Several of the young women from publicity ambled over in their beige Banana Republic slacks and hennaed hair, the smell of Wella Balsam fruit drifting in their wake. These were the very women of whom I was terrified. Not only were they pretty, they smelled nice, were obvious masters of the more complicated fitness machinery at their local gyms, and possessed multiple Ivy League degrees. They also had studied abroad, could speak French and other difficult Romance languages, and had intricate knowledge of independent films and obscure Bordeaux wines. To them, I was just some dopey-eyed, cowlicked white guy from the Midwest who had, through some fabled Kansan miracle, lucked into the job (an impression that wasn't entirely wrong). I always thought of these women as belonging to a well-dressed, vaguely Amazonian breed of corporate carnivores who would sleep with midlevel management not for the purchase of that highly coveted promotion, but merely for an opportunity to be invited to some sacrosanct, inviolable book party. I loathed them. And I stared them down Wild West style. And I wanted to sleep with each of them, to force myself deep into their overly educated, velveteen vaginas.

While these girls were gathering, I watched Lawler Schnoll—an enormous, bespectacled nonfiction editor with a platinum-blond, offensive lineman's crew cut—assault the lemon squares like a polar bear pawing a bucket of Arctic fish. Her monochromatic lime pantsuit was vast and pleated and gave her the air of a publishing-world superhero, as though she would remain intellectually and politically invincible as long as she kept the suit on.

While Lawler Schnoll was moaning about the baked goods, Ford nodded toward one of the editorial laser printers, where his Ayn Rand–slash–Winona Ryder fantasy was hovering with polite office-temp trepidation. Ford waved her over, smiling like a millionaire. He offered a chocolate-dipped strawberry and she accepted mightily.

Harlan Niederlander's appearance was no doubt the cue for all the midlevel managers and their assistants to hustle out into the hallway.

They scrambled around the food and champagne with such over-wrought fanaticism one might have thought they were auditioning to be extras in an earthquake movie.

While Ford chatted up the temp he poured the Korbel into fluted plastic glasses and passed them out with his ironic charm, saying, "Bubbles, ladies. Bubbles for your troubles . . ."

Puck Stickleback, an editor so erudite and gay he brought to mind British royalty, emerged from his office wrapped in a valentine-red smoking jacket. He immediately collected a napkin and started arranging celery on it as though he intended to smuggle it back to his office and feed it to some five-inch, secretly harbored Pomeranian.

Following Puck was Ford's boss, Stafford Davidson, with his un-kempt, meteorite hair and thick-framed black glasses. Stafford wore running shoes without socks and his feet smelled oddly of butter.

Van Von Donnelly and a few other stragglers from the promotions and sales department joined the party while I continued defoiling and uncorking the Korbel. Van waddled about for a moment and then, with an expression on his face like that of a determined star-nosed mole, greeted Lawler Schnoll with a "Hey there, Lawler," and proceeded to shake her hand with the tenacity of an overly oxygenated politician on election day.

Harlan Niederlander whispered something to his assistant, which prompted her to start clinking on her flute of Korbel with a plastic spork. This impotent little tapping garnered a small swell of laughter from the publicity girls, and then Harlan cleared his throat and the thirty or so people gathered drew quiet and smiley in anticipation of some great, holy, congratulatory truth.

Harlan Niederlander unbuttoned his houndstooth blazer, raised his glass in a pose of sincere yet festive bemusement (which prompted everyone else to likewise raise their flutes of Korbel), and proceeded to launch into a deeply felt speech about team play, editorial resiliency, the effort to uphold the corporate mission statement, and the current economic challenges of the industry. While he cataloged the names of all of those fortunate enough to have had something to do with *Wawatosa Sisters* and *Drowning All the Gardeners*, I was attempting to prepare the final magnum of Korbel. Suddenly the cork shot out of its mouth with exceptional velocity and struck Harlan Niederlander square between the eyes. Suffice it to say that there was a stream of crystal white bubbles frothing from the bottle, accompanied by a momentary, earsplitting, car-crash silence. In a geriatric three-part move (aided by Tonya Shunt, his faithful, frosty-haired assistant), Harlan Niederlander dropped to one knee. As such potent manifestations of corporate office shock tend to do, the aforementioned events produced a single, bloodcurdling, gorilla-like snigger from Lawler Schnoll, who, understandably ashamed, quickly attempted to cover her mouth. In so doing she managed to send an enormous chocolate-covered strawberry into her esophagus, where it lodged quite resolutely. Like most educated people of these great United States, Lawler Schnoll was no doubt skilled in the basics of first aid—namely, how to properly execute some version of the International Choking Symbol—and both hands went up to the anatomically correct tracheal positions to indicate mock strangulation. Then, in a thundering explosion of male heroism, with the fleet-footed dexterity of a cow attempting to disembark from a rowboat, Van Von Donnelly proceeded to tackle Lawler Schnoll, engulf her in a vigorous bear hug, and employ a well-studied—I'll even say *legendary*—demonstration of the Heimlich maneuver; after a single, gallant thrust, an enormous glob of strawberry and chocolate, replete with nameless digestive lubricant, was barked out of Lawler Schnoll's mouth and sent missile-like onto the forehead of the already downed Harlan Niederlander. This single mucoidal projectile was followed by another heroic Van Von Donnelly thrust and a smattering of Lawler Schnoll personal vomit whose volume can be captured in prose only by saying it was so epic as to be stygian. This mass of liquid was deposited onto Harlan Niederlander's head, shoulders, and houndstooth blazer, miraculously avoiding Tonya Shunt, who knelt at Harlan's side in a strange, bug-eyed genuflection.

Although Harlan Niederlander never completed his bestseller speech and the celebration was cut grotesquely short, Van Von Donnelly was immediately heralded as a corporate first-aid champion. (That same afternoon an austere memo circulated illuminating his heroism. The bottom of said memo included an invitation from those gentle men and women of human resources to visit their offices and sign up for a free three-hour seminar in rudimentary first-aid training.)

Wawatosa Sisters and *Drowning All the Gardeners* both enjoyed a tenure of double-digit weeks on the *New York Times* bestseller list; Ford McGowan and his fantasy temp (an actress named Barbara Bus) went on to date for several coitally satisfying months; and Lawler Schnoll dyed her hair black and spent twenty minutes or so per week behind closed doors, hyperbolically thanking Van Von Donnelly for saving her life.

Afterward, not one person—temp or executive—would dare touch the mounds of catered office food or the ten or so full magnums of Korbel champagne; the whole of the party's hulking, multicolored plenty was left on the editorial file cabinets for the remainder of that day, gathering fluorescent, temporal power as a tragicomic, sepulchral totem in honor of all that transpired.

Van Von Donnelly's heroism would dwarf the fact that the cork that started it all had come from the bottle of Korbel between my legs.

The Toilet

WITH THE ADVENT OF THE PENITENTIARY HEAT came the failure of certain plumbing utilities.

It was the third week of August. A building on Thirteenth Street had been raided by helicopters. It was a squat full of anarchist, crack-addict heroin dealers. They'd set fire to the roof and were throwing Molotov cocktails onto parked cars. The squad car and EMS sirens squawked and squealed through the sounds of the woofing choppers for what seemed like hours.

Along Avenue A, Tompkins Square Park was still lined with cops in riot gear. The homeless were being slowly extricated like so many bad molars. Occasionally something in the shantytown would catch fire.

Unit three lost their hot water. In the unit above us, the kitchen sink spat brown, gluey rust. The couple in unit one warned everyone not to drink the water with the desperation of cholera-crazed public-health officials, as if some sort of deadly bacillus had contaminated New York City's entire drinking supply.

Signs were posted in the hallways:

No Hot Water!
Kitchen Sink Spewing Rust!
Don't Drink From Any Tap!

In our apartment, the plumbing pestilence manifested itself through the inability of our toilet to properly flush. At first, a simple jiggling of the lever would convince the tank to refill. This sometimes took three to four minutes and required additional waves of augmented jiggling, but with a certain amount of patience, personal waste could be managed.

At first, we thought ourselves lucky. Our kitchen sink was fine. Our shower was faithful and maintained acceptable water pressure. Our only setback was the slow refilling of the toilet bowl. We didn't have to post any warnings.

But like most half-ignored diseases, it was only a matter of time.

After the third week of the heat wave, the water in the toilet tank sank to an alarmingly low level and the jiggling method ceased to work.

The Owl, whose father was a self-taught plumber—a "folk plumber," as the Owl liked to call him—knew a thing or two about toilets and was certain that replacing what he referred to as "the ballcock" would put an end to our worries. So he disappeared for ten minutes and returned with a strange, bulbous, black rubber ball that looked like a thing discovered among the innards of a mammoth, century-old catfish pulled from the loam of some ancient river on the Delta.

The Owl went to work immediately, performing what appeared to be lavatory surgery. His hands disappeared into the porcelain tank and moments later emerged with the old, lopsided, ravaged ballcock. He held it up to the light and turned it between his fingers lovingly, as if it were his own gallbladder, excavated from a jar of formaldehyde. With great concentration he delved back into the tank with the new ballcock, connected it mysteriously, slid the lid back on, and stood with sublime plumber's certainty. The Owl beckoned and Feick and I gathered around the mouth of the bowl as though we were waiting for a magic bubble to burst and anoint the porcelain.

But when he flushed, the only thing that issued forth was a small, watery, not altogether inhuman-sounding burp.

After the failure with the ballcock, Feick retired to his laundry-upholstered room. The Owl pressed on, attempting to outfit the internal flushing mechanism with a wishboned coat hanger in the hope that the fill mode would be continuously engaged, but all this achieved was a strange, incessant, foul-smelling hiss, so we abandoned that idea as well.

We tried several other techniques. The Owl ran the shower extremely hot, thinking the steam might cause some unknown salve to lubricate the pipes. When that failed and induced a tropical rain-forest effect that spread throughout the apartment, I took an old basketball sneaker and whacked the side of the tank for several minutes. This only gave the Owl and me mild headaches. Then the Owl removed the top again and started throwing a tennis ball into the tank, as if he were trying to stun an excited turtle. He reasoned that the plunging tennis ball would drastically change the volumetric pressure and cause a kind of tidal undertow that would restore the water level. When that failed, too, our backs hit the wall and we slid down, sitting shoulder to shoulder, surrendering.

"No westbound buses."

"No westbound buses," I repeated.

"We don't even think about Port Authority."

"Port Authority we do not think about."

"I will not return to Kansas."

"I will not return to Iowa."

"How's your novel coming?" the Owl asked, finally breaking away from our new anti-westbound-bus ritual.

"It's coming," I said. "Slowly but surely."

"Got a title yet?"

"Not yet," I said. "But I have some ideas."

"I see it in the fridge sometimes. It must be satisfying to see it growing like that."

"I'm still pretty much in the dark with it," I said. "How's work?"

"Work's work," he said. "I find myself doing things sort of automatically."

"Like?"

"Like the production manager will call me into her office and I'll just go there. I won't even think about it. My arms and legs start *ambulating* before the thought occurs. It's like I'm meat."

"You're not meat."

"I'm meat that moves, Homon. I walk mechanicals around from department to department. I collect initials. I gather specs. I'll occasionally speak to an artist on the phone. I get this feeling that it's a bodiless voice I'm speaking to. We say things to each other. We exchange information. But nothing really passes between us. I get that feeling about everyone in the office, too."

"What feeling?"

"That everyone is disembodied somehow. The editors. The marketing people. Even the girl in human resources. I see bodies without voices and I hear voices without bodies. Like some weird, corporate pathologist could come in and open us up and he'd find vacuum-cleaner parts or something. The air-conditioning's the only saving grace."

"Yeah, air-conditioning is pretty nice."

"I'm gonna quit."

"When?"

"Tomorrow. I'm giving my notice. I've already decided."

"Well, you're going back to school anyway, so it's probably for the best."

"I wanna teach myself how to play the guitar. Write songs."

"Songs are cool. Songs and grad school."

That's when the Loach appeared bearing an orange bucket of water, like some amphibious mosquito man summoned from the sewers. He took an off-balanced, gravity-deprived step toward the toilet, pushed down his pathogenic briefs, pressed his hams to the porcelain (the bucket of water in his lap now), and began defecating with the timbre of a large helicon tuba.

The Owl and I were too stunned to react in any physical way; we simply looked at each other.

The Loach didn't move. He hardly even twitched. He simply voided his bowels with exceptional gastrointestinal thunder. When he was finished, he wiped, stood, and dumped the bucket of water into the basin.

Surprisingly, the toilet flushed immediately and issued forth a noise not unlike the sound of exploding bowling pins. The perfect whirlpool swirled into the netherworld of New York City's plumbing system. Then the Loach pulled his underwear back up, set the bucket down beside us, and without pride, explanation, or even a hint of confidence, returned to his blue-lit television trance on the sofa, somewhere near the slow wind of the fan.

These were the kinds of things the Loach knew.

These were the kinds of things we learned about when we lived with the Loach.

And this is how the bucket-of-water method was born.

It was surprisingly simple, efficient, and highly interactive. It introduced a rustic element to the apartment. We were roughing it like they once did on the open range, where things like campfires and killing your dinner were done without the privilege of technology, where holes were dug for waste management.

For convenience we kept the bucket in the bathtub. At first, before showering, I would take a moment and set it in the sink so that I could bathe without being reminded of our defective toilet. After a while, though, like most household responsibilities that are eventually neglected due to lack of discipline or communal fatigue or some other natural law of domestic atrophy, I would no longer remove the bucket before my shower and instead watched it fill with soapy water.

There were mornings when I managed to wedge one of my feet inside the bucket and ended up bathing with inadvertent, histrionic, shower-room slapstick.

There was a brief period when a sponge mop joined the bucket, and it was like showering with a headless dance partner.

Thanks to the Loach, our manual flushing system was a great success. At one point, we even drew up a set of instructions for visitors and posted them on the bathroom wall. Friends would compliment us because it was fun.

The system's only danger was that with a large complement of feces you had to be sure not to pour too much water into the bowl, or the turds would leap out of the toilet like so many blackened salmon spawning from the sewers.

Pretty Girl
on a Train

I WAS ON THE DOWNTOWN ONE and she was on the Number Two Express. The encounter happened during that strange, slow-motion interval when the express overtakes the local and you can peer across the gap and into the window of the other train with all of its amber, porch-like dream light.

That particular day, the day I ran out of socks and my feet itched sinisterly, I saw a young woman with dark curly hair and skin so pale it could have been ceramic. Her eyes were enormously sad and so smolderingly green that they looked as though they would warm my hands if I were to touch her face.

I normally wouldn't stare at anyone in a passing train. Perhaps it was her fire-polished skin, or those eyes, or the curls that emerged at her temples like a pair of perfectly positioned hat accessories.

All sounds seemed to momentarily fade: the thunder of the engine; the ruffling and popping of newspapers; the din of music trapped in earphones; the squealing of the train on its tracks.

I felt a strange peace during those three or four seconds. It was as if someone had turned off a small appliance that had been whirring in my head for several days.

After her train sluiced into the blackness, I realized that my hand was poised on the window, as if I were trying to reach through the glass and touch her.

Limping

AFTER MY KNEE EXPLODED, limping became a kind of personal theatre. I call it theatre because with a well-developed limp comes an inherent audience. My audience included (but was not limited to) my fellow publishing-house employees, roommates, anonymous subway denizens, doormen, construction workers, flower cutters, orange-garbed Teamsters, bald religious fanatics, cops (with and without riot gear), bookstore clerks, subway conductors, scaffolding builders, bikers, the Ninth Street cobbler, postal workers (the 10009 branch; such pleasant smiles), hustlers and hostesses, and the homeless.

I limped and they watched. At times it inspired in them a sympathetic need to limp as well, some sort of masochistic desire to vicariously experience afflicted joints.

For the limper, there's definitely a performative aspect as well; a role that has to be fulfilled; a responsibility of eliciting in the onlooker memories of pain or flights of compassion or even bouts of disgust. Each plant of the foot carries with it a display of facial gymnastics not dissimilar to our great soap actors' pre-commercial-break reaction shots.

Certain men are good at pouring cement or tamping freshly laid asphalt or playing games with knives.

I was good at limping.

The limp started in my right ankle and crawled up my leg the way a beetle might crawl on a family of ripe tomatoes. All points between my big toe and my hip were in some way affected. The base of my shin thickened with splints and cramps. The right side of my calf muscle would twitter and ache as if stimulated by an electric current. My right leg would bow out with the flamboyant aping of a rodeo clown. My lower back would buckle and collapse as if I were being beaten with a large and very full suitcase. At times the knee on my foundering side would drop dangerously low to the ground. Then my whole body would pop back up elastically, and the limp would begin again.

Taxis would screech to my rescue. Bus drivers would hydraulically tilt their entrance steps as if I were a geriatric.

After a few weeks, instead of asking after my knee, people would ask me how my limp was doing.

"How's that limp?" Van Von Donnelly would query on the way to the marketing meeting.

"What's new with the limp?" the Owl would ask, attempting to make couscous at the stove.

One morning, on my way to the L train, an obnoxious neighbor who devotedly sat on the stoop next to our building clinging to his mountain bike asked me if I was taking my limp for a walk.

"Takin' her for a walk?" he said.

I replied, "Taking *who* for a walk?"

"Your limp!" he sneered, ducking behind his mountain bike.

The guy could get under my skin.

That morning I kicked his bike three times, seized the handlebars, and honked the horn directly into his face. Despite my throbbing knee, it felt great to kick something hard and in triplicate.

Alexa

ALEXA WORKED IN EDITORIAL, and when I started in the sales department she had recently been promoted from editorial assistant to assistant editor. I understood neither the difference between the two titles nor the significance of their inverted wordplay. I assumed the latter of the two simply meant a slight increase in salary and a box of business cards.

I first encountered Alexa while Xeroxing the bellwether reports. The reports were hulking and the in-house distribution list was so long it read like a page from the phone book. I usually filched an unoccupied chair and sat next to the copy machine while it belched out my morning's work.

If I hogged the copy machine I was instantly resented by multiple departments. Fellow employees would walk by with ferocious gutters of malice gouging their brows. I would ignore them, and they would hate me as if I were an office troll who lived under a mail gurney in the supply room.

I was reading a bound galley that had been left on the free-and-review counter when Alexa entered into my personal space like some domesticated corporate she-ape in pursuit of a banana. I thought she was going to cite a complaint about my monopolization of the copy machine, or ask me if she could cut in (in the spirit of sales department loyalty, I would have said no with detached stoicism).

She was standing so close I could smell the dueling skin products with which she'd slathered herself that morning. Orange and mango and papaya. Coconut and eucalyptus. Something strawberry. I could practically smell these fragrances with my eyes. Her clog-like space shoes were ramped so severely I got the sense that at any moment she might be ejected into the recycling bin. Her dimpled knees were tan and hairless. Her clothes were dark and ominous-looking. An overly stitched, plum-colored riding suit; something from the steeplechase, perhaps. Her padded Wonderbra was employed with such excellence that her breasts seemed somehow military or bionic. Or militarily bionic. Her hair brown as a horse's and pulled back into a severe attorney's bun. Her nails the color of cotton candy and flawlessly manicured. Her face attractive but overly made up. Her lips fully agleam with a high-gloss balm that made her mouth appear to be fireproof. Her teeth so white they sang—or hissed, rather. Her eyes brownish-black and large and lined with great, mannequin-like care. Her brows plucked down to two thin, sleeping serpents. Alexa was harshly pretty the way desk lamps and designer ashtrays can be. She had the privilege of the new fall fashions but the air of a gunslinger.

"You might find this alarming," she said in a rather perpendicular power stance, "but I thought I'd spare you an acre or so of shame and humiliation by letting you know that your fly is open."

I looked down.

My fly was, indeed, open.

"And I'm Alexa."

My fly was so open it was almost sighing. It was a clown's mouth. And to make things worse, the bottom of my pale blue Oxford, complete with a very bright and lustrous catsup stain, was trumpeting through the orifice.

"Thanks," I replied, and continued staring down, embarrassed.

When I looked up, she was marching around the corner, the backs of her legs muscling with peanut-buttery sinews, her head shaking with a kind of vague maternal amusement.

I sat there for a moment, trying to pinpoint when it was that I started to fail at these small hygienic duties.

Hand washing.

Hair combing.

Flossing.

Zipping my pants.

Plucking pubic hairs from the Irish Spring.

After a while I secured my fly and got back to the bellwether reports. There was the distribution to get lost in.

There was always the distribution.

That morning the copy machine jammed four times and I cut my thumb on a staple.

Visiting the Underwood

I WOULD VISIT MY PAWNED UNDERWOOD at the vintage shop on First Avenue (it was called Twice in a Lifetime), sometimes for an hour at a time. I would limp around the Barcelona chairs and surreptitiously stroke the accordions and coo over the twenty-pound ashtrays.

The woman behind the counter watched me the same way a grammar-school principal might watch children throwing snowballs in an out-of-school parking lot.

I would feign interest in the fedora hats and the dwarf guitars and the old three-quarter jazz neckties. I would spy the Underwood out of the corner of my eye while fondling a set of cow and bull salt-and-pepper shakers.

The woman behind the counter kept a close watch with her cat-eyed glasses and her blue bangs and her nose stud, clinging to her nostril like an electroplated deer tick.

To the left of the Underwood was a refinished drop-top desk with a pair of calico bowling shoes placed on the blotter, the laces tied in perfect bows, the strange, mismatched ensemble attempting to upstage my old friend, perched rather austerely on a waist-high marble dais.

The woman watching me.

Walleyed now.

Her face harder than a windmill.

Movie posters and ottomans and lensless spectacles.

Porkpie hats and freestanding cigarette lighters.

Mini TVs.

Oh, the Underwood.

I would turn my yearning into a children's fable. I would wish for the Underwood to sprout little typewriter legs and run out of the shop with me, calliope music wheedling in the background.

Ulysses the Underwood Goes Home.

Pretty Girl Across the Platform

THE GREEN EYES.

The almost translucent pallor.

The twists of hair curling off her temples.

She was standing across the platform, facing me while hundreds of commuters hummed by. Just standing there, poised in a seamless black dress. Somehow out of time. Her eyes enormous and sad, as though they were watching a cherished canoe, empty and sinking in the middle of a foggy lake. A young widow, perhaps. Despite the heat, the dress was strangely long and close to her body, as though painted across her shoulders, down her arms, all the way to her wrists.

She was holding a straw bag. Her fingers like fluted glass. Her face still as ice. Her mouth full and dark and beautifully dead. The girl just standing there like a pilgrim traveler, an effigy of wonderment or penance.

As the express train pulled in, she continued to stand there, facing me.

I was standing, her mirror opposite, mid-limp, my knee tight as a sailor's knot. My newly purchased tie, navy with yellow and red pencil stripes. My khakis with their imperfect, forced, divergently ironed seams. My overly showered hair levitating in an embarrassing cowlick. Those wingtips. My little brother's white oxford gripping me, my pits bleeding a flagrant, chemical yellow. The whole of me stuffed and belted and necktied into some ill-prepared undergraduate's failed attempt at corporate preppiness.

This is the portrait of me she no doubt saw.

And then her arm started to rise. Slowly, strangely absent. Almost confidently, as though the train door would remain open and wait for her to cue her safe entrance. And her hand lifted with equal, sublime listlessness, like a beautiful solitary moon plant leaning toward some runaway vegetal planet.

A hello.

A recognition.

And then I was bumped by a man carrying a pink galaxy of birthday balloons.

I lurched left and then right, until my hand found the very hot and gummy mouth of a large trash receptacle.

By the time I regained my balance and wiped my hand, the train was gone and so was she.

Jack Shank

THERE WAS A VICE PRESIDENT IN SALES who announced his farts. During the early weeks of my tenure as sales assistant he had been away (a much needed monthlong vacation in the south of France), and he and his farts had been spoken of in the same way one speaks of Sasquatch or the Loch Ness Monster. He was physically larger than most of us (he was the size of a retired NFL lineman, actually), so his gastrointestinal proclamations had a kingly quality, as though royal hounds might suddenly appear and start trotting down the gray-carpeted hallway in a synchronized preamble.

The offerings were unbelievably loud and sounded like a grand piano being budged across a cement floor. He'd usually prelude the blasts by saying something Seussian like "Oh boy, Roy!" or "Here she comes, chums!"

Just after announcing the impending flatulence he'd smile mischievously, his incisors gleaming, his eye sockets going wide as eggs. Then he'd bob back and forth a little, heel-to-toe, kind of basking in the pre-blast anticipation. There was a silence that I could feel settling in my throat. And then things would get interesting: I could almost *hear* the methane spiraling through his bowels, sluicing around pounds of intestinal sediment, skidding through clogged diverticula, banking and somersaulting over viscera, gathering echothunder from the alimentary canal, and challenging modern interpretations of fossil fuels at the release point.

And then Jack Shank was suddenly a truck driver on Interstate 80, making a power fist and pulling down. It was either a two- or three-part move. It's hard to reconstruct because there was sleight of hand involved. He'd perfected the art of sneaking up on a group, coiling into the stance, getting his teeth ready to gleam. It didn't matter who was there. Men. Women. Other vice presidents. The pelican-like CEO in his gray landowner's suit. Recent graduates interviewing for jobs. Authors roaming the office, trying to filch bound galleys of their work.

Then the blast would roil up and be released from the clutches of his pyloric sphincter. Time would sort of skid for a moment and the fluorescent lighting would seem to take on a dinner-theatre quality (the way the gels warm a bit during Oliver Twist's "Where Is Love"), and there would be a slightly stunned look on everyone's face, because it *was* a kind of theatre—grand, cut-and-run performance art.

And because he signed our time sheets.

The vice president's name was Jack Shank, and he called himself the Shankler.

One day, after the marketing meeting, the Shankler called me into his office. When the Shankler called someone into his office the meeting had extreme possibilities. It could either mean I was going to be fired or that he wanted me to go downstairs and fetch him a roast beef sandwich (multigrain bread, no mayo).

Aside from experiencing his cathartic buzzsaw fart performances, I had never spent any quality time with the Shankler. I was kept away from the marketing meetings the way dogs are kept away from the table during dinnertime. Once when the regional sales managers came—or *promenaded*—into the office for the editorial launch, and the Shankler had just finished briefing Van Von Donnelly with the intensity of a Big Ten offensive coordinator, they emerged from Van's office like two linemen taking the field. I was about to follow them eagerly down the hall but the Shankler wheeled and pointed at me. His finger mimed a line north to south, literally pointing me back down to my chair. I heeled to my Skinner box with the blind obedience of a cocker spaniel. On cue, Van said, "Keep the midgets in line," as if I were an army recruit assigned to hold sentry over a case of contraband Budweiser. I nodded and sat.

This was, in a nutshell, the god-fearing, sales-department monarchy of the Shankler.

At times I had seen other assistants waiting nervously outside the Shankler's office, pacing choppily, their hands rifling in the pockets of their chinos, perhaps in an attempt to produce a soothing tinkle music with coins and keys and breath mints. Some would disassemble and re-build their neckties, seeking order in the kernels of their Windsor knots. These young Ivy League bachelors would unravel so thoroughly you'd think they were visiting a bookie.

Upon viewing the scene outside the Shankler's office, if one men-tally replaced the company Sheetrock with cinder blocks, one might think the summoned sales department employee was about to be med-ically prepped for lethal injection.

So that was where I found myself, outside the Shankler's office, at-tempting to remain coolheaded. Perhaps I'd written on the job one too many times? Perhaps my recent rash of three-to-five-minute tardiness was unpardonable? Perhaps it was my bestseller-list-party champagne disaster after all?

I started to panic. I think I actually affected a fever. I loosened my tie and tried to put a stop to the flop sweat.

His door was open.

To the naked eye, his office was a quick study in corporate minimal-ism. Unlike other publishing higher-ups, he had no books choking his shelves or drifts of unread manuscripts crowding the corners or star re-ports and distribution updates piled in his in-box. His office consisted of the simple ensemble of a desk with a chair on either side, and four shelves so nakedly poised on the Sheetrock it seemed as though they'd been drilled into the wall only moments before. There were also a com-puter and a phone, neatly centered on the desk like mismatched, inert hardware lovers.

Thumbtacked rather crookedly to the back wall, one could also see a poster of a briefly famous TV actress wearing a flossy, venom-yellow, spaghetti-string bikini. She was lounging on a red sports car and fake-smiling her nose into a little button of lunacy.

Beyond the poster, the office could have been drawn with fewer than twelve lines.

The Shankler was completing a phone debate about the size of the new cookbook editor's ass when we locked eyes and he waved me in.

As I crossed the threshold to my doom he moaned several foghorn-sounding, phlegmatic laughs, as though he were fighting through the vapors of a cough-syrup overdose. He punctuated these sighs with a rather unimpressive burp, hung up the phone, and in the same antihistamine-saturated baritone declared, "Good ol' Slumey," referring to Howard Slume, our legendary rep in Portland. Then, to me, he said, "That new editor, I really like her. What's her name?"

I said, "I think it's Tonya."

"Tonya with a T."

The Shankler started smiling so that his gums showed, so I smiled so that my gums showed, too. This collaborated grin evolved into an oblique head-nodding festival, which ended when I finally offered, "Tonya Trout, actually."

"Yeah, Tonya Trout. What a gal. You like her?" he asked, his eyebrows dancing rather maniacally.

I said, "I like her."

"You sure?" His eyes seemed to get smaller somehow. The dancing eyebrows came to rest and transformed into tense little knives of scrutiny. This was definitely a test.

"Um, sure I'm sure," I replied. "I do like her, Mr. Shank."

"Great set of sticks. I'm not sure about her can, though. What do you think about her can?"

I answered, "Her can?"

"Her *can*, kid. Her *ass*."

I could only come up with, "Oh. Well. Um—"

"I mean, I'd *do* her, don't get me wrong," he testified carnivorously. "Hell, she might be one of these broads who has some kind of weird jack-in-the-box energy. What do *I* know?"

I nodded back at him with the cognitive aptitude of an empty gumball machine.

"God I love vadge in the office," he added. "Hey, close the door, wouldya?"

I closed the door. I turned back. He was grinning like a millionaire again. I took this as a cue that it was my subordinate duty to grin again as well, so I joined him. We were all gums. He was grinning like a millionaire and I was grinning like I had a sheet of food stamps stuck to my ass. Somehow the actress in the poster was setting the tone in the room.

"So I bet you have no idea why I've called you in here," he said.

The Shankler's office suddenly felt smaller than a shoebox. He was a pair of very large loafers, and I was a glob of gum stuck to the sole.

"Um, I guess I don't, Mr. Shank," I responded, a bit of soprano frogging in my voice.

"Call me Jack."

"Okay."

"Go ahead, try it."

"Um, I guess I don't, Jack."

"How did that feel?"

"Great," I said. "It felt great."

"Only in here, though. In here call me Jack."

"Yes, sir. I mean Jack."

"Out there in the trenches call me Shankler."

"Out there it's Shankler."

"Or Mr. Shank."

"Or Mr. Shank. Of course, of course."

"Or Jack Shank, Man of a Thousand Faces."

I was speechless.

"Just kidding."

His sense of humor was bewildering and asinine.

"As you probably already know," he continued, "when I call one of the midgets in here it either means something good or something bad's about to happen. During my twelve years of service I've fired roughly thirty-seven assistants. I've also promoted a few dozen of the little people to greener pastures."

I said, "Greener pastures are cool."

"Strangely enough," he forged on, "with you, it's neither." His shoe-box office was now turning into something that might package a mousetrap. "You get where I'm going with this?" he asked.

I replied, "I'm afraid I don't."

"I'll keep it short and sweet."

"Okay."

"I have this daughter."

"Uh-huh."

"She's twenty-two. Five-seven. A buck-oh-five, a buck-ten, tops. Gorgeous red hair, like her mother. Beautiful, beautiful girl. What are you, six-six, six-seven?"

I said, "Six-three. Six-three and a quarter, actually."

"You play ball, huh?"

"I do play ball. Yes."

"Van tells me you can dunk. That you can get right up there and tear the rim down."

"Well, not right now, actually. I'm sort of still getting over a knee problem."

"Well, anyway, the point is she likes tall guys."

I said, "Oh."

For some reason I pictured a small redheaded, prepubescent girl not unlike Little Orphan Annie.

"I'd like you to take her out on a date."

"Like a *date* date?"

"Man calls woman. They speak on phone. They meet for a Coca-Cola. They take in a movie. Man escorts woman home. They shake hands, they kiss, they take a bath, they play Scrabble, whatever. Here's a few hundred bucks," he said, flipping a knot of rubberbanded twenties onto the desk.

"Her name is Lacy," he added.

"Lacy," I echoed.

"Lacy Elizabeth Shank. L-E-S are her initials, and even though we're one *s* shy, less is more if you get what I'm saying."

"Oh. Right on."

"Like I said, she likes tall guys. So stand up when she walks in the room. Her digits," he added, pushing one of his business cards toward me, her telephone number penciled on the back. "I told her she'd be hearing from you today or tomorrow, so she's expecting your call."

I took the wad of money and the card and placed both in my pocket.

"There's something about you, kid," the Shankler said, extending his hand. "I have every confidence that this'll go well."

"Thanks, Jack," I said, reaching toward his open palm. When my hand met his he squeezed it with the strained athleticism of an overly aerobicized gym teacher.

And then he farted with exceptional volume.

Futons

THE OWL AND I BOUGHT FUTONS.

I folded up my green canvas Marine cot and slid it under the frame of my new futon. The Owl rolled up his corrugated foam-core camping pad for the final time, secured it with gaffer's tape, and inserted it into a vacant umbrella holder.

Thus, the saga of our dueling futons was born.

We slept fitfully but talked about how deep-down dreamy you could get in them. We superfluously manipulated them into sofa mode, not to create space but to showcase the seldom-used utility.

The Owl's futon trundled under effortlessly, whereas mine had to be lifted, pulled, and jointed inversely. I often found myself half-trapped in its wooden jaws like some kind of block-footed nincompoop.

Meanwhile, the Owl would slide his in and out of sofa mode with the ease of a veteran hydraulics specialist.

We asked after each other's futons in the same way one might inquire about a friend who's left the country.

The Owl's futon had a foam-core center, and he constantly boasted of its cloud-like softness.

My futon sagged in the middle and buckled against the wall and afforded about the same quality of comfort as an empty rowboat.

Lacy

I CALLED THE SHANKLER'S DAUGHTER and we met at a bar on Broadway and Sixty-fourth Street. Lacy Shank was a fourth-year conservatory actress studying at Juilliard, and during the first few minutes of our phone conversation I honestly thought she was British. She was at the time mired in tech rehearsals for Oscar Wilde's *The Importance of Being Earnest*. She was performing the role of Cecily Cardew, the young student beauty under the tutelage of Lady Bracknell. After the accent faded, her version of American stage speech took over like so much virgin spring water running down a crystal mountain. Every syllable was seemingly accounted for, every letter crossed or dotted with a slender, well-trained tongue. Experiencing such vocal clarity over the phone was astonishing. I felt as though I'd won a prize, that she was speaking to me from the glossy bowels of some sweepstakes showroom in the Midwest. Strangely enough, I liked her effect on me. She used a new kind of alphabet, not different from my own, but stronger, faster, curvier. In an attempt to feel what it might be like to be a word inside her mouth, after we'd hung up I actually found myself echoing her farewell of "Anon, then."

It was my first time in the Lincoln Center area since Feick's play had closed. Walking up the subway steps I immediately felt that hint of privilege, as though this part of the city had been borne out of some animated catalog of twill and tweed and identical royal blue dealmaker's shirts. The hot-dog carts were polished, the homeless people more articulate. Even the air around Lincoln Center seemed cleaner, as if New York kept a secret tank of purer oxygen in reserve beneath the opera house.

Lacy was seated at a cocktail table next to an enormous copper-etched mantel featuring several nude angels lounging under a stand of olive trees. She was exactly as I had imagined her based on the description she gave me over the phone. She was neither tall nor short, incredibly redheaded in that deep, burnt-orange kind of way, and in possession of perhaps the most mischievous gray eyes I have ever seen. She was wearing old jeans, cowboy boots, and a grim black T-shirt that read, I AM HELL. She was smoking Marlboro Reds like her life depended on it and drinking scotch neat.

I was wearing something absolutely unremarkable: jeans, and an oxford I'd borrowed from the Owl's closet. I was only an XL and the Owl was a double XL, but he had good shirts. It had a collar and was navy blue.

I walked up to her and stood for a moment, hoping that she would recognize me based on my description, which was: "I'm sort of tall, but not that tall."

Lacy Shank stared at me for a moment. The smoke slid silkily out of her mouth, the way it does in film noir. Her cat-like eyes seemed to widen a bit, and then she drained her drink and in a surprisingly husky voice said, "Are you Tall, But Not That Tall?"

"Yes," I said. "I guess that would be me."

Above the fireplace and mounted on a three-foot dais was what appeared to be an antlered, jumping pony. It had been fashioned from cast iron and was hoofed like a horse and wore an expression of a philosopher's supreme, stoic boredom on its bearded face. It was poised midleap, its hind legs heaved up as if the thing were teasing some other mythological half-goat in the room around the corner. For some reason I checked to see if it had genitals, and then sat down.

"Interesting," I said, pointing to our four-legged friend above the fireplace.

"I thought it was a reindeer, but the gentleman behind the bar corrected me."

Men were suddenly gentle. They were gentle men. Perhaps I was one of these men?

"What is it?" I asked, glancing toward the bar, where a Spaniard with a long bullfighter's ponytail was staring back at us with testosterone-charged nonchalance.

"It's an iron wildebeest," Lacy said, taking a drag on her cigarette.

A small Peruvian man in a white smock (perhaps the bullfighter's assistant) came over and took my drink order. I requested an amber beer and immediately felt my gonads shrink. Lacy would find my drink choice to be somehow feminine. She was drinking scotch, after all. I should have at least ordered a stout.

For approximately an hour we talked about inane and utterly forgetful things, roommates and rent money and subway habits. Favorite bands and my glaring Midwestern accent.

"Is it that glaring?" I asked.

"It's totally glaring. Say family."

I said it.

"See?" she prodded. "You say *fam*bly."

I said it again: "Family."

"*Fam*bly."

"I don't say *fam*bly," I squawked.

"You do. You say *fam*bly."

"I don't put a *b* in it."

"Oh, you do, too."

"I do?"

"Absolutely."

"I put a *b* in *fam*bly?"

"See? You just did."

"Huh . . ."

She drank four scotches. I hung tough with my amber beer. Though I had to excuse myself three times to urinate, I matched her drink for drink. Lacy had the bladder of a Norwegian foxhunter and never excused herself to use the bathroom.

After our second round Lacy ordered her scotch on the rocks instead of neat. This is a subtle shift worth mentioning here because I've heard that women who chew ice cubes are horny.

"What?" she asked, ice cubes clinking against her small white teeth.

"What *what*?" I asked.

"You're looking at me funny."

"I am?"

"Yes. You have a look of amazement on your face. Like you have a secret."

"I don't have a secret," I insisted.

"You look like you have a boner or something."

"I do?"

"You don't have a fucking boner, do you?"

"No. I was just sort of wondering why you haven't had to take a piss yet," I explained, trying to adjust my erection under the table. It was firm and angular. "You've drank four scotches and you—"

"*Drunk.*"

"What?"

"You said *drank*. The correct participle is *drunk*."

"Oh."

"And you call yourself a writer?"

This was a low blow.

"My prose is a lot better than my speech," I tried to explain.

"I'm kidding," Lacy said. "You're just a little drunk. Don't be so serious."

She was right. I was a little drunk. I was drunk and I was starting to hate this girl, although I was incredibly attracted to her and had the boner to prove it.

As we left the bar it started to rain and the combined smells of bus exhaust, urine, and baked asphalt rose sharply off Sixty-fourth Street.

We hovered on the corner. Outside, Lacy's eyes seemed even grayer, her skin paler.

"So, where are you going?" she asked, wiping rain from her face.

"I don't know. I guess I was just gonna take the train back downtown."

"Back to your little apartment in the East Village?"

"It's actually not that little."

"Back to safety."

We stood in the rain for another moment and then Lacy did something utterly surprising. It was almost shocking, in fact.

She bit my ear.

And this is how it happened.

She said, "Come here," so I lowered my head. I thought she was going to tell me my fly was open or kiss my cheek, but she bit my left ear rather accurately and with the audacity of a Chihuahua.

"Ouch!" I said dramatically.

"You're the ouch," she teased.

We stared at each other. I tended to my earlobe. I could feel my shoulders hunching so intensely I could have been mistaken for a man wearing football gear for the first time.

Then Lacy said, "*Fam*bly," again.

"*Fam*bly," I echoed. "That's me. The *fam*bly man."

The rain was making me dull and stupid.

"You should come up," she offered.

"I should?"

"Yeah, come up," she said decisively. And then, in a rather unflattering imitation of my own voice, she predicted my response, saying, "Um, okay."

We walked north seven blocks, to her apartment on Seventy-first and Broadway. We bought newspapers to shield us from the rain. As I was adjusting my newspaper on my head I walked into a traffic pole and almost broke my chin. Lacy wasn't the least bit interested in nursing me, or even in making it known that she'd seen me stagger back and nearly be hit by a blaring taxi. She just forged ahead as though we were late for something. We walked like we were lab partners and she had all the results.

Lacy's doorman said, "Hello, Miss Shank," and regarded me rather obliquely, as if I were not a man but rather a thing being wheeled into the building on casters, like an expensive lamp or a grandfather clock.

The elevator ride was slow and torturous. I refused to look at my reflection in the mirror out of fear that the rain had produced some strange mucoidal paste that was now clinging to my face. But I couldn't help looking, and although I was free of facial secretions, I noted that I resembled a very pale and malnourished dental assistant.

During the ten-floor ascent we said nothing. Perhaps in the small, mammalian parts of our brains we both knew that we had very little in common except an interest in performing the sex of dogs and monkeys.

Her apartment was so trashed I couldn't tell if it was a studio or a one-bedroom. Unused tampons and pizza boxes and the remains of so much half-eaten fast food were scattered about in an aimless domestic blizzard. There were clothes strewn about the Ikea furnishings like the deflated carcasses of Halloween monsters. Was that a TV or a microwave? A clock radio or a toaster oven? The positioning of her furnishings was employed with such randomness it appeared that some sort of micro-disaster had ravaged the place, something having more to do with apartment property than with the environment. A Realtor's typhoon. A landlord's tornado.

There was a version of a writer's alcove that was so clogged with laundry and books and the benign remains of things bought without intent of utility or exploit that it appeared that the apartment had somehow been tilted on its axis toward this forlorn and overcrowded corner.

Dominating the center of the apartment was an unmade, king-size bed. It looked like the only place one could go to find refuge.

"So what do you think of my dad?" Lacy asked, suddenly closing the door. I'd expected her to end her question with *home* instead of *dad*. Oh, how one word—a smaller, three-letter word, even—can raise the temperature in a room. It was the one thing we hadn't yet talked about. Jack Shank was the two-ton gorilla that had been silently following us around all night.

"Your dad?" I chirped.

"Yeah, my dad," she said, producing a towel and tossing it to me. I hadn't even realized that I was still holding on to my sopping newspaper. The ink was bleeding down my forearms. "What's he like around the office?" she asked.

"He's pretty cool," I offered rather safely.

"But . . ."

"But what?"

"I can hear the *but* coming."

"You can hear my butt coming?"

"No," she said. "The lingering *but* creeping around at the end of your sentence. He's pretty cool, *but what*?" She could sniff me out, this girl. This Lacy Shank. It was all that acting training. She could feel moments building before they arrived. She could read my energy.

"Well," I said, "he's a great vice president."

"Uh-huh."

"He's like the chief, you know?"

"And you're one of the Indians."

"Yeah, and he, like, leads us."

"He's a leader!"

"That's right. He leads the sales team. He stands over us. Ready to guide. To impart his, um, largeness."

"He leads with his imparting largeness."

"Well, largeness being literal as well as figurative."

"Daddy certainly has a pretty big figure."

"Well, he's a big guy. He sort of, um, takes up a lot of space. I mean, he's great and all, but . . ."

"But what, bro?"

"Bro?"

"Yeah, man, but what?"

"But he sort of like farts a lot."

There.

It was all over.

The following morning I would walk into the office and there'd be a security guard standing over the cardboard box containing my few possessions.

"Oh, Daddy farts around me too," she explained casually. "He used to actually fart *on* me when I was little."

"He farted *on* you?"

"He did, yes. In our *fambly* it's a sign of affection."

"Oh."

"The Shanks, man. When you're dealing with us you know exactly where you are."

This was probably true. In my experience, the Shanks I knew—Jack and Lacy—definitely played their cards. They slapped them right down on the table. No bluffing involved.

"So, did your mother like fart on you, too?" I asked, drying myself with the towel.

"No, unfortunately she was chronically gasless. But she certainly could make it *seem* like she was farting on you."

"How's that?"

"Well, she was sort of into gastrointestinal ventriloquism. Whoopee cushions. Underarm farting. She'd record stuff and play it on the stereo at opportune moments. She actually created a sound studio devoted entirely to her farting projects. Amps. High-end microphones. Various studio accoutrements. A Fostex multitracker."

"Huh," was all I could say in response. For some reason the thought of Lacy Shank's mother and father farting on each other out of familial tradition made me want to sit on the floor.

So that's what I did.

I cleared a space and sat on a rather nice-looking hardwood floor.

"So what did Daddy say about me?" Lacy asked, her head leaning a little to the left, her red hair almost brown from the rain.

"Not much, really. He mostly kept talking about how you like tall guys."

"Oh, he's such a liar."

"What, you don't like tall guys or something?"

"Not really. I think he *wants* me to like tall guys, though. My last boyfriend was like five-five. Daddy just didn't like him 'cause he found out that he dealt a little coke here and there. I'm usually into short guys. The shorter the better, in fact. I even dated a midget for a few weeks when I was in Barcelona. He was a bullfighter. The smallest professional bullfighter in the world. Not a bad lover, either."

"Wow," I replied. "I had no idea they allowed midgets to—"

That's when something darted through the mess. I sprang to my feet and, like a newborn calf, slipped splay-legged and fell on my kneecaps and sprang back to my feet. This did not help my injury or my limp any. The pain was excruciating. Was it a mouse? A rat? An urban raccoon? All I could be absolutely sure of was that a towel, a pair of socks, and a plastic box containing a half-eaten piece of sushi had suddenly animated.

"What was that?" I asked.

"Oh, that was Banjo," Lacy responded casually.

"That was a *banjo*?"

"Banjo," she explained. "My Abyssinian."

I had no idea what she was talking about.

"What's an Abyssinian?" I imagined a French-speaking ferret in designer jeans.

"It's a cat," she explained. "Banjo!" she called out. "Appear, please!"

Moments later, a beautiful orange cat appeared on top of a pile of pizza boxes. Its eyes were so yellow they looked fake. Upon closer inspection, I could see that its fur was almost the same color as Lacy's wet hair. Banjo stared out at us rather omnipotently, poised with a strange stillness, as if a spell had been cast and the cat had been transformed into its own bronzed effigy. I had the strange feeling that he might suddenly break into song.

"Okay, you can go back to whatever you were doing. Thank you," Lacy said, dismissing the genius cat with a flick of her wrist. And just like that, Banjo was gone.

"Wow," I said. "Cool cat."

"Yeah, he's pretty amazing. We have a very unusual relationship."

"Unusual how?" I asked, sitting again, trusting that the phenomenon of things suddenly animating was part of the natural law of Lacy Shank's apartment.

"Well, for one thing, he has an exceptional vocabulary."

"He speaks?"

"Not literally. But we have a kind of telekinesis."

"Really?"

"Daddy thinks we should go on TV. Watch," she instructed, suddenly closing her eyes. Her brows twitched a bit and then, moments later, there was a scuffle of claws and Banjo again materialized on top of the pizza boxes.

"That's incredible," I said, a little freaked out.

"He usually won't perform for guests. He must like you."

For some reason, I felt the moronic need to wave to Banjo. He stared at me with utter feline blankness.

"He's also this total balls-to-the-wall athlete," Lacy continued. "I can throw Jolly Ranchers at him and he'll catch them in his paws."

"I believe it."

"Thank you, Banjo," she said, once again dismissing him with the boredom of a casting director.

Then Lacy Shank took off her shirt. She might have just as easily opened a newspaper or adjusted the blinds. I wasn't surprised to see that she wasn't wearing a bra. She had small but beautiful breasts, and what made their beauty more potent was the ease with which Lacy Shank existed in her nudity. It was a thing she slid into like a silk robe or warm bathwater. There was nothing timid or shy about her. Here was someone at total, utter peace with her body.

I followed her lead and removed my own shirt. It was a slightly more complicated affair, as I had to unfasten what seemed to be three dozen buttons on the Owl's double-extra-large oxford. For some reason my left pectoral muscle started flexing on its own, a spasm that used to happen in the weight room during preseason workouts.

"Your tit's all aflutter," Lacy said, pointing to my chest from across the room.

"Nerves, I guess," was all I could come up with in response.

"Don't be nervous," she said. "You have nice tits."

"Thanks."

"Flutter away."

Things started to take on a strange, pantomime quality after Lacy removed her pants. Moments were happening without words. I had always imagined these kinds of women spending a lot of quality time lounging on nude beaches in Europe.

"Your middle name's Elizabeth," I offered, out of nowhere. I was in my briefs now. They were roughly seven or eight years old, and they had the holes to prove it. "Your dad, um, told me that, too. I had a dog named Elizabeth. She died. Liver cancer."

This was a bald-faced lie. I'd never had a dog in my life. I was in decade-old underwear and lying my head off. It's interesting what near-nudity will do to some people.

"Well, it looks like your new doggie is doing just blammo."

She was obviously referring to the not-so-thunderous erection that was painfully pressing against my briefs.

"Yes." I played along, with forced bass in my voice. "Digger is a healthy young pup."

"Come here, Digger," Lacy said.

Then we stopped talking.

And thank god for that.

Our dumb show took on a strange Eastern European theatre quality when Lacy started meowing.

We kissed and she mewed. I caressed her left breast and she mewed. I stroked her stomach and she mewed. I wasn't sure what this meant, so I decided to meow, too. My meows were deeper and strained with self-consciousness. I descended down her body, kneeling before her. Her bush was small and red and shaped like the state of Delaware. The smell was warm and intoxicating. Lacy stood over me like a priest charging penance to a supplicant. After a quick check for irregularities I performed varsity letterman–caliber cunnilingus (porno-quick tongue, strained face). In between breaths I meowed. She mewed kittenishly. This strange collaboration spurred aggression in Lacy and she forced me onto her bed, which was strewn with laundry and damp towels and other unnameable domestic fabrics. Once the heavy breathing started accompanying the meows we flipped and somehow my underpants were down and her underpants were down and I was inside of her and our feline duet had evolved into full-blown sex on a bed. While my meowing tapered off, Lacy's continued full throttle.

I hadn't been with a woman in a long time and I was having trouble holding back. Just as I felt the rush of orgasm I heard the pattering of paws somewhere behind me. I believe I could hear a thing taking flight as well, the way air can separate. As the flower of pleasure started to bloom through the gases of my brain I suddenly felt claws in my back, four sets of miniature talons sinking into my flesh at the highest point of bliss. Lacy Shank roared when she came. I could feel it buzzing on my face. I had an Abyssinian cat named Banjo riding me bareback. I moaned with pleasure and screamed with food-chain terror. It took a full minute for Lacy to individually disengage each of Banjo's claws from my back. There was a lot of screaming and a little crying. As little crying as possible.

I could feel blood running down my shoulder blades and back. I begged Lacy to lock Banjo in the bathroom, and she finally did—after I threatened him with my fist. I was going to punch a cat, and I felt thoroughly justified.

Lacy treated my back with iodine and Neosporin. Why such a slob would stock such specific first-aid products is a mystery to me. We didn't talk much during this process. I felt sad and strangely lonely. I had been sexually abused by a cat.

It was during the silent nursing segment of the evening that I realized I hadn't worn a condom.

After I got dressed, Lacy walked me to the elevator and waved goodbye, like I was taking a ferry to a faraway island. She didn't kiss me good night. Instead, she squeezed my nose, which I found a little strange. Just before the elevator door parted she leaned into the side of my face and bit my ear again, after which she asked for my phone number.

"Work or home?"

"Home," she said.

I gave her my number while the elevator doors bumped me repeatedly in the sides of my head.

She smiled and backed away, iodine staining her fingertips.

It was still raining and it was a long way home that night.

The subway took forever and there was a man on my train who punched his upper thigh repeatedly.

Tiny

AFTER TWELVE WEEKS of collecting unemployment, Feick landed a role in an Off-Broadway play in Chelsea, at the Atlantis Theatre Company's production of something called *Traffic Lights and Broken Bridges*. He performed the role of Tiny, an adolescent, slightly Peter Pan-ish homosexual runaway who wears only paper underpants.

Tiny is enslaved by Papi, an ex-junkie Puerto Rican hustler with a penchant for lighting blue-tip barbecue matches and dropping them down Tiny's pants. While Papi is out picking up Waspy businessmen in Times Square movie houses, he keeps Tiny handcuffed to the kitchen sink, where the boy is left to count the smoldering burns in his paper underpants and sing lesser-known Christmas carols in a choirboy falsetto.

At one point during the play Tiny brandishes a large serrated carving knife and after a moment of high, screaming melodrama throws it to the floor and jumps into Papi's tattooed arms.

One night, shortly after the show had begun previews, I knocked on Feick's door. I could hear tinny music coming from his headphones. I opened the door to find my brother totally naked, lying belly-up on his bed, masturbating and listening to Prince's "Little Red Corvette." His eyes were closed and his mouth was open and he was breathing intensely. In our family, we rarely saw one another in our underwear, let alone naked. Even on laundry days, bras, panties, and other undergarments were hidden in the bottoms of hampers like Roman Catholic rags of shame. To see my little brother with an erection was nothing less than startling.

A cloud of pot hovered in the room. I watched him for a moment, noting that he utilized the strange method of pinching the foreskin below the head of his penis with his thumb and forefinger, employing a counterclockwise, circular motion. It looked more like some form of meditative Eastern massage involving an obscure pressure point than masturbation. After a moment, he must have sensed my presence, and his eyes opened.

He sat up in bed and cried, "Bro!" disengaging from his extremely white erection. He then removed the headphones, turned off the music, and casually said, "What's up?" as if I'd walked in on him rearranging his old comic-book collection.

"Nothing," I said. "I just wanted to see how you were doing."

"Oh," he said. "I'm great. Come in." He covered himself with a sheet.

I stood there for what felt like a full minute and then took a half-step into the room and closed the door. There was a pile of laundry in one corner that could have provided shelter for a family of raccoons. Play scripts and audition sides were scattered everywhere. Chinese takeout cartons formed what looked like the model for futuristic, windowless, low-income housing projects. And it smelled terrible. I felt as if I'd happened upon some weird ethnology experiment.

"How's the show going?" I asked.

"The show's going great. Early audiences seem to be really digging it."

"Have the critics come yet?"

"This week," he said. "They'll probably hate it. What about you, how are you?"

"I'm good," I said. "Pretty good."

"Work's cool?"

"Cool, yeah," I said.

"And the writing?"

"The writing's coming. I mostly do it at work. On my lunch break and stuff."

"Nice."

He then removed the sheet and put on a pair of white boxer shorts. His penis was still half-erect and I found myself making a mental note of its size and girth. The music from his headphones filled the silence. "Delirious" was playing now.

"I didn't know you like Prince," I said.

"I do," he replied. "Prince is awesome."

At home I remember Feick liking U2, New Order, and Joy Division. Our mother thought Prince was "perverted" and "contentious." Although I disagreed, I understood her misgivings about his sexual ambiguity (she's Roman Catholic, after all), but when I asked her to expound on the contentious idea she would say, "Contentious is contentious. Just look at him!" and leave it at that.

Along with the boxers, Feick put on a yellow T-shirt with a picture of Bruce Lee holding a kung fu pose, his muscles damp and impossibly defined.

"Hey, do you ever miss home?" I asked my brother.

"Not really," Feick replied. His hair was long and messy. I would even say he had rock-band hair, and in that moment I realized that we had been drifting apart for some time, but I couldn't pinpoint exactly when it had started happening. As kids, we were pretty much inseparable. During the summer he loved to follow me to the Loras College gym on Buena Vista Street, where I would play ball with members of the varsity squad who had stuck around town. Feick never even touched a basketball, but he would always watch, sitting Indian-style on the sidelines. Suddenly everything felt so different.

"Have you heard from Mom?" I asked.

"No," he said. "Have you?"

"I haven't spoken to her in a while. I worry about her."

"I don't," he said. "She's exactly where she wants to be."

"I guess," I said. "I still worry."

"You shouldn't."

He was right, and I felt myself nodding.

"Okay, then. Sorry about interrupting."

"No problemo."

"Hey, when did you start smoking pot, anyway?" I asked.

"I don't know," he replied. "A while ago. Why, you want some?"

"Not tonight."

"It's in my underwear drawer. Whenever you want some, feel free."

"Thanks. Maybe some night we could get stoned and grab a few beers or something?"

"That would be chill," he said.

I nodded and then shut his door and stood in the hall for a while.

Loach Encounter #2

"LOACH."

No response.

"Loach."

Nothing.

"Loach, work with me here."

Silence.

"Your dishes have ants on them."

" . . . "

"Your dishes, Loach."

" . . . "

"Ants."

" . . . "

"Hundreds of them. Ants lead to roaches. Roaches lead to rats."

" . . . "

"Rats, Roach."

" . . . "

"I mean Loach."

" . . . "

"If you're not going to clean up after yourself, use the paper plates. We have a cupboard full. They're disposable."

" . . . "

"Just fold them up and throw them in the trash. You can get as messy as you want."

" . . . "

"And why do you always sit like that?"

"…"

"Do us all a favor and close your legs."

"…"

"The smells, Loach."

"…"

"The smells and the general lack of hygiene."

"…"

"Bathing is always an option. Bathing and some kind of personal locomotion."

"…"

"Fitness, Loach. Physical fitness."

"…"

"Toe touches."

"…"

"Toe touches and jumping jacks."

"…"

"Or an occasional burpee now and then."

"…"

"A mild regimen of physical activity is a good thing. It really is."

"…"

"And when you get a chance, take a look at the phone bill."

"…"

"I have to send the check in a few days."

"…"

"Loach, if you can hear me, make some kind of noise. Whistle. Sigh. Something."

"…"

"Give us a grunt, Loach."

"…"

"Fine. But for the love of god, man, please close your legs."

"…"

.

Lunch with Alexa

ONE DAY ALEXA ASKED ME OUT TO LUNCH. We had been exchanging flirtatious barbs ever since the copy machine incident involving my open fly. During the beginning of my limping phase, she was particularly obnoxious with her quips, calling me everything from "the Vet" to "Mr. Attention-getter."

At times, she would suddenly appear at the corner of my Skinner box like a hungry crow on the branch of a hickory tree. If I was working on my novel I would hit the split-screen function and revert back to the call reports.

The third time this happened, she sniggered knowingly and said, "Writing on the job, huh?"

I said nothing, hit the split-screen function, and stared at her vacantly.

"Oh, don't play dumb with me, mister. Every fourth person in this office is writing something on the split screen. There are acres of un-printed novels, short stories, essays, monologues, film scripts, teleplays, prose poems, musicals, and full-length dramas just whirring away on these hard drives."

I said nothing in return and desperately motioned to her to keep her voice down, pointing to Van's closed door.

She leaned in a little closer and whispered, "What is it?"

I looked left, looked right, and wrote "a novel" on a yellow Post-it.

She read the Post-it and smiled.

"Meet me in the lobby. One o'clock," she said surreptitiously. Then she whirled and sauntered away, as though she were traversing some long, wind-blown catwalk.

I met Alexa in the lobby and we walked to a diner on the corner of Houston and Varick. We slid conspiratorially into a booth, as if the subject of our rendezvous involved the outing of war criminals, not the writing of a first novel.

Our waiter dropped two menus on the Formica and pivoted toward another table. Moments later, a busboy poured water and left us a basket of corn bread.

"They have great veggie burgers here," she said.

I smiled awkwardly and stared at my menu. It was my first lunch with a vegetarian.

"So, a novel, huh?" Alexa said, tearing apart a piece of corn bread.

"A novel," I echoed nervously, a little defensively, feeling as though I had to protect myself from the arch, homogenized pitch of her speaking voice and the predatory cut of her editorial pantsuit and her English degree from Brown with its concentration in the late-twentieth-century American novel.

"What's it about?" she asked carnivorously.

I hesitated and drank from my glass. Water sluiced down the wrong pipe and I choked briefly, belching an entire mouthful down my shirt. Then I began frantically swabbing the mess with the napkin that Alexa had passed to me across the table. My red tie with the sea urchins turned a garish, bloody purple.

"I'm not really sure what it's about yet," I finally responded, regaining whatever shred of composure I had left.

Our waiter came over with a very wet rag and helped me wipe up. By the time he finished and took our order, the front of my white oxford showcased a vast gray stain. Alexa ordered a grilled cheese on multigrain, and I opted for a grilled cheese, too.

"Well, you have to be somewhat sure of what you're writing about, don't you?" she said, referring back to the novel. "You're not planting squash. You're telling a story."

"I guess," I said with profound mediocrity.

"You guess?"

"Well, it emerges. It hides from me."

"What is it, a goblin?"

Moments later, our waiter returned with our food—that quickly, as though it had been swiped from underneath a heat lamp, where it had been fighting off the slow, inevitable industry of decomposition.

Alexa cut her grilled cheese into fourths and cleanly inserted one quarter into her mouth as if she were taking a pill. I stared at mine as though it would reveal something wise and useful, something that would help me articulate more literary thoughts regarding my so-called novel.

"You feel that you'll jinx it if you talk about it," Alexa said, placing another quarter of her grilled cheese on the back of her tongue with clinical precision, softening it with the roof of her mouth before swallowing.

"No," I said. "It's not that."

"You're embarrassed."

I shook my head.

"You're making this all up and you just want to sleep with me."

"No, Alexa."

"No you're not making this up or no you don't just want to sleep with me?"

"Neither."

"If you're trying to be mysterious, Mister Feel-Sorry-for-My-Knee-Won't-You, let me tell you that it's coming off as sophomoric."

"I can say this," I said, taking a large bite of my grilled cheese. I chewed for a long moment. It was surprisingly delicious.

"Yes?" Alexa pleaded.

"It contains basketball."

"The novel."

"Yes. And science fiction."

"Oh, dear."

Yes, she actually said that. She said *Oh, dear*, as if we were senior citizens gossiping over hot soup.

"Like *Blade Runner*?" she asked.

"No, not like *Blade Runner*. Just regular stuff. A kind of science fiction of the anatomy."

"Physical metamorphosis."

"Yes."

"Like Kafka."

"It's about acute knee pain and the end of the world."

"Tell me about your main character," Alexa said.

"He's a ballplayer."

"Which means he's basically you."

"No, Alexa, he's not me."

"Is he white?"

"Yes, he's white."

"Then he's you."

"How does that confirm that he's me?" I said indignantly. "I mean, I could be writing about rocks; that doesn't make me a *rock*. Or the rock *me*. It's fiction."

"Are you going to eat the rest of that?" Alexa asked, seizing my half-eaten grilled cheese and chomping down an enormous bite. Her pleasure seemed almost sexual. After a moment she placed the sandwich back on my plate and masticated like a satisfied German shepherd.

"Go on," she said, her eyes swimming in her head epileptically. "Give me the story."

I took a breath and continued.

"So the main character—I'm calling him Opie—"

"Terrible name," she broke in, gulping more water. "Too pre-pube."

"Pre-*pube*?"

"As in, adolescent."

"That's intentional."

"What's his vernacular?"

"His vernacular?"

"His idiom."

"He's American. He speaks English."

"And he's white."

"Yes."

"Ebonics?"

"Excuse me?"

"Ebonics. Street slang. Vocal jazz. Urban lingo, man."

"No way."

"Maybe you should think about it. White boy trapped in an urban game."

"That would, like, make him a rapper or something."

"I'm just giving you my professional advice, mister. Flags pop up."

"Flags?"

"Little red flags, yes."

"It's written in the third person."

"Change it to first."

"No."

"I would."

"Well, I'm not you. I want the narrative to be detached and—"

"I didn't get to be an assistant editor in nine months for nothing, you know."

"Lesbian fiction."

"You didn't just say lesbian fiction," Alexa practically hissed through clenched teeth. "You did not just say that."

I chose not to respond.

"Just because Judy does a lot of women's fiction doesn't make her a lesbian editor," Alexa continued. "I happen to think that her projects are very risky. She's mining a very important market, mister."

I took a drink of water.

"There are hundreds—no, *thousands* of women out there who have been starving for these kinds of stories," Alexa continued passionately. "And Judy is the one responsible for bringing them to the forefront. Authors who were rescued from the slush pile now have careers thanks to her. These are important books. I mean, so what if a few of them take place on islands where vegetarian women rule with macrobiotic intelligence? So what if they've developed their own feminist alphabet, eliminating masculine-looking consonants, using squash and runted endive to model their new characters after? That's totally literary, man."

Alexa was hurt. Her face twitched uncontrollably. Her makeup somehow enhanced the effect, and for a brief moment she resembled the Scarecrow from *The Wizard of Oz*. I genuinely felt bad.

"I'm sorry, Alexa," I said. "You're absolutely right. Have some more of my grilled cheese."

"No, thank you."

Her hands were trembling slightly. "Do you think I'm a lesbian or something?" she asked, seizing my grilled cheese.

"No."

"Yes, you do," she said, biting into it aggressively.

"No, I don't, Alexa. I think you're so totally *not* a lesbian."

She chewed for a full minute and threw my grilled cheese back onto my plate. We didn't speak for a while. Our busboy attempted to clear our dishes, but Alexa stopped him with the sense of entitlement of one who collects rare art. He skulked away apologetically.

I surveyed the gray stain on the front of my shirt and started to notice bits of food on it. Alexa busied herself by gulping large quantities of water, as if she were trying to flush out some unknown microbe that had been discovered in the corn bread.

"So the novel," she said, trying to salvage the mood.

"The novel," I echoed.

"How many pages have you written?"

"I don't know. I'm trying to not count."

"And you say you're doing this on a manual typewriter?"

"I was, yes. A Number Three Underwood. But I had to sell it to pay our phone bill. Now I'm using a Smith Corona daisy wheel. When I type it sounds like I'm deep-frying fish."

"Are you using carbon paper?"

"Can't find any."

"What if you lose it?"

"I'm not planning to."

"But you never know. Burglary. Recycling fanatics. Acts of god."

"I'm keeping it in the freezer. I'm not all that worried."

Then we were quiet again. The waiter came over to ask us if we wanted dessert, but Alexa shook her head before he could open his mouth and he backed away. Moments later he returned and dropped off the check. Before I could feign some feeble attempt to pay for it, Alexa swiped it cleanly.

"So tell me a little bit about this science fiction," she said, rifling though her purse.

"Well, he—"

"*Opie.*"

"Right, Opie."

"Go on."

"Well, Opie wakes up one morning and he has something growing in his knee."

"Something?"

"Something."

"Some *thing*, as in a *thing*?"

"A thing, yes."

"Like what?"

"Well . . ."

"Well, what?"

"Um . . ."

"What's in his knee, man, an alarm clock?"

"No."

"A unicycle? A baked potato?"

"An eye, okay!"

"A what?"

"An eye."

"Are you kidding me?"

"No."

"A fucking *eye*?"

"Yeah, is there something wrong with that?"

"It's so gross," Alexa said, fishing out a twenty and waving down our waiter. "Does it blink?"

"It blinks, yes."

"Jesus!"

"It's a very simple little eye, Alexa. Think of it as an eye from a teddy bear."

"A teddy bear? It sounds like porno! Like watching a fucking house burn down!"

The waiter took the money and made change from a pouch at his midriff. Alexa leafed through the bills and started separating out a tip.

"Let me leave the tip, Alexa," I offered.

"No."

"Please, I feel terrible."

"Absolutely not," she said, getting her purse together. "We're not leaving yet."

She took out a pack of cinnamon chewing gum and offered me a piece. I accepted, unwrapped the gum, and began chewing. She folded a stick into fourths and placed it on the back of her tongue and did not chew.

"So tell me what happens to Opie," she said, negotiating her palate around the lump of gum.

"Well, I think he's going to die—"

"Unless he has the eye removed."

"Exactly."

"I like that. There's a motor. Something to be in pursuit of."

"And there's an antidote."

"An antidote, yes! Sand sifting through the hourglass. What else?"

"What do you mean, what else?"

"In terms of subplot."

"Well, he's also sort of forgetting how to talk."

"As in, he's losing the ability to speak?"

"No, he can speak fine."

Alexa reached into her mouth and tweezed the gum off the back of her tongue. "He has, like, a stroke," she said, folding the gum in a napkin as if it were a small, precious stone she'd found on the beach.

"No, he doesn't have a stroke."

"His tongue is removed."

"Well, no—"

"He gets Alzheimer's."

"He just says gibberish."

"Gibberish?"

"Yeah, gibberish. Like, nonsense words."

"Give me an example."

"Right here in this diner?"

"Why not?"

"No way."

"Come on, man. Just a sentence."

"That would be too weird."

"A half-sentence."

"Why?"

"I'm intrigued, that's why. Gibberish is really literary."

There was that golden word again: *literary*. "It is?"

"Totally, man. Come on. Give me some."

Suddenly she was ending a lot of her sentences with *man*. For some reason I liked this. I surveyed the diner. Our waiter was watching us with keen, wide-eyed interest.

"Are you sure gibberish is literary?" I asked.

"Absolutely, man."

"Okay."

I took a deep breath. I cleared my head and found my center. I didn't want to edit. I wanted whatever bile-saturated word salad was living inside me to burst straight from my literary spleen.

"Strawberry Christmas fish."

Alexa stared at me.

"Black pajamas on a tin-can ham."

I leaned into the table.

"Calico fishbox. Thirty-ton titanium biscuit trip."

Her pupils seemed to dilate with concentration.

"Two-tone thundercrunch banana bone."

Her head tilted to the left.

"Peanut butter Toyota."

She smiled.

"Ambulance bush."

She yelped.

"Cop car on a toothbrush."

Alexa giggled devilishly.

"Zigzag potatoes!"

She started laughing uncontrollably.

"Choochoo surprise. Snowpony in a rabbit stance. Sideways Vance. Chimneysnot in the whatnot pot. Horse gravy! Loose stool on a sideways mule! Porcupine dice! Wagonwheels with rice! Eat 'em on the banana farm! Don't snugglebunch on the baloneyclock! Macaroni johnsonbox! Powpow miniskin chow! Gluetown butterbush! Maw maw tinyside raw! Sixteen wigglefish on a chocolate subway dish . . ."

Alexa stared at me, her red lips forming an enormous, vinyl-looking zero. I'd gone too far. I'd blown my cool. The entire diner was ogling our table. I felt like the room temperature had suddenly dropped twenty degrees.

When Alexa tried to speak she sort of barked.

"Orf," she said.

"You okay, Alexa?"

"Orf-orf," she offered, and drank from her water glass. After a moment the barks turned into words.

"I'm t-t-totally intrigued," she said.

"Really?" I couldn't believe it. My heart was pounding.

"Give me the first f-f-fifty pages. If it's as good as it sounds, I'll pass it on to J-J-Judy."

"Seriously?"

"Seriously, man."

The next morning I took the first fifty pages of my novel to work and made a Xerox of them. I was so nervous at the copy machine that when Van walked by I almost had a seizure. He said "Mornin'" and I said "Mornin'" back, exactly the same way he said it, only with four times the volume.

After I finished at the copy machine I slid the pages into a manila envelope. Inside, I wrote a simple note:

ALEXA,

Thanks for lunch. I look forward to your thoughts. No snugglebunching on the baloneyclock! (Ha-ha).

Thanks again.

I signed my name, sealed the envelope, and left it on her chair.

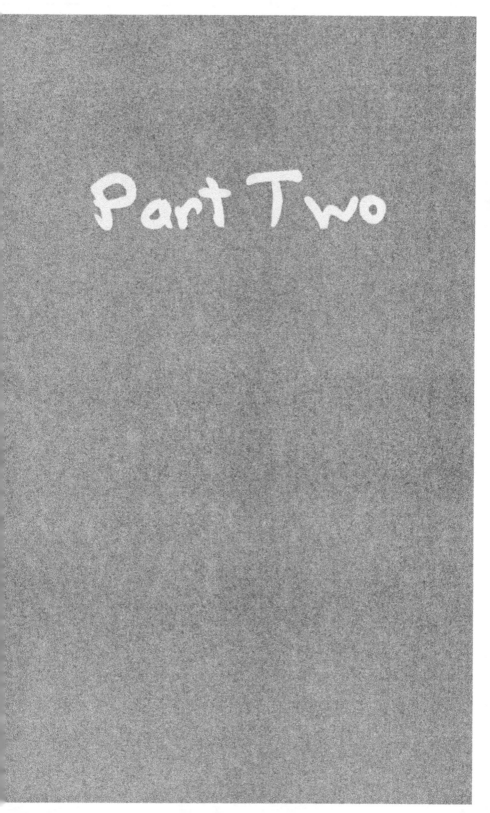

Part Two

Oscar Wilde

BY LATE SEPTEMBER the summer-baked streets of the East Village had finally begun to cool. The barometric drop coincided with a silence in Tompkins Square Park that allowed the less hostile, pedestrian sounds of the neighborhood to drone their more indigenous avenue tones. Taxis sluiced and screeched. Headphoned rockers leaned into the wind with their kitchen-cleanser hair. Distant garbage trucks roared and belched and sputtered. Gasoline-powered skateboards whined across Tenth Street. Junkies spoke to their invisible saviors. Pit bulls barked at less endowed dogs.

The light seemed thinner and the sky was often congested and gray. In the park, the homeless were all but gone; the mayor and his storm-trooping police force seemed to have things well in hand.

Even St. Mark's Place, usually athrob with its caterwauling, Mardi Gras sidewalk lust, took on the more somber tenor of early fall. Exposed, irritated flesh was now covered. Piercings and tattoos were concealed. Socks were employed, turtlenecks revealed. A silly hat became a thing not worn, but upholstered to one's head for the rest of the fall and early winter, at which point an additional item of headgear might be added. The dockworker's skullcap. The transvestite's fashionable, Mexican-style rebozo. The Rasta's African homeland beret. The upper-middle-class Smith grad (in thrift-store glasses) with her third-world babushka tied neatly under her chin.

On Avenue A, the bald woman with scalp trouble stopped pissing on cabs and could be seen sitting in the entrance of a defunct pet store wearing a terrycloth house robe. Refueling, perhaps, for next summer?

In Tompkins Square Park the players on the full courts near the wading pool could barely muster the meager three-on-three half-court game. The shantytown by the bandstand had been disassembled and the few straggling homeless clung to the small parts of their lives with a bewildering ferocity.

One man was living in a tree. He had a prolific, biblical beard and he employed a system of ropes and bungee cords to keep him safely harnessed while he slept. People would throw him bananas and pears, some of which he would eat and some of which he would use as artillery against the police and other municipal officials. Although his eviction was made public through a sergeant's bullhorn, he refused to leave and ultimately had to be extracted by several firemen and a large, subtly mustached woman representing the mayor's office.

There was a black man named Saigon who lived out of a shopping cart, along with his duck, affectionately named Saigon II. Saigon would endlessly push his cart around the perimeter of the park, proselytizing through his chess-piece teeth to Saigon II and anyone else within earshot about the evils of gentrification and capitalism, and how Vietnam was happening all over again.

"It's down in the sewers," he'd proclaim. "A new kind of colonization, Saigon Two. We gotta keep Vietnam out of the mo-fuckin' homeland!"

My novel about acute knee pain and the end of the world was steadily growing. I decided to call it *Opie's Half-life* and began typing an all-caps running head in the upper left-hand corner. I hadn't yet heard anything from Alexa so I distracted myself from my publication fantasies by forging ahead.

At some point I began masturbating with incredible frequency. This seemed to satisfy a need that was athletic rather than sexual—perhaps my sabbatical from basketball caused an overload of testosterone? Regardless, all postures and positions were tried. I masturbated prone, seated, partly and fully nude, standing on one or both legs, left-handed, right-handed, backhanded, forehanded, dry and lubricated (using a wide range of lotions and petroleum jellies), and Indian-style.

My fantasy women included Alexa, Lacy Shank, my sophomore English teacher (Mrs. Stance), Jackie Joyner-Kersee, the novelist Donna Tartt (erotic imagery extrapolated from mysterious graveyard-setting author photo), Elle Macpherson, Madonna ("Like a Virgin" period), and Jane and Bridget Fonda (strange, semi-lesbianic-slash-incest vixen tag team).

Although these women assured hours of autoerotic satisfaction, there were several instances toward the middle of September in which my fantasies were overtaken by a large, featureless Florida orange. There was nothing particularly vaginal about this orange. It was quite simply and irrevocably an orange. Dimpled hide. Human-like navel. Leafless. Without stem. Perhaps even seedless. As round as the Earth as seen from space.

The orange would just sort of take over my fantasies the way vaudeville gorillas storm the proscenium, and often at the precise, unfortunate moment of climax. One might think that with the ejaculative nature of a good old-fashioned quarter hour of prep school–style whacking off perhaps orange *juice* might be an appropriate image, but this was not the case. I was stuck with a perfectly round, inert, uneventful Florida orange. Jane and Bridget Fonda would morph into Sunkist the Orange. Jackie Joyner-Kersee would scissor her legs and then, like a fiery planet replacing a black hole, the orange would emerge.

I assumed that this interloping fruit was somehow a thing that had been inadvertently programmed into my psyche as a result of too much prime-time TV during my teen years, or some other form of subliminal consumer ad media.

Perhaps it was symbolic of the death of summer, and my preconscious mind was arranging citrus metaphors and unleashing them without the consent of my medulla oblongata and other policing gray matter?

Or a simpler scenario: Perhaps this orange was my dislocated basketball?

The fact was that I hadn't even touched a ball since I'd hurt my knee that day in the park.

The Owl, who theorized that my psychosexual orange was a result of a vitamin C deficiency, had begun at Columbia and would return home every night exhausted and on the verge of what can only be described as stunned obedience.

During his exhaustion era the Owl started the strange habit of initiating conversations while voiding his bowels. He called it "throne talk." When I was creatively blocked I would do a lot of pacing in the hallway that connected the living room to the three forking bedrooms at the back of the apartment. This corridor was approximately three yards long and featured two walls that were so overly spackled that they appeared to be suffering from some kind of Sheetrock eczema. In an attempt either to inject a glimmer of eccentricity into a simple habit or to supplement good old-fashioned clichéd writer's pacing with peculiarity (the furrowed brow, the shuffling feet, the staccato of the clicking pen), I should note that on separate occasions, while I was engaged in this activity, both the Owl and Feick accused me of actually speaking to my right hand. I wasn't aware of this being true until one night I was pacing and, from the bowels of the sofa and in a wretched warlock's voice, the Loach said, "If it starts talking back I'd fucking run down a bear to know what it says."

I froze. Indeed, my right hand was poised in front of my face and I was muttering faintly. I don't recall what the words were. I can only cite the fact that I was engaged in a strange, slightly impacted-sounding grumbling.

Only days later, soon after this muttering became conscious, an actual lexis started forming, the content and tenor of which were not dissimilar to the schizophrenic word salads that plagued my novel.

So the Owl was throne talking and I was pacing and muttering nonsensically into my hand.

Once, over a beer, I confronted the Owl about his need to be social while shitting, and in a moment of raw confession he told me there was something about it that made him feel excruciatingly lonely; that he was often overwhelmed with a kind of existential malaise, a sadness one might associate with early frost or naked December trees. He revealed that sitting on the toilet made him feel so horribly alone that he would wind up staring at his hands and commanding his fingers to move (which, truth be told, is not that far from muttering to them). He said he needed to get in touch with his body to make sure he was *still there.* He said his fingers usually *did* move, and that he thanked god for it. At the time, the Owl professed to be a devout atheist, so this sudden notion of a higher power was sort of startling. He said that there were times when he would just surrender to the loneliness and simply turn off the lights and then sit down on the corroded ceramic floor. He said "living inside of it" helped him to come out the other end. I imagined him lost in some wicked sorcerer's cave in the Land of Narnia, evil goblins and syphilitic gnomes screeching at him from the stalagmites, his only light source a toddler's birthday candle.

And this is why the Owl talked to me while on the toilet: like Daddy humming "Silent Night" while watering the Christmas tree, he needed to hear my voice because it made him feel safe.

It was as simple as teddy bears and plastic ponies.

I'm not sure why his toilet habits so often coincided with my writing conflicts. This was a mystery that neither of us wanted to solve. We just accepted it as something that simply *was*, the way two friends might deal with the fact that they share the same middle name or shoe size.

We made a deal: I would mutter into my right hand and the Owl would talk to me from the darkened bathroom. And he would accept my muttering as full-fledged conversation.

I have no doubt that the Owl's existential toilet crisis had something to do with his confusion about enrolling into the New Media program at Columbia. After all, why would a strange, multilingual, highly literary Nabokov freak want to enter the farm system of corporate America? What possible thought process other than one born out of fear or anxiety could lead a poet to crave a life of suits and skyscrapers?

While the Owl was falling apart, my brother was heading in the opposite direction. His play at the Atlantis Theatre Company was a runaway hit, and his time tallied in our building might have been less than that of the mailman. I had no idea what he was up to or where he was spending his evenings. His Tiny in *Traffic Lights and Broken Bridges* was raved about in both *The New York Times* and *The Village Voice*, so of the four of us, he was the one in which we could recognize the soaring eagle wings of artistic success.

One night while I was writing there came a knock on my door. Moments later Feick entered my room. His blond bangs had grown long and were starting to creep down over his eyebrows. He had a look on his face that was equal parts terror and astonishment.

"Hey, Feick," I said.

"Hey, bro."

"You okay?"

"I'm good. Real good."

"You look like you just did something really weird."

"Can I sit down?"

"Sure, take my chair."

Feick sat. I stood. He didn't blink and I wasn't quite sure if he was breathing.

He said, "Tonight Tiny threw the knife."

I said, "Uh-huh."

"And it stuck in the floor."

"Wow."

"I swear, bro. It went straight into the deck."

"Awesome."

"*Wumpf!*"

"Wumpf?"

"They said you could hear it backstage. The running crew got totally amped. High fives and everything."

"*Cool.*"

"It was so moving."

"You must've really had him tonight," I offered.

"I did, bro. I had him."

"You captured Tiny."

"Yesyesyes."

"You captured him like the enemy."

"I did. I totally lost Feick tonight. Totally lost everything that was quote-unquote *Feick*. I'm, like, *soaring*."

"Soar, Feick, soar."

"It went *wumpf*, bro. Totally *wumpf*."

"Awesome."

"*Wumpf!*" he barked.

"*Wumpf!*" I echoed.

Then we didn't say anything for a moment. I thought about Feick *wumpf*ing through his life, and about my lack of *wumpf*ing. There was a sense that luck would follow him around wherever he went, the same way starlings follow certain high-pitched tones. In a terrible bus accident, not only would Feick be the sole survivor, he would probably walk away from the wreck unscathed, find several hundred dollars strewn in the aisle, and then land a book deal to chronicle the events. It was useful to have him around just for the vicarious good fortune it afforded.

"It kind of wiggled for a moment," Feick continued. "You could see the stage lights dancing off the blade."

His eyes were open so wide that if I didn't know any better I would've thought he was tripping on acid.

I said, "Feick, can I ask you something?"

"Sure."

"Are you still Tiny?"

"I don't know."

"Does it feel like he has you, or you have him?"

"It's too hard to tell, bro. It's real hard when it gets to this level."

"Do you want a glass of water?"

"Water. Yeah."

I went to the kitchen and got him a glass of water. The Loach was wearing his yellowed underwear and a black turtleneck, and he looked like a malnourished street mime who had been raped. Where the turtleneck came from I have no idea. But this was the way it was with the Loach; his wardrobe was at once seasonally accurate and mysteriously vast. Months later I would lift the couch cushions to discover a blue mechanic's jumpsuit, three pairs of tuxedo socks, a sleeveless houndstooth coat, a black beret, and a pair of Scooby-Doo pajama bottoms.

When I returned to my room Feick was staring at his hand. For a moment I was worried that he was going to start muttering to it—was this some kind of behavioral gene, like bad arches or schizophrenia?—but he simply gazed as if it were a distant star.

I set the water on my desk. Feick's hand thawed and took the glass. He drank.

After a moment he said, "I gotta tell you something, bro."

I said, "What?" and handed him the glass.

"You have to promise me that you won't tell anyone."

"I won't, I promise."

"Wait for like a week to tell Glenwood." Then he turned his face toward mine and declared, "I'm still wearing the pannypapers."

"You're still wearing the *what*?"

"Tiny's pannypapers. The homemade underwear that Papi makes for him out of comic books. I'm wearing them."

"Wow."

"Tiny love Papi cuz Papi tell Tiny what to do."

"Oh."

"Tiny be Papi's little *maricón*."

"Uh-huh."

"I don't think I'll be able to take off the pannypapers till the show closes."

"When is that?"

"They don't know, bro. It keeps selling out."

Then Feick guzzled the water, handed the glass to me, and exited my room with the same stunned expression on his face. In that moment I was convinced that I could hear a faint crinkling as he crossed the kitchen en route to his bedroom.

Lacy Shank called three weeks after our first encounter and invited me to her Juilliard production of *The Importance of Being Earnest*. Our conversation was limited to eight or nine relatively unrevealing compound sentences and, after I promised to attend, in a rather impressive drawing-room British accent, Lacy punctuated our exchange by saying, "I'll have you know that I'm not exactly *spanning the globe* for any kind of boggy relationship. I think you know what I want. Anon."

She might have accomplished the same communicative function by typing an all-caps memo and sending it to me in an interoffice envelope.

It was clear that she wasn't in the market for a *fambly* man, but like the true Midwestern gentleman I am, I went to see her play anyway; I went out of sheer loneliness more than anything sexual, although the prospect of being inside her again (minus the cat claws) wasn't exactly a difficult thing to get excited about.

The audience at the Juilliard production was largely populated by a species of human so old that among the younger audience members (largely conservatory students) there was palpable youth-community anxiety about natural-cause fatalities. These people were mostly seventy-five or eighty. They were great-grandmothers and grandfathers. This Depression-era audience exhibited an almost flamboyant disregard for the performers. Candy was unwrapped throughout. Noses were blown. Phlegm-rich respiratory ailments were barked, hacked, honked, and snorted during important narrative flashpoints. And running commentary was also part of the evening's fare. These observations included opinions about the acting ("Would she really *talk* that way?"), complaints about the seats (not soft enough, too close together), updates on arthritic conditions and various treatment programs ("There's a hot mineral springs in Vail, Colorado, that did wonders for my hips, Ethel. And boy does it get *steamy!*"), and high praise for the current batch of Burke & Burke tuna salad ("They're putting little bits of *cilantro* in it now. It's *wonderful!*").

Canes, walkers, and other orthopedic and ambulatory support systems clogged aisles, walkways, and the coat check. Hearing aids dog-whistled and chirped throughout the performance.

As Cecily Cardew, Lacy spent most of her stage time pouting coquettishly and lounging on a white wicker patio throne with exceptional, Elizabethan posture. She wore a canary yellow summer gown complete with petticoats, long white gloves, a matching hat-and-parasol ensemble, and a pair of obsidian-looking, lace-up, high-Louis-heeled croquet boots that must have taken two stagehands to put on.

There was a character named Algernon Moncrieff whose British accent was so exaggerated it sounded more like drunk American Southern. The sets and costumes were fantastic, as were the fake mustaches. I have no idea what the actual plot involved, as I was too nervous about possibly having to perform CPR on the elderly lady to my left, whose respiration sounded like the sudsy workings of a distant car wash.

Lacy's American stage speech was nothing less than Olympic. Unlike her bellicose bar voice, onstage she spoke with such startling clarity it sounded as if she had been thoroughly gassed with half a tank or so of pure oxygen prior to taking the stage. I could feel her tongue carving out syllables in my own mouth. Her P's popped. Her O's were like choirboy hosannas, her T's like iron doors slamming shut.

Her character's elderly tutor, Lady Bracknell, wore a wig reminiscent of George Washington's coiffure as rendered in our great nation's more popular grammar-school history books. Onstage there was so much mannered laughter among the actors it almost shamed the audience.

I found my attention drifting between the geometry and volume of the female characters' corseted breasts and the alpha-male, idiotic task of trying to determine how much weight the actor playing Algernon Moncrieff could bench-press. And, like most self-indulgent, egocentric wannabe artists, I also spent an awful lot of time imagining myself as an actual thespian. The makeup. The costumes and vocal warm-ups. The general madness of memorizing lines. All in all, I comprehended very little of the work itself, but greatly admired the wigs and costumes.

Afterward, Lacy and I had a drink at O'Neill's. We spoke not a word about the play. She neither asked me what I thought nor acknowledged that I had been a member of the audience. The only remark remotely related to the theatre was uttered prior to her ordering twin shots of Maker's Mark. While she lit a cigarette, this aside was offered from the corner of her mouth with supreme boredom: "Wilde sucks my dick, man."

A few of Lacy's classmates ran in and out of O'Neill's with a haunted schizophrenia, never actually sitting, but rather revolving between the street, the bar, and the spot under the TV. I wondered what effect Juilliard was having on them. Perhaps they were all perpetually in character.

Lacy seemed annoyed and itchy and anxious to shed the evening. She posed not a single question regarding the quality or tenor of my life. The truth was that things were duller than ever. My knee was slowly recovering. My novel was still collecting mass (to say that it was "growing" would be delusional), and work was turning into a mild exercise of rote compliance and a slow, steady journey toward the safe harbor of good corporate citizenship.

After we drained our drinks, Lacy said, "Let's go," the two-syllable phrase that would become our cue for sex.

So we were off to another round of sport fucking featuring a complex chorus of meows, mild grappling, and the intensity of carnivores hunting antlered prey.

Her apartment seemed to have collected even more coed detritus than before. There was now a small potted cactus on the windowsill (a wad of gray gum at its crown); several editions of the aforementioned Oscar Wilde play splayed about the bed, the floor, and the stovetop; bags of potato chips; a skyline of bottled water (both with and without cigarette butts); a felled dartboard containing what appeared to be Chicken McNuggets sprinkled about its cork face; and an enormous, lopsided pumpkin.

New to the apartment were a false fireplace that I hadn't seen before and a calico ottoman.

There was also a single bobby sock stuck to the ceiling.

Lacy agreed to keep Banjo in the bathroom until we were both coitally resolved.

After peeling off our clothes we made love like two people who are fully aware that they are committing some sort of spiritual larceny. This collusion felt both hollow and delicious. Again, prophylactics were ignored like a body lying under scaffolding. These were the early days of heightened AIDS awareness, and the lack of a condom added a certain kind of bomb-squad tension to the proceedings.

But despite the contraception anxiety, it was nice to fuck without cat claws and blood. We started out quickly and sped up like a go-cart careering wildly down a well-paved hill. I made sure to pull out with plenty of time to spare and wound up ejaculating onto the dented top of a Dunkin' Donuts box.

During this sexual episode I grew fond of Lacy's meows, and of her small, pale frame. And her dark red sliver of a bush now resembled a German soldier's mustache set vertically on her pubis. Her scent was something like Middle Eastern food (chickpeas, onions, garlic) and wet grass. It was intoxicating and made me hungry for hummus and baba ghanoush.

I was relieved to discover that the Florida orange did not make an appearance. Perhaps the only antidote, then, for this psychoactive fruit was live-action, flesh-tearing sex?

Afterward we spoke briefly while Lacy smoked.

"Not bad," she said.

"Not bad?" I asked, not quite sure what she was referencing.

"In bed. You're not half bad. Most guys just plain suck. But you seem to know a thing or two about a woman's G-spot."

The truth was that I hadn't the slightest idea about a woman's G-spot. I'd always imagined it as some randomly positioned control teat commonly found on 35-millimeter cameras and other portable handheld electronic devices; a thing manufactured by Canon or Nintendo and sold at RadioShack.

Inhale. Exhale. Silver, undulating cigarette smoke.

"I hate my hair," Lacy said.

"Oh."

"I'm totally cutting it off and dying it black."

"Can you just do that, with the play and all?"

"Fuck the play. Oscar Wilde sucks my dick."

"Yeah, you mentioned that."

Enormous drag. Bright burning ember. Intake of smoke. Exhale. I coughed and sputtered.

"How's my dad been treating you?" she asked.

"Pretty good, actually."

"Any hints of a promotion?"

"Not really."

"Nothing at all?"

"I'm afraid not. To tell you the truth, it's not something I'm actually expecting."

"I told the jackass he better promote you. I can't believe the walrus is fucking blowing me off."

"Lacy, you don't have to—"

"He won't get away with this!" Lacy said dramatically. She then proceeded to twist her beautiful face into one of the greatest pouts I have ever seen.

"Well, the other day . . ." I started.

"The other day, what?"

"Well. He, um—"

"Bring it on, man."

"Well, he tried farting on me while I was changing the coffee filter."

"He did?"

"He did. Yes."

And it was true. While I was outfitting the coffeemaker, the Shankler had indeed ripped a thunderous blast, the vibrations of which throbbed into my hip socket and actually felt pretty good. He then smiled his big horsey smile and said, "Linguine with garlic and rosemary sauce. Seven ninety-nine over at that little Italian place on LeRoy and Hudson."

"He farted on you," Lacy said. "That's a good sign."

Watching the lights from the street flash on the window. A dish settling in the kitchen sink. The sound of Banjo doing calisthenics in the bathroom.

Lacy then said, "Whatever you do, don't tell him we're fucking, or he'll fire you."

Cat Hair

DEEP IN THE NIGHT, I woke up to discover strange ampersands of what looked like smashed peas in the front of my underwear. It is perhaps a kind of Old Testament cruelty for the predawn to greet one with such a foul and shocking truth.

When I finally drummed up enough courage to go to the bathroom, the act of urinating was so painful that the sound that came out of my mouth was a mixture of sentimental weeping and the maniacal, bone-chilling snigger of a thunderstruck Clydesdale. To say that it burned would be a shameless understatement. It was excruciating. And terrifying. It felt like I was pissing a needle of combustible fuel and someone had lit a match.

After urinating nine or twelve times (in little starts and stops, my bladder contracting and distending painfully), I went back to bed in the hope that a few more hours of sleep would somehow medically correct the irregularity. After all, isn't that what one does when one has a cold? Chicken soup and rest and lots of liquids? I think the harsh reality of what I was dealing with had induced a delicious and potent form of conflict narcolepsy, and when I reengaged with my futon I fell into a deep sleep in about forty seconds.

Sleep was a buoyant, saltwater sea. Sleep was the Mediterranean, and I was a weightless, perfect, nonburning porpoise floating with the starfish.

When my alarm woke me a few hours later, not only had the mass increased, its color had been enhanced, brightened, ripened. And now there was urethral leakage as well—a hot, milky drip that was floutingly disobeying the muscles in and around my penis.

It was Monday morning, so the first thing I did was call in sick.

"Everything okay?" Van asked.

"Everything's fine," I squawked. "Just a little run-down."

"Well, what's wrong exactly?"

"I'm leaking," I said stupidly.

"Leaking?"

"My throat! Is leaking! Postnasal drip!"

"Well, that's no fun."

I quickly feigned a cough.

"I'll call a temp," Van said. "Feel better."

I hung up the phone and went into the Owl's room.

When one is terrified of the infection or possible decay of one's own body, the comfort of a best friend is perhaps the safest place to turn, even if he *is* going a little crazy.

The Owl was sleeping like a man who has been thrown out of a speeding car. One of his arms was wrapped around his neck and his mouth was open so wide I could see all of his childhood dental work. His shortwave radio was sputtering static. I turned it off and nudged his shoulder. His large, strange eyes opened, swam a moment, and then he said, "Homon."

"Hey," I said.

"Hey," he said. "What time is it?"

"Early."

"Aren't you going to work?"

"I called in sick."

"What's wrong?"

"Um, I'm not sure. You mind if I turn the light on?"

"Go ahead."

I turned on his desk lamp and took a breath. There was a nineteenth-century bentwood rocking chair in the corner. I'd previously had no idea there was such a fine piece of furniture living in the Owl's room. The secrets in our apartment were vast and unexplained.

The Owl reached for his glasses and for a moment knelt in a kind of half-fulfilled tornado-drill position. I could see that he had been sleep-ing on several MBA New Media textbooks. His Japanese butt-huggers crinkled about his hams.

When I pulled my underwear down to reveal the mass, the Owl screamed like he had been knifed. I quickly—defensively, even—pulled up my briefs and planted a fist in front of my genital area.

"Jesus, Homon!" the Owl said, bewildered.

"Don't scream!" I begged.

"Holy shit, yo!"

"Please don't scream! Screaming only makes it feel bigger."

The Owl pushed several felt-tip pens to the floor and scratched his armpit.

He said, "What is it?"

"I'm not sure, but it burns when I piss."

"Can I see it again? I promise I won't scream."

I pulled down my pants again.

"That's a serious excretion, Homon."

"It looks like peas, right?"

"It does, Homon, it does look like peas."

"Like when you smash them up with a fork."

"Uh-huh."

"Or when you try to hide them under your pork chops and your mom knows and then she looks at you funny and turns over the chop."

I adjusted my underwear to catch more light.

"There's *that* stuff, too," the Owl pointed out.

"What stuff?"

"The less pea-like stuff."

"Yeah," I concurred.

Then we said nothing for a moment. The early morning light com-ing through the window had an iron quality. In the courtyard there was a bird shrieking, and this didn't seem to help matters.

"Glenwood?"

"Yes, Homon?"

"It's not peas, is it?"

"No."

"Or any other animal, vegetable, or mineral?"

"Nuh-uh."

"What should I do?"

"I would call a clinic."

I left the Owl to his nest of textbooks and felt-tip pens and went into the kitchen, where I found the phone book. After a few minutes of desperate ruffling I contacted a clinic on West Thirty-eighth Street that specialized in sexually transmitted diseases. A woman who was either historically bored or addicted to cough syrup answered the phone and gave me directions. I don't remember grabbing my coat or descending the stairs or even hailing a cab. These events morphed into one another, and strangely all I recall from the ride is a cold, sterile wind and a smashed pigeon on First Avenue whose contorted face gave me the impression that it had died laughing.

The clinic was a former public school with a brick façade that looked charred. The roaring traffic along Tenth Avenue gave it an attendant score of indifferent violence. I saw not a single human soul enter or exit this building. I walked through the front doors the way one walks into a haunted house on Halloween.

Inside I was greeted by a counterwoman whose heroic commitment to apathy was rivaled only by sleeping fish or faceless scarecrows. I filled out several forms that asked for everything from my social security number to my sexual preference to a hard sum of past and present sexual partners. After the woman stapled certain forms to other forms with a rote, administrative perfection that was almost inspiring, she told me in an unwavering Brooklyn tenor to take a seat in the waiting area until my name was called. This particular room was clogged with a platoon of grammar-school desk-chair units, a large color TV that featured an AIDS awareness program, and a species of human I can describe only as being at once terrified, depressed, impoverished, drug-addicted, suicidal, perverted, homicidal, schizophrenic, and starving to death. They were all male, and I surmised that the majority of them were either refugees or derelicts.

The man to my left, at whom I was desperately trying not to look, was lubricating his groin with a gelatinous salve squeezed from what appeared to be a tube of toothpaste. When our eyes finally met he uttered something plaintively in a Slavic-sounding language. I simply nodded and tried to focus on the TV. The enormous, cabbage-faced man to my right was wearing a bathrobe and was sleeping so soundly that I thought he might be dead.

There were several discarded brochures in and around my desk that highlighted all the warning signs and solutions to myriad venereal diseases. I was horrified to discover that my symptoms matched up with syphilis, chlamydia, herpes, hepatitis, gonorrhea, and urethral cancer. My palms were suddenly cold, my tongue stiff and dry. I could feel my testicles shrinking like grapes in an oven. Of the four women in my life I had slept with, Lacy Shank was the first partner with whom I'd failed to use a condom. Right then and there I made a deal with God. Yes I, who, during my final semester of college, immediately after having finished Camus's *The Stranger*, announced rather dramatically and in my wettest baritone that I would adopt rigorous atheist beliefs, was suddenly shedding my pagan ways and falling to my knees in front of the Holy Father. Please, God, I said with the smallest, humblest voice in my head, Please don't let me have a venereal disease. I'll strive to be an honest person. I'll shed all unnecessary possessions and adopt Christ-like ways. I'll speak to the homeless and spare whatever change I carry on my person. I'll reverse all impure thoughts and rediscover the golden road of Christianity. I'll go to church and pray for the poor. I'll take communion and—

In the middle of my spiritual prostration my name was called and the woman behind the counter directed me to a room where my arm would be cleaned with an alcohol swab and a technician in green pajamas would draw blood into a syringe for testing and lab work. Like the woman behind the counter, this person said very little, and I actually had a difficult time determining whether I was being administered to by a man or a woman. Is it possible that STD clinics hire only unisex automatons? Is it some kind of government-instituted social punishment? The sexually marred and morally deviant deserve genderless care? It's the first step of a kind of social deportation. Next would be a trip to a sexual morality theme park, chaperoned by nuns and priests.

Furthermore, there was the paranoia. Would my name go on a list? Would there be bribes and covert responsibilities? I suddenly wanted my social security number back! I wanted all of those forms that were stapled to other forms!

Just as I was about to dismount from the strange throne on which I sat to have my blood drawn, a nurse entered and called my name and directed me to a hallway, where I would sit outside a room to wait for an actual doctor to conduct an examination. At that point I was starving for some kind of human interaction that went beyond needles and forms and instructional videos.

"Hi," I said to the nurse, who nodded silently. Her mouth almost seemed sewn shut, and yet there was a kindness in her eyes. I wanted her to tell me everything was going to be all right. I wanted the simplest reassurance.

"Um. How long have you been working here?" I asked.

She looked at me for a moment but didn't answer. She simply turned and walked back toward the blood room.

While sitting in the fluorescent wash of the hallway, a coldhearted rage started to overtake me. I imagined a confrontation with Lacy Shank. I would knock on her apartment door, and drop my pants to reveal my mutilated genitals. Then, after demanding an explanation and deeming it unsatisfactory, I would brandish an illegally purchased revolver and—

A tall man in a white lab coat was suddenly standing before me. He possessed the reddest mustache I have ever seen and held a clipboard.

"Come in," he instructed. He had a German accent and looked completely exhausted.

The room was clogged with books and desks and the kind of medical accoutrements that one might more readily associate with the psychological testing or training of farm animals. This clinical ensemble was showcased on a large, stainless-steel gurney. In the otherwise nondescript room, the gurney was a kind of radiant altar. I nearly fell to my knees and hugged its cold girth in the hope of achieving a medical pardon.

After the doctor outfitted his hands with a pair of industrial-strength rubber gloves, he asked me to stand and drop my pants and underwear. He hardly flinched at the green mass. During his tenure at the STD clinic I'm sure he'd seen plenty of similar phenomena. Based on his cool, precise bedside manner, I would even go so far as to say he had probably seen much worse.

Quietly, and with the efficiency of a jewel thief, the doctor then procured from the stainless-steel gurney what appeared to be a metal Q-tip. It was approximately six inches long and had a cotton swab at the end.

"What are you going to do with that?" I squawked.

"We'll need a sample for the lab."

"A sample of what?"

"Your excretion."

I suddenly realized the physics of what was about to happen, and my already inflamed and frightened penis receded into perhaps the smallest lump of hard genital flesh that has ever been assigned to a member of the male species. Sure, by all anatomical definitions, it was still a penis (with two equally contracting testicles), but at a glance one might have thought it more clitoral than penile, or even a flesh-colored light switch that, when engaged, would emit a blank, ejaculatory electric current.

"I am going to count to three," the doctor announced rather grimly, "and then I shall insert the catheter and obtain the necessary sample."

"Okay," I squeaked.

With thumb and forefinger he somehow secured the tissue around my tiny knob and zeroed in with his catheter.

"One . . . two . . ."

And then he did it! It was a dirty trick, and one he must have learned from years of practice. He never even started to say "three." When his instrument went in I experienced the most concentrated, acute trauma of violent, hot shock that I ever have or, with any luck, ever will again. I shrieked like a woman, and in the next split second I felt as if every vital breath and blood cell had been sucked out of me and sent flying through a dark and violent prism. Although I didn't faint, my knees buckled and I wound up having to push off of the doctor's shoulder to find my feet.

When he took the next sample (apparently the first hadn't properly done the trick) and smeared it on the tiny, rectangular glass slide, I was already out of my body. In fact, if memory serves me correctly, like some kind of noble gas, I was hovering near the trays of fluorescent lights above.

"Oh, poor boy," my gas self wept to my human self. "Oh, poor, lost, terrible boy."

When the doctor extracted the second metallic Q-tip from my urethra a small, orange hair protruded from the tip of my penis, like tulips from a clown's gun. It was approximately the length and thickness of a spider leg and it was accompanied by a plasmatic sheath of the green stuff.

"What is this?" the doctor queried, half-amazed, half-puzzled. He then plucked the item from the head of my penis with a pair of tweezers and studied it under the fluorescent lights. "It appears to be some sort of animal hair," he said. Then he spoke to himself in German, deposited the hair on a glass slide, and marked and tagged it and placed it alongside my first sample.

"Do you have sex with animals?" he asked clinically.

"No," I said, plunging further into the numbing waters of shock.

"Well, this is very interesting," the doctor said.

"Why?"

"Because, my friend, the only way that animal hair could have entered your urethra was from the aperture in your penis. If ingested, the digestive acids in your stomach would have easily liquefied such a small hair."

"Maybe it's a pubic hair?"

"It's not a pubic hair."

"Or an eyelash!"

"Eyelashes don't look like that. It is from a short-haired animal. A *reddish*, short-haired animal. You haven't been—shall I say—*playing* with any pets as of late, have you? Say, little doggies or ferrets?"

"No," I chirped.

"Squirrels?"

"I haven't seen a squirrel in months."

"Very interesting," the doctor said, and began writing something on his clipboard. When he completed his notations he asked me who my most recent sex partners had been. I explained that I had been with only one person since moving to New York in May.

"Does this person have any pets?"

"A cat."

"What color is it?"

"Sort of orangish, actually. It's an Abyssinian."

"Are you allergic to cats?"

"Not that I know of."

"The dander in cat hair could be extremely irritating to the penis, especially when lodged in as far as this one was."

"I got VD from a cat hair?"

"You may have a case of plain old-fashioned urethritis."

"What's that?"

"Irritation of the urethra. But it could be chlamydia, gonorrhea, or syphilis as well. Did you wear a condom during your last sexual experience?"

"No."

"Well, I won't have your lab results for a few days, and I would suggest calling your most recent partner and asking if this person has experienced any similar symptoms. It is possible that he or she—"

"She."

"It is possible that *she* is a carrier and isn't aware of it."

"Jesus."

"The good news is that it is very likely that this will be cleared up with an antibiotic. It's definitely not herpes. In the future, if I were you, I would strongly consider wearing a condom."

I nodded.

Then, from some unknown fold in his lab coat, he produced a small white container of Doxycillin, which he told me to take three times a day until I ran out. He also said that if my symptoms persisted, I should return to the clinic for something stronger.

I thanked him with the desperation of a starving man who's been given a turkey sandwich. I thanked him with multiple handshakes and a sentimental squeeze of his shoulder. I think I even thanked him in a slightly German accent. After he took his hand back, he stroked his red mustache for a moment and told me to call the clinic in three days and that through some automated voicemail system I would be able to access my lab results by punching in my social security number. The word *negative* would mean that it was a simple case of urethritis, and that would be the end of that.

"How will I know whether the cat hair caused it?" I asked.

"This we may never know for sure," he explained, still stroking his mustache. "But I would venture to say that if your lab results are negative, the cat hair was the cause of your problems. I just don't understand how it got there."

"Me, neither."

"Perhaps your partner has been sexually active with her cat?"

"Huh," I said in response.

"It could be that she has several cat hairs trapped inside of her vagina. If so, I would recommend that she douche. This is the most productive way to clean the vagina."

"I'll pass that on to her."

"Would you like to look at this photo essay chronicling the lives and times of victims of sexually transmitted diseases?" he asked, suddenly proffering a large, coffee-table-size textbook. On the front was a woman sitting on a lowered toilet seat, spreading wide her labia, exposing what appeared to be a toad-like cluster of genital warts.

"No, thanks," I said, swallowing hard.

"I am required to offer this service as educational outreach."

"I appreciate it, but I should get going."

"Very well then."

"I'll pray for that cat-hair theory," I offered as a farewell.

"Good luck."

After I closed the door I stood in the hall for a moment and stared into the fluorescent lights like a bewildered moth. Then I zipped my coat and left the clinic. I decided it would be my penance to walk home.

Putting my head down, I jiggled my bottle of pills and took two immediately. They were huge and went down dry and had the taste of bitter pewter. I recapped the bottle and squeezed it all the way to Tenth Street.

Back at the apartment I called home. I'm not sure why. I guess the threat of a venereal disease can inspire the need to hear the voice of even the coldest mother.

"Hi," I said when she answered the phone.

"Hi," she said.

"Are you okay?" I asked.

"I'm fine," she said.

"You sound weird."

"Well, I'm not," she said. "Not weird at all. I wish you boys would call a little more frequently. I haven't heard from your brother in god knows how long."

"I'll tell him to give you a call."

There was a pause. I could hear the dishwasher running and I was convinced somehow that the dishes were clean but that she was running it anyway, just to have something to do.

"So why are you calling—do you need money?"

"No," I said. "I just wanted to say hi. I've had a couple of funny days."

"Funny meaning what? Did you lose your job or something?"

"No, the job is fine."

"Have they given you a raise yet?"

"No. No raise. Not till after the new year."

"Well, you obviously called for a reason."

"I actually had a dream about you," I lied. Why I went there is anyone's guess.

"What kind of a dream?"

"You were on the subway with me. And we were both wearing shorts. You'd just bought me a kite."

"A *kite*?"

"Yeah, a kite. Like those things that kids fly. A red kite."

"Why on earth would I buy you a *kite*?"

"I don't know. It was a dream. You kept trying to attach it to my wrist with string, but I wouldn't let you."

"Were you old or young?"

"I was the age I am now. And you were the age you are now. And then you turned into a gorilla. Just like that. Weird, huh?"

"Well, that's ludicrous."

I had never made up a dream before. But the gorilla seemed compelling, somehow. I would later actually dream of this gorilla. It would be walking along the shoulder of the highway with a briefcase, and I would wake suspecting that the briefcase contained my unfinished novel about acute knee pain and the end of the world.

"And, by the way," I added after a silence, "I have V.D."

It just came out. I had no idea I was going to say it.

She said, "I have to go now."

"Mom, I'm kidding," I lied.

We didn't say anything for a moment. I could hear her breathing, thick and labored. I wondered how many years she had left. I thought maybe eight or nine. Even though she was a healthy woman who was barely into middle age, I saw her only lasting that much longer. Some people can only go for so long before something clicks in their head. It has nothing to do with health or random acts of violence; they just lie down in a field or on a back porch and expire.

"Was I really a gorilla?" she asked.

"Yes," I lied again. "But you were a pretty gorilla."

"Well, at least I was pretty."

"How's Dad?"

"Your father's fine. He has to have a mole removed."

"Oh. Why?"

"Well, it's gotten a little funny-looking."

"Funny-looking meaning what? Is it cancerous?"

"No. But they think it would be a good idea to have it taken care of. As a precautionary measure."

"I didn't know he had a mole."

"Well, he does."

"Where is it?"

"It's on his person. In a private place."

"Like on his ballsack?"

"Where on earth do you come up with *words* like that?"

"*Ballsack* is a perfectly good word, Mom. In its purest essence a ballsack is nothing more or nothing less than what it says it is: a ballsack."

"I believe the proper word is *scrotum*."

It gave me great delight to say crude things that made my mother squirm. I knew that underneath her Roman Catholic exterior she actually loved it. Once I repeatedly used the word *penis* while talking about the leafy arrangements that my Sunday-school teacher used to describe Adam and Eve's genital flora. "Apparently there was lots of eucalyptus in paradise and it was Adam's favorite choice of *penis* covering," I told her in the kitchen. "This is why the homo sapien's *penis* is so agreeable to vegetation. The *penis* and the female breast." She locked herself in the bathroom and wouldn't come out until I stopped saying it. I swore, though, that I could hear her laughing under her breath and trying to hide it by running the tap in the sink.

"Anyway, it's on his navel," she continued on about my father's mole.

"His navel?"

"Yes."

"Dad has a mole on his *navel*?"

"A brown protuberance, yes. And it's quite large."

"I've never seen it."

"Well, it's there. Plain as day. And it has been for as long as I've known him. I used to joke with him about it."

"Joke with him how?"

"I used to say to him 'Hey, bud, if I unscrewed that, would your buttocks fall off?' "

"You would?"

She was suddenly laughing so hard it almost sounded like she was crying.

"Mom, you would use the word *buttocks*?"

"I would, yes."

She was so beside herself she could barely get the words out.

"And what would he say?" I asked.

"He wouldn't say *anything*! He'd just turn red as a *strawberry*!"

"That's really witty, Mom."

"Isn't it, though?" she cried.

She laughed some more and then started sighing a lot. In our family laughter was always followed by epic bouts of sighing. It was like a household law: no laughing without at least two accompanying sighs. It's why at the age of fourteen I decided to stop laughing; I couldn't bear hearing myself making that weary sound.

"Give your brother a hug for me," my mother said.

"I will."

And then I offered her peace the way a priest would.

"Peace be with you," I said. I could feel a bitter smile hanging on my face.

"And also with you," she said in response. She sounded scared and far away.

Three days later I phoned the clinic and entered my social security number. Within twelve hours the Doxycillin had corrected whatever urethral damage had been done and my urine passed painlessly and with great velocity. The mashed peas disappeared, too, but I had decided to keep my soiled underwear as a reminder of the perils of unsafe sex, general madness, and multitalented Abyssinian cats.

I followed the phone-in system's directions and, after a moment, in a rather dispassionate female voice, I received the following automated reply: "Your results are negative. Thank you for calling."

I opted not to discuss the matter with Lacy Shank.

I simply returned to the general insignificance of my life the way one returns to the favorite roller-skating rink of his or her hometown: as if very little has happened and no time has passed.

Loach Leavings

AS AN AUTUMN PROJECT, the Owl and I constructed a bookshelf with found bricks and scrapped planks we rescued from a Dumpster outside of Spring Street Lumber. We carried the wood back to the East Village on our shoulders like penitent coal miners roaming the foothills of West Virginia.

When we got home the Loach was, surprisingly, gone, so we collapsed onto our displaced sofa and complained about the stairs.

"Those stairs," the Owl said, kneading his thighs with a strange detachment.

"Some workout," I concurred.

"Your limp's looking better," he added, still catching his breath.

"Yeah, it's coming around," I said.

The knot in my knee was starting to unkink itself and I was glad. The trip with the shouldered lumber had been a test. If my knee passed, I would start playing ball again soon.

The Owl said, "I saw a Greyhound parked on Forty-first Street yesterday. Just sitting there, empty. I spit on it."

"Was it westbound?"

"It said Detroit above the windshield. I got this weird sense that it knew my thoughts, Homon. I could feel it mocking me."

After several deep breaths, from between the couch cushions the Owl extracted a small, gland-like cake of gefilte fish. He stared at it, slightly bemused.

"How long do we let this go on, Homon?" he asked incredulously, turning the thing in his hand with mild amazement.

"I can't see it lasting," I replied.

"Has he given anything toward the Con Ed bill yet?"

"Not a cent."

"Still no toilet-paper contributions."

"Not a single roll."

The Owl shook his head and added, "Goddamn cable bill might as well be a paper plate."

"Or a paper plate disguised as a cable bill."

"Con Ed's definitely going to turn us off, Homon."

"Oh, it's inevitable."

"And he's still eating my potato wedges."

"I know."

"I count them, Homon. I literally tally my potato wedges."

"It's a sad state of affairs when one starts tallying one's potato wedges."

"And my shampoo. For god's sake."

"Your shampoo and your toothpaste."

"The urine sample doesn't even own a toothbrush."

"I know, Glenwood, I know."

"Yesterday I caught him again, brushing his teeth right here on the sofa, my tube of Crest on the coffee table."

"What was he using, his finger or something?"

"You don't want to know what he was using."

"Tell me."

"You really don't want to know."

"Oh, but I do."

"He was using a potato wedge, Homon."

"Jesus."

"I know, right?"

"To brush his teeth?"

"Rather effectively, I might add."

"I can't even see how that would work."

"He was spitting into his paper bag."

"Nice."

"Yeah, nice . . ." he trailed off, scratching his neck and accidentally smearing a little gefilte fish on his cheek.

After a moment he added, "Goddamn Loach."

"Goddamn Loach," I echoed.

"Goddamn Loach," we commiserated chorally.

The sofa smelled like a salad of armpits and anuses and foot fungus, undoubtedly our own as well as the various sweats, wastes, and pastes excreted by the Loach.

"Where do you think he is right now?" the Owl asked, looking at his watch.

"I don't know."

"It's the first time he's been gone in, like, weeks."

"Maybe he's out looking for a job," I offered.

We laughed sadly and found that we had been spending so much time working and writing and studying that our own chortling voices had become a lost, exotic sound.

The Owl removed something from the gefilte fish. At first glance it might have been mistaken for a long spider leg, but upon further inspection, it was discovered to be a raven-colored, lethargic-looking pubic hair, certainly the Loach's.

"His days are numbered, man," the Owl said staring at the pulpy mess in his palm.

"Totally numbered."

"I'm counting backward from twenty starting today."

"Twenty," I echoed.

But somehow, in the same way one understands that the pies of dust behind the La-Z-Boy will never be eradicated, we both knew that twenty days later, the Loach would still be in residence, and we would concede to this household constant with something that might be classified as apathetic impotence. Or maybe it was diffident cowardice? Or could it have been plain old-fashioned repressed Midwestern tolerance (a phenomenon not too distant from the subtler side effects of Catholicism)?

Perhaps in some strange way we needed the Loach to remind us of how far down the male species could go? Perhaps our daily diet of him was a kind of vaccine? To ingest part of the disease will create the antibodies necessary to bolster a good defense. Even with laboratory experiments, distinct baselines are crucial in establishing what is necessary (or even vital) to deviate from.

Perhaps we needed him?

Perhaps he was saving our lives after all?

Longhand

A FEW MONTHS AFTER I sold the Underwood to the vintage shop on First Avenue, a woman who called herself my great-aunt Rollie sent me a crisp hundred-dollar bill. I had never heard of this person before, but when charity falls from the sky, why should one suddenly become preoccupied with cloud formations?

In her brief note—penned on heavily weighted, lilac-colored stationery and executed in a meandering, jittery penmanship—she wrote that she lived in Zuni, New Mexico, and that she was my mother's grandmother's sister. Due to "an illness involving her thyroid," she was trying to reengage with whatever familial strands were still left to her.

Feick was also the recipient of one of these epistolary miracles, although he hadn't been home for days. Where he was spending his nights I had no idea. For a fleeting moment I was tempted to commit larcenous, brotherly theft, but in the end I lacked the courage.

I imagined expensively packaged, equally crisp hundred-dollar bills flying like little green sparrows all over the country. I found it curious that a fatal illness would inspire an old widow to blindly spend her money on unknown relatives three generations her junior.

After sending my great-aunt Rollie a rather sentimentally pitched, hyperbolically punctuated thank-you note, I ran downstairs to Twice in a Lifetime in the hope of reclaiming my Underwood.

The hard truth is that things had slowed down considerably with *Opie's Half-life*, and like all superstitious writers I had attributed my sluggishness to ridiculous externals. It was the advent of fall. My healing knee was thawing the dumb-jock part of my brain and the neurotransmitters attuned to higher, more intellectual pursuits were suddenly overwhelmed. Like a deficiency of certain essential vitamins needed to run competitive long-distance races, my narrative muscles had somehow atrophied. Having Uncle Brad's typewriter back would solve my novel, inspire velocity, and usher me to the finish line. Perhaps it would also minimize my compulsion to masturbate. There's nothing like a well-used writing machine to cut down on pathological sexual behavior. After all, one can't effectively masturbate with one's knees.

I think.

The other hard truth is that at the vintage shop, the woman with the blue bangs reported in a dispassionate, nasal voice that the Underwood had been sold to a small, off-off-Broadway theatre company that very morning. (Oh, the brutal irony!) With the vitality of a bowl of soggy cornflakes, Blue Bangs informed me that said theatre company (the Workhorse Ensemble) needed it for a show they were producing on White Street in TriBeCa.

I jog-walked down First Avenue, crossed Houston, skip-hopped west, hit Broadway, and headed south, my knee cauliflowering painfully. After a quick rest I rubber-banded my way through the snarls of Broadway like someone suffering the recent effects of faint and sublime electrocution, the hundred-dollar bill gripped in my white-knuckled fist.

When I arrived at the theatre, the stage manager–slash–house manager–slash–coffee girl person wouldn't let me pass beyond the cafeteria table disguised as a box office because she said the company was in the middle of a "tech" rehearsal. I imagined a small troupe of frightened actors being hypnotically manipulated by some sinister, hulking mainframe.

During a lull in our conversation I heard the actors shouting onstage. It was a man and a woman. They were screaming at each other at the top of their lungs.

The girl at the door wore black pants with a black turtleneck and a headset that she adjusted compulsively. I couldn't decide whether she was dressed like a street performer or a thief. The bill of her black baseball cap was flipped up in some failed attempt at comedy or defiance. Her face was a dimpled corn muffin of obedience.

I pleaded and waved my money and explained the sentimental weight of and my psychic attachment to the Underwood, but she just continued to stare at me, periodically adjusting the dial at her ear, leaning against the door, an arm bar poised in front of her.

I was boring her socks off.

I was boring her to smithereens.

The actors screamed. They howled. They were murdering each other onstage.

Then, suddenly and with the velocity and inspiration of a gospel-choir leader, I started miming the composition of my recently titled novel on the Underwood, fingers spidering wildly, left hand finding the manual return, exaggerating its horizontal sweep with Christmas-morning eyes, adding a little vocal *ding*. I squatted down slightly so we could view each other on a level sightline.

The actors were crying now. They were sobbing from places deep inside themselves. The theatre was drowning in grief.

My stage manager–slash–house manager–slash–coffee girl person finally thawed out of her arm-bar pose (now diagonal) and told me she would put me on the list for their dress rehearsal, scheduled for the following night. She handed me a beige, five-by-seven postcard and wrote my name down on what appeared to be a waitress's order pad. She said I could take up the matter of the Underwood with Luke, the director, after the dress rehearsal.

There was hope.

For the briefest moment I saw myself united with the Underwood in playful romance. I would never betray our relationship again. I would sell my own ass on the Bowery instead. Or, better yet, I would do without Con Ed! I would survive the winter cold by doing hourly calisthenics! We could build fires in the flueless fireplace! We could throw living room barbecues!

Moments later, two actors came walking through the front door, a man and a woman, wearing identical velvet vampire capes. They were hugging with the kind of bereft desperation one might associate with people who greet loved ones in hospital waiting rooms. They hugged for their lives as they crossed White Street, headed west, and rounded the corner at Broadway.

Oh, to be a thespian and feel so much.

I looked at the flyer, which read:

Boots, Bats, and Sticks
a new play by Sherman Furl

In a crude Rorschach test of black ink was an image of the two actors who had just exited the theater, as well as a third, female figure clad in what appeared to be a World War II Nazi greatcoat. Her posture was both threatening and provocative.

While I was folding the flyer in half, Luke the director came through the stage door shaking his head. He was thirtyish and bitchy and sported a perfectly sculpted goatee that was both satanic and Elizabethan. He wore black leather pants, snakeskin cowboy boots, and an enormous turquoise belt buckle. His T-shirt was four sizes too small and in big, black letters read BACK OFF, BITCH!

"They're just not getting it!" he proclaimed, seemingly frustrated to the point of tears. In an impressive three-part move he then produced a clove cigarette, made a flame whose source went unnoticed, and inhaled oceanically. "They're indicating the whole fucking final scene, Petey!"

I don't think I have ever known a woman called Petey—a name I'd always thought was reserved for adolescent boys and Jack Russell terriers.

Petey shook her head and said, "Frankly, I think François is more concerned with how we're displaying his head shot in the lobby."

"Fucking François. Why did I hire a frog, anyway? Never let me do that again."

Luke twittered bitchily for a moment.

"And that fucking stage-left Fresnel keeps frying the gels," he added suddenly.

"Big Apple Lights is sending someone over to replace it," Petey explained. "How's Sherman holding up?"

"He's backstage hitting on Basha again. Another breeder playwright desperate for a pretty muse. I need a fucking mint julep or something."

Luke paced and smoked for a moment. I found it interesting that he hardly looked at me, let alone gave the slightest acknowledgment that a tallish, desperate-looking member of the human race was standing three feet in front of him holding a hundred-dollar bill.

Petey must have sensed my anger and said to Luke, "This gentleman would like to speak with you."

The director said, "You're not another breeder playwright, are you?"

"Actually, I'm a breeder novelist," I said. "But I'm also seeking a muse. Preferably breasted." I offered my hand.

With the cool suspicion of a cardsharp, Luke the director regarded me and then shook my hand. His grip was stronger than I expected.

"What can I do for you?" he said.

"Well," I replied, "I understand from the woman at the vintage shop on First Avenue that you purchased an Underwood manual typewriter from her this morning."

"What about it?"

"That typewriter is mine."

"If it's yours, then why was it on sale in a nonreturnable vintage shop?"

"That's a good point," Petey chimed in.

"I sold it to her a few weeks ago to cover my Con Ed bill," I explained. "I'm prepared to buy it back from you. I have a hundred dollars right here," I said, opening my fist and revealing the crinkled, woman-ish face of Benjamin Franklin.

"I'd love to help you out," Luke said, smoking his lips off, "but it's already in the show."

"Is there any way you can get another one?"

"I went prop shopping in Vermont for an entire weekend just to find that typewriter. The author of the play wouldn't settle for a cheap imitation. I rented a car. I came back from Montpelier with nothing. Twice in a Lifetime was one store in thirty. Besides, I bought it for one-eighty."

"You did?"

"I talked her down from two-twenty."

"Jesus."

"It's been welded to a Doric pillar," Petey said, adding vinegar to an already bitter salad of disappointment.

My heart suddenly felt like a toad in my chest.

"I'll tell you what," Luke said. "Come see the dress rehearsal. At the end of the run I'll sell it back to you."

"How long is the run?" I asked.

"It's an Equity Showcase, so we can only go for fourteen performances. She'll be yours in two weeks. How's that sound?"

"It's gonna be hell getting it off that pillar," Petey informed us.

"It's a deal," I said.

"I'll take the hundred as a deposit," Luke said, his fingers pulling at the hairs of his goatee.

Then Petey held out her hand as if she were a dental assistant requesting my insurance card. And like the Midwestern fool that I can more than occasionally be, I handed the money to her and felt relieved—perhaps even a little thankful.

Then Luke and Petey continued their criticism of the actors, the faulty cue lights, the soundboard, and even the muse-seeking, immoral advances of the playwright as if I had turned to chalk dust in a room with a good, clean breeze.

By the beginning of October, it was becoming more difficult for me to write at work. This was mostly due to increased responsibility. Van Von Donnelly put me in charge of monitoring and running down all marketing and promotion materials for the reps, which required lots of interdepartmental liaising. When I wasn't summarizing bellwether numbers or transcribing call reports I was hopping around between the publicity, promotions, and editorial departments like a confused chicken.

At home I had grown weary of the assembly line, robotic staccato of the Smith Corona daisy wheel. Despite its affordability (twenty-five bucks at a used electronics store on Canal Street) and relatively compact size, I banished it to the Tenth Street curb and tried to write longhand. I would serve my two-week sentence for betraying the Underwood with newfound maturity, at which point I would transcribe whatever longhand sentences, paragraphs, or chapters of *Opie's Half-life* I could eke onto a yellow legal pad pilfered from the supply room at work.

Despite my increased responsibilities, my sales-assistant salary was still making the consumption of a well-balanced dinner a difficult economic task, and after work I'd usually eat a bowl of industrial-tasting ramen noodles and swallow an orange, spaceship-shaped Centrum multivitamin, and then head to the cafés on St. Mark's Place. There I would sit and brood over the loss of my Underwood, a three-dollar cappuccino mugged and saucered between my hands, its luxurious contents somehow not intended to be ingested with regularity but rather appreciated the same way one might appreciate the perfection of a handsomely arranged bowl of copper pears or ancient African mask art.

There was a man I often saw making the rounds at the same cafés. Café Mogodor. Café Gigi. St. Dymphna's. Café Orlin. Small and Sephardic-looking, with the blank, expressionless face of a Suffolk sheep, he was balding rather tragically and had black, unibrowed eyes above a pristinely manicured mustache.

His usual meal consisted of the rack of lamb with mint sauce (a special request) and a Diet Coke with lots of ice. He spent most of his time poring over the details of a horse-racing form and twisting the gold-nugget oil-sheik rings strangling his fingers.

Somehow I assumed we had a silent brotherhood, a kind of East Village private café camaraderie, something small and wordless and telepathically respectful.

I would scratch out my novel with a blue felt-tip pen and he would eat his lamb chops carnivorously while wringing every infinitesimal bit of information from his racing form. Though there was no evidence of him actually being a fellow East Village artist—oh, how deliciously pretentious that would be!—there was still an air of creative mystery between us. I imagined we were transatlantic spies. Or Red Sea spies. Or something like that.

One day while I was pretending to drink my cappuccino, he finally broke the silence.

It went like this:

"Don't stare at my food!" he said.

"Huh?"

"You ogle like small dog!"

"I'm not ogling."

"You're killing my lamb with your eyes."

"I am?"

"You mangle my tabouli!"

"Your what?"

"Look at you! Stop mangling! Waitress!"

"Dude, I'm not—"

"Murder your own food!"

I focused on my novel, vowing to never look at his, or anyone else's, food again.

In general, writing longhand gave me cramps and I became superstitious that too much of it would somehow corrupt the release of my jump shot. It was a chance I couldn't take, given the recent improvement of my knee and the promise of a return to the courts ripening before me.

As a result I tried to write left-handed, but that made me feel like I was suffering from a mild stroke.

I melodramatically came to the decision that it would be the Underwood or nothing.

So the following night I attended the dress rehearsal of *Boots, Bats, and Sticks* by Sherman Furl.

My name was on the list, which made me feel dumb and important at the same time. There was a brief period after my arrival in New York when I thought that having your name on such a list was a thing to be envied. New club openings. Gallery showings. Author readings and signings. Dress rehearsals. I would later learn that list-landing is actually a resilient, agoraphobia-inducing virus disguised as social capital;

the same kind of condition that sets in when the voice of the bill collector keeps you from checking the messages on your answering machine. I discovered that the more lists I landed on the less I felt like leaving my apartment.

The Workhorse Ensemble Theatre's capacity was maybe eighty seats, all of which were filled. Unlike the Juilliard audience, the Workhorse crowd consisted mainly of youngish downtown people. Lots of them wore combat boots, Dickies, and intentionally nerdy glasses, and those who did not don a clever hat possessed hair so twisted, snarled, tousled, and weather-beaten it had a kind of mad theatricality unto itself. Thus, in addition to the formal play about to be enacted, I was subject to what can only be described as a kind of strikingly hirsute performance art.

During the ten or fifteen minutes before the play began I became distinctly aware of my own ordinariness. I didn't have facial hair or distressed thrift-store clothes or quirky eyewear. What I did have was a math teacher's haircut and a sense of fashion that was pretty much mall-bought. Even my authentic limp—perhaps my one true eccentricity—was starting to evolve back into a regular pedestrian stride. But my homogeneousness could always be remedied. Oh, to be an artist and *look like one!* In that moment I vowed to experiment with facial hair, to start sporting a cool hat, and to haunt the vintage shops for an ironic, filling-station wardrobe.

After the houselights dimmed, Luke the director performed a self-effacing curtain speech that included an insincere apology for the lack of programs; a quick cataloging of the three actors, the designers, the playwright, and the stage manager; and big smooching thank-yous to three or four people without whose help the play wouldn't have had a chance (he actually brought the tips of his fingers to his mouth and sent a chef's fellatio to the rear exits).

There was a man pacing at the back of the house who I assumed was the author himself. Sherman Furl had his own wild proliferation of black hair (more theatre) and he shrugged his shoulders and cracked his knuckles incessantly.

The play was set in an East Village apartment not unlike mine. The hyperrealistic set featured a lopsided coffee table choked with junk mail, a saddlebacked sofa, a functioning stove and kitchen sink (they actually made tandoori chicken during the course of the production), a microwave oven with a turntable, a velvet painting of an eagle, and my Underwood typewriter, set on a four-foot Doric dais.

The play was about a writer–slash–furniture mover, his hypnotist wife, and their abusive relationship. She wanted to take a trip to the Pacific Palisades but he needed to finish his novel. She wanted a massage. He wanted space. She wanted to be pregnant with twins. He wanted to get a vasectomy. She wanted him to "fuck her Cadillac style," but he was in love with the heroine of his novel (called *Boots, Bats, and Sticks*), the Baltic femme fatale, Katrajina.

The mutual spousal abuse included spanking, biting, water dousing, finger bending, larynx thumping, skillet throwing, boxing, spitting, pinching, mouth taping, wedgie employment, joint manipulation, condiment dodgeball, one-on-one Red Rover, and kung fu. There were also onstage fireworks (magic snakes and firecrackers—the audience jumped like spooked chickens).

In the last ten minutes, after the wife removed her black cape (for some unknown reason they wore the capes throughout the entire play) and finally left her husband (she boarded a train for a small cabin in Saskatchewan, Canada) another woman materialized through a blue mist. She was green-eyed, noir-like, and clad in a tight-fitting turquoise sweater dress and high heels. Her hair was pulled back severely. At her side she held what appeared to be a forty-ounce ball-peen hammer. She was both beautiful and murderous-looking. There was something hauntingly familiar about this woman, and after the mist cleared I realized that she was the girl I had twice seen on the downtown express train. She had the same round, beautiful green eyes. The same black hair. The same porcelain skin.

I was completely agog.

To put it modestly, I was rendered, in essence, a small petting-farm sheep.

I almost started bleating.

In some vague, theatrical leap, the audience was supposed to believe that this woman (my distant subway love) was actually Katrajina, the Baltic heroine from the husband's novel. They exchanged several erotic, heavily accented sentences and then he professed his love for her. But when he actually made a move to take her hand she reared back with the ball-peen hammer. I believe the intent was to have the mysterious, fictitious heroine–slash–muse–slash–metaphysical lover (my unattainable subway fantasy) attempt to strike the novelist, but what actually happened was that in her rather clumsy hammer hoist, said tool came crashing down on my Underwood typewriter, making solid, earth-separating contact with the Doric dais and splitting it in two like a chunk of lumberjack's sidewood, both halves timbering to the stage. My uncle Brad's beautifully restored No. 3 Underwood typewriter—my beloved graduation gift and the literary salve for whatever momentum I had lost with my novel—came crashing down directly, generating a noise comparable to the sound that might be made if a piano were to fall several stories to the pavement. The Underwood caved in as if it were made of gingerbread and pipe cleaners.

I have never seen so much damage done by a single tool.

The requiem for *Opie's Half-life* was surely being composed by literary angels in heaven.

As indicated by the dropping of the ball-peen hammer (the truest moment of the play, no doubt), it was obvious that this was a major mistake, and both stage manager Petey and director Luke charged the stage EMS-style. Moments later, the houselights were brought up and yet another person whose gender I can only describe as unisex (s/he was dolphin-shaped, had a low-cropped white man's Afro, wore blue mechanic's coveralls, and spoke in a choirboy soprano) stormed the stage. Along with the two actors, these three attended to the actress playing Katrajina with the intensity and desperation of an overly caffeinated and underused SWAT team.

After the actress was calmed, given a Dixie cup of water, and seated on the sofa, the director, in a speech that almost seemed plagiarized from his earlier one, thanked everyone and added a half-sung apology, informing those of us in the audience that the rest of the play wouldn't be performed. This was followed by a foghorn of groans and guttural complaints, and a fish-fry smattering of applause. My focus was torn between the beautiful actress and my caved-in typewriter.

As people filed out of the theatre I found myself glued to my seat. I was both aroused and infuriated. I felt like I was on the bad end of some existential prank, and yet I was overwhelmed by a strange warmth flowering in my chest.

At some point the other two actors cleared the proscenium and the stage manager and the unisex person walked through the house lighting cigarettes. Luke the director followed them and I was left alone with the actress.

Still holding her Dixie cup, she had a look of blank shock on her face, and yet there was something full about her expression, as though whatever feeling was living behind her eyes was being experienced with great intensity. She was beautiful the way things made out of glass are beautiful. She was almost petite, not quite curvaceous. Her hands were slender and perfect.

"Are you okay?" I asked.

She looked at me but neither of us said anything for a moment. During this pause it was as if she knew intimately the details of all of my scars, cavities, Little League batting slumps, various adolescent haircuts, sacred baseball cards, the horrible night I lost my virginity and got crabs (a five-foot-ten, large-breasted orthodontist's wet dream at Island Lake Summer Camp), BMX bike injuries, basketball shoelace styles, Catholic Church sacraments (minus confirmation), and that time I urinated in my sleeping bag while camping in a National Park in Bergdorf, Idaho (acute fear of local, legendary wapiti elk).

These kinds of pauses are not meant to be written about. They exist only as themselves. Words pollute their purity. I was in the presence of such extreme beauty that if I could have named the feelings I was experiencing during this interval I believe I would have been able to solve all that was wrong with my life.

"You are man from subway, no?" she asked in her voluptuous eastern-bloc accent.

"Yes," I replied woodenly.

"I see you three times now," she said. "Each time I am molested by confusion and some peculiar business occurs."

"What happened the other two times?"

"The first time I forget what subway stop to get off and wind up dismounting in Greenpoint, Brooklyn."

"Where were you supposed to get off?"

"Street of Chambers in Manhattan."

"What happened the second time?"

"The second time I get out at Street of Chambers in Manhattan and go on bus for no reason. The bus take me to the ferryboat of Staten Island. I go to Staten Island and walk up hill and purchase several chocolate milks at Korean deli grocery store."

"Were you planning on going to Staten Island?"

"No. I was planning on going to Greenpoint, Brooklyn."

"Wow."

"You see? And now I ruin play. What are you doing here?"

"Well, it's sort of a strange story. That was my typewriter, actually."

"The typewriter that I destroy?"

"Yeah. I had to sell it to pay my electric bill and your director purchased it from the vintage store I sold it to. I was planning on buying it back after the play closes."

"Was this typewriter important to you?"

"It was sort of a personal good-luck charm."

"You are writer?"

"Yes."

"And now I crush it."

"Yes."

"I destroy your personal good-luck charm."

"Yes."

"This is no good."

"Not really."

"The hammer is very strong."

"Yes."

"I never want to touch this hammer again. Perhaps it is cursed, no?"

"Perhaps."

"My duties are that I am supposed to crush *plate*, not typewriter."

"Maybe you should work on that backstroke."

"I make such terrible mess. They will fire me like whore."

"I'm sure things will work out."

"Typewriter is supposed to be metaphoric symbol of penis."

"It is?"

"According to Sherman Furl, yes. I do not understand this."

"Interesting idea."

"So I kill the play's penis."

"That's one way to think about it."

"I would like to smoke cigarette. Will you join me outside?"

"Sure."

The actress crumpled her Dixie cup, let it fall to the stage, rose off the couch, and stepped down from the lip of the proscenium. I followed her through the fire exit and out into an alley.

"Do you smoke?" she asked.

"No," I said, and watched her light a Marlboro Red. Up close I could see through the knit of her turquoise sweater dress. The sight of her skin underneath just about took my knees out.

"So you write heart-wrenching American dramas?" she asked, smoking.

"I'm writing a novel, actually."

"I just finish nonfiction novel about the famous actress Shirley MacLaine. She is very interesting American celebrity. I enjoy books very much." She exhaled and crossed her arms. "You are very tall for writer."

"I am?"

"Yes. Most writers are short."

"They are?"

"In Poland every writer is short. You are not like this."

"I guess."

"And you are boyishly handsome."

"I am?"

"Yes, but you dress like employee of New York Public Library."

"I know. I have no style."

"But this is perhaps good thing. Like you have secret. Do you have secret?"

"Not that I know of."

She smoked lethargically. In the alley light, her eyes were sad and beautiful.

"What's your name?" I asked after she exhaled.

"Basha," she said.

"Basha," I echoed.

"In English I would be Barbara. Like Barbra Streisand. What is yours?"

I told her my name and she said it three or four times with different inflections. Then she told me what my name would translate to in Polish, which sounded like some kind of ancient music sung by Baltic mermaids. This made me start to sweat in a way that I hadn't since the last time I'd played a full-court pickup game in Tompkins Square Park.

Then she smoked for another moment and I said, "Can I, like, get your phone number or something?"

"You wish to take me out on romantic date?"

"Um. Sure."

"We go see Chevy Chase movie?"

"Sure. Is he in something right now?"

"I don't think so. But perhaps we could rent one? *Vacation. Vacation Two.*"

"That would be fun."

"Do you have VCR?" she asked.

"Uh. Yeah," I lied. "I do."

"I like this Chevy Chase person very much. He is exceedingly funny. And profoundly tall. *Kittyshack* is one of my all-time favorite American movies. I view this movie when I am little girl in Poland.

"My phone number is five-nine-eight-one-eight-eight-two."

"You live in Manhattan?" I asked.

"In the Village of Stuyvesant, yes. Please call me. I feel very attractive to you."

Having no pen on my person, I had to start memorizing her phone number.

"Now I must go back inside," Basha said. "I promise Sherman we consume a large steak dinner."

I said, "Are you and Sherman, like, dating?"

"No. He would wish this to be true I am sure, but I think he is fool. He always—how you say—cramp his knuckles."

"Crack?"

"Yes. He always *crack* his knuckles like little boy. He does not interest me in this fashion. He does not dress like secret librarian."

"Could you repeat your phone number again, please?" I nearly begged.

"Five-nine-eight-one-eight-eight-two. You memorize this, no?"

"*Fivenineeightoneeighteighttwo. Fivenineeightoneeighteighttwo. Fivenineeight . . .*"

Basha watched me for a moment and then said, "You have handsome chin."

"Thank you."

"When I see you on subway platform I feel like we kiss. This is strange, no? Perhaps we will kiss next time?"

"*Cool*" was all I could come up with.

"And I would advice wearing cold weather jacket or fleece-style pullover from Eastern Mountain Sports at intersection of Street of Broadway and Street of Houston."

"Okay."

"It is too aloof to be walking around like secret librarian."

"Aloof?"

"This is the same as chilly, no?"

"In terms of one's attitude, yes," I explained gently. "But in terms of weather, no. The wind can't be aloof. But a person who is standoffish can be aloof."

"Standoffish?"

"Distant or quiet."

"I see."

"But it would be sort of cool if rain or wind *could* be aloof," I offered in consolation.

"Now we are next to the point," Basha said. "November is season of the cold and flu, no?"

"Yes."

"So please be wise person and dress with accordion."

"Accordion?"

"I mean accordingly."

"I'll wear a coat," I conceded.

The truth was that my sole item of legitimate winterwear was my electric-gold varsity basketball jacket, which featured my surname written in cursive across my heart, my number (33) on the left shoulder, and the name of my obscure, only recently turned coed (there were maybe eighty male undergraduate students, most of whom were athletes) Catholic college across the back in big purple block letters.

I wouldn't have been caught dead in that thing.

Basha flicked the butt of her cigarette into the alley, turned, and reentered the theater through the fire doors, her turquoise sweater dress slightly undulating.

I was tempted to pick up her cigarette and press the still-smoldering end to my wrist just to make sure I wasn't dreaming. I watched it burn all the way down to the filter, at which point the various smells and sights of the avenue invaded my senses: a soiled mattress; a scallop of shat-upon newspaper; a fallen, violently dented air conditioner; and a squad of pigeons marching about with a strange, almost human fanaticism.

The entire way home I recited Basha's phone number, complete with eastern bloc accent.

Somehow I had forgotten about the Underwood.

The Owl Cracks

THAT SAME NIGHT THE OWL walked into the apartment and sat down in the middle of the floor, textbooks spilling out of his book bag. I was boiling water in preparation for my first attempt at pasta. After my encounter with Basha, even this simple act seemed difficult. Using a jumbo-size Sharpie, I wrote her phone number above my desk in large black numerals:

598-1882

BASHA

I was anxious to tell the Owl about her.

The Loach was on the sofa, wrapped in what appeared to be a large medical curtain. He was watching TV with the sound turned down, engrossed in something that was casting a metallic, blue light on his face, giving him the air of a malnourished warlock.

The Owl took three laggard, slightly pigeon-toed steps into the apartment, didn't close the door, dropped his book bag, and with the morale of a third-grader forced to play duck-duck-goose at recess, sat down Indian-style. He stared at nothing with his mouth slightly open, his mammoth head falling forward enough to make my neck hurt just watching him.

"Glenwood," I said, greeting him.

"Homon."

"What's wrong?"

"You sit in class," he offered.

"Uh-huh."

"You watch the professor."

"Yeah."

"The slacks. Tweed jacket. The occasional turtleneck."

I crossed the living room and closed the door. "Go on," I said, returning to my post in front of the stove.

"He scribbles things on the blackboard."

"Uh-huh."

"In white chalk. Scribblydoodly things."

"Scribblydoodly, sure."

"Words and phrases."

"Keep going."

"Little things. Tinytinytiny."

"Right."

"Eensyweensy."

"Don't stop."

"To be copied down, Homon."

The Loach was picking his nose again. I had an impulse to slap him and send him to his room.

"Homon?" the Owl called out as if suddenly blinded. His hands formed fists and it appeared that he was trying to screw them into his eyes. He said, "What's a *cash cow* mean to you? Because I'll tell you what *I* see."

"Okay."

"I see a cow. Lowing."

"A lowing cow. Sure."

"A large, lowing cow with warm, hot-chocolaty eyes. A kind cow. The type of cow you can stare at for hours. I see that cow. Hear me out on this, Homon."

"I'm right here, Glenwood."

"I see that large, kind cow with the warm, hot-chocolaty eyes lowing in the middle of a pasture, Homon. And then I see cash. Slightly off to the left. Large stacks of cash. In consecutively numbered, unmarked bills. I see a cow. And cash. And a silo kind of leaning in the distance . . ."

"Nice touch with the silo."

"And another thing."

"Glenwood, my water's boiling."

"Eye-Pee-Oh."

"Huh?"

"Initial public offering, Homon. Eye-Pee-Oh."

"Gotta throw in the farfalle."

"Ee-sop."

"Eye soap?"

"Ee-sop."

"First crack at real pasta. Big night, Glenwood."

"Eye-Pee-Oh."

"I'll fix you a bowl."

"Gross-Pee-Pee and Ee."

"That's catchy."

"Ee-bit-dah."

"Let me just—"

"Cash cow. Eye-Pee-Oh. Ee-bit-dah."

I turned and dumped the pasta in the boiling water.

"Gross-Pee-Pee and Ee."

I stirred thoroughly.

"Ee-sop."

I added a bit of salt. I'm not sure why.

"Eye-Pee-Oh."

The froth rose up, so I lowered the flame.

"Ee-bit-dah."

I poured the jar of primavera into a saucepan.

"Gross-Pee-Pee and Ee."

I started a low flame on the opposite burner, slid the saucepan over the grill.

"Ee-sop."

I stirred the farfalle.

"Ee-bit-dah."

I stirred the primavera.

"Gross-Pee-Pee and Ee."

I stirred the farfalle yet again, staining the pasta froth a sickly orange.

"Cash cow."

The primavera started to pop like a bed of lava.

"Eye-Pee-Oh."

The farfalle suddenly looked like a clown's head.

"Ee-bit-dah . . ."

The Owl was still going on like this long after I strained the pasta, mixed in the sauce, killed the burners, placed the pans in the sink, and fed him a bowl of crunchy, undercooked farfalle in a sauce that tasted like catsup mixed with a small box of finely ground number-two pencils.

The Loach continued to watch Feick's TV with the sound turned down. It was a wildlife program about migrating wildebeests trying to cross crocodile-infested waters of the Mara River in Kenya. They showed slow-motion footage of the wildebeests leaping gracefully through the water in a ballet of infallibility. I rooted for them. I mentally applauded their superior athleticism, their ability to perpetuate their species by their gift of jumping. It was as if God himself was lifting them with a divine miracle wind.

And then I grew suddenly cold when I saw them being ripped limb from limb by tag-teaming crocodiles.

Some of the wildebeests got across the ford.

Maybe twelve percent.

"Loach," I said, momentarily ignoring the Owl and my farfalle.

His face was as expressionless as the seat of a rarely sat on piano bench, the blue light throbbing into his eyes.

"Hey, Loach," I called to him again, but there would be no response, so I opted for bully tactics.

"Loach," I said, "if you don't start answering me I'm gonna put you in a fucking headlock."

A wildebeest's foreleg was ripped out of its socket.

"A headlock or a full nelson. Your call, buddy."

The feasting crocodile masticated with a sneer.

"You owe us forty bucks."

"Cash cow," the Owl contributed.

A previously unseen wave of wildebeests cleared the riverbank and continued running.

"The Con Ed, Loach. Three months' worth. A hundred and sixty-six bucks. The bill's sitting right there on top of the TV. Split four ways, that's forty-one-fifty each."

One of the wildebeests looked back at the waters, now boiling with its half-alive, half-eaten brothers and sisters.

"Your time on the sofa is getting, like, ethnological, man. People our age are supposed to have jobs."

Somehow, the Loach was a crocodile and Feick, the Owl, and I were wildebeests. The food chain in our apartment defied logic.

"Ee-bit-dah," the Owl chirped.

"Loach, you're an educated white male."

Through the warfare of sloth and inertia he was slowly tearing us limb from limb.

"You're perfectly capable."

The sole wildebeest turned to join the other survivors.

"Everyone else in this apartment works," I croaked.

"Ee-sop," the Owl bleeped.

"Well," I added, thinking out loud, "the Owl's back in school, but at least he's making himself useful. At least he's got, like, a *loan* to live off of."

Was I that sole wildebeest?

"Even Feick works."

Do wildebeests acquire knee problems and compulsive masturbation habits?

"And I have trouble believing that he's even fully gone through puberty yet."

"Eye-pee-oh," the Owl babbled.

For a moment, the Loach's mouth opened slightly, as if he were going to finally respond.

"There was a HELP WANTED sign in the window of the used-book shop on St. Mark's," I informed him, genuinely trying to help.

But he simply gulped a small portion of air and closed his mouth.

"I'd even write you a recommendation."

And then he started scratching his crotch.

"Employment can be a good thing."

The nature show had moved on to the migratory habits of caribou now.

"Just a few hours of work a day, Loach. Enough money to cover your share of the bills."

I was expecting to see caribou at the banks of the Mara.

"We all gotta pull our own weight around here. Forty-one-fifty, Loach. You can even round it down to forty-one."

"Ee-sop."

"I'll cut it to twenty if you move into your room," I heard my own voice saying.

The Loach was using telekinesis now.

"How 'bout fifteen?"

"Gross-Pee-Pee and Ee," the Owl tweeted.

The Loach was one with the caribou.

"Ten and no headlock."

I made my way back toward my pasta.

"Ten bucks, Loach."

The Owl was still sitting on the floor, making a Parkinson's face now.

It was the second week of November, and at twenty-three I felt I suddenly possessed a crystalline understanding of the concepts of sanity and insanity.

"Gross-Pee-Pee and Ee," the Owl cheeped.

From my own bowl I dive-bombed spoon-filled airplanes of pasta into his blabbering mouth.

He *ee-sopped* through the farfalle.

He *eye-pee-ohed* in between mouthfuls like a stammering victim of electroshock therapy.

He *gross-pee-pee and eed* earnestly, usually following the gulps of tap water I poured down his throat from a rinsed-out peanut butter jar.

He blipped and chirped and tweeted through the entire serving, sitting Indian-style, punctuating crocuses of primavera sauce all over my T-shirt.

The beeping gibberish would continue long into the night.

For approximately nine hours.

I woke up several times to check on him. He was always sitting in the exact same spot, still Indian-style. I considered calling the hospital, but I thought that might be borderline dramatic. Instead, I gave him more tap water. I spoke to him in a soothing voice. At one point I brought him his pillow and blanket, fashioned a kind of kitchen-nook cocoon about his knees, shanks, and stomach, and patted him on the head.

The Loach didn't seem to mind the Owl's verbal spin cycle and slept through it all like a freshly nursed baby, dreams of wildebeests no doubt flying silently behind his blackened eyes.

I eventually returned to my bed a final time, unleashed a few primavera belches, and fell asleep staring at the phone number above my desk, hoping to dream of Basha.

Facial Hair

I EXPERIMENTED WITH FACIAL HAIR.

During the Owl's pre-Columbia days he had the beard of a Saskatchewan tree-splitter. The man generated a skin of black pepper only a few hours after a close shave. I, on the other hand, had to farm my beard as if it were stubborn topsoil. I pulled it and stroked it. I twiddled it self-consciously between my fingers. I coaxed it out in hushed tones. I sang to it and shaped it. I licked it and gelled it and brushed it tenderly. Then I tried to give it space, some life of its own, a little room to figure things out and develop.

The Owl looked great with facial hair.

I looked like the guy who washes your car in the parking lot of the Jewel Food Store on Sunday afternoons.

Cable Man

THREE DAYS BEFORE THANKSGIVING our cable was turned off.

Looking back on it now, I'm surprised that we made it that far into November with Time Warner.

I had spent a long day at work mailing things to reps in preparation for a sales conference that was to take place in White Plains. I had cut my knuckles with the tape gun and was licking my still-zinging wounds when I walked through the door of our apartment.

The Loach was on the sofa and the Owl was in the john running bathwater in an obvious attempt to disguise the fact that he was taking a crap.

Moments later our apartment was buzzed. I answered the monitor and the baritone of some bloodless android stated that whoever (or whatever) it was that owned the aforementioned voice worked for Time Warner and that he had "come to seize our cable hardware." This was so intimidating that by the time the three knocks issued from the other side of our front door, I had the box thoroughly disconnected and ready for the handoff.

When I opened the door I was greeted by what appeared to be a steel-bending maniac who might have lived on a derailed train. He was small, boasted a thick, intricately muscled neck, and had the skin tone of one of the Loach's gefilte fish cakes. He wore a gray jumpsuit and steel-toed combat boots. He also possessed hard black eyes, a cauli-flower ear, and several tattoos that traveled over both forearms like violent, multicolored ivy.

This guy was straight out of Rikers.

After a greeting that was more canine than human (a guttural *hroof*), he seized our cable box as though he were bullying a bawling calf off to the slaughterhouse. Working with a remarkable economy of movement and sound, he performed a thorough, quick, and utterly wordless inspection of the hardware.

Strangely, and perhaps through some form of self-preservation, the Loach slept through the entire event.

After the cable man completed his inspection, he said, "Remote, please."

I had to fish the remote from the crack of the sofa, where it was wedged between the Loach's *Wolverine* comic book and a graying athletic sock containing a shaggy, septic-looking toothbrush.

Once he'd inserted the remote into a small, diagonally zippered pocket, the cable man simply nodded and saw himself out.

When the Loach woke up an hour or so later, he didn't seem to mind that we had no reception; he simply pitched himself off the sofa, lurched toward the TV with the velocity of an astronaut in need of a toilet, flicked it on, turned, and found his way back to the malarial cushions, where he watched the receptionless set with the sound turned down as if it were a beautiful blue snowfall feathering across some moonlit window.

Two days later the Owl and I would carry Feick's TV to a used electronics store on lower Broadway, where we would sell it for sixty dollars. We would use the money to make a partial payment to Con Ed so they wouldn't turn off our electricity.

Upon our return home we would find that the Loach had pulled out the summer fan and placed it where the TV had been. Somehow—and I'm not quite sure why—the fact that he was nude was upstaged by the substitute TV.

"He's nude," the Owl said.

"Yes, he is," I said bleakly.

"That's his penis," the Owl pointed out.

"Unfortunately it is."

We watched him for a moment and then, in my best Shakespearean voice, I said, "The winter is upon us, Loach. The fan has been retired for the season."

As usual, there was no response.

The Owl left us in the living room, shaking his head slowly.

"*Loach!*" I screamed. "You're watching the fan, man!"

For some reason, I wasn't going to simply resign myself to the pond of entropy that was slowly drowning our apartment. I would talk this through with the Loach, even if I was the only one doing any talking. I was determined to crack through.

I tried lowering my voice.

"That's a fan, Loach, and you're, like, *engrossed*."

His eyes might as well have been the buttons on a navy peacoat.

The Loach conjured an oyster of phlegm from the wetlands of his lungs, let it sit in his mouth for a moment, and then swallowed it.

A door opened, then closed, and moments later the Owl started the shower.

"And what happened to your clothes, Loach?"

His stomach made an odd digestive noise that sounded like a heavily lubricated casserole being mopped off the floor.

"Loach," I said, "it's Thanksgiving tomorrow. The final Thursday of November. You're gonna catch a fucking cold, man."

His nudity was almost terrifying. The yellow, slightly sweaty skin. The little knobs on top of his shoulders. The caved-in chest. You can go to the zoo and find creatures with fewer limbs that are more human.

In the bathroom, the Owl started singing a Christmas carol. It was "The Little Drummer Boy" and there was something almost horrific about his plaintive interpretation.

"You gotta let go, man," I said, covering the Loach with Feick's boyhood blanket. "The TV's gone."

The Owl was *pa-rum-pa-pum-pumming* now.

The Loach kept the velocity dial on low and aimed the fan's blades squarely at his head so that there was a slow, late-November wind blowing through his fishmonger's hair.

Authors and Editors

AT WORK, Alexa invited me out to lunch again. I assumed this would be the moment she would disclose the fate of my novel. Either she liked the first fifty pages and was hungry for more, or she would slide the same interoffice envelope I'd given her back across the table and offer a diplomatic, semi-encouraging sentence-and-a-half basically saying thanks but no thanks.

We went to a small Italian bistro on Hudson Street, where we both ordered exactly the same thing, which was penne pesto with walnuts, a side of focaccia, and a Diet Coke. I was so nervous and eager that she could have ordered a bowl of dead fruit flies and I would have followed suit.

I silently waited. I cracked my knuckles and then sat on my hands. I couldn't stand it anymore so I prompted her by saying, "I came up with a title."

She said, "A title for what?"

"My novel."

"Oh, that," she said. "I haven't gotten to your novel. But it's creeping up the pile."

That was that, then.

No novel talk.

Instead we talked about editors. We talked about their hair and their funny glasses. We talked about who had an ass and who didn't have an ass. We talked about general editorial asslessness. We talked about how we spied them eating with their hands at lunch. She mauled her puttanesca. He massaged his mackerel. How they knocked a few back after the salmon fettuccine. How he was obsessed with the *Times* crossword puzzle. How it was rumored that she would close her office and masturbate with the phallus of a butternut squash she kept on her windowsill, how she wouldn't necessarily put it in.

We talked about editors who were screwing their authors. We talked about editors who were screwing other editors. We talked about how we talked about them. We hated them for their presumed intellectual superiority but loved them because they were eccentric and well read.

We also talked about authors. He's in the window. She's on the end cap. He's midlist, but rising. She doesn't do interviews. Two hundred people go to his readings and he pulls out kazoos and does voices. She wears an ear clip to pull focus from a scar from harelip surgery. He performs magic tricks with motorized kitchen appliances. She's midlist, but falling. He's literary. She's commercial. He's literary-slash-commercial. She's infomercial. He drives a brown-paneled station wagon. She rides a scooter down Fifth Avenue every Sunday around four. He walks around his house nude except for a single leather driving glove, which he doesn't wear, but rather carries sort of elegantly between his thumb and index finger.

At the end of our lunch, Alexa dabbed at the corners of her mouth, sat very still, and said, "Speaking of editors, I have a confession to make."

"Oh," I said. "What?"

"I have a crush. But I think he's gay—will you tell me if he's gay?"

"Sure."

"I can't stop dreaming about him. Last night we were playing beach volleyball with these Cuna Indians and during a service break he went down on me and I came four times."

"Jesus."

"I know, right? I can't even make *myself* come four times."

"Well, who is the masked man?"

"Puck."

"*Puck Stickleback?*"

"Uh-huh."

"Are you serious?"

"Deliriously serious. The man knows how to use his mouth. Myths are born from that kind of cunnilingus."

I tried to imagine Puck Stickleback going down on Alexa, but just as his head was nestled between her thighs I suddenly envisioned them both wearing lime-colored haute couture pantsuits and seated at some famed West Village café, eating Caesar salads.

Alexa said, "You think he's gay, don't you?"

"Well, Alexa, I have to say—"

"Look. I know he's a bit effeminate."

"This is true."

"And he closes the door to his office and listens to 'Forever Plaid' on continuous replay."

"He certainly does, yes."

"And he'll don the occasional sarong."

"Or the occasional tube top."

"And I'll even concede that from time to time he'll wear eyeliner and a hint of pink lipstick."

"A *hint*?"

"It's practically *invisible*."

"Ha."

"Hey, don't you *ha* me. No one's gone down on me like that, ever. Period."

"Alexa, he was wearing a T-shirt the other day that said I GOT FELT UP AT THE DUPLEX."

"So?"

"Have you ever walked by the Duplex?"

"You're just pissed because I didn't read your manuscript."

"That's so not true! Puck Stickleback's gay!"

"Oh, you're so homophobic! Not every effeminate man is gay, you know! Puck's just in touch with his softer side."

"I am not homophobic, Alexa."

"You are seriously homophobic."

"Not true!"

"Have you ever kissed a man?"

"God, no."

"See?"

We sat for a moment. I was genuinely angry about her accusation, even hurt.

After guzzling some water I said, "Alexa, you're basing this on a dream you had."

"My dreams are frighteningly real."

"Haven't you ever dreamed that you could fly? Or breathe underwater? Or that a giraffe can speak in Old English or something like that?"

"Sure."

"This is my point."

"Well," Alexa said, "I'm just going to have to test those waters."

"Good luck."

"Perhaps you're just trying to cock-block me."

"Um, I don't think so."

"You told me that you think I'm attractive, did you not?"

"Well, Alexa—"

"DID YOU NOT?"

"I did, Alexa, yes. I certainly did say that. And you are. But that doesn't mean that I'm, like, pining for you or anything. I'm just trying to be honest. I sincerely think that Puck plays on the other team."

"Check," Alexa called out to the lone waitress, who had no doubt heard our entire conversation.

The waitress came over and in a hasty three-part move Alexa paid our check, pushed away from the table, and exited the restaurant.

That same afternoon, while I was contemplating a letter of apology to Alexa, a children's book illustrator from Ketchum, Idaho, who had been spending the past week in the office poring over her final page proofs made several insouciant, lazy-hipped sweeps by my Skinner box. Through my now highly developed corporate peripheral vision I detected a kind of sly, grinning appraisal.

She was a legitimate six-footer with curly blond hair, widow's glasses, and a cowboy's walk that was so exaggerated I can only describe it as being unmistakably and flauntingly Texan.

At the end of the day, she stopped in front of my cubicle holding what appeared to be several sketches composed in black ballpoint ink on assorted cocktail napkins.

"Hey," she said.

I said, "Hey."

"I'm Babs," she said. "Babs Hancock."

"Nice to meet you," I said.

At a closer look I could see that the drawings were all male nudes rendered in various pornographic poses.

"You like the job here?"

"Sure," I said.

"They treat you okay?"

"I can't complain."

"Salary, health insurance, 401(k) plan?"

"Um, all of the above, yes."

"How long you been here?"

"Going on seven months."

"I worked in an office for this lawyer-slash-landlord guy. It lasted three weeks."

"Oh," I said.

"Everyone breathing the same air. Sharing the potty. Gets me too worked up."

Harlan Niederlander walked by furtively, as if he were the lone survivor on a wild-game safari.

"Hey, Babs," he whispered through radiant teeth.

"Hey, Harley."

After Harlan disappeared down the hall, Babs said, "What a stiff." Then she rifled through her collection of napkin art for a moment, plucked one out, handed it to me, said, "That's you," and walked away with a vague, serpentine half-smile.

The picture was a rather crude rendering of a long, rubbery-looking, half-human, half-simian ectomorph whose pubic mound was adorned with what appeared to be the down and small flowers indigenous to high-Alps edelweiss. My art self's facial expression was one of either supreme bliss or semi-bored sorrow. On the back of the cocktail napkin was the Manhattan phone number where she was staying with CALL ME written below it.

Later that afternoon, after I had finished another batch of call reports and Van Von Donnelly had left for his three o'clock meeting, I dialed the number on the back of the cocktail napkin and a woman answered.

"Is Babs there?" I asked.

"This is she."

"Hi," I said, "this is—"

"I know who this is."

"You do?"

"You're the tall kid from the office. Sort of shy. Sort of Midwestern. Big hands. You call because I've spurred something, correct?"

I didn't answer. I counted three Mississippis.

"So, what do you think?" she asked, emitting what sounded like an exhalation of cigarette smoke.

"Well," I said. "It's—"

"It's my interpretation of your primal sexual self. A dripping gesture of the lover inside you."

I thought of sexual love and dripping gestures and in a flash was reminded of the various symptoms of my recent urethral nightmare.

"Have you met the lover inside you yet?" she asked.

"Um," I said. "I think so."

"Is he armed and dangerous?"

"Well—"

"Perhaps he's soft and sensual."

"I—"

"Sometimes this person stays away from us for a very long time. I met the lover inside me back in eighty-eight on a bus to Atlantic City. It made for a very exciting ride. I never even got off the bus. Drove all the way back to where I had departed from. Tell me what you really think."

"About what?" I asked.

"The picture. Tell me what you really think."

"Honestly?"

"Yes, please."

"Well, I must admit—and don't take this the wrong way."

"Just say it."

"Well, Babs," I said cautiously, "I look sort of ape-like."

"That's intended."

"And there's this sort of weird, foresty, Jack London bush vibe going on."

"You're referring to the berries and oak leaves."

"Yeah, what's with that?"

"It's the pubis and nature coming together. I was thinking of adding a wasp's nest, too. And fractals of bull dung."

"And you're a children's book author?"

"Yes. I've written and illustrated over twenty picture books for early and middle grade readers. You might be familiar with *Big Moon, Lots of Milk*?"

"Sure. That's the one about—"

"Milking heifers during the final full moon of Carlotta Crow Beauchamp's life. She was the Great Fertility Witch of Eastern Massachusetts."

"Right."

After a brief lull, Babs Hancock got right back on her naughty horse of kink and porn and told me she wanted to balance a hard-boiled egg on my anus while we performed "impure puritan sex" in the missionary position.

There was a harrowing silence during which I counted five more Mississippis, followed by my query of "What are f-f-fractals of b-bull dung?"

But she was interested only in reiterating the hard-boiled egg on my anus thing. I couldn't quite understand this scenario—neither the pleasure she would receive nor the raw physics of it.

Then things got intense when she started talking about strap-ons, black hoods, mock strangulation while coming, and a small particle-board affliction chamber she had built next to her solar-heated home in Ketchum.

I hung up rather disoriented.

Later, I showed the cocktail-napkin art to Ford McGowan, who confided that he, too, had been the recipient of one of these nude Hallmarks and that, like me, he'd also called Babs Hancock, but instead of the hard-boiled egg scenario, she wanted to construct a papier-mâché model of his erect penis and use it to sodomize him while she drank a smoothie made from a mixture of bananas, strawberries, bee pollen, honey, soy protein, and eight ounces of his urine.

A few days later, while I was copying the star reports, Ford McGowan sidled up to me and through clenched teeth informed me that he'd actually visited Babs Hancock during her final evening in New York and indulged her arts-and-crafts fantasy.

"What was it like?" I asked.

"It was pretty weird," he explained. "Before we started she made me read picture books while she flogged herself."

"Wow."

"Dr. Seuss's *Green Eggs and Ham*, over and over. She used a whip made of horsehair."

"And then?"

"Then she molded a cast of my erect penis, made that smoothie, and, well, you know . . ."

"Did it hurt?"

"It fucking killed."

"Papier-mâché, huh?"

"Papier-fucking-mâché."

"Ouch."

"Oh, but the pain was worth it, man."

For nearly a week Ford walked around the office slightly bemused and conspicuously bowlegged. A few times I visited his cubicle in an attempt to mine, quarry, and excavate the various details of his Babs Hancock episode, which included African jungle poetry, an exploding firecracker, a phalanx of incense pods and "spell" candles, a large linoleum butt-spanking flap, a magic trick involving a military saber, and an incessant score of chanting monks.

I noted that Ford's chair was vacant and practically begged to be sat upon. While performing his administrative duties, he displayed an obvious, almost sadomasochistic need to stand.

Smile, Unsmile

LATE-NOVEMBER LIFE ON TENTH STREET seemed crueler, shrunken, even bitter. The bald trees trembled in the Novocain breeze like arthritic hands. Along window ledges the once ripe and colorful flower boxes were suddenly barren. A lonely flotsam of newspapers, plastic bags, and nameless other Dumpster castoffs gusted along the sidewalk like the husks of strange, earthbound birds that had failed in their search for a warmer climate.

For Thanksgiving, the Owl and I had treated ourselves to the turkey dinner special at a Ukrainian diner on Second Avenue, where we witnessed two female prostitutes enact a full-blown fistfight, which was broken up by a cook and two extraordinarily tired waiters. We invited Feick, too, but he never showed.

The Owl told me how he walked into Port Authority on Forty-second Street that afternoon.

"What happened?" I asked.

"I just wanted to look around," he said. "The people there are like . . ." He trailed off and took a breath. "This one guy was standing in front of a kiosk that sells hats and mittens. He was holding one of those jumbo pretzels. It had mustard on it. Big white guy with a sad face. He was wearing a Green Bay Packers coat. He was just standing there, Homon, staring at stuff. It was like he'd been there for weeks.

"Then I took the escalator down to the Greyhound terminals. There's this waiting area. It's penned in with Plexiglas. The people are all bundled up and hardly moving. They're totally wearing hats, scarves, mittens. And their eyes are just staring out. At nothing in particular. Like they've been drugged or they're waiting to die or something. I kept wanting to yell at them to get up and start running. *You can do it!* I wanted to yell. *You can do it, you really can!* But when I opened my mouth nothing came out because . . . well, because there's all this *orange tile* down there, Homon. Everywhere you look. Orange tile with cement grouting. On the walls, the floors, everywhere. It's like it has a hold on them . . ."

His enormous brow was locked in a tense cauliflower. I didn't press him about what happened next, nor did I remind him of our "no westbound buses" pact. Our Port Authority moratorium. Eventually, his forehead relaxed and we ate our turkey dinners in silence.

The early-December light was wan and gray. It was as if the sky had been plated with a dreary tin ceiling.

The chic East Village pets (boa constrictors, pit bulls, ferrets, toucans) were now seldom seen on the streets and it was only the resilience of rats, pigeons, and the occasional jumbo-size, Orwellian sidewalk roach that reminded one of the subsistence of urban wildlife.

The two constants were the puffy-coated drug dealers on the corner of First Avenue and Tenth Street and the hieroglyphs of graffiti on the shit-brown north wall of Lina's Deli.

I had a sudden hankering for oatmeal. At the onset of cold weather, while idling, certain makes of cars start to violently rev; I believe it has something to do with a corrupted carburetor. Similarly, through some early childhood seasonal comfort system born of overly attentive mothering or the grammar school desperation of pre–bus stop winter mornings, I suddenly needed oatmeal.

Luis was at the deli buying several liters of bottled water. Despite the cold weather he was still wearing flip-flops, cutoff jeans, and a T-shirt. His black hair seemed to have doubled in volume and chaos since the last time I'd seen him.

He greeted me with a big, bright smile. "Hello there," he said.

"Hey," I said. "How are you?"

"Fine, and you?"

"Hanging in there," I replied. "How's the garden?"

"Well, I've moved just about everything inside. They're predicting snow tonight. How's the puccoon?"

"Oh, she's fine. Flourishing on my writing table."

This was a bald-faced lie. After several weeks of wellness, my neighbor's gift was starting to wither. Despite continued care (watering, pruning, sunlight rotation) the plant was dying, as if the puccoon had some sort of invisible, umbilical link to my stalling novel. Perhaps fatigue, general privation, and the lack of artistic velocity can vicariously poison even the most promising puccoon?

"It's a *she*?" Luis asked, referring to my pronominal gender choice.

"Plants and cars, you know?"

"What's her name?"

"Just she," was all I could come up with.

"Most of my plants are men," Luis declared. "But that's neither here nor there. How's the novel coming?"

"It's actually been pretty slow-going as of late."

The truth was that I hadn't written a single syllable in over a week and doubt's ugly elbow was starting to nudge me around. My authorial ribs were aching.

"Blocked?" Luis asked.

"Sort of."

"I'm sorry to hear that."

"I'm hoping it's just a phase. Seasonal change. Internal thermostat. A temporary early winter slump."

"I know a remedy," Luis offered.

"You do?"

I imagined some kind of potpourri-smelling botanical stew involving yak dung.

"It's a game called Smile, Unsmile," Luis explained. "I use it whenever things are slow with my garden. It spurs growth and a sense of well-being."

"Smile, Unsmile?"

"Smile, Unsmile, yes. It's quite effective."

"Does it involve smiling?" I asked.

"It does, yes."

"And, um, *un*smiling?"

"Exactly. You should come over. I'll teach it to you."

Despite Luis's obvious homosexuality and mildly eccentric ways, somehow I trusted his invitation. After all, the man had given me a plant. And on top of that, taking him up on his offer afforded the opportunity to prove to Alexa that I was *not* homophobic!

In addition to a small cylinder of Quaker Oats, I purchased a half dozen packets of ramen noodles, a box of powdered doughnuts, and two slim, discolored bananas. I carried my plastic bag of depressing provisions across the street to Luis's apartment building, the spleen-colored hallway of which smelled like fresh paint and Mexican takeout. The buzzing light created a tense, laboratory-in-the-stairwell vibe.

When we reached the second floor we encountered a small girl who possessed a terrific explosion of curly, white-blond hair that looked as if she could use it for personal storage. From the recesses of this glorious nest I imagined her extracting gumballs, jacks, doll parts, and cereal-box prizes.

She was leaning against the balustrade as if she were appraising the deck of a recently boarded cruise ship. Thoroughly costumed, she wore Scooby-Doo pajamas, an improvised pantyhose scarf, dark sunglasses with pink daisy frames, a pair of oversize mules (her mother's, no doubt), and several beaded bracelets. The ensemble was punctuated with a yellow Wiffle-ball bat, which she clutched as if it were an all-powerful scepter. The bat was almost taller than the girl.

When we passed her on the stairwell, in a voice whose purity can only be equaled by certain springtime songbirds, she said, "Luis has microwave popcorn."

This remark seemed to be a shared truth intended to edify not only the two large mortals passing her in the stairwell, but also all gnomes, fairies, cherubs, and other hard-to-see East Village sprites.

Luis simply said, "Hello, Doris," and gave her a pat on her miraculous head.

Doris then abandoned her cruise-ship posture, crouched behind her yellow bat, and announced that she was invisible and that only the *purple people* could see her.

"Am I one of the purple people?" Luis asked playfully.

Doris replied, "Yeah, but he's not." She pointed at me from behind her quickly erected railing–slash–Wiffle-ball-bat fortress.

As we continued up the stairs, I realized that aside from the few kids who hung around the full courts in Tompkins Square Park, Doris was the first child I had actually encountered since moving to New York City.

For some reason, I imagined a municipal child-catching task force secretly sweeping through the predawn neighborhoods of Manhattan and capturing all the children and shuttling them to an underground bakery, where they were transformed into Gotham's greatest pies and casseroles.

Luis's apartment was a quick study in domestic minimalism. Outside of a nondescript tan sofa and a leather Barcelona chair, he owned very few pieces of furniture. The walls were bare except for an enormous, fire-engine red shelving system that housed what appeared to be thousands of vinyl records. There was a single halogen lamp that cast a cool, noir-like light across the room. For entertainment, apparently Luis did without the aid of a television and obviously preferred the warm, analog murmur of an immaculate, omnipotent-looking platinum turntable whose connecting speakers were either invisible or nonexistent.

There wasn't even the slightest indication that there was an at-home garden on the premises. This was both odd and confusing.

Luis disappeared with his bottled water and returned moments later with a long-stemmed glass calumet from which we proceeded to smoke two potent bowls of marijuana, the crystal-forming buds of which smelled like some faraway, uncharted, peppery island where beasts believed to be extinct alighted to mate.

Luis sat in the Barcelona chair while I chose the tan sofa. It had been a while since I had been stoned and between the pain of my knee injury, the nine-to-five publishing grind, general exhaustion, the acute anxiety of my recent brush with the world of venereal disease, too much reading, no basketball, fitful sleeping, and a slow-burning cumulative creative futility, it was just what the doctor ordered.

Into our second bowl, Luis confessed that the marijuana was his own batch of homegrown but vowed that he was neither a dealer nor a baiter, and that his fire-escape nursery was not some kind of legal camouflage; his intentions as a gardener were indeed pure.

He simply enjoyed getting stoned.

When I asked about the plants, he explained that his winter gardening was performed in a room toward the back of the apartment whose photosynthetic light could be seen seeping into the hallway through the crack beneath the door. When Luis emerged from this room with the stuffed pipe it was as if he were a time traveler who had just passed through a starlit, vegetal portal.

The pot went straight to my head. Or perhaps it would be more accurate to say that the pot actually *became* my head. I felt as if all neural and cortical tissue had been hollowed out of my skull and replaced by some kind of ethereal gas. In a matter of five minutes, my head had been transformed into a big, dumb balloon.

Luis, on the other hand, partook of his marijuana with the sophisticated, acquiescing nonchalance of the leader of a great mountain hike, inhaling and exhaling smoothly, not coughing once, and handling the pipe and lighter with sleek, minimal movements.

After we passed the bowl back and forth twice and I barked out the desperate, lung-seizing coughs of a drowning victim, Luis explained the tenets and a brief history of Smile, Unsmile.

"It started in Puerto Rico," he explained, "where my brothers and I would lounge under the guava tree in our backyard. Pablo and Jorge—they were twins, five years older than me—had perfected the game during a trip to the United States with my grandmother. They were both poets. Pablo would perform his verse to Jorge's mandolin and Jorge to Pablo's xylophone. They found that the game had quite a magical, inspirational effect on their work. After they played it, a productive period would often follow . . ."

The story of Luis's twin brothers went on for fifteen or twenty minutes. He chronicled their teenage travels through Europe, their coincidental bout with an odd case of shingles, Jorge's drinking, Pablo's brief affair with a Spanish princess, and the various travails of their rise and fall from artistic prominence. Luis then confessed that he hadn't heard from either of them in over ten years and suspected that they were both opium addicts, living under a shoe store in Bangkok.

After the room got uncomfortably quiet for a moment, Luis swallowed the wistful lump in his throat and explained the rules of Smile, Unsmile, which were simple enough: Luis would say "Smile"—he would command it—and then I would smile. After holding the smile for a period of time—the duration to be determined by the smile commander—Luis would then say "Unsmile" and I would release my smile. In a successful execution of the game, my face would unflinchingly return to its pregrinning state. After I smiled, it would be Luis's turn and I would become the commander.

"And this will somehow help my writing?" I asked.

"I can almost guarantee results," Luis assured me.

The marijuana not only made this seem logical, but, as described by Luis, the idea of the game seemed to take on a thing of historical—even *supernatural*—genius. I was ripe to be awed. I was more than excited. I was falling in love with a game suited for toddlers and lobotomy patients.

When Luis commanded me to smile for the first time I was immediately seized with the inexperienced pot smoker's spell of the giggles. After a dozen laugh attacks I gained control and was ready to begin the game with grave seriousness. After all, Smile, Unsmile obviously wasn't simply an entertainment; it was a deeply felt solution for South American poets! It was a technique honed and crafted with the vision to achieve creative resurrection!

In the voice of a rather energized vampire, Luis declared, "*Smiiiiiiile,*" which resonated throughout his apartment in a long, prayer-like fermata.

I held my first successful smile with the rigor of a veteran lumberjack. My lips receded into my gums almost epileptically. I curled my toes. I clenched my dueling fists. My eyes seemed to expand with ether or some other highly effective giggle gas. I could feel muscles in my face that had lain dormant for months.

"*Unsmiiiiiiile*," Luis commanded rather dramatically.

My smile dissolved and my face returned to its neutral state.

We sat there for a moment and said nothing.

Luis watched me the way one watches a cow urinating in a pasture, with a subtle yet zesty curiosity.

"How was that?" he finally asked. "Did you give over to the smile?"

"I think so."

"Did you feel anything start to unlock?"

"I'm not sure."

"Shall we do it again?"

"Okay."

"*Smiiiiiiiiile*," Luis commanded again.

And, just like the first time, my face bloomed into a glorious, slightly painful smile that made me feel as if I were ludicrously a-dance in an enormous, multicolored Easter basket.

Luis held my second smile a little longer than the first. When my face thawed back to its natural state, while I can't say that paragraphs of purple prose were suddenly bursting out of my head, I have to admit that I could definitely feel something starting to happen.

"Now your turn," Luis offered, and he squared his body to mine as if we were about to engage in the sacrament of religious confession.

"Smiiiiiiiiile," I announced in an overly oxygenated baritone.

When Luis smiled, his mouth produced what appeared to be hundreds of perfectly arranged white teeth. They had such symmetry that they seemed to possess a quality more endemic to fine art than to anatomy. His face was frozen in a brown sarcophagus of equal parts joy and spiritual illumination. His eyes were flawlessly round buttons of rapture.

And that's when I did perhaps the most surprising thing I have ever done in my life: I kissed him.

It was a dry, *toast-like* kiss, but it was a kiss nonetheless. It lasted for eight or nine seconds. His lips tasted like salt and peppermint. About three-quarters of the way through it I realized the kiss was being executed with about the same quality and excitement as one of my aunt Norma's eggnog-saturated, 'neath the mistletoe pecks.

After the kiss was over I sat back and Luis returned to his smiling state as if nothing had happened.

"Unsmiiiiile," I finally commanded.

Luis easily thawed and returned to his presmiling state.

"Whoa," I said, a little stunned.

I'm convinced that the kiss was more inspired by one man's simple human generosity than by anything sexual, as there wasn't any evidence of genital swelling, stirring, or tingling.

I cannot deny that Luis was *arresting*, and that certain men possess a salient beauty that defies gender. I'll even admit that the kiss itself, despite the lack of salivary lubricants and absence of hormonal fireworks, elicited a kind of curious natural harmony that I had never before experienced; something approaching the feeling one might have when a rare butterfly alights on the back of one's wrist.

We sat in silence for a moment, and then Luis rose, crossed to his wall of records, removed an LP, and started his turntable. The needle drop revealed a hiss of gentle static and then David Bowie's voice filled the room.

Luis and I continued our game of Smile, Unsmile through "Suffragette City," "Ziggy Stardust," "Starman," "Space Oddity," and "Changes." No doubt aided by the pot, I found that his sound system was nothing less than an audio crystal waterfall.

For my next smile, Luis held his command for close to a full minute, and my face started to feel like it was suffering from a slight sprain. It had been so long since I had knitted together a collection of grins that the infinitesimal fibers that made up my smile muscles were exhausted, perhaps even experiencing a strange kind of facial shock. My cheeks, my mouth, and the wings of my nostrils suddenly felt heavy and overused.

My final smile was executed largely internally as my lips, chin, tongue, cheeks, eyebrows, and forehead were completely spent. I was hardly able to bare a few teeth. I could feel the corners of my mouth twittering with fatigue. What started out as a delightful stoners' game had suddenly morphed into an exhibition of my failure to sustain facial joy.

"Good," Luis commended. "That should do the trick."

After the rounds of Smile, Unsmile, the munchies seized me and I wound up eating both of my bananas, several powdered doughnuts, and a package of ramen noodles (dry).

Luis and I not only didn't kiss again, we never spoke about it. I would even go so far as to say that he bent over backward to make me feel like nothing had happened at all. His strange, episodic presence in my life defied definition. He had the empathic, practical concerns of the proverbial Good Samaritan and yet was somehow more shaman than neighbor, more sage than citizen.

When I got back to my apartment, I stood staring at my legal pad for a full five minutes before sitting, turning a page, and beginning work. I wrote until five a.m., churning out nearly thirty pages of my novel about acute knee pain and the end of the world.

At around 4:30 the first snowfall dusted across the Tenth Street rooftops and the sky took on a strange cotton-candy quality that made me think of clowns at the circus.

I fell asleep at my desk, my face next to my female puccoon, its aroma strangely luxuriant. I would dream of nothing in particular and wake early the following morning almost completely unaware that I had kissed a man.

Basha, an Unexpected Mentor, and Sudden Snow

THE FOLLOWING DAY I called Basha.

It was a Sunday and there was a hushed quality in the East Village. Heavier snowfall continued throughout the rest of the morning and left Tenth Street looking eerily virginal. It died for an hour or so, but by the afternoon, the flurries increased to the point of being almost blinding and there was talk of a blizzard. Platoons of snowplows scraped north on First Avenue like some kind of municipal-vehicle exodus. Men threw salt from the backs of four-by-fours like it was parade candy. Garbage trucks armored with additional plows were called upon for relief.

Out my window, pedestrians could be seen knifing through the wild ribbons of snow, their heads wrapped in scarves, their shoulders hunched as though they'd been recently beaten. Naked, gloved, and mittened hands formed impromptu visors over brows.

I finally tired of watching the effects of the whiteout from my bedroom window and, layered in a T-shirt, a sweater, and my trusty jean jacket, ventured out.

I spent the rest of the afternoon at Café Orlin reading through and attempting to line-edit my new chunk of *Opie's Half-life*. In a reckless, celebratory spirit of my thirty-page coup, I splurged and ordered the nine-dollar eggs Benedict.

At one point a woman passed across the café window on a pair of cross-country skis. A few minutes later a Jeep drove by pulling three men crammed in a makeshift toboggan jerry-rigged from a gutted refrigerator, several bungee cords, and plywood. For just a moment I imagined that it was the refrigerator from my apartment being pulled by this Jeep. I envisioned pages of my novel fluttering about the snowbound streets of the East Village and avenues farther west. And was it possible that the three men manning the toboggan could have been the Owl, Feick, and Burton Loach? I loathed their sudden solidarity: a secret beer party; late-night gatherings on the roof; a conspiracy hatched to prevent the completion of my novel. I imagined the Loach flinging shredded chapters of *Opie's Half-life* all across St. Mark's Place, manuscript confetti blending with the snow and turning into gutter slush.

While a Latin busboy arranged potted poinsettias along the windowsill I wallowed in the hollandaise tang of my eggs Benedict. Oh, the luxury of poached eggs and their soft, flavorful bellies! How far I had come from the predictable Midwestern staple of scrambled eggs and catsup. I was certainly poor, and I was by no means even remotely versed in the ways of Sunday-morning East Village café culture, but at that moment I was having brunch and no one could take that away from me, damnit! At that moment brunch had become a *verb* in my life. I was brunching, like Yoko Ono!

The snow continued to bleach the café window, and, inspired by the sudden brook of good feeling that was burbling inside me I set my manuscript pages down, walked over to the pay phone, and dialed Basha's number.

Over a rather zesty chorus of exclamatory background Polish, I fabricated a story that while I was very much looking forward to Chevy Chase's comic expertise, we wouldn't be able to rent *Vacation* or *European Vacation* because as of that very morning our VCR had mysteriously disappeared.

"Such bamboozling activity," Basha commented.

"Yes," I said. "I believe we were indeed bamboozled."

Despite the slight language barrier and general over-the-phone awkwardness, we were able to devise a plan to meet later that night at Downtown Beirut, the infamous dive bar just around the corner from my apartment. After a few drinks, if we couldn't get a bus, we would slide, skeetch, sled, or ski over to Chelsea and see Feick in *Traffic Lights and Broken Bridges* at the Atlantis Theatre Company. After all, Basha was an actress, and I figured taking her to a hit play would prove my interest in theatre arts (oh, and how I would milk that one!) and give us something to talk about. It would also afford me an opportunity to finally view Feick's second critically acclaimed performance.

Basha seemed happy to hear from me. She referred to me as the "Secret Librarian Man" and confessed that she'd wondered if I would ever call.

This was not a bad start to an otherwise dull Sunday evening in the East Village.

After paying the check and gathering my new pages (in a white-knuckled grip), I went home and showered twice, washed and conditioned my hair, shaved off the pathetic goatee I had been farming, applied the appropriate amount of musk-scented Speed Stick under my dewy arms, brushed my teeth with athletic gusto, changed clothes, descended the ever-darkening stairwell, and slipped and slid around the now snow-impacted southeast corner of Tenth Street and First Avenue.

Downtown Beirut was choked with perhaps the most disparate sect of East Villagers ever assembled in the same watering hole. There was an enormous transvestite with eyelashes so long and obnoxious they might have been appropriated from the lids of a sleeping giraffe. He was wearing black pumps, long white gloves, a gumball-machine brooch, the largest pink gown I had ever seen, and a black netted snood whose funereal dreariness clashed with the neon glare of the gown.

Despite the flamboyant attire, the drag queen spoke in a thick, penetrating baritone that was both chilling and disorienting.

"Oh, I love the snow," he announced, host-like, to no one in particular. "It hides all the doggie poo."

Seated next to him was a man in crisp, pinstriped Wall Street attire who was staring into his pint of lager as if it might pardon him for all past and future sins.

There was also a triumvirate of chain-smoking middle-aged women who were not only more stoic and clamp-jawed than most high-school varsity football coaches, but also bore a striking (and mysterious) collective resemblance to Ernest Borgnine. To their left sat a homeless man who kept arguing with the Amazonian bartender about her Superman tattoo (he kept claiming that the S was actually a symbol for certain European secret agencies, whatever that meant). Other patrons included a thin black woman who bore a less-than-striking resemblance to Sammy Davis, Jr., and Donald Amblin, the recently let go, highly respected author of the critically acclaimed *Elect Mr. Rouge.*

Amblin was staring into a rocks glass of what appeared to be bourbon with a blank, almost pleasant expression.

I grabbed the stool next to him and with feigned beer-drinking experience ordered a five-dollar pint of an Eastern European stout that tasted like stale bread and licorice.

Out of the corner of my eye I did a quick study of the man. He wore faded blue jeans and low-quarter scuffed black shoes. Over an old, paint-splattered white T-shirt he layered a cardigan that was either navy blue or black. He was sitting on an Army-issued snow parka with a fur-trimmed hood. His almost rock and roll–length hair was dark brown with gray strands and parted somewhere between the center and the side of his head. He had a few days' growth of salt-and-pepper beard and a large Adam's apple. The backs of his hands were pleasantly hairy. He had oval-shaped, penetrating brown eyes that sat heavily over the gloomy, multilayered bags of an insomniac. He did not wear glasses. He was both unkempt and hygienically admirable. He was neither handsome nor homely. He did not sit with a notebook or any discernible writing utensil. In five words or less I would describe him as being an utterly anonymous-looking human being.

While Donald Amblin jingled the melting ice cubes in his glass, I brilliantly offered, "Hey, you're Donald Amblin."

He turned and looked at me with the kind of shock and disbelief one might associate with a person who has recently suffered a severe knife wound.

"I mean you are, right?" I continued.

"I am," he said. "Do I know you?"

"No," I said, and pivoted so quickly on my bar stool that I nearly wound up on the floor. "I mean, we've been associates in a kind of indirect way," I continued, regaining my composure. "It would be safe to say that I probably know more about you than you do . . . I mean know about me, I mean."

"Do I owe you money or something?" he asked, understandably incredulous.

"I work at the company that published *Elect Mr. Rouge.*"

"Oh, then I do owe you money."

"Nah."

"That book won't earn out in a million years."

"It's a great novel," I offered.

"Thank you," he said sincerely.

"I read it one day when my boss was out meeting with the regional sales managers."

"Who's your boss?"

"Van Von Donnelly."

"Oh, that guy hates my book."

"He does?"

"My editor told me that at a marketing meeting he was referring to it as 'The Book That Should Never Have Been Bought.' "

"I think Van's more into the good old-fashioned detective novel. And those cookbooks about meat—he's crazy about those."

"I doubt he inspired too much enthusiasm in the reps. They didn't exactly write me Christmas cards."

"Trust me, I was so swept up by your novel that I took it to lunch with me. And when I finished it I read it two more times. I practically dated that book."

"Well, I'm glad to hear that. Unfortunately, not enough people have been equally smitten."

"I particularly loved that sex scene on the electric lawn with all the crocodiles on leashes. By the way, was that Astroturf or common sod?"

"Astroturf."

"I thought so. That was really cool."

"Yeah, that chapter tends to make an impression."

"I mean, the short-of-breath lust dialogue was so totally funny.

'Oh . . . Wow . . . Yeah, there . . . *There?* . . . Yes . . . Yes? . . . No, not *there!* No? . . . Watch the croc.' "

"It has its moments."

"I don't laugh out loud at novels very often. I mean, 'Watch the croc!' That rocks!"

"May we all rock a little more often," Donald Amblin said, toasting the air with his empty glass, ice cubes clinking.

"I thought you really captured both the humor and pathos of postapocalyptic American domesticity. I mean, how intimate can we possibly be if our fate is to erect chain-link fences around our own homes? And that whole thing about tripping neighborhood land mines with great works of American literature. *Moby-Dick* becoming the sacrificial throwing stone for safe passage to the Seven-Eleven. Total genius."

"You should be my publicist."

"And it got great reviews," I rallied.

"Yeah, it did pretty well with the critics, but that's not enough anymore."

"I don't get that."

"These days you gotta do signings and readings and that whole dog and pony show."

"So you won't do it?"

"I just don't feel comfortable. When they got wind that I wasn't going to do the twelve-city tour they cut my first print run by twenty thousand copies. Your marketing VP called me a pussy. She literally called my agent and told him I was a pussy, the dyke."

"Darla Nordtgard's gay?"

"I don't know, probably not. What do I know? I'm so homophobic I can't even look at myself naked."

Donald Amblin ate a few ice cubes and continued: "The bottom line is that I think the book should speak for itself."

"Absolutely," I testified.

"Some of these authors go out there and perform magic tricks and serve sushi and play the twelve-string while they read and three hundred people line up around the block. It's all becoming a stunt show. I guess I'm old-fashioned."

"Well, I respect your integrity."

"Thank you."

Then Donald Amblin ordered more bourbon and said, "What's your name, anyway?"

I introduced myself and we shook hands. I noticed that my hand was larger than his and it gave me a false sense of superiority, albeit brief. The bottom line was that I was classically awestruck. Although I had been at the publishing house with the mirror-smoked windows for over seven months, this was the first time I had ever engaged in a legitimate conversation with a respected author. Sure, I had bumped into a few of them at the office, but there was always that strange corporate gravity pulling me back to my Skinner box, not to mention the dull-yet-penetrating nine-to-five sellout embarrassment evinced by my homogeneous sitcom haircut and moderate, acceptable office wear. "I'm a writer, too!" I'd wanted to holler from behind the burlap hide of my cubicle. "I'll slip you some bound galleys," I'd declared so often with the voice in my head, longing to collaborate. I was so excited to be speaking to Donald Amblin that not only were my palms sweating, but so were my ears, brows, armpits, the gully between my shoulder blades, and the backs of my knees.

I took a sip of my stout and said, "I don't mean to be nosy, but have you found a new house?"

"Not yet," he said. "I'm gonna finish this new thing I've been working on before my agent and I come up with a strategy."

"The Abraham Lincoln beard thing?"

"You know about that?"

"Your editor's assistant told me about it."

"Good old Ford," he said, Gatsby-like. "I'm gonna miss that guy. I abandoned that piece, actually."

"So this thing is *new* new."

"Yeah. It's still pretty unformed," he explained. "But I'm moderately sure it has something to do with a mildly depressed, fortyish, vaguely alcoholic novelist who becomes ensnared in an anarchist plot to bomb a wealthy, chickenshit publishing house gone commercial."

At this we both chuckled mightily into our drinks. Donald Amblin's laugh held an undeniable hint of sadness. Mine was a nervous chortle that could have served as the beginning of a Saturday-afternoon variety show for children involving large Nerf puppets and an asexual, slightly demonic host with pointy shoes.

"Do you live in the neighborhood?" I asked after our laughter subsided.

"Tenth, between Second and Third."

"I'm down the street, between First and A."

"Neighbors."

"Neighbors!" I echoed, so in love with the world that I could have been robbed by a Girl Scout.

"Are you able to pay the rent with the writing?" I asked sophomorically.

"Every once in a while I can steal away for a few months. But I teach on the side."

"Where?"

"This low-residency MFA program up in Vermont. Most of my students are older than me, but it's cool. You basically find a way to get by."

I sipped my beer and Donald Amblin stared into his glass for a moment.

"Do you write, too?" he finally asked.

I could have served my heart to him on a plate.

"I do," I said, trying to hold back the excitement that was about to gush forth.

"Prose?"

"Fiction."

"Short stories or novel?"

"I'm actually writing a novel."

"Your first?"

"Yeah, my first."

"The first one's like falling in love."

"It so is!" I concurred.

"You swoon."

"Yes!"

"You sing and dance."

"You *do* sing and dance!"

"You take extra-long showers."

"I totally waste water!"

"You get that beautiful ache in your chest."

"Yes yes *yes!*" I sang.

"Then eventually you forget to eat. You stop changing your underwear. You learn how to hate anything and everything that is a direct threat to *her.*"

"She's the only one."

"Then things shift pretty drastically and somehow you wind up actually hating the cunt, which may lead to such activities as wall-punching, fasting, heated arguments with household appliances, compulsive masturbation, or the consumption of inordinate amounts of Kentucky bourbon."

"I've actually been masturbating a lot," I offered matter-of-factly. Why I shared this with a man I hardly knew still mystifies me.

"Yeah," he said. "Unfortunately one can't fuck one's manuscript . . . I mean, I guess you could take a small chunk of it and roll it up—"

"To create a kind of vaginal funnel!" I exclaimed.

"But then there's things like paper cuts to deal with."

"And Wite-out!"

"Hey, there's a lubricant!" Donald Amblin proclaimed.

At this we erupted into laughter again. What collaboration!

Our synchronized outburst couldn't have been better captured in a state-of-the-art recording studio. And at the apex of this choral orgasm, the tsunami of all that I wanted to tell this man—the details of my novel, the saga of my sofa-bound roommate, my state of economic squalor, my now ruined Underwood, the struggling puccoon on my windowsill, my brush with the world of venereal disease, my peasant's wardrobe, my embarrassingly boyish skin, my perpetually recovering left knee, my lack of a normal sex life, and a slowly encroaching, shoulder-pinching insomnia—all of it was concentrated, packaged, and delivered in one monstrous, rather wet-sounding croak. Make no mistake, this was not a beer-induced belch; it was an authentic, frog-like croak that came from some region below the recesses of my abdomen. It had in it equal parts sorrow, glee, hatred, starvation, lust, terror, god-fearing desperation, and shock. This noise was then followed by a deluge of tears more like weather than any kind of anatomical phenomenon. My head suddenly became very heavy and my brow met the top of the bar and I sobbed for a solid three minutes while Donald Amblin patted me on the back, saying, "I know, I know. It hurts and it always will." He then bought two shots of Maker's Mark and we toasted the inexorable force of the American novel.

"In the face of darkness," Donald Amblin declared, "may the American novel be our brightest, most fucked-up star! Cheers!"

"Cheers!" I said, my chest heaving.

"Cheers!" grunted the triumvirate of chain-smoking Ernest Borgnine look-alikes.

"Cheers!" cried the transvestite in the enormous pink evening gown. And so it was.

My new life of sorrow, poverty, and drinking had been officially anointed. If Donald Amblin was any example, perhaps I was on my way to the long, liver-ruining road to artistic apotheosis.

Moments later, Basha entered the bar looking like the most beautiful thing I had ever seen. She was wearing a long black greatcoat, a red scarf, a green wool hat, and thin, velvety gloves. Her eyes were so huge I wrote an impromptu three-line poem about them.

Eyes so huge
Woman so pretty
Green hat over black hair

"Hello," Basha said.

"Hello," I echoed with similar inflection.

In an idiotic attempt at European social grace, I tried to kiss her on each cheek but nearly licked her nose instead.

"Basha, this is Donald Amblin, a great American Novelist. And that's Novelist with a capital N."

"Pleased to meet you, Donald," Basha said, extending her gloved hand.

"The pleasure is mine," Donald Amblin reciprocated. They shook and then Donald removed a pack of Marlboro Lights from his pocket, tapped one out, pinched the butt with his lips, produced a silver Zippo, lit his cigarette, and smoked. He offered one each to Basha and me but we both declined.

"I thought you smoked," I said to Basha.

"That was just for Sherman's play. The director believed it contributed to Katrajina's midnight diva stylings."

"Are you an actress?" Donald asked.

"Yes," Basha replied.

"I recently saw her perform in this very cool play down in TriBeCa," I said.

"I am only just commencing," Basha explained. "But I now possess head shot and I am to take professional classes at Lee Strasberg Institute or perhaps Herbert Bergdorf Studios in the West Village on Bank Street."

"Well, you're very pretty and you have a great speaking voice."

"I am exceedingly flattered," Basha replied multisyllabically.

"I hope it works out for you," Donald said, toasting Basha with his rocks glass.

"Thank you," she said, genuinely appreciative.

"You're very welcome," Donald returned, drinking more bourbon. Basha then turned to me.

"Hello, mister," she said.

"Hi," I said.

"Are you okay?"

"Sure," I said. "I'm good."

"You look terribly wounded," she observed, bending a black curl behind her perfect ear.

"He just lost his cherry," Ernest Borgnine number one announced, inspiring a barful of laughs.

"And I don't think it was a maraschino!" honked the enormous drag queen across the bar.

Everyone laughed and high-fived in alcoholic solidarity. It could have been a scene from *Oliver Twist*.

"I'll explain later," I told Basha. "Are you ready to go?"

Basha nodded.

I turned to Donald Amblin with a full heart.

"It's been a pleasure talking to you," I said. "I look forward to reading your new novel. I'm sure it will find a house."

We shook again.

And then he said something that I have written down several times since, a sentence that has found its way onto napkins, paper plates, toilet paper, the gutters and margins of novels, and the thighs of several pairs of faded blue jeans. Someday I will cull together these various pieces into a makeshift canvas, frame it, and fashion a spiritual wall hanging.

He said: "I'd wish you luck but to wish luck upon another writer is bad luck, so I will simply say goodbye."

To which I had no reply.

The guy had nothing but grace.

I nodded and Basha and I turned and walked out into the snowy night.

The Atlantis Theatre was on Nineteenth Street between Eighth and Ninth avenues. We were fortunate enough to catch the M8 bus at the northwest corner of Ninth Street and First Avenue. After thirty minutes of sitting in traffic and being stalled by snowplows and salt trucks, we finally arrived in the West Village, where we got out at Christopher Street and Seventh Avenue and slid the rest of the way to the theater. Basha performed several arabesques while humming the music to some ballet that was no doubt being performed in the ether of her mind.

During the bus ride I couldn't shake the memory of my conversation with Donald Amblin. I was both exhilarated and a little heartbroken. Here was a real live novelist who had amassed critical success and the respect of many, but he was alone (did I notice a slight drop in his face when I introduced him to Basha?) and very likely on his way to drinking many more bourbons at a bar in the East Village.

"Are you very sad?" Basha had asked as the bus crossed Third Avenue, where NYU students were playing tag football and sliding around in front of their building in what appeared to be socked feet.

"I'm fine," I said. "It's just that that guy from the bar said some stuff that sort of got to me."

"Donald possessed very much, how you say . . . melancholy, no?"

"I think so, yes."

"And this makes you feel sorrow for him?"

"I guess it does."

"Do you love this man?"

"I admire him very much."

"Writing must involves much toiling, no?"

"It does," I answered. "But sometimes it can be pretty rewarding."

"Rewarding is good, yes?"

"Yes."

"So is writing more toiling or more rewarding for you?"

"I think it's about half and half."

"Half on half. This is American dairy creamer, no?"

"Yes, but I mean to say fifty percent of the time the writing is rewarding and fifty percent it is sort of toiling, but I can't imagine myself doing much else. I mean, I work a job and everything. You know, at an office. With cubicles and phones with intercoms and fluorescent lights, and I get a paycheck, but it makes me really restless."

"What is cubicle?"

"It's like a little square where my desk is. With these four-foot walls around it. And the walls are covered with this denim-colored burlap material so that you can tack things up, like memos and to-do lists and pictures of Barry Manilow with aviator sunglasses. And everyone drinks coffee and does the *New York Times* crossword puzzle in ink and pretty much wears the same thing every day. Lately it's been indigo blue, button-down shirts from the Gap and khaki pants. Like everyone phones in the wardrobe to each other at seven-thirty in the morning.

It's all pretty depressing if you ask me. I don't know . . ." I trailed off.

"Sorry. I don't mean to dump all of this on you."

"It's okay," Basha said.

At Third Avenue a woman wearing a black garbage bag boarded the bus. In some indecipherable, hateful convulsion of words, she announced that the snow had "extraterrestrial knowledge," as if she wanted to brawl, but the bus driver, who obviously dealt with this on a daily basis, simply waited for her to complete her outburst and then effectively pointed her back down the stairs.

"Is there nothing that is pleasing about your job?" Basha asked after the woman in the garbage bag exited.

"Well, I do get free books. And every once in a while they have these weird celebrations with catered food. And there's this new thing called direct deposit, too."

"Do you love to toil and to write?" Basha asked after the bus lurched west.

"I guess so, yes."

"Then this is all that matters, no? Perhaps someday you will not have to work at this job with the blue blouses? Perhaps you will write a book that becomes famous, no?"

"Maybe."

"And if your friend Donald is always sad, then he is always sad. This does not mean that you will always be sad, too. Perhaps he is sad for other reason? Perhaps he cannot have childrens or perhaps he suffers from being a victim of depression or other mental illnesses?"

"No, you're totally right, Basha," I concurred. "Totally, totally right."

"My uncle Jerzy is plumber in Sheepshead Bay, Brooklyn, and sometimes people feel sad for him but he is very happy to be plumber so I tell them to take a bath."

"You do?"

"Yes."

"You actually tell them to take a bath?"

"I hear this expression on American TV program *Hill Street Blues*, but this is next to the point. Uncle Jerzy is happy to be plumber. For some reason other people see this as very sad job, but Uncle Jerzy is happy and drinks Miller beer with his crones and watches many American movies starring Robert De Niro, particularly *Raging Bull* and *Taxi Driver* costarring Jodie Foster. Jerzy has good life. You should do what you do because it bestows you pleasure to do it, no? Even though Uncle Jerzy is most of the time putting his arms into toilet bowl doesn't mean he is unhappy person."

"It sounds like you admire him very much."

"He has wife and two beautiful childrens. To me this is happiness."

"And what about you?" I asked. "Are you happy?"

"I do not think a person can be always happy. Sorrow is in the world all of the time. Like fog in a cloud. But sometimes the cloud surpasses. For instance, when I am performing as actress, this sorrow is not so present. Even if the play possesses sorrow or my character possesses sorrow I don't not feel this so strong."

"So even if the material is sad, acting makes you happy."

"It makes me feel alive, yes. And possessing less sorrow, this is true."

"Isn't that business hard, though? All of that auditioning and rejection and stuff?"

"It is difficult, yes. And as I continue to make more excellent improvements to my American-style accent, this will become less so. But the jobs that I am bestowed are gratifying even though they are sometimes small. It would be nice to have American TV show like *Who's the Boss?* or *Full House* starring John Stamos. This way I could help my family and purchase large apartment for them to live in Bay Ridge, Brooklyn, and one for myself in Santa Monica Village, California. But if this does not happen I would still be happy. Performing as Katrajina in Sherman Furl's top-notch drama *Boots, Bats, and Sticks* at Workhorse Ensemble Theatre in TriBeCa two blocks south of Canal between Broadway and Church made me very happy. The only night I was not happy was when I destroy your typewriter machine with hammer of destiny. But then I meet you in your secret librarian costume so this was perhaps okay, no?"

"I think I'd really like to kiss you," I said suddenly. "Would it be okay if I kissed you on this bus?"

"I think this would be okay, yes."

Then we leaned in close and I kissed perhaps the softest, fullest lips I have ever felt against my own. Though there were no grinding jowls or darting tongues, the sweet sap of her saliva alone was enough to erotically charge me and hormonally endow my progeny for thousands of years. During our kiss, Basha's gloved hand rose and stroked the side of my overly mentholated face. It was at this moment—on a New York City bus traveling west while snow was passing diagonally across the aquarium-like windows, while two seemingly insignificant lives were converging like windswept birds approaching some rapturous shore at the beginning of the last decade of the twentieth century, on the cusp of our great holiday season, in late December of 1991—it was at this precise and overly written about, verbally investigated moment that I knew with the certainty of a diamond cutting glass that I would fall face-first in love with Basha.

I could practically feel my chin hitting the snow-impacted pavement.

After the kiss we sat in silence. It was then that I realized that, besides the driver, we were the only people aboard the bus.

At Sixth Avenue a young kid in a red snowmobile suit attached himself to the side of the bus and street skied, unnoticed by the driver, all the way to the Stonewall Memorial at Sheridan Square.

For the rest of our bus ride Basha and I didn't speak of the kiss, nor did we try to repeat it. That kind of perfection is best left untainted.

I felt more alive than I had in my life and the silence on the bus was nothing less than orchestral.

That Sunday evening's offering of *Traffic Lights and Broken Bridges* was attended by fewer people than it takes to populate a bush-league sixteen-inch softball team. The snowstorm had obviously done a number on the box office of the critically acclaimed Off-Broadway hit. Normally $32.00, on that night the tickets for the eight p.m. performance were going for $10.00. I could have gone through Feick and scored comps, but I wanted to surprise my brother and impress him with the mysterious, beautiful Basha on my arm.

The Atlantis Theatre Company made their home in a former church whose Byzantine narthex had been transformed into the box-office and lobby area, where previous Atlantis Theatre play posters, framed production photos, and a periodic chart of company members' head shots adorned the walls. On either side of the box office and garishly displayed on three-foot-by-five-foot foam-core placards were blown-up easel reviews from *The New York Times*, *New York Post*, and *The Village Voice*, all testifying to the immortal genius of *Traffic Lights and Broken Bridges*. In each of these, Feick was featured in a black-and-white, noir-like action shot looking almost naked and very pale as Tiny the Runaway.

After our tickets were torn, a geriatric man outfitted with the largest hearing aid I'd ever seen led us to our seats and handed us programs. His Neapolitan ice cream–colored summer golfwear was highly confusing and gave him the air of a person who thought he was working a dinner theater in Boca Raton.

Basha and I sat fourth row center. After we shed our hats, scarves, mittens, gloves, and multiple torso layers, we fiddled with our programs for a few silent minutes and shared an awkward glance or two and then, without the slightest warning, Basha slid her hand into mine, which immediately made me feel like my stomach had disappeared. Basha's hand was white and delicate and beautiful, like a thing one might find amid the nettles of a magic forest. I was starting to believe that my whole encounter with her was some sort of mirage. My right hand was holding her left with a slight, almost imperceptible thumb stroke. The prominent carpus bones, sharply peaked ivory knuckles, and slightly raised, colorless veins in the top of her hand added a tinge of blue-collar suffering to her beauty.

While we awaited the dimming of the houselights, I became pathologically obsessed with this hand and couldn't help imagining it not only touching me sexually, but also shelving books, dicing vegetables, removing the empty toilet-paper tube from its spring-action dowel, performing amateur magic tricks, turning off and on a high-fidelity sound system, applying mascara, and starting coffee on the coffee-maker, as well as a host of other domestic, sensual, and beauty-related activities. Part of this imagining involved the hand independent of Basha, floating in black, negative space like a tentacled sea creature.

When the houselights finally dimmed (after the box-office guy managed to lure a few more pedestrians into the theatre), Basha leaned in and gently kissed my cheek and I all but turned to pollen.

Despite the somewhat disorienting, thoroughly intoxicating spell that Basha had induced, I was able to take in the play. In fact, I would argue that my narrative wits were somehow heightened by her proximity.

Traffic Lights and Broken Bridges could be summed up by highlighting the various wants, compulsions, and performative actions (songs included, although the program made a point of insisting that the play was *not* a musical) of the three characters.

PAPI:

Papi is Cuban and eats a lot of beef.

Papi wants a color TV.

Papi pines for Blake Drake, the seemingly straight, sexually confused number-cruncher who has been hanging out a lot around the seedier sections of the late-eighties Times Square porno district.

Papi wears a wife beater T-shirt and complains about the heat in his Chelsea SRO.

Tea-colored stains hang wetly under his arms and bleed down to his rib cage.

Papi occasionally wears a white Panama hat when he's feeling loud and elastic.

Papi likes to have sex in the hat.

Papi occasionally plays with a yo-yo and is particularly good at "walking the dog."

Papi sings a song about red meat and anal sex called "The Bull and the Bunnyhole." He sings the song vigorously, with lots of Spanglish thrown in. The song has a percussive military marching band vibe.

TINY:

Tiny subsists on lollipops and miniature boxes of Froot Loops breakfast cereal.

Tiny wears only a pair of underwear fashioned from the pages of old comic books.

Tiny's "pannypapers" make for a very leggy performance (nothing but hams and thighs and shanks).

Tiny occasionally dons a similarly fashioned, comic-book chaplet-like coronet, but always removes it when Papi is home.

Tiny likes to huff airplane glue out of small brown paper bags and fantasizes about growing an aquarium of Sea-Monkeys.

Tiny wants Papi to "take his buns Mike Tyson–style."

Tiny sings a song in a castrato-like falsetto called "I'm Tiny, I'm Me, Nudity Is Free." The number is punctuated by Tiny tearing off his pannypapers and flexing his butt muscles with a power fist thrust ecstatically in the air.

BLAKE DRAKE:

Blake Drake hates his anchorman hair.

Blake Drake is desperate for a promotion but simultaneously wants to throw the office mainframe computer out the window of his Wall Street building.

Blake Drake wants to take it up the ass, and at a crucial point during the play he screams this—verbatim—into the receiver of the phone mounted on his office desk.

Blake Drake wants Papi but can't wrest himself from the talons of his purportedly large-breasted fiancée, offstage secretary Bonny Lee Bush, from Buffalo.

Blake Drake doesn't know what he wants.

Blake Drake likes to rifle through the pockets of his suit trousers, which makes for a continuous, jangling score of loose change.

With his back to the audience, Blake Drake often masturbates after spitting into his left hand. His nudity is hidden under a candy-striped, flat twin sheet, and through a series of self-loathing moments in a bathroom mirror the audience learns that his opinion of his body is that it is both ludicrous and shameful.

About halfway through the intermissionless play Blake Drake sings a song about the madness of big corporate calculus and the power of the number two called "Loosen Your Deuce and Drink All Your Juice." The song is a kind of old saloon rag that requires karate kicks, a full-fledged cartwheel, and an inordinate amount of bad softshoe.

THE STORY:

There's a rift in the Brooklyn Bridge that leads to a secret cave full of runaway young gay men who inhabit an unseen netherworld where art and fantasy merge with utopian whimsy. Through some sort of unexplained pheromonal process, at approximately nine p.m. every night Blake Drake finds himself drawn there, where he happens upon Papi, who, in a sinister Latino baritone, sings a discomfiting yet potently seductive song of lust and salsa power called "Breaking the Breeder."

The song involves a stiletto dagger and several unwrapped condoms. At one point one of the condoms is sheathed over the dagger. Moments after the final chorus of the song subsides and the audience's sporadic applause degenerates into the listless smattering of an unsuccessful bag of microwave popcorn, Tiny emerges from the rift in the bridge. His face is powder-white, with red, peripatetic crow's-feet marking his cheekbones. The Native American imagery is at once ghostly and kitschy. Tiny is barefoot, his hair an electron cloud of chaos, his complete nakedness disrupted only by his Marvel Comics pannypapers. In the audience, though populously anemic, there was a constant tension surrounding the question of whether the pannypapers would actually stay on.

In a later scene we learn that Tiny is actually from McCall, Idaho, a small resort town on the cusp of eight hundred miles of uninhabited national forest. Most of his childhood was spent swimming in glacial lakes, bathing in lithium-infused hot springs, and communing with elk and deer at an elevation of over five thousand feet. The rustic upbringing and exposure to thin levels of oxygen have given Tiny the ability to hold his breath underwater for several minutes at a time. This is demonstrated by Tiny's continuous self-inflicted, headfirst plunges into bathtubs, kitchen sinks, a fifty-gallon drum of Del Monte apple juice, and the Hudson River.

The entire play was performed in just over ninety minutes and the love triangle that developed between Papi, Tiny, and Blake Drake culminated in a heated, bongo-scored scene in which Tiny, cuckolded, freshly slapped in the face, and spat upon by Papi, threatens to return to the utopian netherworld of the Brooklyn Bridge rift, at which point he brandishes Papi's dagger and then throws it into the floor, where it sticks, almost perfectly vertical, with an audible *thwunk*. Papi then removes the knife and, after Blake Drake enters his apartment wearing skintight soccer shorts and an equally snug black T-shirt bearing the words OUT AND PROUD, and holding a single red rose, Papi slowly approaches Tiny, puts him in a haunting, almost gentle, embrace-like full nelson, and proceeds to slash his throat with scary realism, a horrible smile of blood connecting Tiny's young, blond ears. After a terminal run of slower-than-a-heartbeat bongos, there are some tears, a primal scream, and complete cast nudity.

The lights dim slowly to black during a chilling embrace between Papi and Blake Drake, after which Papi takes the red rose and feeds the petals to his new lover, grape-like, one by one.

At the curtain call, all three actors wrapped each other in matching bloodred terrycloth bathrobes and took their bows with smears of tears, snot, saliva, and other emotional fluids shellacking their cheeks and necks, Tiny's throat marked by a blurry, pink, murderous rope of diluted stage blood.

By the time they took their second encore, all thirteen audience members were standing, crying, heaving, and shouting "Bravo" and other hyperbolic European testimonials.

To say that my brother was utterly transformed by this role would be an understatement. He was so convincingly Tiny that I was never even the slightest bit aware of the process of the suspension of disbelief.

The play hunted me down and held me captive. I was a small sheep tethered to a fence. The ninety minutes of theatre galloped along like a derby horse, and Tiny was the tragic jockey (and Papi the steed!).

After Basha and I gathered our things and relayered ourselves, we managed to help each other to the stage door (perhaps there's nothing more physically disorienting than old-fashioned theatre shock), where we waited in silence for Feick.

The snow continued its diagonal assault, quickly attaching itself to Basha's eyelashes. We huddled next to the stage door. At one point Basha took off her gloves and slipped her hands into my pockets, over mine. This act of unadulterated affection further underscored my mirage theory. Up until that moment, my life had been a rote, generic, vaguely suburban survey of a typical Midwestern man's upbringing that included First Communion; Cub Scouts; paper routes; Sunday school; Little League (center field); family picnics; the occasional fishing trip (Lake Manteno, Illinois); three consecutive summer camps (Burlington, Wisconsin, twice-awarded "Best Camper," once "Fastest Runner"); waning participation in the Catholic Church (I was never confirmed); countless tornado drills, sightings, warnings, and alerts; mall walking; stone skipping; BMX riding; Atari, Colecovision, and Sega Genesis home video-game systems; multiple varsity sports; clichéd, almost romantic pet discovery in field (Scooter, a half-Chihuahua, half-miniature dachshund, deceased junior year of college due to acute kidney failure); PSATs, SATs, ACTs, college applications, college acceptance, college choice; overly disciplined study habits; inaugural coed sexual experience with high-school-cheerleader-turned-promiscuous-sorority-girl (uneventful, under-two-minute ejaculation); mild partying (mostly cheap American beer tapped from a Friday-night keg, first marijuana experience occurring in an empty Lost Nation, Iowa, corncrib; a rather enlightening episode of "shrooming" in an Elizabeth, Illinois, field dotted with extraordinarily solemn brown cows); college basketball; occasional newspaper photo (conference-leading scorer, MVP, purported halfhearted interest from CBA pro scouts); burgeoning, unrequited romances with J. D. Salinger, John Updike, Frederick Exley, Haruki Murakami, and Don DeLillo; bachelor of arts degree (double majors in English Writing and Psychology); surprising accelerated foot growth (size twelve to fourteen in just a few months following twenty-first birthday); and, finally, the hopeful abandonment of Mississippi River regional history and a move to the big city.

If it was a color it would have been beige.

With blue-ribbon trim.

It was in the darkness of a theatre that my first moment of connec-

tion with Basha had been made, and here we were again, this time huddled near the exterior of one, falling into each other like the evening's
ubiquitous snow into a warm, urban puddle.

Perhaps our destiny would be forged by new American drama?

Perhaps I would someday write a play in which Basha would star as
my leading lady–slash–muse?

When the stage door opened, my little brother emerged hand in hand
with the actor who played Papi. Feick was wearing gray flannel trousers,
a navy peacoat, large waterproof hiking boots, and a dockworker's skullcap that was so black it made his pale face appear to be lit from within.
When he saw me, their hands quickly broke apart and Feick said, "Bro!"

"Hey," I said.

"You came to the show," he said, his voice somehow more tinged with
the sobriety of concern than with the genial lift of welcome surprise.

"I did," I concurred. "It was great. Really powerful stuff."

"You liked it?"

"*Totally*. Didn't you see us standing up at the end?"

We were suddenly overtaken by a tundra-like wind.

"HE CRIED," Basha shouted, which was true, although I thought I
had made sure to weep silently. I would even go so far as to say that my
weeping was spy-like. I had no idea Basha had witnessed it.

"YOU CRIED?" Feick asked, surprised.

"HE BECAME FILLED WITH GREAT EMOTION DURING THE
SCENE WITH THE KNIFE," Basha explained. "I WITNESSED SEV-
ERAL TEARS. HE WAS VERY MASCULINE ABOUT IT," she added,
poking me in the ribs a little.

"YEAH, THAT KNIFE SCENE TOTALLY GOT ME," I admitted.

"*WHAT WAS THAT?*" Feick asked.

"I SAID THE KNIFE SCENE TOTALLY GOT ME."

Then the wind died for a moment and we stopped shouting. The
snow briefly assumed a vertical cant, as if it were between violent
thoughts.

"I had no idea you were coming," Feick added, taking us in as
though we were all mild acquaintances who were about to board an un-
stable pontoon boat.

"I wanted to surprise you."

"Well, it's definitely a surprise," Feick replied, smiling through his obvious unease.

Papi smiled as well, turning up the collar of his too-thin tweed blazer. He then secured the top button of Feick's peacoat and pinched his cheek maternally.

"Some snow, huh?" I offered in an effort to avoid the enormous Chelsea elephant that was now looming among us on the corner of Ninth Avenue and Nineteenth Street.

Feick said, "I think it's a blizzard."

"WHAT?" I cried, losing his words in the newest rush of wind.

"I SAID I THINK IT MIGHT BE A BLIZZARD!"

"OH," I announced, cupping my hands around my mouth, bullhorn-like. "RIGHT!"

Above us, apartment windows glowed with an amber omnipotence. It was as if the entire neighborhood were watching some inevitable brother scene that they had witnessed innumerable times, and through all forms of inclement weather.

"THIS IS BASHA," I shouted to my little brother.

"HEY, MARSHA," Feick shouted back pleasantly.

"*BASHA!*" I corrected him.

"OH. SORRY. HI, BASHA," Feick came back at us, not quite as embarrassed as I'd hoped he would be.

"HELLO," Basha returned, matching his volume now. "I VERY MUCH ENJOY YOUR PERFORMANCE."

"THANK YOU."

"AND YOURS, TOO," she hollered to Papi. "YOU WERE VERY SCARY AND SAD SIMUL . . . *TAN* . . ."

"SIMULTANEOUSLY," I helped.

"SIMULTANEOUS, YES!" Basha exclaimed.

"THAT'S VERY NICE OF YOU," Papi yelled appreciatively. "I'M RUBEN," he then offered. He accented the second syllable of his name in a way that was both sophisticated and inexplicably threatening.

"HI, RUDY," Basha said.

"RUBEN," he shouted, correcting her.

"I MEAN *RUBEN*," Basha replied. "I'M VERY SORRY TO DE-STROY YOUR NAME."

"DON'T WORRY ABOUT IT," Ruben retorted, loud and kind.

Then Basha and I took turns shaking hands with him.

"SORRY," Feick apologized. "I'M SO BAD AT THIS KIND OF THING. RUBEN, THIS IS MY BROTHER!"

"I'VE HEARD A LOT ABOUT YOU," Ruben screamed.

"OH, NO," I said.

"ALL GOOD THINGS," he assured me.

Then we all stood there on the street in the swirling snow. Several people slid, shuffled, and skied by us, their heads bowed, embracing themselves as if trying to keep from sobbing. Some were actually ambulating backward with strange, peasant-like, pedestrian faith.

"YOU WERE BOTH EXCEEDINGLY HEROIC," Basha announced, injecting a few more syllables of public address–like flattery, deflating yet another expanding silence.

"Basha is an actor, too," I stated, lowering my voice in accord with another lull in the snowstorm. "I just saw her in a play a few weeks ago."

"Cool," Feick said.

"It was called *Boots, Bats, and Sticks.* By this genius Sherman Furl." I have no idea why I felt the need to barb Sherman Furl. "Down on White Street, at the Workhorse."

"It was small part," Basha said. "But I learn how to smoke for it."

"Are you working on anything now?" Ruben asked, his hands wedged under his armpits, snow glazing his dark eyelashes.

"Not at the moment," Basha answered over the grate of a passing snowplow. "But I forestall several highest profile auditions awaiting my future."

"WHAT?!" Feick asked.

"SHE SAID SHE HAS SOME AUDITIONS COMING UP!" I yelled over another squall.

"EXCELLENT!" Feick blared.

"SHE DOES A GREAT AMERICAN ACCENT! SHE'S REALLY, REALLY GOOD," I offered enthusiastically, blaring a little myself. But that didn't seem to register with either Feick or Ruben. Perhaps this was because at that very moment the actor who played Blake Drake appeared through the stage door wearing a red snowsuit.

"SEE YOU TOMORROW, FELLAS," he called to Feick and Ruben with his head down, seemingly poised to attack the elements. I imagined him going off to ice-fish on some upstate lake.

"GOOD NIGHT, TIM!" Ruben called after him. "GOOD SHOW."

Blake Drake–slash–Tim then bounded through the snow, turned the corner, and disappeared in the whiteout.

After that Feick said, "WELL, THANKS FOR COMING. I WOULD LOVE TO HANG, BUT WE'VE BEEN INVITED TO THIS SORT OF PRIVATE DINNER PARTY THING IN LITTLE ITALY."

"COOL," I announced through my hands.

"NICE TO MEET YOU," Ruben shouted gladly, offering his bare brown hand. We shook. I looked in his eyes and saw neither predatory lust nor any other Papi-like vice. He was at once both gentle and strong. "AND YOU, TOO, BASHA," he added.

"VERY NICE TO MEET YOU BOTH," Basha replied. Then they shook as well.

"I'LL SEE YOU AT HOME, RIGHT?" I said to Feick.

"WHAT?"

"I SAID I'LL SEE YOU AT HOME!"

"SURE, BRO," Feick said. "SEE YOU AT HOME."

Feick and Ruben turned and walked south on Ninth Avenue. Their figures were quickly obscured by the expanding, snow-shaggy nimbuses of oncoming traffic lights.

Basha and I walked to Seventh Avenue and Charles Street and caught the eastbound M8 to St. Mark's Place and First Avenue. On the bus we resumed our hand-holding and did our best to engage in a postplay discussion.

"Ruben was superbly powerful when he was exposing his nude membership," Basha said.

"Yes, indeed," I responded with Chekhovian formalism, half-hearing her. I was obviously distracted by Feick's new, unannounced lifestyle.

"Are you sure you're not deeply troubled?" Basha asked for the third time as we passed Astor Place, where students, street performers, and the homeless were collaborating in the dueling activities of spinning an enormous cube sculpture and building a ten-foot snow gorilla with a titanic, saber-like erection. The affair was nothing less than Dionysian, and it seemed as if the rotating cube was powering the communal industry of raising the winter beast's boner.

"I'm fine," I said. "Just a little surprised is all."

"You did not know about your brother."

"Um, no," I said. "Actually, I had no idea."

"This must be exceedingly astonishing for you, then, no?"

Was I surprised?

Certainly, yes.

Up until that point, until I'd walked in on him masturbating some months back, I'd had a hard time imagining my little brother possessing *any* sexual orientation. I had always believed Feick to be categorically blank, the way houseplants can sustain profound domestic neutrality on the most well-lit windowsill. Even when it came to his reproductive anatomy, despite sharing a bedroom for several years—perhaps through some catechistic behavioral heredity—I either imagined the vacant, polyurethane loins of a CPR dummy or the smooth, unthreatening bump of an acorn squash. But then again, is it possible that all younger siblings are thought of in this way? Or do we simply assign these blank reproductive spaces to our younger brothers and sisters because we feel threatened by a newer, more virile, genetically improved version of ourselves?

Was it true that Feick possessed a larger, more sexually endowed cock than I?

But he was almost four years my junior!

And six and a half inches shorter!

No way!

While shoe-skiing north to Stuyvesant Town, Basha and I were relatively quiet. For a brief minute the wind died and the snowfall slowed to the velocity of fish food floating through aquarium water. Along First Avenue there were only a few patches of visible pavement. Everything else—the sidewalks, the streets, the curbs—was covered with a pristine quilt of snow. The taxicabs took on a luminous, dream-like quality, somehow hovering futuristically.

The shop lights gave off amber hues as a woman from Rose's Pizza, dressed only in her counter clothes, pulled the gates down over her storefront. A few blocks later an elderly man slipped and fell in front of David's Bagels. Several pedestrians stopped to help him, and one woman was already calling the paramedics on the corner pay phone.

As we weaved through the brick and mortar warren of Stuyvesant Town, after making a few benign observations about a stalled snowplow and the men attempting to revive it, I stupidly asked Basha if she had a boyfriend.

"Oh, boy," was her reply.

"What?"

"Ohboyohboyohboy," she said. "This is not such a dazzling question to bestow in the moment."

"You do, then."

"Yes," she said.

"Where is he?"

"Lublin."

"Is that in Poland?"

"Yes."

"What's his name?"

"János."

"Why isn't he here in New York?"

"He is concluding university."

"What does he study?"

"Medicine."

"He's going to be a physician?"

"Yes."

"What kind?"

"I forget the word. The doctor who helps pregnant women with their cozy feminine issues."

"Cozy?"

"Cozy means personal, no?"

"Yes, it does. But personal in the way sitting around a fire can be personal. But not in terms of hygiene."

"I see."

We continued through the snow for a moment. At the base of a building there were five or six bundled kids jumping into a snowdrift from the ledge of a recycling Dumpster.

"So Jelco's gonna be an obstetrician?" I asked.

"János, yes. He wishes very much to move here after he completes his residency in Warsaw."

"To New York?"

"Yes. To live with my family."

Suddenly I felt like there was an indigestible stone turning hotly in my stomach. "Do you talk to him a lot?" I asked.

"We do talk sometimes, yes."

"It must be difficult to maintain a relationship, being so far away from each other," I offered, suddenly sounding like some neutered friend from a church meeting.

"The long-distance telephone system is very expensive, no?"

"Of course."

"We compose romantic letters. But this takes much patience, as the United States airmail system is exceedingly painstaking and arduous," she explained in her beautiful, thesaurus-rich English.

"Do you and János have some kind of agreement or something?"

"What does this mean—agreement?"

"Sometimes when two people are in a romantic relationship but they are away from each other, they, um, *agree* that it's okay to see other people."

"What is *see*?"

"Date."

"Oh," Basha said. "János and I do not possess such agreement."

"So tonight probably wasn't the best idea."

"Perhaps this is true," Basha concurred.

As we walked on, I grew increasingly leery of the romantic possibilities.

"But I would still very much like to *see* you," Basha said.

"You would?"

"Yes. Perhaps we shall have another interview?"

"*Interview?*"

"I mean rendezvous."

"Sure," I said. "But I'm sure János wouldn't be too thrilled."

"He would not be pleased, no. But I am not professionally obliged to discuss this high-octane information with him."

We shuffled across a basketball court, its half-mangled nets frosted with snow. Oh, if only my knee were healthy! I would jump up and grab the rim, exhibiting my leaping ability!

When we reached the other side of the basketball courts, Basha slipped and I helped her up. It was the least dangerous winter fall I have ever witnessed. She slid on her heel for a few feet and simply sat down in the snow. It looked almost choreographed. "So if we continued to see each other, that would make me like your paramour or something," I offered, hoisting her off the ground, giving her an arm to hold.

"Is paramour like stallion?" Basha asked.

"Um. Sort of."

"I like the horses," she digressed rather impressively. "They are swift and powerful beast of the plains. I prefer the horses to almost all other animals. In Poland we have the Wielkopolski, which is popular for its hearty blood."

"Wow."

"And a superlative constitution."

"Well," I said, "that's really quite interesting."

This talk of Polish horses was indeed interesting, but although I wanted to get back to the talk of *us*, I was distracted by a Technicolor flash-fantasy of Basha and me atop an enormous white unicorn, naked and damp with a sultry humidity, riding into a fragrant, purple literary forest of giant heliotropes.

And then, lurking at the edges of the flora, was the giant woodsman János, a gigantic ax resting on his burly shoulder.

"By the way," I said, passing under the far backboard, "is your boyfriend a big guy?"

"János is very massive, yes."

"More massive than me?"

"You are a little more taller. But he is thick like grizzly bear and he possesses much bone-crushing strength."

I pictured a giant grizzly bear in pursuit of our unicorn.

"And he is karate expert, two boots," Basha added. "He holds most superlative degree black belt."

A grizzly with martial-arts skills!

Shit, I thought. Shit, shit, shit, man.

At the door to her building the sodium entryway lights made the snowflakes look like tiny, stunned seagulls descending.

"Are you and János planning to get married?" I asked.

"I think our families would desire this with great force, but I am not so sure," she said, again slipping her hands into my coat pockets.

"How long have you been dating?"

She did some quick Polish math under her breath, which caused her to look up. Exactly three snowflakes landed on her velveteen eyelashes.

"Three years and seven months," Basha said, bringing her Polish computations back across the Atlantic and retranslating.

"It sounds pretty serious," I offered.

"Yes."

"How old is János?"

"He will revolve to thirty next month. Let's stop proclaiming his identity, okay?"

"Okay."

"It makes me feel like he is hiding in my bush."

"Your bush?"

Basha kicked a small, snow-encrusted shrub that had been planted next to her building's entrance.

"I'll stop saying his name," I conceded. "I'm sorry."

Basha removed her hands from my pockets and poked me playfully in the stomach.

"Perhaps you could come by and visit me at my place of toiling tomorrow?" she suggested.

"Where do you toil?" I asked, poking her back.

"A new bistro-style restaurant on Fifth Street between First Avenue and Avenue A called Polly Parker's. I will be toiling at my shift from five p.m. to close."

"I'll come by."

"Good. This makes me exceedingly gay," Basha said, smiling.

"It does?"

"I mean glad."

"Me, too," I said.

Then we kissed again. It was even better than the one on the bus. The warmth of her lips was like the slow, passing perfection experienced on the shores of certain windless summer beaches. I was suddenly seized with a kind of apoplectic, scarecrow-like loss of coordination. I teetered a bit, and then found my balance against a snowdrift.

To this day, there are still long, sleepless hours when the only thing that knits my thoughts together is the memory of that kiss in front of Basha's apartment building.

I watched her walk down a fluorescently lit hallway, call the elevator, and board it. She looked back at me the whole time. The doors converged indifferently, finally ending our night together.

As I walked south on First Avenue, the snow returned to its relentless, diagonal attack and the squalls came in fits. The northbound salt trucks and snowplows rumbled past as if they were herding toward some silent war in midtown.

In front of David's Bagels the crowd had dispersed and whatever emergency medical service had been called had come and taken the fallen man away.

———

Back at the apartment, the Loach was seated on the sofa, wearing what appeared to be a British grenadier guard's uniform, complete with white ducks, red wool, brass-buttoned parade tails, synthetic patent leather low-quarter shoes, and a black bearskin shako that was chin-strapped to his head. The expression on his face made him look as if a larger man had forced him to wear the costume and perform a series of monologues, and then had raped him repeatedly.

"Hey," I said, shutting the door.

"Hey," he said in return, staring straight ahead. His normally gray and sunken cheeks were now two rosy apples of rouge.

"What's with the costume?" I asked.

"I got a job."

"You did?"

"I gained employment, yes."

"Doing what?"

"Standing in front of FAO Schwarz in this monkey suit."

"What are you supposed to be?"

"Roger the Toy Soldier."

"Roger?"

"I could have been Mac or Benny, but I chose Roger."

Then the Loach pointed to an area near the upper brass buttons, where ROGER was stitched in black cursive lettering over his right breast.

"Congratulations," I offered.

To which the Loach replied, "I didn't win the fucking lottery." He adjusted his chinstrap and snorted some phlegm.

"Do you, like, open the door for people or something?" I asked, genuinely curious.

"I just stand there. At parade fucking rest. And little kids stare at me. All those little brats with their mommies. I'd rather contract a terminable disease."

"Does it pay well?"

"Twenty an hour."

"That's great cash."

But the Loach didn't respond, and after a pause that didn't involve the TV, the fan or any other electrical stimulus, I said, "Is the Owl around?"

"He's in his room, sleeping."

I peered down the hall to see if the crack under the Owl's door was illuminated. It wasn't.

"Guess what?" I offered stupidly.

"Is this, like, call-and-response?" the Loach quipped, ineffectual as ever.

"No," I said. "I just want to share something with someone."

"Share away."

"Feick's gay."

After a moment the Loach said, "Good for him."

"And I think I'm in love."

"With Feick?"

"No, with a woman. Her name is Basha."

"Is she hot?"

"Yeah, she is."

"Nice rack?"

"Um, sure."

"What about her ass?"

"She has a great ass."

Why I was indulging this idiotic line of questioning, I have no idea. "She's beautiful," I added. "And she's a beautiful person, too."

"Good for you," the Loach rejoined bitterly. "Good for everyone."

The following day, while eavesdropping on a phone call to some unknown Burton Loach associate, I would learn that during his first tour of duty, after merely an hour and a half on the job, the Loach had walked away from his front-door post at FAO Schwarz. He flipped off the famous toy store while shouting "Merry Christmas, shmuckos!" boarded a southbound bus, and came home.

The Loach ended the phone call saying, "I'm doin' a show soon. You're comin', right? Yeah, I'm funny! I swear to god I'm fuckin' funny! You promised you'd come see one, you fucking dick! I said I'd comp you!"

He would continue to wear the toy-soldier uniform as an alternative to obtaining proper winter bedding. In the middle of the night, well into late December, while on the way to the bathroom, I would see the Loach using the shako as a pillow, the white ducks and brass-buttoned coat pulled up to his chin, faint wintry smoke slipping out of his mouth in troubled exhalations.

Lunch with the Shankler

AT WORK, IN PREPARATION for the winter sales conference in White Plains, like so many migrating birds threatened by early winter winds, the hardcover sales department flapped and fluttered into crisis mode. Temps were called in for reinforcement. Lunches were skipped. Tempers flared. Non-remunerative overtime was expected ("It's just not in the budget, kid. Sorry"). The biweekly rep mailing accrued triweekly status. FedEx slips drifted about desks and countertops with the careless extravagance of never-used grocery-store coupons. Everything from editorial videos to book briefs had been stockpiled at the mouth of my cubicle. While the mountains of snow continued to grow against the sides of buildings, I had my own little administrative blizzard to worry about. On any given night, I was lucky to make it home by seven p.m.

One morning I was preparing boxes for a rep mailing when the Shankler sidled up to me on his way to the marketing meeting.

"Hey, Romeo," he said by way of a greeting.

"Hi, Jack," I answered, attempting to wrest a sales blad for Chico Serengeti's *Tuna's Not the Only Fish in the Sea!* from the gummy teeth of my tape gun.

"Lunch later?" the Shankler asked, although I knew this was not an invitation but a declaration. Our working relationship was a small but potent monarchy in which he was the king and I was his lone, royalty-fearing subject. Van Von Donnelly (my boss) had less impact on our little government than would a moth perched on the wing of a Boeing 747.

"Lunch," I said. "Sure."

"I already put in a reservation at that gay joint on Hudson where all the editors go to max out their company plastic."

He was talking about The Painted Bird, a classy, white-tablecloth café a few blocks north of our building. I had no idea it was a "gay joint," but its popularity with the publishing elite was no secret. On any given afternoon you could find a half dozen of the more fashionable editors there, drinking wine or cappuccino with their favorite authors.

"I'll just need to clear it with Van," I said.

"Oh, it's crystal, trust me," the Shankler assured me with the smile of a well-fed lion.

"Crystal," I echoed idiotically.

"One-thirty. See you there. And don't forget your galoshes; it's brutal out there."

He exited toward the boardroom.

For the next five minutes I stood in a rather beleaguered attitude of what one might liken to the doomed, predator-prey attitude of a rabbit frozen beneath the gaze of a starving wolf: pigeon-toed, my shoulders hunched, my mouth hanging open, an infinitesimal bend at the waist as if self-generated invisibility were possible.

As my coworkers and temps passed by loaded with sales materials, I played off my mild terror stroke by feigning halfhearted attention to my tape gun.

I spent the duration of the rep mailing trying to come up with a few reasons why the Shankler hadn't attempted to fart on me.

Had I graduated beyond a certain scatological threshold?

Or had I simply slid down the sales-department food chain?

What could Lacy possibly have told her father?

At one-thirty I met the Shankler at The Painted Bird.

In one corner, Puck Stickleback penned a crossword puzzle. At another table Stafford Davidson was entrenched in a very grave-looking conversation with one of his new authors, an unkempt, gauzy-haired Englishman named Apian Bradwell who kept using the word *solipsistic*.

And in the corner opposite Puck Stickleback was one very large and kingly-looking Jack Shank, his mass dwarfing the table, giving the whole dining ensemble the feeling of a dark, portentous fairy tale. He waved me over like a coach trying to impart strategy in between the opposing team's free-throw attempts.

I scooted over and took my chair.

"Order the lamb," is the first thing he said. "It's the closest thing to vadge you'll ever taste. Whattaya drinkin'?"

"Well . . ." I said, sitting.

"Come on, order some gasoline, kid."

"Like alcohol?"

"No, *bull's blood*. Of course alcohol!"

"Do you think that's such a good idea, Jack? I mean, I wouldn't want Van to get the wrong—"

"Don't worry about Van. I sign off on just about everything in Van's life. How 'bout a martini?"

"Um, sure."

"Vodka, straight up, two olives, right?"

Before I could answer, the Shankler flung his hand in the air and moments later a white-aproned waiter materialized. The Shankler ordered two vodka martinis and a pair of lamb entrees, prepared medium.

"And two house salads," he directed. "Blue cheese, right, kid?"

"Perfect," I conceded.

The waiter nodded and backed away.

The Shankler then chugged half a glass of ice water and said, "So I understand you went to see my daughter's play. *The Importance of Being in Cleveland* or whatever it's called. She any good?"

"As an actor?"

"No, as a parking meter. Of course as an actor."

"Oh, she's very good, Jack," I said. "Very very very good, yes. I would even say that her performance was sort of mind-blowing."

"Well, that little kitty cat's nothing less than mind-blowing."

For a moment I thought he was referring to Banjo the Abyssinian and I momentarily left my body while I imagined a single phantom cat hair passing Seattle Space Needle–like through my urethra.

"Sounds like things between you and Lacy are moving in a good direction," the Shankler continued. "I'm glad to hear that."

"It's been fun," I responded, back in my skin now, suddenly guzzling my ice water, not able to fully imagine what Lacy had been telling her father.

"She said she really enjoys you," the Shankler said with what might have been a lascivious twinkle in his eye.

"Oh," I said, "that's very nice. Lacy's a great talker. We've had several interesting conversations. And her apartment is quite neat."

The waiter returned with our martinis and then the Shankler proposed a toast.

"To Lacy," he mused.

"To Lacy," I testified.

"And to the future," he said, lifting his glass a little higher.

"And to the future," I aped, not entirely sure whose future he was referring to. We clinked glasses and drank. It was my first official martini and it tasted like refrigerated furniture polish.

The Shankler impressively gulped half of his drink and set his glass down.

"So, you're probably wondering why I asked you to lunch, right? Don't worry, you're not getting a promotion anytime soon. With this recession crapping all over the carpet that's not in anyone's cards. So far we're lucky we haven't had to make any cuts. And we're not takin' you up to White Plains for the sales conference, either. We gotta have you back here holdin' down the fort, so I'll cut to the chase," the Shankler said, knocking back the rest of his martini, hailing our waiter and ordering two more drinks before the next full exhalation. "I'd like you to take Lacy to the company Christmas party," he began. "And it can look as romantic as you'd like, just don't do anything in front of me 'cause I'll most likely be crocked and want to crack your head open with a freestanding ashtray or somesuch thing."

"Okay," I said, gulping my martini.

"The last few Christmas parties Lacy attended got a little out of hand," the Shankler explained.

"In what way?"

"Let's just say she had a few too many visits to the punch bowl if you get my driftola."

He drank again and I followed suit. I was sure to match him gulp for gulp, which might have been the dumbest thing I had done since moving to New York.

"I always bring her 'cause the local reps get a big bang outta her," the Shankler went on. "She's liable to grab the mic and start doing a 'Copacabana' at any moment. And I'm not referring to the Barry Manilow version."

"Huh," I said, imagining the possibilities.

"I like to enjoy myself at these parties, so I'd appreciate your help. Just show her a good time."

"No problem," I said.

"And if she starts takin' her goddamn clothes off I give you permission to tackle her. Just watch where your hands land."

The waiter returned with round two of our martinis. I speared the olives out of my first one, ate them, and downed the last gulp, hoping to not expose my martini naiveté any more than I already had.

Then the Shankler leaned a kingly lean, reached into his pocket and removed a hundred-dollar bill, shimmied it under his cloth napkin, looked left at Stafford Davidson, then right at Puck Stickleback, and slid it toward me.

"Let's keep this between you and me, huh?" the Shankler said collusively through nicotine-stained teeth.

I nodded and slipped my hand under the napkin, taking it, feeling like a publishing gigolo.

Suddenly, Van Von Donnelly was standing over our table. I never even saw him enter.

"Hey, Van," the Shankler greeted him.

"Hey, Shankler."

"Hey, kid," my boss said to me.

"Hey, Van."

"How goes it?" the Shankler asked.

"Oh, it's goin'," Van responded, "it's goin'. How 'bout yourself?"

"I could use a few more of these and a pair of private dancers," the Shankler said, gesturing to our martinis. They broke into Big Ten laughter. I followed suit with my own laughter, which stopped just short of the lunatic banana screeching of a caged chimp.

"Get the rep mailing done?" Van asked me, suddenly sober.

"Called it down to the mailroom just before I left," I answered. "The guys were on their way up."

"And the forecast numbers?" Van asked, his eyes crawling all over my martini.

"He was pullin' 'em outta the printer when I invited him to lunch," the Shankler said, lying. Oh, our little monarchy was getting ever so complicated. The king lies for his serf! The truth was, I had barely started printing the spring forecast. Shit truly does roll down hills.

"The digits for the midgets," Van said, smiling again, a bit of a nervous heel-to-toe bob undoing his tableside stance. "Gotta keep 'em happy in marketing."

"Gotta keep the wheels greased," the Shankler added, stabbing his new olive and making it disappear in his large, walrus-like mouth.

"He's a good one, this kid," the Shankler said to Van while chewing his olive. "Works real hard."

"Oh, I'm pleased as puppy piss. I just hope we can keep him around without some other department luring him away. I see the way the gals in marketing look at you," Van said to me, smiling now.

At some point shortly after the Shankler's lie I had mentally or astrally projected myself to the sales department, where I was pulling the spring forecasts out of the laser printer with my thumbs and index fingers. I was begging them out with corporate desperation. I was pulling for my dear life.

Then the Shankler changed the subject, saying, "See the Gopher game last night?" and their voices became indecipherably one.

"Oh those Gophers . . .
    What a buncha . . .
        They ever hear of the line of scrimmage?

. . . I'm tellin ya . . .

    Buckeyes murdered em . . .

      Third quarter was a massacre . . .

    Like the friggin Boston Tea Party . . .

      Like cabbage and creamed corn . . .

It was biblical . . .

  No backfield . . .

      And all they do is run the option . . .

Faggiest play ever created . . .

Don't talk too loud, Stickleback's over there in the corner.

He might throw some panty hose at us or somethin' . . ."

It was at this point in their conversation that I returned from the sales-department laser printer. Listening to them deftly juxtapose Puck Stickleback's homosexuality with the University of Minnesota Golden Gophers football team, I somehow gained a new appreciation for these two men. There was suddenly something heroically Russian about them. If Anton Chekhov were to write modern American men in their early midlife, I'm almost certain he would have penned Van Von Donnelly and Jack Shank ice-fishing on a glacial lake. Prehistoric loons crying. Antlered elk barking about the big timber. A hockey stick in the Shankler's hand, an unpainted circular saw in Van's.

TWO LARGE MEN FROM MINNETONKA
by Anton Chekhov

There was a pause.

The Shankler looked around surreptitiously and leaned toward Van.

"Hey, Van," he said through gritted teeth.

"Yeah, Shankler?"

"I farted on Holtzman's arm this morning."

"Jeezus. Really?"

"Right when those guys from the superstores blew through the door."

Then they laughed again, and I did, too. There could have been a string with a plastic loop attached to my back, the way I let them control me. After this final wave of hysterics dissolved, the Shankler guzzled his martini.

And I followed suit, my burgeoning buzz and the Shankler's protective royalty giving me newfound, almost antagonistic courage in the face of my generous, professionally impotent boss.

Van jingled the change in his pockets and said, "Well, I better get back to the office."

"Don't expect the kid too soon," the Shankler said. "I'm takin' him to Atlantic City. We're gonna use the company plastic to shoot craps for a coupla hours."

Van was suddenly breathless, no doubt terrified about those spring forecasts.

After a pause whose discomfort is perhaps rivaled in emergency waiting rooms, the Shankler broke into one of his Seussian smiles and aimed a naughty, lounge singer's finger gun at Van (perhaps one too many sales conferences in Las Vegas?), and Van then thawed into a chuckle, squared off with his own naughty finger gun (shorter, stubbier, a snub-nosed revolver), backed away toward his table, almost moonwalking now, reholstered his artillery, paid his check, became one with his Arctic-like snow parka, and left in an ensemble of moves that should have been videotaped and shown to the reps at sales conference in an attempt to highlight the charming, albeit savant-like abilities of their national sales director.

"Gotta love that guy," the Shankler said, finishing his second martini. "Took him under my wing fifteen years ago. Started out selling mass-market spinner racks in the Ohio-Pennsylvania territory and now he's director of the whole goddamn hardcover sales force. Taught him everything he knows. Which is a helluva lottuva very little." He shifted his weight and added, "I gotta go talk to a horse trader. Order me another one of these." Then he pushed the table away from his veteran home-plate umpire's stomach, got his legs under him, and headed toward the men's room.

While he was away I ordered him another martini and ate my second olive. I looked wistfully around The Painted Bird. I knew in my bones that this was perhaps the only time I would ever be lunching among this holy literary pedigree. Would I amount to nothing more than a failed novelist stuck in the provincial biweekly mailing mediocrity of the sales department?

Would I ever pass through the invisible glass wall of working on books to publishing one of my own?

Oh, the sour despair of glimpsing one's future!

I gulped the last of my second martini. I was starting to feel drunk and bitter, and I was thankful that the Shankler was either constipated or lost in the men's room.

Just after our house salads were delivered, Alexa entered the restaurant in a Yankee bean–colored, knee-length ski parka and walked a direct line to Puck Stickleback's table. Just before she reached it Puck shed his crossword puzzle, stood up, took her hands in his, and kissed her rather obliquely on the cheek. It took her what seemed like several minutes to wrest herself from her winterwear.

As she was about to sit down, Alexa and I made eye contact. She then handed her parka to the maître d', excused herself, and walked over to my table.

"You," she said.

"You," I said.

"Here with?" she asked, brushing off her gray flannel pantsuit.

"The Shankler. He's in the men's room."

"Wow. Promotion?"

"Just lunch."

"Ooooh."

"Ooooh what?"

"Mysterious."

I chose not to clarify.

Alexa bobbed on her rather tall heels for a moment and said, "I'm over there with Puck."

"Yeah, I saw."

"We started hanging out a few days ago. I'm not sure what it is yet, but what the hell, you know?"

"Sure," I said, my lingering bitterness starting to taste very much like an olive.

"Well, I just wanted to say hi," Alexa added, suddenly seeming more disarmed and sweeter than I'd ever noticed.

"Hi." I smiled, and then attempted to drink the martini I forgot I had just finished. The olive spear clanked against my teeth.

"By the way," Alexa said, almost as an afterthought, "I read the first fifty pages of your novel. I think it's brilliant."

"You do?"

"Yeah. The best first fifty pages I've read since I've been with the company. I passed it on to Judy. She's going to take a look at it this weekend. If she likes it she's probably going to ask for the rest of it. You're very talented."

"I am?"

"A little off the wall, but you have a real voice."

"Wow. Thanks, Alexa."

My bitterness suddenly started to wane.

"Well, I better get back to my table. Puck and I have a lot to discuss. I'll keep you posted."

"Good luck," I added.

"Puck luck," she said rather sweetly, and then turned and walked back to her table. Puck Stickleback stood as she approached, came around to the other side, and pulled out her chair for her. His chivalry was surprisingly masculine. After he sat, he took her hand and they stared at each other wordlessly, as if they were in the south of France, overlooking the Mediterranean.

Mine and the Shankler's matching entrees were served shortly after he returned from the bathroom. We drank yet another round of martinis and ate in total silence, except for his rather impassioned observation of the lamb, which was: "Tastes just like pussy, don't it, kid?"

I simply nodded and smiled.

The Shankler ordered us ricotta cheesecake and cappuccino for dessert. While he pawed about the last bits of crust and gnawed the little graham-cracker molds off the pads of his thumbs, he reminded me about the company Christmas party and my Lacy duties.

"You'll come through for me, right, kid?"

"I'll totally come through, Jack," I said. "I'm your man."

"Loyalty is a beautiful thing," he said finally, punctuating a very strange lunch.

Then the Shankler hailed our waiter, slipped him his corporate American Express card, and excused himself for one more visit to the men's room. "Take care of those forecasts," he gently warned.

"Will do," I responded.

After he left I sat for a few moments, taking in the quiet din of editors and their guests. I tried to make eye contact with Alexa a final time, but she and Puck were in the throes of some deeply felt conversation.

I stood, relayered my extra sweater, hooded sweatshirt, and jean jacket, and exited The Painted Bird on rather rubbery legs.

Hudson Street was dizzy with snow. I zigzagged a little, pushing off of nearly every available parking meter.

I reached the Leroy Street baseball diamond and somewhere near home plate I seized the chain-link fence and vomited three martinis, a slice of cheesecake, and the finest lamb I would ever eat.

While heaving the various expensive liquids and solids from lunch, I couldn't help imagining Van peering down at me from his fourth-floor office window, plotting my demise.

After I got back to the office, I rinsed my mouth out in the men's room, drank a cup of acidic black coffee, and printed the spring forecasts.

The Owl's Faint Ringing, Snow Bullets, and Sublime Effervescence

SO FOLLOWING MY LUNCH with the Shankler, there was this nonstop thing with the weather.

New York City was in the throes of what was perhaps its worst snowstorm in three decades. Now officially declared a blizzard, the extreme conditions inspired an exaggerated neighborhood narcosis that resembled the hibernation habits of the grizzly bear. The good people of Tenth Street seemed to be hiding behind drawn blinds, drapes, sheets, quilts, and other makeshift window dressings. The entire city was blanketed in a pristine, white hide. Tenement buildings looked like odd, shaggy ramparts. The chain-link fence along the First Avenue Housing Project was a parapet of solid snow. Even the corroded pig iron on the arches of the Cooper Union building was obscured. The East Village looked like some kind of fabled, overly frosted gingerbread world.

The snow continued to fly diagonally across my bedroom window at a velocity that seemed to defy physics. I found myself still slightly repelled by the space that my Smith Corona daisy wheel used to occupy. The typewriter's vacancy was accruing a loathsomeness that only reminded me that there was this novel I wasn't writing. Born more out of good old-fashioned monotony than any real botanical concern, I periodically tended to my anemic puccoon, watering it with the brownish, fecal-looking liquid that slogged through our half-frozen pipes.

Despite the Owl's efforts at duct-taping the cracks along the living room window moldings, the baseboard heat had little effect on our apartment. The only consistent warmth was drawn from a lozenge-shaped electric heating pad that I found in Feick's room (under a box, under a trunk, under his installation of pasty, moldering laundry), which had a trilevel control tooth (low, medium, high). It was utilized most effectively when placed under the small of my back, where its affiliation with the surface of my futon would create an unexceptional circumference of thermal relief, upon which I would rotate my various body parts throughout the night while staring at the film of frost slowly creeping across my window.

The Owl had purchased a three-foot-long electric space heater and slept with a kidney-colored rubber heating bladder that looked like a prop stolen from some half-realized Noël Coward play. He'd fill the bladder with hot water, brought to a boil in a saucepan we seldom used for actual cooking. He would then set the bladder on his stomach and sleep with a look of troubled concentration, as if he were awaiting a penal sentence. Though still clad in one of his many pairs of rice-colored Japanese underwear, the Owl now added a thick turtleneck and a dock-worker's skullcap. His partial nudity coupled with the burly sweater-and-cap ensemble gave him the air of a logger who'd been caught cheating on his wife.

Through some unknown supplier, the Loach procured an orange, multizippered snowmobile suit. Where this item of winterwear came from was anybody's guess. It eventually replaced the toy soldier's uniform altogether, although the Loach continued to sleep in the shako. Despite its bright, vitamin-rich hue, the snowmobile suit did nothing to improve the perception of his phlegmatic lifestyle on the sofa. If anything, by contrast, it only emphasized his limp-limbed, slow decay.

I compulsively peeked through the curtains in my room (two mysteriously stained muslin strips hung by the previous tenant), hoping to spot another north-side-of–Tenth Street loner with whom to share silent glances of snowbound commiseration. When the wind is bawling through the poorly caulked cracks in one's windowsill, a simple look from an anonymous stranger can do wonders.

Those who did challenge Mother Nature and took to the streets were forced to employ a farcical mode of pedestrian transport that went far beyond the improvised techniques of walking backward, skate stopping, and inadvertent foal-legged snowplowing. Even for the most talented big-city walker, venturing outside became a semi-exceptional athletic challenge that involved sliding, slipping, groping for the snow-impacted fenders of cars, hopping around islands of unpoliced dogshit, navigating through the graveyard-like minefield of miniature snow-banks, catching, grabbing, and hugging fellow East Villagers, accidental senior-citizen tackle prevention, and the occasional twelve-foot hydroplane.

The wind and snow and all the accompanying urban matter (candy wrappers, street salt, voided tampon applicators, loose coins, rooftop debris, etc.) attacked one's face like an agitated school of invisible flying piranhas.

Over the Owl's shortwave radio we heard a constant, dreary litany of public service announcements advising the listening audience to wrap their faces, cover their eyes, and limit outside venturing to a three-block radius.

Per usual, the Loach seemed oblivious to all that happened outside of his life on the sofa. To him, the blizzard might have been a distant rock concert or a flock of startled birds. Aesthetically speaking, he was entering a new phase. In addition to the orange snowsuit, he was growing a vast, apocalyptic black beard that, coupled with the slowly filling-in tonsure, made him look like one of the Twelve Apostles trapped in a Devo video.

As for work, despite the impending sales conference, the offices were closed for a forty-eight-hour period, and Mayor Dinkins himself urged the citizens of Manhattan to keep their cars off the major transit arteries so the snowplows and other makeshift automotive blizzard units could restore the avenues and streets to acceptable driving conditions.

I purchased a beige corduroy coat for twelve dollars at a thrift store on Ninth Street. It was missing three buttons and smelled faintly of cat urine and clove cigarettes, but the felt lining was in acceptable condition and the pockets had been mended.

That same evening, when I'd entered the apartment the Owl had been standing motionless in the middle of the living room like some wayward, prehistoric iceman fighting through a slow thaw. Despite the weather, he was wearing only a pair of Feick's sunflower boxer shorts, which were entirely too small (he'd clearly run out of the Japanese butthuggers). I had grown used to the turtleneck and skullcap so it was strange to see him suddenly revisiting his old ways of complete torso nudity.

The flesh between his shoulder blades was gluey with perspiration. A comet of pepper-black pubic hair protruded through his fly and a lone testicle dangled from the crotch of the boxers like a bulbous ganglion of Silly Putty. His knees were slightly bent and his large cinderblock head was tilted to the left at about forty-five degrees. His eyes looked strangely close together, as if his skull were trapped in a vise. His right hand was pressed against his right ear; his left arm hung limp at his side. There was obviously something horribly wrong with him and it put a bit of a damper on my excitement at sharing the news of Alexa's response to my novel.

Also in his underwear (festooned with his own natural, uric sunflowers) and equally impervious to the cold, the Loach was on the couch, watching the fan.

"Loach, where's your snowmobile suit?" I asked.

In all honesty, I was more disgusted by his appearance than concerned for his health.

"I crapped it," he answered matter-of-factly.

"You crapped *in* it?"

"Affirmative."

"Jesus. Where is it?"

"Hanging in the bathroom."

I sniffed the air, fearing the hot, horrible stew of Burton Loach's feces, but fortunately it was too cold in the apartment for the odor to penetrate even the most finely tuned Midwestern olfactory process.

"Aren't you cold?" I asked.

"I ate your ramen noodles," was his response.

To which I said, "Of course you ate my ramen noodles."

A painter might have found the image of Burton Loach and the Owl in their tableau vivant of twinned, pubic-themed stasis worthy of the canvas. There was an air of monstrous solemnity to it, a kind of grotesque inertia that called to mind the only thing I remembered from my undergraduate art history elective: a sixteenth-century Bruegel painting titled *Parable of the Blind* in which six men holding canes and linked hand-to-shoulder are attempting to cross a seemingly harmless stream. The front two have fallen on the rocks, and it doesn't look good for the others.

I slowly closed the door.

"Glenwood?" I called to my best friend.

Without moving any other part of his body, the Owl slowly, almost ominously, raised his left hand to hush me. The expression on his face was both utter bewilderment and deep, oceanic peace. His enormous forehead was furrowed in rubbery, cabbage-like folds.

Basically, he looked like he was in a lot of pain.

"Can you hear it, Homon?" he asked me.

"Hear what?"

"The ringing."

I listened for a moment.

"Um. I don't hear anything, Glenwood," I offered gently.

"Calliope music, Homon. Tinkling, chiming calliope music. Listen."

"I'm listening, buddy."

"Tinkle tinkle chime."

"*Tinkle tinkle chime?*"

"Jingle jingle skinnyclink."

"*Skinnyclink?*"

"Like it's hundreds of miles away, Homon. Skinnyclink jingle-jingle. Twinkle twinkle tambourine ring. Hundreds and thousands of miles away . . ."

I turned to the Loach.

"Loach, do you hear anything?" I asked, but he'd doled out his daily ration of language and was all about the fan now. I would even go so far as to say that he was mentally making love to it.

"Loach?" I pleaded.

"I ate your ramen and three bowls of Wheaties. Are you fucking pissed?"

I turned back to the Owl.

"Do you wanna kick my ass?" the Loach egged. "You should kick my ass. I'm such a dick."

"Glenwood," I called to the Owl.

"Yeah, Homon?"

"Can you move?"

"I can move," he said, almost comfortingly.

"Are you in any kind of physical pain?"

"No, there's just the ringing."

"It's probably from reading. You read way too much."

"It's not from reading."

"Maybe it's tinnitus."

"What's that?"

"When you experience buzzing in your ears."

"It's not a buzzing."

"Well, can you describe it?"

"It's astral."

"*Astral?*"

"Like stars, Homon. Little stars. Weeping."

I listened again. I tried to tilt my head at the same isoscelean angle the Owl was employing.

I concentrated.

I even stopped breathing.

I heard nothing.

"Or a dog whistle," he continued.

"An astral dog whistle?"

"A weeping astral dog whistle, Homon. There's a sadness at work. A deep-space melancholy. Like a lost astronaut. A lost astronaut playing the saw."

"On a little weeping star?"

"Yes, Homon! And he wants to come home!"

"I'll bet."

"But no one can hear his tiny . . ."

". . . Space song?"

"His tiny space song, exactly!"

"Maybe you should go to the hospital, Glenwood."

"No, Homon, this is bigger than the hospital."

"Tell him one of his balls is dangling," the Loach blurted out in his dehydrated, lugubrious baritone.

And for some reason, despite the fact that winter was upon us and these two were still living in their underwear; despite the three ribbons of insect-peppered flypaper that had been tacked to the ceiling since the end of August; despite the enormous hide of snow that was amassing on the northern ramparts of Tenth Street, seemingly adding a full story to an already congested tenement skyline; despite the dishes in the sink that were starting to fossilize with a pasty rigor mortis; despite the fan, whose indifferent propeller noisily sent the sour, milky-smelling air of half-naked men throughout the living room; despite all that was askew, off track, absent, unfulfilled, unpaid for, unwashed, and forlorn, I took the Loach's advice.

"Glenwood," I called to my best friend.

"Yeah, Homon?" he answered.

"One of your balls is dangling."

But he did not respond to this, so I simply left him there in Feick's boxer shorts, an index finger lightly prodding his ear, his black shock of pubic hair somehow accruing a kind of arboreal mythology, like that of the small, highly revered West Indian divi-divi tree.

Later that night I met Basha at Polly Parker's on Fifth Street. The café had maybe fifteen tables and the menu—a single sheet of laminated white papyrus—listed several sandwiches, salads, and a few homemade soups. On the back were domestic and foreign beers and a wine list so vast you would have thought important epicureans from all over the world frequented the small café.

The walls were decorated with a mosaic of ceramic tiles, shards of broken mirror, and what appeared to be artistically rarefied pieces of shattered coffee cups.

Over the sound system Johnny Cash's *Live at Folsom Prison* played at a low volume.

There were maybe five occupied tables and Basha was waiting on an old man wearing a red hunter's hat who couldn't decide between the Caesar salad and the chicken pesto sandwich. When our eyes met she looked at me in a way that almost made me lose my balance and I had to quickly sit. Her hair was pulled back and her eyes looked enormous. She wore a dark turtleneck and black pants with a white apron. She continued to wait on the man in the red hunter's hat, recommending the chicken pesto sandwich, saying that it was "inexplicably miraculous." The man thanked her for the tip and Basha moved to the kitchen counter to put the order through. Moments later she returned to the dining area and slowly, almost teasingly, made her way to my table.

"Hello mysterious boyish man," she said.

"Hello mysterious girlish woman," I replied.

"Are you horribly destroyed by the unrelenting snow?"

"Not too horribly."

"Many ruffian boys in puffy, rap-style winter blouses were hurling snow bullets at the buses earlier. It was fastidiously entertaining. Look . . ."

With her perfect, delicate hand, Basha pointed toward the east-facing window, where a thoroughly bundled woman wearing a football helmet was waiting under the First Avenue bus-stop shelter. Despite being protected by its roof (not to mention the football helmet), she was holding a black umbrella. Moments later, the northbound M15 emerged, stopped, and silently intercepted her, and just as it started to pull away a band of five or six young boys clad in enormous winter parkas and multicolored ski masks materialized, double-fisted with snowballs, and pelted the bus ambush-style. After their assault, a few of them slipped and helped one another up, and then they disappeared around the corner.

"Such urban pandemonium," Basha observed beautifully. "Are you terribly famished?" she asked.

"I'm starving, actually," I replied.

"The soup is hearty Yankee bean with ham," Basha offered, gently placing her hand on the back of my neck. This simple, effortless gesture almost knocked the wind out of me.

"I'll have the soup," I said. "And a grilled cheese sandwich."

Basha took her hand back and wrote my order on a check.

"For suitable hydration?" she asked.

"Just a Coke."

When Basha turned away I felt a strange sense of loss that I can only identify as self-indulgent, artificial pathos. Part of this, I'm sure, stemmed from the fact that she had to attend to other customers. I had never thought of myself as the jealous type but suddenly I didn't want to share Basha's attention.

I had the distinct impression that the other customers in the small café (four or five middle-aged East Village veterans) could see through me, that underneath my clothes was an inexperienced, naive schoolboy wrestling with his hysterical, romantically deprived nervous system.

"Hi," I greeted a woman who was staring at me in a manner that made me feel profoundly bovine. Her face had the unfortunate consistency of wet Kleenex. She was bundled in several layers of shirts and sweaters and was so thoroughly ensconced in a corner of that café she could have been a disgruntled tenant squatting on her few square feet of brick-colored ceramic tiles. At her table was a bowl of the Yankee bean soup, around which she had carefully arranged several weather-beaten paperback novels, a carton of Parliament cigarettes, and a geometrically perfect star of orange dominoes.

In response to my greeting she simply nodded and thrust her spoon into the blond bog of her soup.

In the opposite corner a fiftyish man with long gray hair was reading Samuel R. Delany's *Dhalgren*. A highly respected college professor once said that this novel was the only way we unfortunate, end-of-decade, precentennial babies could truly experience the sixties. The man was blank-faced and ate while he read, a skill I'd always admired but could never seem to master.

When Basha returned with my Coke and soup she sat down across from me and took my hand under the table.

"Your hand is terribly frozen."

"My hands and feet are like that," I explained.

Her fingers were warm and delicate, and I was finding it hard to concentrate. Her large green eyes were making me feel like time was in the process of some strange, penumbral distortion, that these few precious moments had an unbearable, historical magnitude, that the reality of the café with all of its simple, cozy comforts was skidding a bit. "It has something do to with long extremities," I continued, attempting to excuse my clammy hands.

"Extremities?"

"Arms and legs," I explained. "The longest parts of us."

Basha took her hand back and wrote my definition of extremities on the cardboard base of her menu pad, alongside several other English words and their accompanying definitions. I helped her spell out the word, as I could see she was clearly struggling. After she finished, she returned the menu pad to the pocket of her apron and again took my hand under the table.

"So are you having a superlative day?" she asked.

"Certainly more superlative than most days," I answered. "I actually have some good news," I added, forced nonchalant.

I went on to tell her about Alexa's response to my novel. To this news, Basha smiled and said, "This is cause for vigorous celebration, no?"

"A vigorous celebration might be a little premature at this point. She only read the first fifty pages. She's passing it on to her boss. But it's a good start, nonetheless."

"I am filled with much pleasure for you."

Briefly, I imagined Basha filled with "much pleasure," and it wasn't the magnanimous, neighborly kind.

"How's this going?" I asked, referring to the general surroundings in an attempt to discuss things practical.

"So-so. Not a pleasurable amount of extraordinary tips. The supreme shifts are Saturday and Sunday for the famous Polly Parker's brunch with secret Bloody Mary alcoholic beverage. But these aren't bestowed to you until you pay the deuce. So now is my time to pay the deuce." She squeezed my hand for another moment. "Would you like to see me when I am presented with relief of my professional duties? Perhaps I can visit you at your apartment on Tenth Street between First and A," Basha suggested. "And we can not quite celebrate the effervescent news about your novel."

For a moment, the Roman Catholic–reared, all-around-good-guy part of me wanted to ask her if she was sure, if this would upset János in Eastern Europe, but I simply said, "Okay."

Basha then released my hand and walked over to the woman playing dominoes, dropped off her check, and made change for another customer. When she was finished she came back.

"I accomplish my duties at eleven p.m. Please write your address on this parcel," Basha instructed, handing me a pen and a napkin. While printing out my address I felt as if I were passing into some unknown East Village vector of neighborhood space that only a few privileged Midwesterners are allowed to encounter.

What could possibly happen on this snowy night?

I folded the napkin in half and handed it and the pen back to her.

"Enjoy your soup," Basha said and turned away, tending to the other patrons and all of their less important needs.

For the next twenty minutes I ate my soup and grilled cheese sandwich and thought about how much had changed in the past few days: Feick and his new lifestyle; the Loach's attempt at gainful employment; my steadily healing knee and the excitement about my novel; Basha's unflinching, totally welcome advances.

For a few brief moments the world seemed so full of possibility, and even things that I hadn't eaten yet tasted delicious.

———

When I got home from the café the Owl was in almost the same spot in the living room, now wearing a hooded burnoose with vertical blue stripes. He was kneeling over an enormous piece of butcher's paper like some desert-blown Moroccan Berber.

An assortment of markers and colored pencils were strewn about and it appeared that he was using them to create an arts-and-crafts project.

The Loach was still on the sofa. The fan had been turned off and he was napping in a seated position. His *Wolverine* comic book had been rolled and inserted into the waistband of his underwear.

I watched the Owl at work for a moment. With a black Sharpie he was thickening a long line that was punctuated here and there with hash marks.

"Glenwood, what are you doing?"

For a moment I thought he was completing one of his group projects for business school, but there was a quality to the drawing and color scheme that was more evocative of the path of a child's first bike ride without training wheels.

"Don't you have class tonight?" I asked.

"I dropped."

"You can drop classes in grad school?"

"I mean *out*, Homon. I dropped *out*."

"Oh."

The dull, persistent sound of flying snow could be heard and for a moment I thought the fan had somehow commenced autogenously.

"You, like, *dropped out* dropped out?" I asked.

"Out of Columbia Business School, yes."

"Whoa," I said. "Do you have a plan?"

"I'm gonna play the guitar."

"The *guitar*?"

"Six-string acoustic guitar," he said, breathing heavily. "I already went over to Mojo Guitar on St. Mark's. Put fifty bucks down on a Fender. I'm gonna go pay off the rest of it tomorrow, as soon as my student-loan check clears." He took a few rapid breaths and continued. "I bought a chord book, too. Gonna grow my hair long. Maybe buy a van."

"Seriously?"

"There's a seventy-one VW Bus for sale on Sixth between First and A. Only forty thousand miles on it. Rebuilt engine, new curtains in the windows. The guy's asking twelve hundred."

"You're really gonna do this?"

"I'm gonna write songs, Homon. Drive around and write the great American novel on the guitar. That's all I wanna do."

"What about your student loans?"

"They'll still be there."

"What about our no westbound buses agreement?"

"It's not a westbound bus, Homon, it's a VW bus, which is quite the opposite. In fact I would even say that it's the antithesis of a westbound bus. My plan is to head in every direction *but* Kansas."

Then the Owl spun around and started writing numbers below the hash marks, consecutive numbers starting with twenty-two and ending at thirty, the kind of bright, colorful numbers that might be found on the sides of Formula One race cars.

"Glenwood, does this have anything to do with the ringing in your ears?"

"It has everything to do with it and nothing do to with it. Everything and nothing."

When I stepped closer I could see that the Owl was creating a timeline of his twenties. Next to "22" he had written:

Graduated from KU Phi Beta Kappa. Bought Dodge Dart from Dad for three hundred dollars. Drove to Ojai, California. Slept on the side of the road. Stole oranges and avocados from local orchard. Saw Pacific Coast rattlesnake coiled on a dirt path. Turned and walked in opposite direction. Later that same night encountered a small mountain lion. Made myself big like they say you should. Stared at each other for several minutes. Learned more in that stare than anything taught at KU.

Next to "24":

Taught English in Kromeriz, Czechoslovakia. Learned to speak Czech. Fell in love with beautiful student. Her husband was a lumberjack with a vast and terrifying beard. On Easter Sunday he punched me in the jaw and later that night we slow-danced to several Elvis Presley songs at the local tavern. A place where they serve beer for breakfast. A single American dollar can feed you for two days. Learned more in my tourist ignorance than anything taught at KU.

Next to "25":

Took train ride in Thailand. A thin, ailing man spat in the aisle for several consecutive hours. Had to walk over his monstrous pool of bloody phlegm on my way to the bathroom, where I defecated into a hole that had been cut into the floor. There was a bowl of sanitary water next to the hole, mosquitoes swirling about its surface. I learned more staring into that hole than anything I learned at KU.

The strange, vignetted autobiography, which also chronicled his seven months in New York, was oddly moving. I wasn't sure if the timeline was intended to be presented to fellow MBA candidates or if it was an entirely personal endeavor. I had never seen the Owl more passionate about anything in his life.

"Acoustic six-string," the Owl said, his burnoose bunched around his legs, a red Sharpie clutched in his right hand now. "D-A-G. E-A-B. C-G-F."

In the street someone had engaged some sort of vertical floodlight and the snow was suddenly backlit in the window.

"Verse, chorus, verse, chorus, bridge, solo, chorus, outro."

Its angling flight seemed to possess a kind of omnipotence. For a moment, the Owl turned to it as if it were whispering lyrics to him.

Basha buzzed the apartment just past midnight. After I let her in I opened the door and listened to her steady, careful ascent up the four flights of stairs. I shone a flashlight down through the stairwell so she could find the railing, as the common-area Con Ed service had been interrupted yet again. Her shadow sawed through each landing, noir-like.

When she reached the fourth floor she was brushing the weather off of her navy peacoat. Illuminated by the flashlight beam, the snowflakes in her eyelashes looked like the silvery dust of precious gems.

By this time, the Owl was bivouacking in his bedroom with his timeline project. The Loach was sleeping on the sofa. His toy soldier's uniform, hidden before, had been pulled over his thin, hairy shoulders as an improvised blanket. He looked like some vagrant Civil War soldier who had expired before finding the triage site. He was clutching the bearskin shako as if it were something that would absolve him of all transgressions.

I quietly led Basha to my room. This served two functions: (1) a home-tour deflection, so she wouldn't have to experience the general decay of our unkempt bachelor pad, and (2) a quick escape; the sooner I got her out of the living room the less likely it was that she would have to be introduced to a waking Loach.

In my room I closed the door and quickly kicked a few pairs of dirty underwear under my futon. I apologized for the mess and Basha shooed off my act of contrition, calling the room an "expedient bear's nest."

My desk had been overrun by reams of blank paper (stolen from the office), my versatile dictionary-slash-thesaurus, and the floes and drifts of typed manuscript, legal pads, spiral notebooks, doodled envelopes, napkins, Post-its, and other compositional flotsam that I had failed to work into my novel. Stupidly, I attempted to tidy things, as if restoring order would somehow ease the tension that was mounting like the very snow settling on the Tenth Street rooftops.

After I made a few neat piles of papers, while Basha continued to politely stand, I closed the curtains and attempted to configure my futon into sofa-mode, but its joints wouldn't budge. With the side of my hand, I hammered dumbly at the frame seven or eight times and then finally gave up after Basha insisted that we simply sit on my "lair" in its present state. I suggested that we keep our coats on as the room was only fifteen degrees or so warmer than the street. To Basha, huddling in full winter regalia was "exceedingly romantic" and she said that the only thing that could possibly "further accent" such an "amorous situation" would be if it was actually snowing in the room. I told her about how during the previous evening the Owl swore that he could see his breath smoking out of his mouth in silvery plumes. I then showed her my small, lozenge-shaped heating pad, and we took turns switching it on and off.

Outside of a digital alarm clock whose reception was limited to an AM, Spanish-speaking station, my small room was tragically ill-equipped with music or any other form of electronic entertainment.

After we'd exhausted all possible fun with the heating pad, we sat on my futon and said nothing. The spill of wintry light from between the curtains gave the room a dank lunar quality that seemed only to further deepen Basha's beauty. From here on in we sat largely in silence, with the exception of a brief exchange about where I got so many books. I told Basha that I acquired most of them at work, that this was the nicest job perk I had. Then she asked what "job perk" meant and I expounded on what I'd started to tell her on the bus during our first date, conveying some poorly thought out half-truth having to do with freebies, the catered bestseller celebrations, and employee benefits. She then wrote "perk" in a small notepad that she removed from the pocket of her navy peacoat. Next to it, she wrote "frisbees," "bestsellers," and "employee benefit." For the moment, I let "frisbees" go, as the English lessons were starting to feel a little tedious.

From there our silence took on an apprehensive chill that felt prompted by the snow falling outside my window. We stared at my bare walls, riddled with nail holes, water stains, and the faint lightning of cracked plaster.

When Basha finally took my hand we both exhaled nervously and lowered our overly bundled bodies to the futon. Outside, the sounds of the East Village—a distant, forlorn police siren; pedestrian chatter; the occasional car alarm; the soft, inevitable thrum of mounting snow—

seemed not only suddenly beautiful, but somehow essential. These noises became the quiet, unremarkable score to perhaps the most unforgettable night of my life.

Eventually, Basha would unbutton my corduroy coat and place her head under my chin. Her hair smelled faintly of chicken soup and cigarette smoke. I could feel the heat in her cheek radiating through my sweater and T-shirt.

We passed the next twenty minutes wordlessly. We shared a strange, mutual desperation that was both gentle and frightening. When our mouths finally found each other, their union was followed by groping hands, interlocking legs, awkwardly shed clothes, and a vision of female nudity that surpasses all flora, trees, birds, waterfalls, lily pads, unicorns, mermaids, lightning storms, spiderwebs, robin eggs, twilit buffalo, celestial corona, and other prodigy and phenomena of Mother Nature's various manifestations of perfection.

Making love with Basha wasn't so much a physical act as it was a kind of time-travel lesson in the origins of human feeling and quixotic pleasure. It was like falling into a deep, dark, soporific pond whose breathable, velveteen waters were derived of the purest opiate; a standing volume of narcotic liquid to which there was no foreseeable bottom.

And there was nothing to do but sink further down.

Just before dawn I walked Basha back to Stuyvesant Town in the snow.

When I woke, she was sitting up, my Midwestern prep-school blanket bunched around her waist. She was still naked and looking toward the spill of window light as if she were utterly lost, even scared. There was a small constellation of tiny moles between her shoulder blades that looked as if it had been artfully arranged. Her strange, quiet vulnerability inspired in me an impulse to hold her, but I opted for restraint, as one who is wandering through a museum is wise to refrain from touching the art.

In the bluish moonlight, I watched Basha gather her clothes and slip into her bra. Her slight, round breasts were aroused by the cold air. She stopped for a moment and took the heating pad and pressed it to herself, gazing at some unknown space that held her stare so intensely it was as if she were glimpsing something profound that was inaccessible to the rest of the world.

Through a series of simple gestures she communicated that she had to use the bathroom, and I gave her directions with my thumb. She then put my corduroy coat on in such a way that I wished she would never take it off and exited.

While she was away I watched my alarm clock clip away a full minute. It was five-twenty a.m., and I decided this was the most perfect needle of time in the history of the world. It was better than N.C. State's Lorenzo Charles's last-second tip-in to win the 1988 NCAA Championship, better even than Kirk Gibson's walk-off home run to win game one of the 1988 World Series (his only at-bat of the series). For a few fleeting moments I honestly couldn't decipher whether the events of the past few hours had actually happened or if they were part of some half-remembered idyll.

After Basha returned from the bathroom, she sat and leaned against me for a few minutes, her nudity warm and soft under my coat. My alarm clock read 5:27 a.m. now.

Basha said things would not "be exceedingly swimming" if "Dragan" knew she had spent the entire night somewhere.

"Who's Dragan?" I asked.

"My father."

I imagined a large, fire-breathing man with massive, reptilian shoulders.

We dressed quietly. The floor was freezing and, as the Owl had reported, we could indeed see our breath animating in front of us in silvery gusts.

I'm not sure how much guilt or shame contributed to Basha's need to leave. I have no idea how often she thought of János. Perhaps she saw him while we made love, his face floating, sentry-like, over my shoulder. While putting on my jeans I did recall a stanza or two of Polish that she had whispered hotly in my ear. The words were mysterious and hard and cut directly through me.

On the street it was still snowing, although the volume had thinned and the blizzard's diagonal cant had redressed perpendicularly, as if Mother Nature herself had admonished it for poor form.

Basha and I held hands while we walked to Stuyvesant Town. Shop owners, defiant of the blizzard's power of economic devastation, were busy behind their dimly lit storefronts, wiping down counters and mixing egg salad and preparing hopefully for another day of neighborhood commerce. Taxis slowly slalomed between lanes, adopting a newer, gentler form of driving. The M15 bus glided north, almost dangerously close to the thoroughly salted eastern curb. The sidewalks were quiet. Even the stoplights had an air of wintry solitude.

During our walk Basha and I said nothing, and before she entered her building at Twentieth Street, we hugged and kissed wetly and stood there leaning against each other. While there was no doubt that whatever we were feeling was mutual and that the strange, subtle desperation that precipitates between two people who fall into the warm, breathable sea of love had already submerged us, there was also a palpable, almost crushing feeling of fear and uncertainty.

"Will I see you again?" I asked, scared as hell.

"You will see me again, yes," Basha said assuredly. Then she turned and entered her building. As before, I watched her call and board the elevator.

The walk home was crushingly lonely.

I took note of very few things, except for the rim of eastern light and how within the span of a few blocks it was turning decidedly gray.

Coke and Sunny

AFTER I GOT HOME I had trouble falling back to sleep. I was at once exhausted and filled with a caffeine-like buzz. Love, I discovered, will dope up your anabolic chemistry more treacherously than most over-the-counter antihistamines.

On our answering machine there was a message from Van instructing me to not bother coming to the office because of the blizzard. My first day off in seven months would no doubt be a lazy, cold, monastic reprieve of much-needed privacy, complete with a trip to the corner deli for coffee and ramen noodles, a few hours of dedication to a good book (Haruki Murakami's *A Wild Sheep Chase*), and pleasant thoughts of the night before tumbling through the chilly air of my bedroom like invisible, inebriated butterflies.

Of course, the literary soldier in me, though weakened as of late, would also forge ahead on *Opie's Half-life*. I vowed that no less than half the day would be spent at my desk, my lozenge-shaped heating pad warming my lap.

At around eleven o'clock, after I had settled into a complicated reading cocoon, someone buzzed the apartment.

When I engaged the push-button two-way communication system so wondrously featured on our PA–slash–surveillance monitor unit, I was greeted by a pure, virginal-sounding young woman's voice announcing she was half of a duet called "Coke and Sunny."

"Hello," I called into the nebula of New York City apartment surveillance.

"It's Coke and Sunny!" the voice called back on the other end.

The first thing that came to mind was a pair of conservatively dressed, look-alike Mormon debutantes—perhaps twins—who were the highly entertaining, scripture-quoting hosts of some corporate-sponsored Christian-rock variety show involving Say No to Drugs parables, Good Samaritan–themed spiritual anthems (with accompanying hand-clapping, tambourines a-ringing), and a menagerie of life-size, genderless Nerf puppets. The woman went on to explain that they had arrived to "move Feick's stuff."

On the other end of our connection I could hear the wind and the snow and a few pedestrians barking like wayward sea lions in the face of a monsoon.

"Move his stuff where?" I asked.

"Chelsea," she said.

"Did Feick know you were coming?"

"We arranged it over the phone this morning," she explained. "He paid us a hundred bucks."

"How do you know him?"

"He came and spoke to our class yesterday. It was Visit with the Artist Day."

"Come on, dude, it's rough out here," a young man's voice croaked into the PA. My tag-teaming Mormon debutante fantasy was debunked. The other half of the duo was male! For a moment, I could almost make out their forms on the blurry screen of the monitor. For some reason I came to the conclusion that Coke was the male.

"Fourth floor," I instructed, and I buzzed them in.

Not more than thirty seconds later I was greeted by what appeared to be two teenage siblings geminating up the stairs, each hauling a bundle of flattened boxes. The male was also carrying a tape gun not unlike the one I used for rep mailings. They were both blond and outfitted in knit green hats, brown corduroys, puffy ski parkas, and low-top canvas basketball shoes. In addition to their coordinated outfits, they each possessed enormous, doll-like blue eyes.

"Hey!" the girl said through her load, her face smiling as though she was not performing a physically challenging task, but rather toting a small galaxy of brightly colored helium balloons. She was pretty in the way that young women in department-store catalogs are pretty, and she had a smile that boasted dental perfection. "I'm Coke," she added. "This is Sunny."

How does one acquire a name like Coke? I wondered. Sunny I could buy. But Coke?

"Are you the Owl?" Coke asked. Already I could tell that she was the kind of person whose sentences, regardless of their punctuation, ascended a light major scale as they neared their conclusions.

"I'm Feick's brother, actually," I explained.

"Oh, that's right," Coke said, her eyes sparkly and unblinking. "He *did* mention a brother. You must be so proud of him."

"We're all proud of Feick," I offered obliquely.

"He said his room was down the hall to the left," Sunny noted, getting to the business of the day. His voice was the direct opposite of Coke's, unusually deep and hoarse, as if he'd just awakened from hibernation.

"Down the hall to the left, that's correct," I replied.

"Well, he's paying us by the hour so we better get to work," Coke added, smiling her glycerin smile.

"Tell him about the books," Sunny grumbled.

"Oh, that's right!" Coke chirped. "Feick said you guys could have his footlocker and he wanted to know if he could leave his books! Apparently, Ruben's having new shelves built and they won't be ready for another month or two! They're being custom made by this total artisan down in Peru!"

Why she felt the need to share Ruben's exotic interior-design plans with me, I had no idea.

I said, "Leave the books. No problem."

"And the bills, too," Sunny bellowed.

"Right!" Coke tweeted. "Feick said he'd pop a money order in the mail for his share of the phone and Con Ed."

"Great" was all I could muster.

Before Coke turned and headed down the hall, she examined me closely for a moment and said, "It must be really special having someone so talented in the family."

"It's a blessing for us all," I said.

"Weren't you a professional volleyball player in Tortola or something?" Coke asked.

"Um, no. I played basketball. In college. I never played pro."

"I swore Feick said you played volleyball in Tortola. That's too bad, cuz Sunny and I play on this really great coed intramural team at NYU and you're allowed one ringer per team. We were gonna get this girl in Park Slope who makes these Native American spirit rugs with a loom. She actually *did* play professionally in Brazil. Feick told us about you so we thought we'd offer you a spot first."

"You're probably better off going with the rug-maker," I offered.

"Yeah, you're probably right," Coke said sweetly. "Oh, well. Basketball's fun, too! You're younger, right?"

"Three and a half years older, actually."

"You're joshing," Coke responded, genuinely surprised.

This was a bit of a blow to my self-esteem that went far beyond the obvious. When I was sixteen and still genitally hairless, one day, at a whopping twelve years old, Feick had come out of the shower and while he walked down the hall his towel fell, exposing a veritable fleece factory of nappy white pubic hair that caught the light in such a way that it looked almost divine. It would take me another six months before my own pubic hair would start to sprout. Despite my being the starting guard on the varsity basketball team I was tragically prepubescent, and my very little brother had already pulled well ahead of me in the area of pubic sophistication.

"Don't I look older?" I asked with a little added volume.

"Well, taller, yes, but not necessarily older," Coke answered sensitively.

"Is Feick's voice, like, *deeper* or something?" I asked desperately.

"Totally deeper, dude," Sunny answered, his boxes perched on his head now.

"Well, not that much deeper," Coke said, no doubt sensing my teetering pride.

Just then, the bathroom door opened and the Loach appeared, half in his snowmobile suit. I made a point of not looking for evidence of the purported crapping episode.

"This is Burton Loach," I offered politely.

"Hi there, Burton!" Coke said, bursting with her endless morning vigor.

"Hey, dude," Sunny added.

"Call me the Loach, twatfucks," my roommate ramrodded.

"Yeah, he goes by the Loach," I said.

Then we all just stood there in the hallway for a moment. Sunny cleared his throat and shifted his bundle of boxes to the floor. For a second I thought he was preparing to fight. Part of me honestly hoped that Sunny would kick the Loach's ass.

"People with titles are so cool!" Coke then offered.

"What?" the Loach said, sour-faced as ever. His beard contained bits and remains of indescribable things. His bare chest was grotesque and alarming, the tonsure a hippodrome of dandruff, psoriasis, and other lesser-known scalp conditions. There was also some sort of rash forming an inflamed halo around his left nipple. After a moment he shouldered past us and, in five or six monster-movie strides, reclaimed the sofa.

"Okay, then," Coke said, exhaling mightily, and she and Sunny took their bundles down the hall, opened Feick's door, closed it behind them, and got to work.

For the rest of the day I attempted to work on my novel while fighting a persistent, seven-hour bout with conflict narcolepsy. My protagonist suddenly felt inactive. Useless paragraphs started to mount on the page like drifts of clipped hair on a barbershop floor.

I drank about seven cups of coffee, but that only loosened my stool and I ended up spending more time on the toilet than at my desk.

I was also distracted by a desperate need to hear Basha's voice. I tried to call her several times but her phone was busy. I imagined her engaged in a heartfelt, dramatic conversation with János, one filled with newfound promises, absence-induced sweet nothings, and the heightened poetry of the lovelorn.

Eventually, I drifted off in a fitful pontoon boat of sleep that was plagued by strange and elusive dreams, one of which involved the task of assembling enormous boxes for a rep mailing that contained not selling samples or star reports, but several hundred pounds of freshly fallen East Village snow.

I woke up in the middle of the night with my sheets twisted around my limbs and a bad case of cottonmouth. When I went into the living room for a glass of water there was yet another palpable absence in the apartment.

The Owl was gone.

The door to his bedroom was wide open and his room appeared to have been ransacked. All of his bedding had been stripped and his wardrobe had been cleared out of his closet. Only his books and his map-of-the-world time-zone clock were preserved in their usual well-proportioned positions on his monolithic brick-and-scavenged-lumber bookshelf. His nineteenth-century bentwood rocking chair was vacant, so I sat down and rocked a bit.

Then I went to the kitchen and opened the storage fridge, only to find that the white plastic cylindrical forest of his various contact solutions was also gone.

I closed the fridge and went back into his room.

Bunched under his futon was the large piece of butcher paper he had used to craft the autobiographical timeline of his twenties. I opted to leave it under the bed.

I closed his door and went into the bathroom, where there was a letter taped to the toothpaste-splattered mirror. In a sloppy penmanship scrawled in green ink it read:

DEAR HOMON,
I know this is not the best way to say goodbye, but I couldn't stand sticking around any longer. I had to get away while I still had the balls.

I bought the VW bus and I'm off. By the time you read this, I'll probably be on some great interstate heading toward the horizon. I promise on the eyes of my periwinkle soul that I'm not heading back to Kansas, Homon.

Not to worry, the bus is in good condition and I have enough cash to get by. Feel free to take any of the clothes that I left behind, as well as my books. I think you'll particularly enjoy The Alexandria Quartet. *And the clock is yours. Please say farewell to Feick for me.*

I would advise getting Burton out of the apartment as soon as possible. My gut is that the fucker is a lot darker than we think. I don't know. I just have a weird vibe about him.

Good luck with the novel, Homon. And don't let the machine grind you up. You are meat, but be meat that moves.

No westbound buses!

Stay warm, my friend. I'll be in touch.

AS EVER,

GLENWOOD

I removed the letter, folded it in half, and headed back to the Owl's bedroom, where *The Alexandria Quartet* was indeed waiting for me in its cardboard omnibus sleeve.

I have to admit that when I took *The Alexandria Quartet* into my arms I cried. And although these tears were few and unaccompanied by song, sob, or heave, they were no doubt the tears of serious melodrama, and for a fleeting moment I felt like a clichéd fallen hero. After a brief recovery period I made my way back to the living room.

On the sofa, the Loach was reading his *Wolverine* comic book for the fortieth time, his snowmobile suit snapped up to the chin.

"So who's the Russian chick?" he asked, flipping through the comic book like a man searching for his favorite month in a pinup calendar.

"She's Polish," I responded, still a bit stunned by the Owl's departure. "Great ass."

He flipped through a few pages and laughed through his nose. It was the maniacal laugh of some wicked, syphilitic clown on the lam. The laugh died almost as quickly as it had erupted. "Not bad-looking, either," he added, still turning those pages.

"Burton, I think we need to talk."

My tone was firm yet amicable.

"Burton's a small town outside of Flint, Michigan, where people in trailer parks fuck each other with car parts. Call me the Loach or call yourself a cab. What's her name, anyway?" he asked, still flipping through the comic.

"Basha. But you're not listening to me."

"Basha," he snorted and adjusted his testicles. "That rhymes with Kasha: a hearty buckwheat hot-breakfast cereal. Yum-yum delicious. Did you get any stank on your hangdown?"

"Did I get any *what*?"

"Stank on your hangdown."

It took me a moment to process the possible meaning of the phrase.

"Did your dick achieve wetness?" the Loach queried on. "As in vaginal fluids, juice from the gash-goose."

"I'm starting to have violent thoughts about you, Burton."

This was more of a statement of fact than a confession.

". . . slot syrup, cunt cola . . ."

The door, I said to myself. Just move toward the door to your bedroom. Put one foot in front of the other and start walking.

I thought about snapping his neck in an efficient three-part move.

". . . flounder froth, beaver bisque . . ."

Or stabbing him in the kidney with a paring knife.

". . . twat soda, camel-toe flow . . ."

Or strangling him with guitar strings.

". . . labia lava, fallopian fizz, genital jiffy lube . . ."

Or asphyxiating him with a deli bag.

Part Three

John Anderson-Allensworth

THE SNOW GOT DIRTY.

My East Village winter wonderland was short-lived. Brown, septic-looking floes of slush now pooled at curb corners. Dog shit resurfaced like some strange breed of limbless, cooked rodent desperate for oxygen. A sickly, viral rime of street salt clung to the trunks of garbage cans, the skeletons of abandoned ten-speeds (still chained to the stems of street signs), and the fenders and wheel wells of parked cars.

It had been three weeks since the Owl's departure and I still hadn't heard from him. I would go into his room periodically and stare at his clock of the world, wondering where he was off to, romanticizing his travels to places like Corsica and the south of France (VW Bus improbably included), the Owl donning only a sarong and hemp sandals, smoking kif with Paul Bowles in Morocco, his acoustic guitar slung over his shoulder, the strings rusted, the neck scarred.

Nor had I heard from Feick, last seen amid the squalls of Chelsea. The closest thing to contact with him had been my brief interaction with Coke and Sunny. His room felt so empty I swore an audible drone murmured off the walls.

For a few weeks, the Loach and I learned to live in a communicative moratorium. Between us there was neither animosity nor the slightest gesture of goodwill. It wasn't so much a solidarity of silence as the kind of rote social subsistence that the elderly sometimes exhibit on buses and park benches. When I'd come home from work I'd either go straight to my room or open up the freezer to greet my yet-to-be-completed first draft of *Opie's Half-life*, running my hand over its surface, feigning interest in the other things that were taking up space in our warm refrigerator (more comedy flyers, a voided tube of Bengay, an orphaned navy blue Chuck Taylor low-top Converse All-Star basketball sneaker, size ten), and then head to my room.

While we gathered the garbage the only thing that spoke was the plastic skin of the deli bags. We did not share looks or nods. Nor did we mime, gesticulate, or improvise sign language. Besides the whirring of the fan, the occasional far-off bloodcurdling East Village scream, or the chorus of car alarms refraining from the street below, the common area was quiet.

In the bathroom, I would carefully remove the Loach's body hair from the drain while he stood at the sink, scratching the eczema that had begun forming around his lint-filled navel. In the living room, while I collected the yellow toenail clippings that he'd scissor off with the Owl's utility shears, he would simply stare at the cracked plaster above the fireplace, and through some process of domestic adaptation he would accrue a kind of human furniture quality, slowly sinking deeper and deeper into the cushions of the sofa.

Things actually almost grew to be polite.

On any given trip across the living room the Loach could be seen watching the fan with his hand down the front of his snowmobile suit. Every so often he would remove his hand and sniff his fingers. Once I saw him pick his nose after sniffing his fingers and then put his hand back down the front of his snowmobile suit. Perhaps he was gathering data for his purported stand-up audience?

After all, the Loach was an artist!

He was wielding his cultural mirror!

The waves of silence that precipitated in the apartment were occasionally scored by hacks, belches, snorts, and an assortment of the Loachian farts that ranged from the decaying cry of a beleaguered oboe to the foghorn-like detonations of the lone tuba player preparing for marching-band duties around the local high-school track.

Although there's no doubt we were quietly opposed to developing even the most marginal friendship, I'd like to believe that in those weeks there were the beginnings of a strange, protracted evolution of domestic grace at work, the kind of primordial, creature-to-creature acceptance that had perhaps occurred in firelit prehistoric caves.

Or to bring the trope into the ovine world, we were like rival Suffolk sheep that had strayed from our flock and were forced to share a few acres of some unknown English countryside.

Although warmth was not a temperature I could rely on from Burton Loach, in terms of human thermodynamics Basha had become a dependable, passionate oven radiating all the heat I could ever need. We would often meet at Polly Parker's toward the end of her shift, where she would sneak me a lidded Styrofoam cup of their homemade chicken noodle soup and a packet of oyster crackers, slyly charging me a dollar for takeout coffee. I would always tip her two dollars, but days later, invariably, these crumpled bills would turn up in the breast pocket of my corduroy coat or under my desk.

We made love on my futon with regularity and I looked forward to her company with a quality I can describe only as acute joy-terror. Joy for obvious reasons. Terror because there was *so much* joy, and this exultant happiness often ends with a profound absence of itself, which, in turn, can only be replaced by its darker, more depressing converse.

I knew I was swimming in very deep water and I was happy to naively pretend that there were porpoises circling playfully, not hammerhead sharks.

In addition to my professorial duty of mentoring Basha's always-expanding English vocabulary, I occasionally helped her with her acting auditions, most of which were open calls she would find listed in *Back Stage* or hear about through the small but thorny grapevine of downtown New York theatre. One character she went in for was a genderless singing zebra at the center of a children's holiday fantasy being produced in Elizabeth, New Jersey, called *Oh Dear, the Animals Are Here!* Another was for a blind peasant girl–slash–chorus member in a silent, Dostoevsky-inspired farcical mime-dance of something called *War and Peas* at P.S. 122, the whole of which was to be performed to a live orchestra of Fisher-Price instruments.

At her audition she was asked to bring kneepads, perform a five-second handstand, and reveal her "inner vegetable," which turned out to be cabbage.

"How did you, like, *do* cabbage?" I asked after an evening of love-making.

"I just executed myself," Basha explained. "I think to my brain, 'At this precise moment I am four thousand cabbages and all of their childrens in the most superlative garden in the world.' And it was so."

Basha was offered the *War and Peas* job but had to turn it down because it conflicted with her Polly Parker's shifts, upon which her parents were economically dependent. Her dad, a retired machinist, was earning a meager under-the-table living working maintenance at a furniture warehouse in Astoria. Her mother, who'd been a schoolteacher back in Poland, took a job waiting tables at a small Ukrainian diner on First Avenue, not far from Polly Parker's. They had moved to New York the year before, Basha explained, because they wanted her to have the chance to follow her dream of being a television actress.

We never spoke of János. His presence in our lives was both enormous and invisible. He was like some portentous, undetectable zeppelin slowly approaching our side of the Atlantic. When he would descend on North America, and then on our lives, was anybody's guess. I chose to simply ignore that possibility and enjoy my time with Basha, who was the one bright spot in my otherwise gloomy December.

Outside, as the snow was gradually reduced by Manhattan's thermal underworld, the city's unharvested garbage slowly emerged, ton by putrefied ton. The temperature remained at a level just around freezing, which at least kept the smells away.

Approximately one week before Christmas a strange man entered our apartment unannounced.

When the door opened I was pacing in the hallway, attempting to detangle the mess I was making of my novel.

The man didn't knock; he simply walked through the door the way one walks into a pool hall or the dry cleaner's.

Like he owned the fucking place.

He was a strange man not only because of the propriety with which he entered our home, or his subtle, pigeon-toed limp that bordered on the gait of a war hero, but also because of his attire. It must first be pointed out that he wore a wig. And this was not like the sophisticated toupees that subtly grace the well-concealed hairless crowns of thousands of middle-aged men. This piece, with its bile-brown color and slightly slimy exterior, looked like it might have been fresh roadkill scraped off the highway. In addition to the questionable wig he donned a false mustache whose spirit gum was leaking down the corners of his mouth. Like the incongruous pubic thatch of a whore with a cheap peroxide job, color-wise, this mustache was several shades removed from the wig.

For his wardrobe, he chose (as all true eccentrics *choose* their wardrobes) a powder-blue, polyester-blend suit that featured shoddy white stitching and extra-large lapels. His collared shirt was white, his tie profoundly banana. He also wore black imitation-leather wingtips, streaked with what appeared to be dried semen.

He didn't say anything, but simply looked around like some legendary gunslinger who'd just entered a frontier saloon. He regarded the street-facing windows with arched eyebrows, the fireplace with a friendly nod, and the Loach with a lopsided, nicotine-yellow smile that featured a chipped gray incisor and coffee grounds riddling the cracks.

After he sized me up a business card was offered. His fingernails were filthy, his left hand either extraordinarily tan or subtly gloved. The card was of the plain white variety and, stamped in shiny Times Roman print, it read:

JOHN ANDERSON-ALLENSWORTH

Below the name was a 917 number—no doubt beeper digits.

I stared at the man, his ludicrous ensemble acquiring an almost dream-like quality. It was as if the costume had created the character inside of it, and not simply in a conventional theatrical way, but perhaps through some mystical or supernatural process.

The Loach seemed utterly unfazed by our trespasser and continued to watch the fan.

I looked at the card again, hoping it would provide more information.

"You know who I am," the man finally said by way of introduction. He stated it; he did not query. There was not a question mark to be found on the guy. He possessed the deep, sonorous voice of a world-class radio host and spoke with an authentic Spanish accent.

"I don't know you," I replied.

"Oh, but you do," he assured me.

He swaggered toward the fireplace, disco-like, kind of letting his head go on a swivel. He touched the fan and then rubbed his fingers together. Things were suddenly less supernatural and more ridiculous. This guy was all Caesars Palace. He was Morley the Bit Man, live from San Diego, Lear-jetted to Las Vegas for the entertainment of thousands!

"John Anderson . . . *Allensworth?*" I read aloud from the card.

"It's been a long time," he said, almost sentimentally.

"It has?"

"Indeed it has, my friend."

He bobbed on the heels of his imitation-leather shoes and added, "Now I think we hab things back under control."

I looked to the Loach, who was sucking on a nine-volt battery.

"What things?" I asked.

"You know what I'm talking about," Mr. Anderson-Allensworth said assuredly, with a high roller's gleam in his eye.

He walked a slow parabola across the living room, stopped, bent down to pick up a wire coat hanger that the Loach had been using to scrape away his athlete's-foot-turned-trench-toe, regarded the hanger for a moment, then crossed to the front door, promenading backward now, practically moonwalking, still somehow casing the joint, and hung the hanger on the knob rather thoughtfully.

"Um. What exactly is back under control?" I asked.

"The seeshuashun," our visitor replied.

"What situation?" I asked.

"Oh, I think you know what seeshuashun I'm talking about."

He moved to one of the street-facing windows, opened it, and let it drop. This was done scientifically, as though he were gathering important data.

Perhaps he was a hit man who specialized in defenestration?

"Does this have anything to do with Glenwood Ledbetter?" I asked in earnest. Although I'd never known the Owl to be a gambling man, perhaps he was fleeing from a bad bet and this guy was some down-and-out bookie coming to collect?

"Is that a trabel agency?" the man asked rather sincerely, milking the hell out of that soft V, twiddling the ends of his gummy mustache.

I didn't answer.

Travel agency.

Was this further obfuscation? Or part of some double-helixed riddle that all Midwesterners are faced with approximately seven months into their tenure in the East Village? Sure, trump him with the old *trabel agency* number! And season the sauce of ambiguity with the old follow-a-question-with-a-question routine! And was Mr. Anderson-Allensworth's question rhetorical, or one of garden-variety sincerity?

"I'm sorry, but I don't have any idea what you're talking about," I declared rather plaintively, my hands clenching into sweaty fists now.

The temperature in the room was definitely rising.

"Things are going to change around here," Mr. Anderson-Allensworth said, wagging his finger with the affected propriety of a congressman. "We're going to return to the old ways."

"Really," I rejoined.

"Yes, really," he said, his voice in a higher register now, almost pitying. "Berry much really."

"What are these quote-unquote *old ways*?" I asked with a bit of gusto.

To which he responded: "It is cold outside, my friend. Many trees die at this time ob year. The winter is long and the birds hab to stay away for a berry long time. Ebentually, the begetation withers and loses its color. In other words: it is not easy to sleep next to a bast and boluminous snowman. Let's not play games."

Then the Loach finally chimed in. It was the first complete sentence he'd uttered in weeks:

"He thinks he's collecting rent from us."

"He does?" I asked.

"I'd bet my balls and cock on it," the Loach said. His voice seemed to resonate from somewhere deep inside his nose.

When I turned back around the man in the powder-blue suit was gone. He left the front door ajar, and I could see the murky hallway light almost oozing its way in. The wire coat hanger seesawed infinitesimally on the knob. I went out into the hallway and peered over the fourth-floor railing. Although I could hear Mr. Anderson-Allensworth's footfalls faintly padding at the bottom of the stairwell, I could not see him.

Was this man some sort of illusionist?

Was he, in fact, real, or was he some architectural or anthropological phantasm?

When I reentered the apartment, I promptly closed the door and turned the deadbolt.

"Should we, like, call the police or something?" I asked the Loach, who was still orally preoccupied with the nine-volt battery. Its nutritional value was probably better than anything he'd set his lips to in recent months.

"Loach," I called to him, but he had checked out.

The Tins

LATER I WALKED DOWN to the third floor and knocked on unit three's door. From somewhere within, a strange symphony of what sounded like melancholic whale music could be heard. Outside of the occasional mailbox encounter, after seven months I had still yet to make much of a connection with any other tenant in my building, so I had no idea what to expect. According to what the Owl told me before he left, the current squatters in unit three were a husband and wife and their toddler son. At some point they had replaced the guy who owned the cricket bat with human hair embedded in the grain. All I knew of them was that the husband, like the old tenant, had a pretty big beard and rarely left the building. I knew nothing about the wife or son.

There was no answer, so I knocked again. Despite a lull in the music during which I heard the distinct shuffling of feet, there was still no answer, so I waited a minute or so and tried a third time. Moments later the husband answered the door to reveal a black-lit, velveteen darkness whose only light source came from the combined efforts of a UFO-shaped sodium desk lamp looming precariously over a sink full of dirty dishes and the midnight blue spill of a vacant fish tank that featured a drowned G.I. Joe doll lying in a prone position, his face half-buried in a bed of salmon-colored coral bits.

My bearded neighbor was wearing only a pair of long thermal underwear bottoms that had been mended with silver duct tape. His hair was a shoulder-length dried casserole of clumps and cowlicks. His equally unkempt blond beard was twisted, knotted, braided, singed, dreadlocked in patches, and ponytailed here and there with orthodontic rubber bands. His flabby, prolifically tattooed torso had the pasty constitution of a storybook pirate. His breasts verged on mammary and boasted hairy, inflamed-looking nipples.

This man had acres of interesting flesh.

"What's up?" he uttered through a half-collapsed mouth. His breath smelled unmistakably of prunes.

"Hey," I said. "Sorry to disturb you. I live above you, in unit four."

"We too loud or somethin'?" he asked rather unthreateningly.

"No," I said. "You're not loud at all. In fact, I never even hear you."

"Right on," he replied.

I briefly lost his mouth in the vastness of his beard but quickly found his eyes.

For a moment a hurdy-gurdy rose over the whale music.

"Who is it?" an exhausted woman's voice called out from some unseen bedroom. "If it's Tron tell him I ran out of beeswax and the candles won't be ready till tomorrow."

"It's the guy from upstairs," he responded. It seemed to cost him a great effort to increase his vocal volume.

He stood there thumbing at his navel for a second, and that's when the toddler appeared—as though my neighbor's belly button had activated some sort of silent paging system. The kid emerged into the hallway light like a large fish walking upright in a dream and came to rest at his dad's side, hugging his leg. Like the larger person next to him, he was bare-chested and rather zonked, but instead of long underwear, he sported an enormous droopy diaper that was kept together with the same silver duct tape.

"This is Bert," the man said, blindly indicating the small child with a hitchhiker's thumb. "Bert, this is our neighbor from upstairs."

"Hi, Bert," I said.

"Spooky likes the taste of poop!" Bert announced in a rather excited bubble-bath soprano.

"Oh," I said. "Who's Spooky?"

"Spooky was our German shepherd. He died a few days ago," his dad explained, running his hand through Bert's wheat-colored mullet.

"Spooky likes the taste of poop!" Bert sang again.

"Okay, Berty," his dad said. "That's enough now."

According to my neighbor, Bert had just drawn that very statement on the wall with Pert Plus. He gently pulled me into the apartment by my elbow so I could have a look.

"Bert, go see if your mother needs anything," his dad said, closing the door. The music was louder now, the whale cries sadder. With the apartment sealed off, some enormous, unnameable smell started to materialize, and it wasn't prunes.

"So what's up?" the man finally asked.

"Well, I was wondering if anyone has been in touch with you regarding the rent."

"What rent?" was his response.

"Exactly," I corroborated.

Through his teeth my neighbor then scoffed in solidarity, and like scree sliding down a high desert slope, several unidentifiable particles fell out of his beard. Whatever it was must have been important, as he quickly retrieved the mysterious matter, some of which he reinserted into the depths of his facial nest, the rest of which he ate.

"This guy came into my apartment and demanded rent today," I explained, watching him chew.

"Who was he?"

I went on to describe John Anderson-Allensworth, his unforced entry, and the nature of our conversation. I cited his wardrobe and strange disguise. I tried to re-create some of his gestures and quoted from his abstruse snowman parable.

"Sounds like a fucking charlatan to me," my neighbor offered. "Here," he said, suddenly producing the legendary unit three cricket bat, seemingly out of thin air. "Next time he swings by, let him have it right in the shins."

He handed me the bat. In the dim light I couldn't determine whether there was human hair embedded in the grain. I couldn't even see the grain.

"That little number's gotten me through a fair number of long nights," my neighbor said. "The nutsack's not a bad target, either."

"Thanks."

The bat handle was gluey with some sort of adhesive and its face was riddled with half-embedded staples and carpenter tacks.

I rested the cricket bat against the wall and refocused on the man, who was fingering something out of his ear. My eyes had adjusted to the light now and I suddenly realized that every single tattoo on his torso was the same. Featured on his arms, shoulders, neck, belly, and aforementioned mammary-like breasts were roughly twenty-two three-color images of Jesus Christ carrying a Coke Machine on his back. There was an enormous version of it set between his shoulder blades as well.

"How's your heat, anyway?" my neighbor asked.

"It's not been too bad. We had to duct-tape some of the windows," I explained. "The nights can get pretty chilly, but it isn't alarming or anything."

"We've been augmenting with a hibachi two or three times a week," he explained. "It's a bit of a downer finding charcoal and lighter fluid in the middle of the winter. Lina's over on the corner sells Duraflames, so that helps. The smoke's doing something to the walls, but it's tolerable. And our oven's busted, so it's a decent cooking option. Throw a couple of dogs on the grill, a few burgers, you know?"

"Sure."

"What about your plumbing?" he then asked.

I explained our bucket-of-water toilet-flushing method and he seemed genuinely impressed. He even praised me for my ingenuity.

"Now there's using one of the four elements," he said. "If it ain't mud, it's water. After that, fireworks'll fix up just about anything. Never underestimate good old-fashioned arson's logic."

When asked about the state of his plumbing, he said, "Our shitter's shot. We urinate in the sink and wear diapers. And my lady works at Wholesale Liquidators twice a week so we get good deals on the Depends."

"Hey!" the woman's voice called out again. "You comin' back to bed or what?"

"Spooky likes the taste of poop!" Bert blurted out from the hidden room.

"Just a sec!" my neighbor called back to them.

I stood there for another moment while the whales and the hurdy-gurdy swelled a final time. The apartment's courtyard-facing window was obscured by frost and smoke stains. I might be wrong, but I had the distinct impression that G.I. Joe was now sitting up in the fish tank. There was a different kind of natural law in this apartment and its subtleties were elusive and stupefying.

Moments later, what sounded like a rocket launch seared through the music, followed by an atonal string arrangement that was no doubt some sort of maddening coda.

It was at that very moment that I identified the smell that had been thickening. It wasn't death or food, nor was it sex or menstruation or feces. It was the smell of wrongness; that's the only way I can describe it. And not wrong because there was something amiss or amoral with regard to my neighbors. It was wrong because there was something wrong in the *place*, in its walls or pipes or beams. Perhaps this smell was lying dormant somewhere in our apartment as well, behind the Sheetrock or under a section of ancient floorboards, waiting to attach itself to some foul strain of mold or rot or damp and be released. Perhaps the whole fucking building was cursed with wrongness and John Anderson-Allensworth was a specter materialized from its invisible, primordial ooze.

"What's your name, anyway?" the man with the tattoos asked.

I introduced myself and we shook.

"My name's Tim," he said. "Tim Tin. And that's my wife Kim in the other room."

"Nice to meet you," I said.

"Just let us know if you ever need anything else. Knock on our door anytime, okay?"

"Thanks," I said. "And don't hesitate to knock on number four, either. Use the facilities or whatever."

He said, "Thanks, bro," and we continued shaking hands.

When he finally released my hand I saw that there was yet another tattoo of Jesus carrying the Coke machine in the center of his palm.

"Take care," I said by way of a farewell.

"You, too. Remember," he advised, "straight for the shins."

He turned and closed the door to his apartment, locking the deadbolt.

I took the cricket bat and headed back upstairs, where I first set it in the corner by the door, but then thought better of it after seeing the Loach, who was snoring in a way that sounded like he was making love to a go-cart. His snowsuit was starting to take on the color of the sofa and his troglodyte beard seemed to be going through a process of radioactive decay. Tim Tin's was much cooler, I'd decided. Compared to the Loach's attempt at facial hair, Tim Tin's beard was a Roald Dahl novel.

I wound up stashing the cricket bat under my futon, where I would learn to sleep with my right hand curled around its gummy handle. Upon further inspection I did excavate what appeared to be a lone, iron-colored human hair from a rough patch of wood grain.

Slowtrane

TWO DAYS LATER I met Basha at Habib's Place, where we ate overstuffed falafels and held hands. Other than Habib, who was shaving shawarma and silently testifying to the sounds of Miles Davis, we were the only two in the small Middle Eastern café.

"How was toiling?" I asked Basha while she was attempting to excavate a jalapeño pepper.

"Toiling was so-so," Basha said. "I make commonplace tips and rebuff flirtatious man who invite me to ride a snowmobile car with him in the upstate New York," she continued.

"Wow," I said, and left it at that.

"So toiling was nothing special," Basha said, picking some shredded lettuce out of her pita. "But what is this thing everyone is talking about—this computer for the lap?"

"Laptop computer," I said through a mouthful of hummus and diced tomatoes. "It's portable."

"What is *portable*?"

I gave her my best definition, which included the words *lightweight* and *small*.

"Do you possess one of these portable laptop computers?" she asked.

"I don't," I answered.

"But this would be superlative item for your writing, no?"

"It probably would be, but I prefer a manual typewriter," I said.

"But the portable computer is exceedingly more popular, no?"

"No, it totally is," I agreed. "I guess you could say I'm sort of old-fashioned."

"I see," Basha said and started to play with my thumb. She made little assembly line noises while erecting and bending it at the joint.

Miles Davis changed to Charles Mingus while Habib did some spatula accompaniment, scraping grease off of his grill in little percussive scats.

Through the window a filthy NYPD squad car squawked by, its pursuit light a scramble of blue and white.

I thought of all the meals we would have together; all the pierogi and beet soup and stuffed cabbage; the smell of cooking permeating our future upstate home; the warm, comforting scent of garlic and potatoes lingering in her hair, soaking into her pillow, wafting through the ether of my dreams.

Out the window a man in gym shorts and a ski mask walked by. His legs were cadaver-white. Basha watched him pass and her stare held such an unexpressive, flat intensity it almost drew an audible sigh from my loins.

Basha wiped some hummus away from the corner of my mouth with her thumb.

And that's when I dropped the bomb.

I said, "I love you."

I'd wanted to say it for at least a week, but I had no idea I was actually going to do it. It just came out like lake water through my nose.

Basha replied, "I love you, too," and kissed the space between my nose and eye.

We touched foreheads, kissed some more, and then Charles Mingus changed to John Coltrane's smoky, unsentimental "Slowtrane."

Habib himself was the sole witness to the first time Basha and I verbally declared our love.

So what happened to me during this kiss, one might wonder?

Well, first of all, my stomach disappeared.

And then I turned into a sunflower.

And then several hundred smaller sunflowers sprouted around me and sang the entire collection of poems anthologized in *The Prophet* by Kahlil Gibran.

Life was suddenly a warm, fragrant field and Basha was the sun.

"This computer for the lap must be very valuable and chief," Basha said, returning to our more earthbound subject matter.

"I think to many people it is, yes."

"If I win ingenue-style role on network television situation comedy, perhaps I will purchase one of these computers for the lap for my secret librarian."

"That would be really sweet of you," I replied.

"Then you could compose beautiful, heartbreaking novel about a young writer with a tall, sad face, and a slightly happier actress from Poland who meet in New York City subway tunnel."

"I could, huh?"

"Yes. And the novel would possess much tragedy and copious amounts of comedy and many effervescent scenes of their superlative lovemaking."

"I might just do that," I said. "Let's just be sure to stay away from those ball-peen hammer things."

And this was largely how we spent our time together: we ate falafel and sometimes talked about deeply important things like the difference between the words *humidity* and *humility*, as well as unimportant things like the advent of the laptop personal computer.

And I stared at her a lot and felt enormously happy and scared at the same time.

To this day, if I hear Coltrane's *Slowtrane* it takes my legs out from under me so suddenly that I simply have to go to a knee.

I have actually genuflected in the middle of a busy sidewalk, and it had nothing to do with my Roman Catholic upbringing.

Reduced

AT WORK FORD MCGOWAN SIDLED UP to my Skinner box with his bouncing blond bangs and a Herculean manuscript that he was transporting in the bottom of a stationery box. The fact that the manuscript traveled in its own vessel made it seem sacred, as if it were being delicately chauffeured to some sort of literary altar where other precious manuscripts in stationery boxes were lovingly stacked, anointed with oils, and secretly prayed to by all members of the editorial staff.

Ford was wearing his customary khaki chinos and a long-sleeved sales-conference T-shirt over a blue oxford. The T-shirt featured the book jacket for the upcoming surefire *New York Times* bestseller written by our most commercially successful author, Selden Kong. Record-setting advance orders were the hopeful salve to the now arthritic joints of our recession-riddled bookmaking operation. The title was *The Cop Who Ate a Bear*, and the novel's accompanying artwork was a screen print of a large, rather amused-looking grizzly bear wearing a state trooper's uniform, a broad-brimmed hat, and aviator sunglasses. In its paw it was clutching a cafeteria spork.

"Cool T-shirt," I said.

"More butter for the bread and butter," Ford said alliteratively. "This smegma of mediocrity will make it possible to keep our last few midlist gems in the catalog. Books like *The Glorious Whores of Zaragoza* by Willie Volinda and Charlotte Indiana's *Fewer Vowels* will find some shelf space thanks to Mr. Kong."

"That guy really churns 'em out," I offered.

"Oh, Kong's gone on record saying that it's all about volume for him. If he writes eight pages a day for thirty days he has a novel. He's the authorial equivalent to the Quarter Pounder. And his work has about the same nutritional value."

The thought of a Quarter Pounder made my stomach gurgle.

"The guy puts out three titles a year," Ford continued. "He makes well over a million a pop."

"But the critics murder him."

"Kong's above the critics. People in airports buy his books and read them on the plane. They usually finish the by the time the landing gear is engaged, and many of them buy the next title at the bestseller kiosk on their way to the baggage claim. The effect is similar to that of MSG or cocaine."

"There must be something to them," I said, wondering what it would be like to hover above the critics like that. I pictured a big hot-air balloon, clown-nose red, a hundred of our finest, most erudite book critics herding below, attempting to bring Selden Kong plummeting back to earth with *New York Times Book Review* lawn darts.

"His books are horrible," Ford whispered and came closer. "His own editor refers to each new one as 'the latest in a long line of shake 'n' bake fiction.' Every one features a totally predictable, full-on sex scene. The orgy always, without fail, hits at around page one-forty. Erect cocks and Silly Putty labia. Titanic cumshots. Hot, churning flesh. It's unbelievable. The scene just sort of materializes out of nowhere, like on a veranda or in the frozen-foods section or something. And invariably one of the participants is murdered. Or they're kidnapped and eaten cannibalistically. It's total snuff porn."

"Sounds like you know a lot about them."

"Oh, I've read every one. It really is like literary cocaine."

Ford rested the manuscript on the corner of my Skinner box.

"So did you hear about the layoffs?" he said surreptitiously, changing the subject.

"Layoffs?" I echoed, split-screening away from *Opie's Half-life*, to which I had devoted the entire day since Van and the Shankler were at the sales conference in White Plains. I was one of three employees in the entire sales department left behind to "hold down the fort," and I figured I would make them pay with the creation of art.

"Stafford was telling Staley about it in the bathroom," Ford explained through the side of his mouth. "A thirty percent downsize. Closed-door exit interviews starting after the holiday party."

"Whoa," was my response.

"Just liquor up the steak and cut away the fat, right?"

"Some holiday spirit," I said.

"Recession, recession," Ford sighed.

"Do you have any idea who they're targeting?"

"My gut is telephone sales is a safe bet. Those guys just do bong hits all day and play Pong on Niederlander's old Mac Classic."

A temp from mass-market promotions passed by holding a life-size cardboard cutout of Selden Kong in a bear costume. He was holding the costume's head in the crook of his elbow and staring back at the onlooker with a grave poker face. For a fleeting moment it seemed that the temp was smuggling the thing out of the building, and I was worried that the missing marketing gem would somehow compromise the future of all of those midlisters trying to hold on to the few slippery vines of literary integrity still clinging to our publishing house.

"That chick so wants me," Ford said after the temp was a safe distance down the hall. He watched her for a moment and shook his head as if the possibility of them having sex was not only inevitable, but slightly depressing as well.

"What's in the box?" I asked Ford, pointing to the manuscript.

"Oh, it's this first novel by this MFA stud from Brown."

"Wow," I said, genuinely admiring its girth.

"Yeah," Ford said, "the kid's like twenty-two or something."

"It's huge."

"Yeah, thirteen hundred and forty-seven pages huge."

"Jesus. What's it about?"

"Apparently some South American soccer star who wakes up one morning with a chick fetus growing in the well of his collarbone."

"Really?"

"Yeah, and this Nike swoosh birthmark thing mysteriously appears on the fetus's prenatal forehead. So there's this, like, whole corporate marketing subplot with television rights and commercial endorsements. Oh, and the soccer player is dying."

"Jesus," I said again.

I could almost feel my heart cleaving in two in my chest.

"What's it called?" I nearly croaked.

"*The Reduced Life of Nestor Delgadillo.*"

I was suddenly light-headed.

My elbows hit the desk and I almost fainted.

Ford reached for my shoulder. When he lunged, the entire manuscript tumbled out of its box and avalanched rather abusively onto my neck, back, and shoulders. Although the blow certainly rattled me in the same way one is perhaps rattled after being bitch-slapped in front of a convertible full of attractive girls in swimwear, it didn't do any serious damage.

Drifts of paper were everywhere.

Somehow my keyboard split-screened on its own and *ffffffffffffffffff ffffffffffffffffffffffffffffffffffffffffffffffffffffffffffffffffffffffffffffffffffffffff ffffffffffffffffffffffffffffffffffffffffffffffffffffffffffffffffffffffffff* was invading my novel at a horrifying velocity.

My desk was smothered in *The Reduced Life of Nestor Delgadillo.*

"Are you okay?" Ford asked.

He was no doubt referring to my hyperventilating and acute flop sweat.

"It's my blood sugar," I lied, panting, my head reeling. "I'm . . . borderline hypo . . . glycemic. I'll just . . . eat a candy bar . . . or something."

I pulled all the pages off the *f* key and split-screened again, attempting to regain my composure.

It took us roughly fifteen minutes to gather all of the one thousand three hundred and forty-seven pages, and another half hour to repaginate.

During this editorial first-aid session Ford cited two other temps whose phone numbers he'd acquired earlier that day. One girl was over in mass marketing putting mailing labels on Jiffy bags. Her name was Keiko and she was Asian and he was sure that he would be licking her pussy by week's end. The other girl was covering for someone in permissions. Ford referred to her as "Fatty" and confessed to a rich fantasy life that involved females who weighed over two hundred pounds.

I simply listened to Ford the way one listens to a foreign radio in the back of a taxi: I tried to enjoy the music his voice was making.

Although I'd like to believe that I refused to look at a word of our triaged manuscript, I have to admit that I read the final sentence on page 1,347, which was:

> If there was one thing that Nestor knew more than anything else it was that, above all things, he did not want to die under the black Tortola sky.

The Christmas Party

THE CHRISTMAS PARTY WAS HELD in a large ballroom at the Doral Park Avenue on Thirty-eighth Street. I met Lacy Shank in the hotel's bar and grill. I sat patiently on my Naugahyde stool, nursing a seven-dollar pint of wheat beer that tasted like a slightly bitter, liquefied English muffin.

It was the Friday night before Christmas and I was becoming acutely aware of the fact that my clothes were hanging off me. My one-meal-a-day diet was obviously starting to take its toll.

Lacy arrived forty-five minutes late and exhibited the agitated, fidgety disposition of someone who'd been on a long caffeine-and-doughnut-fueled road trip. She appeared at once highway-lulled and desperate to urinate. Her auburn, Raphaelite hair corkscrewed down to her shoulders in silky ribbons so thoroughly styled that they looked edible. She had donned black, oddly tined earrings and carried a matching handbag that didn't have tines but looked like it should. Under her oversize navy peacoat she wore something purple and vaguely see-through that had the consistency and sheen of expensive panty hose. The décolletage alluringly featured her perfectly small-to-midsize breasts. Her nipples were so erect they made me want to touch my own.

The first thing that she said was: "I'm going to tear your head off if you get all thoughtful and boring tonight."

I nodded dumbly.

She then said hello in some Mediterranean language and kissed the air near my cheek. I kissed the air near hers, which smelled like scotch and frozen cigarettes. Her earring nearly lanced my jugular.

She rifled through her handbag in a little fit and raged, "My fucking smokes have, like, anal lube all over them or something!" She groped for unseen items and cursed through her teeth. "I need a bartender, and that anorexic gorefest in the taffeta jumpsuit needs a sandwich."

Lacy was referring to an elderly lady at the end of the bar, who was indeed very thin. No less than seventy, with skin like fading papyrus, she was drinking a large glass of red wine and within easy earshot. Lacy took no prisoners.

After she and our neighbor exchanged wicked glances, Lacy wiped the said lubricant off her soft pack of Camel Lights with a cocktail napkin.

"I'm going to behave very badly tonight," she warned, mischief already brewing in her absurdly dilated gray eyes. "I don't care what Jack told you."

She crumpled the cocktail napkin and tossed it onto the silicate bar top.

"I apologize in advance if I do something to jeopardize your job," she continued. "But we shan't walk on eggshells, right?"

It was somewhat bewildering how in a matter of sentences Lacy Shank's idiom could shift from foul-mouthed Hell's Kitchen dive-bar broad to Gatsby-like heiress.

She unloaded her navy peacoat, which was four times heavier than it looked, onto my lap.

"That tie is so shoe salesman," she added, referring to the pencil-stripe number I'd recently purchased for twelve bucks from the sale bin at the Gap. I thought it was sure-handed yet understated. I adjusted my feeble attempt at a Windsor knot and checked for stains.

Lacy then produced a cigarette, lit it herself with a cheap Bic lighter, and took a long drag.

"You look like a really bad blend of Harrison Ford and Ron Howard," she said, exhaling almost directly into my face. Then she did something to my hair that hurt a little. "That's better," she added. "How's my lipstick?"

"It looks fine," I said. "What color is that?"

"Calf's liver. I'm so fucking coked up I feel like I ate too much chicken fried rice. Can you see my thong?"

She turned around and I inspected. Her ass looked impossibly perfect.

"Thong-free," I offered.

Lacy turned around and took another drag. "By the way," she said, exhaling, "Banjo died."

"Oh," I said. "Jesus. Really?"

"Yeah, really," she replied, seizing my beer and gulping impressively. "I came home after rehearsal last week and he was lying facedown in his litter box. Vet had no explanation beyond acute heart failure. What kind of beer is this?"

"Wheat."

"It tastes like a fucking breakfast cereal. You look thin, by the way. Are you fucking dying or something?"

She took another gulp and shoved it back at me, took a drag from her Camel Light, expelled a cloud of smoke that turned blue through the spill of the stylish indigo halogen lamp above the bar, and added, "I'm still mourning, thus the coke splurge and accompanying bitchiness."

I noticed that her nails were the same purple shade as her dress, as were her heels, whose stiletto stems looked like they could puncture just about anything.

After Lacy finished my beer, I paid my tab and checked our coats, and we made our way to the ballroom.

"On Monday, if Daddy asks if I smoked any cigarettes, tell him two fucking packs," she instructed as we passed through the mistletoe-and-Christmas-tree-light-festooned portico.

Lacy walked with feline, marauding intensity. She was slinky and selfish. She was a rapacious meat eater and she let everyone know it. I noticed that her shoulders were dusted with peach-colored freckles that I didn't remember from our previous two encounters.

While trailing Lacy to the party, I was for some reason reminded of a fairly pretentious platitude that my writing professor, Dudley Vanderhal, had shared with my fiction workshop at the end of my final semester in college. (I should preface his literary maxim by pointing out that Dudley wore turtlenecks and tweed blazers—with suede patches at the elbows—well into the third week of April. He also had chronic halitosis and possessed perhaps the most unpredictable case of bedhead that I have ever seen.)

In his reedy, effeminate voice, while theatrically holding a pomegranate out in front of him as if to sketch its still life, this is what Dudley imparted:

Dread, my lemmings, is perhaps the most powerful force in storytelling. If you can potently inject the sense that something *terribly bad* is going to happen, you will stir your reader's humors, and he will undoubtedly turn the page with a shameless, wicked velocity.

Then he lowered the crimson fruit and made a grave face.

Three of my female classmates took offense that Dudley Vanderhal had assigned the male pronominal modifier to his universal readership, to which he rejoined, "But feminine humors are *always* churning, my XY lemmings."

As we joined the throngs of my coworkers and their well-dressed dates, I was acutely aware of the indigestible cold paste of Dudley Vanderhal's beloved dread settling in my intestines.

When we entered, Belinda Bush's identical twin daughters, Uma and Una, dressed as rather shoddy-looking, recently admonished Christmas Elves and standing on festively decorated chairs, covered our heads with Santa hats.

"Happy hollandaise," they said in unison through very few adult teeth. "Don't trinka drive."

"Trinka this," Lacy barked, removing her Santa hat and tossing it over her shoulder.

The ballroom was garishly punctuated with a platoon of potted firs electroplated in holiday gold and silver. In random celestial arrangements white Christmas-tree lights hung from invisible wires. From the center of the ballroom ceiling, a gargantuan storybook chandelier loomed with precarious indifference, serving as the nucleus for countless rays of red and green crepe paper.

Everywhere were long tables dressed in snowy, woodland-themed linens and crowded with catered food. Chilled jumbo shrimp and multicolored grapes seemed to be the staple of some holiday seafood theme. In addition to the shrimp there were scallops simmering in stainless steel pans of oil, and what appeared to be an ancient Russian troika of sautéed calamari. Laid out on a block of ice and adorned with lemon wedges and sprigs of parsley was an enormous Alaskan salmon, its head still on, wearing a wily expression. It was the most intelligent-looking fish I had ever seen. Most of the bullheads, crappies, and anemic carp that I had encountered on the banks of Midwestern lakes and rivers had possessed faces full of mild boredom. Even in profile the salmon looked as if it had died while learning something enormously important.

In each of the four corners of the ballroom there was a fully stocked bar wagon, the featured drink being a room-temperature brew of rum-infused eggnog that could be ladled from a large, stainless steel soup tureen. The four bartenders were costumed in cheap tuxedos, red bow ties, and crowns of what appeared to be authentic reindeer antlers.

At the far end of the ballroom a stage had been erected and a multiracial, tropically costumed band was playing Prince's "I Would Die 4 U." The lead singer was a curvaceous white woman in a white jumpsuit. While atavistically channeling Prince, she scooted around the stage in a manner reminiscent of my junior-high homeroom teacher supervising a tornado drill. The bassist and drummer were middle-aged black twins who smiled at each other with such willful tenacity that I feared their teeth might fall out. Conversely, the lead guitarist, an incredibly tall, mustachioed Hispanic man with plum pleather pants and Menudo hair, wore an expression that was profoundly cryonic.

While the band kept good time and seemed to execute even the subtler parts of the songs they played (The Time's "Jungle Love," The Gap Band's "Outstanding," and Kool and the Gang's "Celebration"), their overall effect inspired more dance-floor grope than groove.

Several of the good people from my publishing company were enacting a genre of corporate boogie that included cardiac flailing, off-tempo undulating, pelvically challenged ghetto grinding, inadvertent parade marching, inspired revolutionary-style fist-pumping, full-fledged running in place, and a constipated, foal-legged bunny hop, all the while wearing the bug-eyed, pained smiles of recently escaped lunatics.

I would be remiss if I didn't cite the following injuries:

Besserman Staley, while caught up in a ferocious, off-tempo, gospel choir member–like hand-clapping demonstration inspired by the band's call-and-response version of "The roof is on fire," broke into a complicated, almost impossible one-legged whirling dervish, arms spastic, at the height of which she slipped, shattered her two-inch Louis heel, corkscrewed into a bewildering, high-speed contortion of limbs and centrifugal hair, and landed smartly on her tailbone. She had to be dragged off the parquet floor and was administered to with several makeshift ice packs by Haley Bartizal and Jensen Hope, the new plump-in-a-pleasant-sort-of-way coordinators from human resources.

Next was Harlan Neiderlander, who threw out his back during the final chorus of a slightly speedy cover of Cameo's "Word Up." Virtually every assistant and midlevel manager stopped to lend a helping hand, but Harlan waved off the aid, heroically resisting succor and limping to the periphery, continuing to shoo away his subordinates while clutching his lower back like a man who'd just lost control of his bowels. For the rest of the night he would drink multi-olive gin martinis while clinging to a rubber ficus tree.

There was also an epileptic fit, induced by a strobe light that the drummer triggered during the highly energized triple-harmony a cappella outro of D Train's "You're the One for Me." For a few minutes no one knew whose fit it was, as the only thing you could see was a pair of tuxedo-trousered legs extending cadaver-like from under the front of the stage, as well as two extraordinarily long black patent leather Clancy straight-tips vibrating oddly to the beat. An instantaneous rumor materialized that the legs and shoes belonged to the protean, six-foot-eight Don Svoboda, executive editor–slash–head of publicity, who some sincerely believed to be Thomas Pynchon—a dead ringer, according to Ford McGowan, who emerged from the cyclonic dance floor chaos double-fisting plastic champagne flutes of eggnog and with a large

Christmas wreath around his neck. In that moment, I realized that I had lost Lacy.

"Nice wreath," I said to Ford, scanning the crowd for her purple dress.

"It's my subliminal mating call. Taut, fleshy head penetrating verdant aperture. Very neoclassic, Garden of Eden imagery. Taboo, taboo."

"You think that'll really work?" I asked, genuinely curious.

"Give 'em twenty minutes and the banditas'll start cueing up for burrito time."

How could I question such unwavering conviction? Ford would no doubt make headway with several of the young post–Ivy League women who were in attendance on this festive night (the best-dressed under-twenty-thousand-dollar-salary sect of humans I had ever seen).

"Where's your cerveza, chap?" Ford asked.

"I'm pacing myself," I replied, noting the carefully selected Briticism invading his taco-stand vernacular. Perhaps the British/Spanish blend was part of his holiday persona?

"Now there's a stragedy. Lay back and let the ladies soak in the marinade. Then the band starts kickin' out the Peaches and Herb ballads and they're all peeling off your pantalones."

"Hey, have you seen the Shankler's daughter?"

Ford then licked a mustache of eggnog from his upper lip and said, "Haven't seen her yet, but I look forward to it. You catch Pynchon's seizure?"

"Only from the waist down," I replied.

"Who knows? Maybe it stimulated the reader's empathy center of his brain and he'll decide to translate *Gravity's Rainbow* for all us retards."

Ford then toasted an invisible future sex partner and broke away like a man on a swinger's cruise ship in pursuit of the nude shuffleboard deck.

Despite the dance-floor first-aid necessities, within the first hour, the party forged ahead as all good-clean-fun–themed, end-of-the-year corporate celebrations do.

I turned to look for Lacy and almost bumped into the newly hired subrights assistant, Garner Kerr (I guess they weren't "cutting back" in subrights). Garner was the closest thing to a true seven-footer I have ever seen away from the basketball court, and I actually had to shout upward to have a conversation.

"HEY, GARNER," I shouted through cupped hands. "FROM YOUR VANTAGE POINT CAN YOU SEE A REDHEAD IN A PURPLE DRESS?"

He looked out over the crowd for a few moments and replied, "I SEE NOT A HEAD OF HAIR NOR A DRESS OF THAT DESCRIPTION."

"THANKS!" I cried, and moved on.

During a rather jumpy rendition of the Tom Tom Club's "Genius of Love," a temp named Gwynne approached me in a poinsettia-colored pantsuit. She had been filling in in publicity for the past week and somehow got herself invited to the party. Gwynne was tall and bore an unfortunate resemblance to John Wayne and didn't move her arms very much when she walked. Like Ford, she was holding a plastic champagne flute of eggnog. In addition to the pantsuit, her wrist was decorated with a festive green velvet bow. She was already crocked and had a big red splotch of cocktail sauce on her white shirt to prove it.

"So this is where the reindeer play," she said in greeting. Atop my head I made little finger antlers, attempting reindeer cleverness. Gwynne made little finger antlers as well and we dueled. I was a stoic Donner and she was a feisty Blitzen. We locked antlers and bared our teeth. We turned a full circle and almost took out a catering woman wielding a tray of chopped vegetables and dip. Tall, square-chinned Gwynne was so amused by our sporty reindeer play that she almost pitched sideways from an attack of the Christmas giggles and had no recourse but to yank on my tie to keep her balance. This action pulled me face-first (and rather violently) into her upper torso and I was wetly greeted by the aforementioned cocktail sauce. I wiped my face and helped her stand, and composure was restored.

Through a cacophonous break of dueling bass and jungle drums, "Genius of Love" somehow turned into the Wang Chung hit "Everybody Have Fun Tonight."

Everybody on the dance floor began flexing and Wang Chunging their heads off.

Gwynne jogged in place to the music a bit.

"Hey, have you seen Lacy Shank?" I asked.

To which she replied, "Is that the author who wrote her novel while living in that nudist colony in Loxahatchee, Florida?" and continued jogging in place.

Then Manda Shoutly of mass market promotions sidled over wearing a look of party-girl-for-a-night supremacy on her face. She had been struck with the unfortunate inspiration of wearing a red reindeer nose. Gwynne was radiant with joy.

"Oh, that nose, that *nose!*" she cried.

After it was fussed over, removed, squeezed, poked, prodded, tried on by Gwynne, guffawed about, and ultimately returned, the two ladies quickly spoke to the success of the sales conference in White Plains, which I was amazed that Gwynne actually knew about considering her limited company history. Manda then shared an anecdote about a tennis match that she had played against recently promoted regional sales manager Rollie Goldfarb in the Marriott Hotel's winterized air lung. In the third person and seasoned with shameless hyperbole, Manda cited her ferocious backhand, multiple first-service aces, crafty net play, and other bewildering athletic feats as if she were chronicling the performance of a great Wimbledon legend.

She basically kicked Rollie's ass six ways to Sunday (in straight sets) and didn't even break a sweat.

Through all of this Manda Shoutly neither greeted me nor acknowledged that I was any sort of visible matter involved in her space-time continuum.

"You try the salmon yet?" Manda asked Gwynne, finally abandoning her third-person tennis heroics and reaffixing her red nose.

"No. Why, is it good?" Gwynne answered.

"Oh, it's *divine,*" Manda testified. "They must have gotten it at Dean and Deluca. You simply *must* try it."

"Manda, have you seen Jack Shank's daughter?" I asked, cutting in.

"Like nine thousand hours ago. She's so hot, she's like fucking *white hot*, right?"

"White hot," I replied. "Sure."

Then the two girls executed a European air kiss-kiss goodbye, Manda moseyed in the direction of the dance floor, and tall, square-chinned Gwynne waved farewell to me as if she were on a tarmac, about to board a jet, and loped away toward the eggnog tureen.

Wang Chung morphed into Men at Work and then the band returned to their staple of seventies funk and Top-40 soul.

I finally caught up with Lacy and her purple dress, undulating in front of Van Von Donnelly who, despite the song's having faded several minutes before, was still Wang Chunging as if his life depended on it. Lacy playfully grabbed his clip-on Frosty the Snowman bow tie, affixed it to her neckline, mock-seductively ran a purple nail down the front of his shirt, returned the bow tie, and twirled away, entering the slightly sluggish sequence of a clichéd, unimpressive, half-memorized Electric Slide that had materialized in front of the stage (the girls from publicity, no doubt inspired by the band's high-octane, twelve-minute Janet Jackson medley and led by tall and square-chinned Gwynne).

I called out to her and aggressively charged through the crowd, but just when I thought I had reached her, Van slipped and fell into my arms and I spent the next twelve seconds or so attempting to hoist him back up while he giggled like a toddler who'd just pooped on the linoleum.

Back on his feet, Van said, "Thanks, kid. Havin' fun yet?"

"A blast," I said.

I leapt in the air, trying to see over the crowd, but again, I had lost Lacy. Utterly this time. I looked desperately in all directions. Nothing. And now my knee was throbbing.

"Drunk yet?" Van asked.

"Not yet."

"Well, then, you're fired!" he roared. "Just kiddin'."

He laughed, as did I. He was having the time of his life and I envisioned us spending many years together.

"Well, I gotta go get a picture with that bartender babe with the antlers," Van continued. "Merry Christmas."

"You, too," I said, watching him waddle toward one of the liquor wagons.

"So that's festive," I heard. I turned around to see Alexa. She was pointing to my Santa hat. I'd forgotten I was still wearing the thing. By this time most everyone else had shed theirs. Even in college, I was always the ass at the meet and greet who forgot to remove his name tag.

"Where's yours?" I asked.

"Puck's eating his watercress salad out of it, the little herbivore."

Alexa looked better than ever. I would even say she was aglow. She motioned to her effeminate paramour, who was standing near an enormous, holly-wreathed cheese wheel and leaning toward it as if he were receiving important financial advice. Utilizing Alexa's Santa hat as an improvised salad bowl, he was indeed spearing some sort of vegetation with a spork. He wore a forest green turtleneck and a navy velvet blazer, and his hair was coiffed in an undeniably rockabilly fashion.

"So Judy's here and she wants to talk to you," Alexa said. "I told her I'd make an introduction."

"Wow," I said, only half-believing her. "Really?"

"You bet your ass really. So keep the chives out of your teeth."

I ran my tongue over my teeth, searching for chives and other substances.

Alexa then said, "The novel's finished, right?"

"Yeah," I lied. "I finished it just the other day."

"Congratulations."

Alexa teetered a bit and then toasted me with her eggnog. I tapped her plastic champagne flute benignly with my fist.

"How many pages?" she asked.

"Three hundred something," I lied again.

The truth was I had stalled out at around two-forty.

"Three hundred something's a good length. A little thick, but good. After the fat gets cooked out of it it'll be nice and trim."

"What fat?" I asked.

"Oh, every book starts out with a weight problem, trust me. Editors are like dieticians. Or butchers, for that matter."

"Huh," I responded, imagining large sides of beef hanging in private refrigerated editorial meat lockers.

"Believe it or not," Alexa continued, "I've actually seen Judy measure a manuscript, literally wrap her little yellow tailor's tape around it, and say, 'This one needs to lose an inch and a half.' Then the green pen comes out . . ."

"Don't you think that's simplifying things a little?"

"Hey, it's practical. The thinner the book the less it costs to produce."

Suddenly the Shankler was all over us. His tie was flipped over his shoulder and he was clutching a large tumbler of rum and Coke.

"There he is," the Shankler roared, smiling through his enormous, recently bleached teeth.

"Hi, Jack," I offered, shaking his warm and sweaty paw.

"I know you," he said to Alexa. "You work for Dyketits."

"Hi, Jack," Alexa said.

Jack then slapped me on the back a little too hard and said, "Where's your drink, kid?"

"Oh, I've already had a few," I lied.

"What, are you impersonating a counselor at a Christian sports camp or somesuch?" he said, enlisting Alexa in a multiscaled chortle. He then slapped her on the shoulder a little too hard, too, and Alexa slapped him back. During their chucklefest I noticed that Alexa had recently bleached her teeth as well.

"Come on, slim," the Shankler continued. "It's the friggin' holiday party! You're s'posed to get all ribald and Dickensonian—drink!"

I'm certain that *Dickensonian* was supposed to be *Dickensian*.

Which was probably supposed to be *Dionysian*.

I actually wondered if he was so trashed that he'd forgotten about hiring me to watch his daughter.

Jack then said, "Nothin' better than the old end-of-the-year shindig. Free booze. Good grub. Shenanigans galore, right, Franchesca?"

"Alexa," she corrected him.

"Look at Niederlander clinging to that tree. It's prolly the closest thing to poontang *he'll* get tonight. May we all get a little of what we didn't have earlier," the Shankler added, toasting us and moving on like some large domesticated polar bear in need of a toilet. "Party on, kids."

The Shankler plowed his way over to a cluster of female temps who, like Gwynne, had been invited to the festivities and partied on.

"Why aren't you drinking, anyway?" Alexa asked.

"I'm on duty, actually."

"What, in some sort of *writerly* way?"

She pushed her champagne flute at me and I drank. The eggnog was warm and thick and dangerously intoxicating.

"Observing the folly, are you?" she said, taking her champagne flute back, and downing the rest of the eggnog.

"Not really," I said.

"Oh, come on," Alexa said, teetering yet again. "I see the way you watch people."

I was starting to become acutely aware that everyone around me was completely crocked and it wasn't even nine o'clock yet.

"Mister People Watcher. Taking it all in. Mister Invisible Witness. By the way, you look thin. Aren't you eating?"

"I eat."

Alexa's forest green blouse seemed to pulse with its own light source. I briefly took note of her hair, which for a change she wore down in a sophisticated, self-consciously casual holiday style.

"How do I watch people?" I asked, feeling a little indignant.

"You get that—what's the word?—*prosaic* expression on your face. Like you're inhaling the horrible truth or something."

"I'm not inhaling anything, Alexa," I replied, defensive now. "And just for the record, I don't think faces can be prosaic. Dialogue can be prosaic. Or, like, a turn of phrase or a passage or something."

"Whatever. The girls in publicity talk about it all the time. They call you the *Grave Guy*."

"They do?"

"The other day when I was distributing the weekly review roundup, Brie Hunter-Blooton asked me what I thought of the Grave Guy and I was like, Who's that? And she said that young sales assistant and I told her that despite being a bit of a lone wolf I thought you were a nice enough member of the male species and sort of cute in this Tom Sawyer–meets–junior-high P.E. teacher sort of way, to which she replied—and I quote—'His intensity frightens me a little. I always feel like he's *gathering evidence*. Like he's *preparing to chronicle our great fall or something.*'"

"Brie Hunter-Blooton said that?"

"She did, indeed."

"Well, Ford told me she does colonics and walks around the Upper West Side wearing a surgical mask," I retorted immaturely. "I mean, look at her right now. Doing the Electric Slide."

"Brie can *go*," Alexa said, defending her.

"But that's not the point."

"Well, what's the point?"

"I don't know. It's like she's desperately afraid that she won't be perfect or something."

"See what I mean? Always zeroing in. Spinning the beginnings of yet another great cultural artifact."

I said nothing and tried to summon an image of the little cultural artifact that was resting in my freezer. It seemed far from great. It also seemed hardly cultural. I saw it withering like an old, forgotten pile of spinach leaves.

"You should let it go for a night, bro. Forget the pathos and bathos and all that. Get a little sloppy. Frederick Exley devoted his whole adult life to sloppy, and he won a blinkin' Pulitzer. Down a few flutes of this stuff—it'll be good for you."

The way Alexa could drop the occasional *bro* was sort of stupefying.

"But I'm literally on duty, Alexa," I tried to explain. "I'm better off staying sober, trust me."

"Are you, like, working for hire or something?"

"You could say that."

"For who?"

"The Shankler."

"Ohmygod, are you watching Lacy?!"

"Sort of, yeah."

Her hand covered her mouth.

"Ohmygod ohmygod ohmygod!" she cried, genuinely terror-stricken. "She's, like, evil!"

"That's a little extreme, Alexa."

"I wouldn't be surprised if her head does three-sixties! Did you hear about what happened at last year's party?"

"No."

"She got out-of-control wasted during a Donna Summer song and totally tasered someone."

"She did?"

"Oh, it was the stuff of legends. I can't believe you never heard about it."

"Like, *taser* tasered?"

"Yeah. Like, acute voltage blast from a taser gun."

"Who'd she taser?"

"This totally sweet young guy who used to work in telephone sales."

"Lacy has a taser gun?"

"She *used to*. She got the thing in, like, Aix-en-Provence or Copenhagen or someplace."

"Jesus."

"And then, while the paramedics were gurneying the poor kid to Beth Israel or Mount Sinai or wherever, Lacy commandeered a blinkin' banquet table and pissed on the Christmas ham!"

"She did?"

"Full-blown urine jet."

"On a *ham*?"

"On the holiday pork, brotherlove. To 'Love Will Find a Way' by Pablo Cruise."

"Whoa."

"Yeah, whoa. And the guy from telephone sales never came back to work."

"As in, he quit?"

"As in he was conveniently let go. The Shankler asked *him* to watch her, too. Paid him, like, four hundred bucks or something."

"Four hundred?"

"Yeah, it might've even been five."

"I only got a hundred."

Just then Puck Stickleback sauntered over, all hips and wrists. His velvet navy blazer turned sort of purplish as he drew closer. He wore a sly smile and walked like a leading lady who'd just inhaled a large quantity of ether in her honey wagon. When he reached us, he did not speak but simply ran a manicured finger across Alexa's forearm. He was no longer in possession of her Santa hat.

"Did you finish your watercress?" Alexa asked.

Puck nodded and pursed his lips. I swear he was wearing lip liner.

"Where's my hat, Pucky?" Alexa asked.

But Puck didn't vocally respond to his pet name and his hand flitted about in a dismissive manner as if to tell the coy story of the hat's fairy tale–like disappearance. Then Puck pouted cutely again, delicately pinched his turtleneck while issuing a complaint about the heat, wagged a finger derisively at Alexa as if to say, "Be a good little snow bunny, now," and sauntered away, perhaps in search of some other foliage to nibble on.

"What's with all the miming?" I asked.

"Oh, the little Adonis is just in one of his moods. His voice gets tired, talking to agents all day. And frankly, I think he's a smidgen intimidated by your breeder energy."

I suddenly had the distinct, displeasing feeling that Alexa was taking on the characteristics of an elderly gay man.

Then Alexa's boss—the august and legendary Judy Klooszch—materialized from the dance floor. She wore a gray flannel suit with the sleeves rolled up and a lesbianic Peter Pan haircut, and in the half-moment before our introduction I could see that she would not fail to live up to her editorial reputation, which was that she possessed the kind of book-publishing savvy and poise that one acquires through years of knitting together a handful of small literary successes in an afghan of economic insolvency.

Despite the small print runs and lack of advertising budget devoted to midlist literary titles, to be published by Judy Klooszch was nothing less than an honor.

Alexa introduced us and we shook hands. Judy had hard, bluish hands, venous forearms, and an uncle's grip, yet when she spoke her voice was surprisingly warm and feminine.

"It's nice to finally meet you," she said. "I enjoyed the first chunk of your novel very much."

I thanked her in my most authorial voice.

"So when do I get to see the rest?" she asked.

"Soon," I said. "I should be able to get the kinks out in the next few days."

"Well, I leave for the Vineyard tomorrow. I'll be gone through the New Year. When I get back I'd love to be able to close the door to my office and sit down with a big box of caramel corn and finish it."

"Excellent," I said. "I'll definitely bring it in."

"Enjoy your night," she said by way of a farewell.

We shook again and then she headed in the direction of the Alaskan salmon.

"Well, that was promising," Alexa said.

"You think?"

"Judy doesn't even speak to her *established* authors that way. So don't fuck this up."

Alexa then removed my Santa hat and handed it to me in a gentle, parochial-schoolteacher fashion. "She rarely takes such a shine. I better go find Puck."

And with that, she was off, leaving me to briefly indulge in the fantasy of *Opie's Half-life* attaining actual book form, with a dust jacket and sewn signatures and an inlaid copper title on the spine and eloquent front matter and insightful flap copy and a moody yet not too moody author photo and subtle yet potent, slightly abstract cover art and an austere interior design with ten-point Jansen typeface and an odd-numbered-only folio arrangement and rough-cut pages. I saw my novel resting on an end cap in some superstore in the Midwest, those fortunate enough to know me in my former life lining up to buy multiple copies (teachers and cousins and coaches!). I also saw the book in more obscure circumstances, shelved in such a way that you would have to *find* it; noting that it was a thing to be *sought out*, that the person in search of the little-known title would be rewarded by its discovery at the Strand or some small, highbrow store on one of those diagonal cobblestone streets in the West Village. I would do only a handful of readings and signings, at select places.

People would buy me drinks and give me their phone numbers!

Just as my fantasy evolved into a kind of literary orgy populated by a dozen or so attractive NYU English majorettes (in the back of St. Mark's Bookshop), Ford returned with a wily grin, sans the Christmas wreath, again double-fisting flutes of eggnog, saying, "The bartender with the Kim Carnes hair totally wants my johnson."

"Which one?" I asked.

"The one serving drinks next to the calamari sleigh."

I looked over at her festive bar wagon, on top of which Ford had laid the wreath, an obvious offering.

Ford toasted her from across the ballroom and she smiled.

I said, "She's, like, forty, Ford."

"At *least!*" he replied, enthused. "Haven't you ever wanted to be with a chick on the cusp of menopause? There's something so—I don't know—*reverse Graham Greene* about it. Look at the way she ladles the nog, man."

"She ladles it."

"Ladle, ladle, welcome to my stable," he said through clenched teeth. "Man, there's nothing like tits in a tux! What I would be willing to part with just to give her the old Dirty Sanchez!"

Ford's sexual digestive system could be likened to an eight-year-old's insatiable desire for Oreo cookies and gum.

"I gotta get to work on her," Ford said, turning and heading toward the calamari sleigh.

Moments later, just as I was about to resume my hunt for Lacy Shank, Van Von Donnelly yanked me onto the dance floor and I was suddenly the fourth member of a quartet that included Stafford Davidson, Van, and Van's Heimlich maneuver damsel in distress, editor

Lawler Schnoll, who was wearing an anti-holiday, all-black ensemble that gave her the troubling air of a cold-blooded ninja.

The song was Michael Jackson's "Billie Jean" and Van boogied like a man who was resigned to—or perhaps even comforted by—the knowledge that he was ruining his clothes.

Stafford Davidson employed a style of dance that was undeniably frat boy as he hopped up and down, working not with the beat but rather to some strange, unheard counterpoint that yielded a result martial yet impressionistic.

Van failed to harness even the slightest measure of rhythm and basically wound up vibrating a lot. He periodically utilized a burlesque-like torso jiggle, offering his male mammae to Lawler, who was deeply steeped in a cauldron of dance that involved a lot of freezing into action-hero poses, complete with bicep flexes and the employment of an invisible ray gun. Every ten seconds or so she would shoot Van or Stafford and they would feign expiration, briefly clutching their stomachs, necks, and chests.

It took a lot of hand-clapping and snapping to find the beat, and after Lawler gave me a gigantic and shocking titty-twister (in the seven months I had worked on her floor, Lawler Schnoll had never even said hello to me, let alone touched me), somehow the rust shook loose and I found the groove.

During the song's climax, when the woman impersonating Michael Jackson started to screech with the simian ecstasy of a classically conditioned rhesus monkey, Lawler, a large, mannish woman, executed a rather inventive series of undoubtedly ninja-inspired karate kicks, leaped in the air, and jackknifed into a full split, landing between Stafford Davidson and the now thoroughly enraptured Van Von Donnelly, whose perspiration stains were so vast they were forming gluey continents at his paunch.

Despite the inordinate male-to-female ratio, there was a strange heterosexual democratic comfort at work, as Lawler was surprisingly fair about doling out plenty of individual attention. There was one moment when she was riding Stafford gangsta-style and Van and I partnered off and danced with a feeling of spirited, almost heroic collaboration. It lasted perhaps thirty seconds, but during the interval it was as if we were the only ones on the dance floor. Van wiggled and shook his male breasts at me while I clapped and snapped to his inventive turn-and-pivot footwork.

The woman impersonating Michael Jackson wailed and screeched about the woman who had purportedly birthed his child while my boss and I were in the midst of some sort of vaguely homosexual dance-floor communion.

Toward the end of the song, Lacy materialized in front of me and reached around and seized my left buttock, squeezing almost too hard, pulling me close, pelvis to pelvis. The rhythm section dropped out while an unseen keyboard started the intro to George Clinton's "Atomic Dog." When the drums and bass kicked in Lacy entered a mode of dance that was both raunchy ghetto-kink and deeply felt club trance, undulating her hips and torso in an overtly sexual way, yet wearing an almost beatific religious expression that was something between sentimental joy and narcotic rapture.

I must admit that during at least three BOW-WOW-WOW YIPPEE-YO-YIPPEE-YAYs I felt profound relief that nothing bad had happened—so much relief, in fact, that it was almost erotic in its effect on me.

"You're going home with me later, right?" Lacy asked with a surprising hint of vulnerability in her eyes. I felt suddenly sorry for her. She seemed so lost and alone in that moment, as if I were the only one who could remind her that there was still a place for her in the world. Her grip on my ass released and I watched her slowly spin with her eyes closed. Where she went in her head I have no idea. Maybe she was in a field behind the house she grew up in, bits of milkweed sticking to her hair. Maybe there was an apple tree. When she completed the spin, her eyes opened and she reclaimed my ass and we continued as before. Her grip hurt more now and I could feel myself grimacing.

"Come home with me," she said, sensing my hesitation, still seemingly half asleep in her trance state, her voice softened.

I said, "I can't, Lacy."

"Why not?"

"Because I'm sort of seeing someone."

"Oh . . . Is it serious?"

"Yes."

"Jesus fucking H. Are you in love with her or something?" she asked, looking directly at me now.

"I am, yes."

"Well, what are you doing here?"

I couldn't answer.

"Another quick fuck and I'll be on my way?"

"Lacy . . ."

"A little fuck her while she's down but make sure she's got a dress on?"

"Come on now."

Her breath was thick with the spiked eggnog.

"What's her name?"

"Why does that matter?"

"I can just imagine the cunt. Some Midwestern mini heifer with milky skin and born-again eyes. A bright blue blouse and pleated office pants."

And then in desperation to end an uncomfortable situation I feared would spin wildly out of control, I said it: "Your dad paid me a hundred dollars, okay?"

Her eyes got small and hard.

"He paid you a hundred dollars to what?"

"To . . . hang out with you tonight."

Lacy continued dancing and did not respond. This new information only seemed to send her back to that place behind her eyes. I thought she was going to slap me or elbow me in the ribs—I actually braced myself—but she stopped clutching my left butt cheek and actually took my hands and positioned them on the back of her neck. Then she looked at me for a moment, almost pleadingly, and placed her head gently on my chest. We slowed down, defying the music, and as she pulled me close I could feel the warmth of her body radiating through her dress. Her skin smelled faintly of peppermint and patchouli oil. Things were suddenly oddly romantic—the music was purely incidental at this point.

Toward the end of the song, Lacy pulled my hands away, kissed my cheek, turned, walked off the dance floor, wove through the throngs of stinking, sweating publishing professionals, found the Shankler (who was completely crocked and attempting to master an invisible high wire while negotiating a triple-olive, half-drunk gin martini), and proceeded to rear back and kick her large, totally shitfaced father squarely in the balls, causing him to drop his martini glass, clutch his groin, and land on both knees so thunderously I'm almost positive there was an echo.

Several of the same underlings who had rushed to Harlan Niederlander's aid during the bestseller celebration some months before leaped, skidded, and flung themselves to the Shankler's side. He made a noise not dissimilar to a large diesel eighteen-wheeler downshifting in Midtown traffic. Appropriately, the music stopped, the lights were brought up, and across the ballroom Lacy could be seen removing her lovely purple dress, a look of sublime petulance on her face.

Wearing only her heels and a thin purple thong now, she draped the dress over one shoulder. Any impulse I had to stop her from whatever it was she was about to do was somehow paralyzed by the crude reality of what she had just done. I found myself mesmerized, as if she were a great lion appearing before me in a dream. And for the slightest moment I thought I might indeed be dreaming. We locked eyes and then she turned back to the frenzy of people tending to her father and cried, "Hey, geeks!"

For a moment it was so quiet you could have heard a penny landing on a pillow. Even her father's groaning had died down. Then, with catlike quickness, Lacy mounted the main catering table, squatted, and urinated on the enormous, half-eaten Atlantic salmon. Sprigs of parsley, lemon wedges, and cocktail napkins were suddenly floating. Her small, perfect breasts faintly wobbled while she concentrated. No one said a word, and her urine stream actually sounded oddly peaceful. When she was finished Lacy said, "Merry Fucking Christmas," and then she let herself down from the table rather gracefully and exited in her heels and thong, her purple dress trailing down her perfect, pale back.

Let Go

TWO DAYS LATER—the following Monday, to be exact—I was fired. After I had transcribed the call reports and collected a fresh batch of bellwether numbers, Van Von Donnelly intercommed me into his office, closed the door, took his seat behind his kaleidoscopic haberdashery desk arrangement, and told me swiftly that I was going to be "let go."

To chronicle the actual conversation seems meaningless, even farcical. It wasn't Van's fault, after all. Despite being my direct boss, he was simply the messenger. Van blamed it on the "cutbacks" that he knew were imminent and said he had tried to find a way to "get around it" but the "higher-ups" wouldn't budge.

It was a fiscal reality, of course.

It was the recession, of course.

It was happening all over the company and every department would suffer.

I was one of many.

Of course.

Van was so kind he even went so far as to say that he would be happy to write me a referral letter.

After the news we shook hands sadly and I turned and walked out of his office, collected my few things, and left.

When I walked past a batch of unwanted free and review titles I had an impulse to violently sweep them off the counter and roar in mighty, primal disgruntlement, but instead I picked one of the books off the floor and placed it next to the coffeemaker.

On my way to the elevator banks, I stopped by Jack Shank's office.

Armed with a mouthful of equal parts varsity-jock expletive and the pure, unknown result of already inflamed bitterness, I was determined to tell him off in my deepest, most masculine voice.

However, when I threw open the door I was greeted not by the Shankler but rather by the life-size point-of-sale promotional cardboard cutout display of novelist Selden Kong, our company's bread and butter, as it were, on whose face a grainy, poorly magnified Xerox copy of Jack Shank's big grinning visage had been pasted. And where our great bestselling author was normally clutching a copy of *The Cop Who Ate a Bear*, there was now an eight-by-eleven-inch piece of Xerox paper with the following message scrawled in black Sharpie ink:

> ### Gone Skinny Dipping in Sarasota
> ### Get the hell out of my office!

When I recall my final walk to the elevator banks, the thing that seems to endure most tenaciously is not a feeling of sadness or the ache of regret or even the slow-burning fury that I could almost feel oozing through my pores. It is, rather, the quality of the light, an almost blazing, color-flattening fluorescence saturating the hides of cubicles, the pleasant faces of my now former coworkers, the seemingly endless miles of corporate Sheetrock, the lifeless abandoned mail gurneys, and even the gray carpeting. It is an indifferent radiance whose barely audible yet penetrating accompanying buzz still occasionally refrains in the back of my mind like the detested church music of my adolescence.

Unemployment, Eccentricity, and Subterranean Fathers

COLLECTING UNEMPLOYMENT WASN'T SO BAD.

As with many of the great government-subsidized programs for taxpaying Americans, unemployment had its perks.

Like the $212.00 a week, for instance.

And the simple, user-friendly process of dialing my social security number into a touchtone phone.

Which bore the technological genius of the automated voicemail service for New York City's much-celebrated Unemployment Program.

Which, in turn, yielded a strange, soothing comfort experienced during the brief, short-declarative-sentence interaction with the digitized female automaton on the other end.

Sure, there were other new challenges, but your scrappy, pliant narrator would not be overwhelmed.

To begin with, I had no real sense of what the hell I was supposed to do with my time. Oh, sure, I was in a city full of infinite opportunities. There were museums and parks and bookstores and vintage-clothing shops and used-record stores and the cinema! Even a simple stroll down the street of my East Village wonderland offered a stimulating menagerie of drug dealers, pit bulls, and the homeless! Yet despite the wealth of culture just beyond the threshold of my apartment building I was somehow content to remain inside, which forced me to accept certain domestic truths that, perhaps due to my usual post-work, bleary-eyed, low-salary exhaustion, I hadn't really dealt with before.

Like coming to the realization that during unit four's daylight hours there were many more mice and mouse-like rodents scurrying about than there were at night.

And the scathing, almost cathartic discovery of the corroded grouting plaguing ninety percent of our household tiling.

And the identification of a damp, sour odor not unlike the smell of rotten trout wafting from underneath our dead refrigerator.

Or noticing for the first time the plexus of zit guts, boogers, dandruff, toothpaste spittle, and other unknown Loachian personal matter clogging the margins of the bathroom mirror.

Or the moist, corduroy-like hide forming on the dishes in the sink.

Or the dead black squirrel I found oddly contorted in Feick's old room.

Or the unfailing waste-management nightmare of lifting the toilet seat to discover log after Loachian log.

The embarrassment of collecting unemployment was intellectually molded—metaphysically transformed, even—into the idea that I was actually receiving an "artist grant" from our generous, sympathetic state government agency.

It was like getting one of those New York Foundation for the Arts awards.

NYFA was saving your slightly down-and-out hero.

And he deserved it, damnit!

So like a humble, prostrated servant of truth and beauty, your good-citizen narrator kept his head down and attempted to complete his novel about acute knee pain and the end of the world.

I even called Judy Klooszch's office and left her a message saying as much.

"Judy," I said to her automated voicemail, "I'm just about done with the novel. I'm really putting my nose to the grindstone. Hope all is well with you."

I left her my phone number and, for several days, any time the phone rang I practically sprinted to it, but it was never Judy Klooszch. More often than not it was either telemarketers trying to get me to buy magazine subscriptions or the phone company itself, calling with disconnection threats.

I had also lost track of Feick. I hadn't seen or heard from him in weeks. I imagined he and Ruben were taking trips to Fire Island or Provincetown or Cape Cod, where their lifestyle could flourish without the shadow of an uncomfortable older brother. I actually stopped by the Atlantis Theatre and left Feick a note with the box office. It was a simple, three-sentence greeting written on spiral notebook paper. It read:

> FEICK,
> Hey. Hope all is well. Would love to hang out and catch up sometime.
> LOVE,
> YOUR BRO

But I never received a response. There were new stakes at play as starvation, daytime loneliness, and the general threat of penury were lurching around my East Village apartment like agitated, invisible polar bears.

On Christmas I spoke to my mother for the first time in months. In the background I could hear Nat King Cole singing an old holiday standard.

"Have you gotten a raise yet?"

"No," I said. "Not yet."

I didn't have the heart to tell her I'd been fired.

"Are you eating enough?" she asked.

"I'm eating fine," I said.

"How's your little brother?"

"He's good."

"You're keeping an eye on him, right?"

"Of course," I lied.

"Your father thinks he might be eccentric."

Eccentric was the term my parents used when they spoke about nontraditional sexuality. To utter the word *gay* or *homosexual* would no doubt have triggered some acute psychic break that would require a large amount of Valium.

I can't deny that Feick's new life was shocking to me, in the way that discovering a stray cat in your underwear drawer can be shocking, but I firmly believe that despite the obvious gulf that had grown between us, at least I was on the road to acceptance. Where my parents were concerned, there surely would be no road. Or if there was one, it was populated by Pope John Paul II, his magisterial retinue, the current head of the N.R.A., Sisters Joan, Alice, and Mary Elizabeth (a triumvirate of casually dressed but severe-looking Sisters of the Blessed Virgin Mary nuns from my parochial grammar school), an outfit of armed U.S. Marshals, and all of our Republican presidential candidates from the last four elections.

Although my mother hadn't actually said anything for a moment, I could hear her voice wavering a bit on the other end.

"He's not eccentric," I said of my brother, trying to calm her.

I'm almost certain she was covering the phone now, as Nat King Cole's "White Christmas" was suddenly muffled on the other end.

My mother unblocked the receiver, sniffled a bit, and said, "We sent you boys a card. Did you get our card?"

"I got the card, Mother," I said. "Thank you."

It was Frosty the Snowman smiling through a perfect twilit snowfall. Inside were two twenty-dollar bills: one for me and one for Feick. I put Feick's in a used paperback edition of Kurt Vonnegut's *Breakfast of Champions*, hoping I would see my brother again soon.

The inside of the card read:

MERRY CHRISTMAS, BOYS.
LOVE,
MOM AND DAD

"How's Dad doing?" I asked after a pause during which my mother's labored, overly dramatic exhalations almost drove me to rip the phone out of the wall.

"He's fine," she sighed.

"The mole removal was a success, I assume?"

"It was a success, yes. There's just the smallest scar now."

"Where is he?"

"He's in the basement pretending he's not trying to sneak all the holiday crumb cake. His feet are the new problem."

"What's wrong with his feet?"

"Oh, he says they hurt a lot. Dr. Quigley just remolded some new orthotic insoles for him."

My father had terrible pain in his arches and spent half of his adult life soaking his feet in a solution of hot water and Epsom salts. I knew I would no doubt eventually inherit this condition, and I resented him for it.

"You know they honored him at the plant the other day," my mother continued. "Gave him an engraved plaque and everything. Thirty years of service. What that man has sacrificed . . ."

I said, "Tell him congratulations for me."

"I think he resents you not going to work for him."

"Merry Christmas to you, too, Mother."

"Now, don't be snide."

"You started it."

"Oh, I did not."

"Oh, you did, too."

With my mother, when it came to the subject of who "started it" one could get buried alive in a discussion of limitless philosophical perplexities.

"Well, it's true," she said, finally breaking. "He offered you a *good* salary. A *union* position. With *benefits* and *perks*. You don't know how it *hurts* him. I think you're spiteful. You and your brother. So full of vinegar."

"Mother, I've said it a million times. I didn't go to four years of college to become a tool-and-die man."

"You could have at least *tried* the apprenticeship."

"I'm a writer, not a machinist."

"Oh, you and your *higher calling.*"

"Don't start guilt-tripping me just because you're miserable."

"You watch your step, young man."

"Watch *your* step," I snipped childishly. "It's *your* misery."

"I am *not* miserable! *You're* the miserable one! The *tortured artist!* What a bunch of *hooey!*"

That's when I said, "I'm going now, okay?" I started to hang up.

"Don't go!" she cried out.

I stared at the phone and tried to make it melt in my hand with untapped superpowers, having heard of hundred-pound mothers lifting the back ends of cars to save their infants from getting crushed. Unfortunately, I was handicapped by earthbound, mortal human skills, and the phone remained room temperature.

I could hear my mother weeping on the other end. She was no doubt fondling one of her three hundred and forty-seven Hummel figurines; most likely the doe-slash-fawn team featured genuflecting amid an oval of field grass and nettles. This prized and oft-fondled collectible was showcased on one of my grandmother's eighteenth-century lace doilies, carefully placed on the antique tea tray next to our monolithic, ancient Zenith console television.

I slowly put the receiver back to my ear.

"I'm sorry, honey," she said, sniffling now. She could go from inflamed, nonalcoholic Roman Catholic rage to pathetic self-pity with the best of them. "I shouldn't have done that."

We were silent for a moment. She wasn't breathing and Nat King Cole was crooning "O Little Town of Bethlehem" in his impossibly silky baritone. I was making fists and staring at a coagulated blob of soup that the Loach had left on the kitchen counter. There was some sort of insect trapped in it, and I wished it would drown.

"Please don't hang up," my mother begged.

"I'm not hanging up."

"I just wish you boys would've come home."

"It's too expensive."

She said, "Greyhound has very affordable fares."

I thought about getting on a Greyhound and my heart sank. I would never hear the end of it from the Owl.

"Feick's got the show, too," I offered.

"I feel like you're both so lost in that awful city. Where is your brother, anyway?"

"He's out."

"But what does that *mean?*" she whimpered.

"It doesn't mean anything. He's just out. He has a life."

"Why aren't you *together?*"

"He's having dinner with some friends from the play."

"Well, didn't he *invite* you?"

"I'd already made other plans."

"You did?"

"Yes," I lied.

"Romantic?"

"Romantic plans, yes, Mother."

"With a woman?"

"No, with an octopus."

"Who is she?"

"Her name is Basha."

"Is that foreign?"

"She's Polish, yes."

"Oh."

"Don't worry, Mother, I'm fairly certain she's been baptized and confirmed."

"In the Catholic Church?"

"No, in the Church of the Roving Zebras."

"Are you sure she's Catholic?"

"Positive."

"Well, that's a relief. I hope you're still going to Mass."

I didn't answer this and she was smart enough to drop the subject.

For some reason I couldn't shake the image of my father in the basement, foisting off marital avoidance as crumb-cake theft. I knew he was down there to escape my mother's eternal whining. Of course, there were his copper etchings and fly-fishing lures, too. He could spend hours attending to the surgical enterprise of threading and knotting artificial flies, and although he had lifetime subscriptions to *Bass Fisherman* and *Field & Stream*, he rarely, if ever, actually went fishing.

After a deep breath and a prodigious sigh, my mother said, "Are you positively certain that Feick's not eccentric?"

To which I answered: "Well, Mother, to be honest . . ."

"To be honest *what*?"

"To be honest, I, um . . ."

The heel of my free hand was pressing into my right eye. Oh, had I blown it now.

"You *um*? What does that mean, you *um*?"

"Well, Mother, I wouldn't say I'm positively certain."

"*What!?*" she shrieked.

"I just can't be absolutely certain!" I shrieked back. "Stay calm!"

"OH, DEAR JESUS!" she cried.

Now she had totally lost it and was hyperventilating and wailing whole-hog.

"NORMAN!" she called to my father. "OHMYGOD, NORMAN!"

It was like listening to a person with brain damage being terrorized by their first roller-coaster ride.

"Please don't cry, Mother."

"HOW DID YOUR FATHER AND I PRODUCE TWO *BOHEMI-ANS*?!"

It took a few minutes, but after a full-blown howling session that degenerated to dreary, exhausted sniffles and maternal sighs, I eventually got my mother to calm down, and I was able to dodge what would turn out to be the first of many epic holiday family sagas regarding my bohemian lifestyle and Feick's damning eccentricity.

Later Basha and I had Christmas dinner at Leshko's on Avenue A. She wore her hair down, and no makeup, and during the short interval between sitting down and our menus being dropped on the table I had to resist the pathetic urge to touch her face several times.

"You seem filled with a terrible sadness," Basha said after our waters were served.

When it came to my emotional existence, her powers of observation were always frighteningly accurate.

I detailed the conversation with my mother. Basha was especially intrigued by my father's time spent in the basement.

She said, "This is very strange, no?"

"Honestly, we never thought it was strange. It's just the way things were. We always knew he was down there doing his thing."

"Perhaps he has some great secret?"

"I don't know," I replied. "Maybe. He's a pretty quiet guy."

"Perhaps he is—how you say—dragon queen?"

"Dragon queen?"

"This is when a man dresses in the clothing of his mother and goes dancing to disco sensation ABBA, no?"

"Sort of," I explained. "It doesn't necessarily have to be his mother's clothes, though, nor is dancing a requirement. And it's, um, *drag* queen."

"Drag queen, yes!"

I said, "I highly doubt that my father is a drag queen."

"There is this movie called *Some Like It Hot* starring Tony Curtis and Jack the Lemon in which they dress up like women. It is exceedingly funny and causes many fastidious riots in the belly."

"But that was a farce."

"What does this mean?"

"It means it was comedic. There was a certain amount of irony and silliness involved. My father is about as far from irony and silliness as you can get. He's about as comedic as a mailbox."

"It caused Tony Curtis and Jack the Lemon to possess copious amounts of joy to wear the dresses. In Poland, my cousin Zygmunt wears his mother's dress on Thursdays and he is a very handsome person and likes to dance to ABBA's 'Dancing Queen' and also Michael Jackson's *Thriller*. He is exceedingly masculine and happily married and has two childrens."

I tried picturing my father wearing one of my mother's Sunday dresses—the yellow one with the blue anemones cascading down the midriff, a starfish on either sleeve. The image was far more disturbing than funny. For some reason, I imagined him chewing a plug of long-leaf tobacco and posing in front of his gun collection.

"I'm not sure my father has those kinds of secrets," I explained.

After all, one should always opt for simplicity when faced with confounding mysteries. My father's stoicism and private world were as impenetrable as the reinforced stainless steel Fort Knox Yeager 66 safe in which he kept his various shotguns and hunting rifles and the prized .357 caliber Glock pistol he would take apart and clean once a month as if it were a precious model airplane from his youth. His tour in Vietnam was like an invisible, silencing vapor that perpetually hung in the air of our house. As boys, starving for myths and legends, if Feick or I ever brought up the subject of our war-hero father and his time spent "over there," my mother would turn on us so fast we could see her pupils contracting in her head like those of an agitated mountain lion.

"I think he just likes to be alone," I added.

"If he prefers this then you should not be sad."

"Maybe you're right."

Eventually the topic of my father faded. Basha and I held hands and sat in silence. Through the diner window we saw a band of four or five East Villagers run by with a Christmas tree that they had stolen from the corner deli. They were dressed as ninjas and the two without black masks looked like mimes who hoped to become ninjas. Moments later, a man wearing an orange baseball hat ran after them brandishing a hockey stick.

"I love you," I told Basha after our turkey dinner was served. It was only the second time I had said it and it leaped out of my mouth like burnt soup.

Basha smiled sweetly, clutching my thumb. The thumb-clutch was a recent development; I liked it so much that I found myself periodically clutching my own thumb when she wasn't around.

Our eyes locked and I felt a naive surge of warmth and hope.

Basha then bowed her head toward her lap for a moment, and when she looked back up her eyes were filled with tears.

"I'm pregnant," she said.

"Oh," I said. "Wow."

"Yes. Wow. Very much wow."

"How long have you known?"

"Two days. I was afraid to tell you."

"But I'm so glad you did. Wow."

"A million wows, yes."

Then I stood and leaned over our turkey dinners and hugged her. She hugged me back and gravy got all over just about everything I was wearing.

"Well, how do you feel?" I said after we both sat back down.

"I don't know. How you say . . . ?"

"Excited?"

"Terrif . . ."

"Terrific?"

"Terrified."

"Terrified."

"This means extremely scared, no?"

"It does, yes."

"How do you feel?" she asked.

"Um . . . Well, I don't know. It's sort of a surprise. But this could be a good thing."

"You are terrified, too, no?"

"I am terrified, yes."

And it was true. I was as terrified in that moment as I have been my entire life.

Basha then said, "We finish eating, okay?"

"Okay," I said.

We ate the rest of our dinners in silence.

Later that night we attended a revival of *Manhattan* at Theatre 80 on St. Mark's Place. Woody Allen's Isaac Davis was heroic and romantic and possessed an elastic physicality, and as Tracy, Mariel Hemingway broke my heart.

During the two-and-a-half-block walk back to my apartment there was a light, advent-calendar snow and I almost dropped to one knee in the middle of First Avenue and proposed marriage to Basha, but while it appeared to be clear all the way to Houston Street, the promise of traffic was imminent.

And I was too much of a coward.

We spent New Year's Eve in my room nursing a bottle of six-dollar Wild Irish Rose.

With her tip money, Basha had recently purchased a portable boom box and we were listening to Tom Waits's *Rain Dogs*. Basha sang along to "Cemetery Polka" and performed an impromptu dance with my corduroy coat that involved lots of high-stepping and a rather doting relationship with the coat. She punctuated the routine by buttoning it up to her chin, somehow removing her sweater and bra, and then flinging them across the room in an illusory, multipart move.

Later that evening Basha taught me about the more practical thermal uses of candles and we positioned several beeswax cylinders on the windowsill to create a potent front line of heat, but a good share of the winter draft still crept, sluiced, and leapfrogged by, around, and over our lighted shrine.

Aesthetically speaking, the candle effect was almost cathedral-like. The flame shadows sawed on the walls and flickered in Basha's big round eyes. I fought off the Catholic imagery, determined to keep my former life as an altar boy at a safe distance.

Prior to her announcement in Leshko's, in my little cold room, making love with Basha had taken on a survivalist purpose, and we were somehow comforted by the advantages of friction, increased heart rate, and cardiovascular conditioning.

Sex doubled as winter fuel, and we were proud of our resourcefulness.

"Shall we use more," I would ask archaically, as if I were some doomed Bolshevik talking about firewood in a Russian novel.

"Yes, we shall," Basha would respond, lifting the covers for me.

Post-announcement, understandably, our sexual relationship entered a new phase that went far beyond the obvious coital pleasures of intercourse. Now that she was carrying our child, even though she was only early in her first trimester, I found her body to be more beautiful, magical—supernatural, even—and I treated it as a totem of worship, not a thing to gain pleasure from. I bathed her and washed her hair and clipped her toenails and rubbed lotion into her arms and sesame oil into the pads of her feet.

To be totally honest, the constant pampering got to be a little tedious, but I was in love and scared out of my mind so I tricked myself into believing that nursing a pregnant woman was like participating in some great artistic process.

Every belch was a percussive masterpiece.

Her flatulence was the sweet breath from the mouths of madrigal fairies.

Basha had transformed into a vessel containing our miraculous creation, and I was her humble, devoted servant.

I lobbied hard to keep the child, an idea born perhaps of some ridiculous notion of male heroism. I convinced myself that, if this were to indeed happen, during the course of the next several months I would grow into the kind of man who could sustain a full-time job and bring home groceries and wake up multiple times during the night and coach Basha through Lamaze and paint our room robin's-egg blue and create a safe place for a young couple and their child in a city as unforgiving as New York.

"And poopy diapers?" Basha would say.

"Poopy diapers are nothing," I'd respond. "I'll change them with my eyes closed."

"I will become ugly and fat like Roseanne."

"I don't care. Get as fat as you want."

"I will crush you in bed. You'll have to sleep in cage."

"As long as you let me out in the morning."

There were extensive naming lists.

Male names included Bob, Sam, Feick, Glenwood, Chevy, Jaroslaw, Zygmunt, and Dragan.

Female names included Cherry, Sonia, April, Helena, Miriam, Cornelia, and Cesia.

That New Year's Eve, after all the candles were lighted and a silence had fallen in the room, I said, "So, should we have it?"

"I do not know this answer," Basha replied.

She looked out the window longingly, as if she were waiting for some sort of winter bird to bear a prophecy.

On January 2, through the kindness of a pro-choice hotline, I was able to locate an unnamed private clinic on the Upper East Side, and a few conversations later, I discovered that we could have what was described to me as a "very safe and tasteful procedure" for six hundred sixty dollars cash.

Other than the occasional trip to the deli, for weeks I left the apartment only to check the mail. I felt that *Opie's Half-life* was more important than ever. Child or not, I was determined that there would be a novel, and a Great American Novel at that.

Basha exhibited brutal morning sickness, and I often spent the early hours holding her hair while she vomited into our functionally challenged toilet. She was spending more and more nights with me, and I have no idea how she was justifying her perpetual absence to her parents (whom I had still never met). And what about János, for that matter? When I asked her about her man back in Poland she was vague and reticent.

"Have you told him yet?" I asked one morning after she'd been sick.

"No."

"What do you think he would say?"

"János is János," was her answer. And the vaguer she was about him the more his shape in my mind resembled that of an enormous grizzly bear.

At some point during the day I would meet Basha at Polly Parker's, where I'd do my best to satisfy her strange hunger cravings. Black licorice and tins of sardines were her early favorites. In exchange for her nightly snacks, Basha would sneak me halves of sandwiches wrapped in napkins. These small, furtive meals helped my weekly $212 unemployment check go a long way.

Beyond Basha and entertaining thoughts of fatherhood, I was tethered to my task and to a replacement Smith Corona daisy wheel I purchased from an Avenue A flea market for twelve dollars. It was uglier than the original, heavier too, but I made the best of it.

I'd spoken to Alexa on three different occasions, apologizing for my repeated delays in getting the completed manuscript to Judy Klooszch.

"Judy said she's happy to wait," Alexa assured me after the new year.

According to her, everyone at work was shocked by my dismissal. Ford and I spoke about it briefly one day after Alexa was kind enough to transfer me to his extension.

"It's like that thing from your childhood that you don't realize you miss till it's gone," Ford said. "You're like the pogo stick that got sold at the garage sale or something."

"Thanks, Ford," I said.

Ford and I agreed to meet for a beer in the near future, but we both knew that was a remote possibility. No one who is firmly positioned on the ladder of employment wants to hang out with someone who has just fallen from its lowest rung.

I jokingly promised Alexa that in addition to the manuscript I would deliver a month's supply of caramel corn to Judy Klooszch.

"Just bring the novel," she urged me.

So, like some indigenous hunter and his prey, *Opie's Half-life* and I became one and the same. The novel was my elephant, and I was also the elephant-hunter king responsible for its destiny. I would wake up in the middle of the night regurgitating vivacious word salads, reacting to my half-remembered dreams in dialogue that Opie himself would use in the novel.

Opie was speaking through me in a logorrhea of abstract violence, and I was writing it down. I was simply a vessel, a kind of metaphysical canoe for my alter ego's wants, needs, and nocturnal insanity.

Converse to my newfound hermitage, the Loach seemed to be away from the sofa more and more. In fact, there were times when he was noticeably absent from the *apartment*—sometimes for days at a time—which made me both happy and acutely paranoid. I had no idea what he was up to. Perhaps with spring somewhere on the horizon he'd recently pupated from a kind of larva state and was undergoing a major transmutation?

He was venturing out into the world, after all!

He was actually *walking* places!

One night I was heading toward the refrigerator with the day's completed work. It was perhaps two or three a.m. and Basha was spending the night in Stuyvesant Town. I'd written two new chapters and edited another three. I was feeling satisfied and kind of sleepy in that warm, saggy way that melts down the back of the neck until I heard the Loach's voice emanating from somewhere deep inside his snowmobile suit. He hadn't been home for a few days and the surprise almost made me jump into the kitchen sink.

He said, "It's getting bigger."

My blood pressure skyrocketed and I almost tore my new pages in half. I placed them on the counter and smoothed them a bit.

"Maybe *fatter*'s the better word," the Loach continued in his dehydrated voice. "Watch out for tubby."

"Loach, what are you talking about?"

"That thing you're writing."

"It's called a novel."

"Right. Injured hoops player screwing around in the East Village, trying to get laid, trying to make sense of his miserable life. You know, the, like, science-fiction fantasia *rudiments* or whatever don't mean it ain't you."

"You've actually read it?"

"You don't mind, do you?"

I replied, "I guess I don't, no."

"I like the talking dog a lot. He's probably my favorite character. The way he's, like, obsessed with sniffing his balls. Him and the chick with two names."

"KellySarah."

"Yeah, her. She's fucking hot, yo. I imagine her thirty-six-twenty-four-twenty-eight. With fuck-me eyes and a Brazilian. She's a wacko, but what a fantasy."

For a moment I wasn't sure if I should be flattered or furious.

"What do you do with a story like that, anyway?" the Loach asked.

"Well, the hope is to publish it."

"That's gotta be pretty hard, right?"

I said, "It's not easy."

"Does it pay?"

"It could, I guess. But first-time novelists rarely get very big advances."

"It's gotta at least be six figs, though. A hundred, a hundred and fifty K, right?"

"I'd get maybe a tenth of that."

"Ten grand?"

"Maybe less, maybe more," I said. "I really don't know."

"Still, ten G's can buy a lotta burritos."

"More burritos than I can afford right now, that's for sure."

"Do they, like, put your head shot on the back?"

"Sometimes they do, yeah."

"I'll bet the chicks dig that."

"Maybe."

"Yeah, I'll bet that that guy—what's his name? The schmuck who writes all those weird horror books with the orgies—Selsnick something?"

"Selden Kong."

"Yeah—Selden Kong. I'll bet that fucker gets pussy galore."

"I wouldn't know."

"Yeah," the Loach said. "I should be an author."

"It's not that easy."

I tried picturing the Loach as an author: looming over a desk; cleaning up his act and wearing blazers; autographing books at some super-store in West Palm Beach. It was about as far-fetched as Big Foot.

"Tell me this much," the Loach said. "How do you make sure no-body steals your ideas?"

I said, "You copyright it."

"Is that, like, expensive?" the Loach asked.

"It's, like, thirty bucks. You send it to the Library of Congress and they register it."

"Have you done it yet?"

"No. But I'll do it when I'm done. Why?"

"I was just wonderin' 'cause I have all this, like, material I might wanna put in a book."

I said, "Your stand-up stuff?"

"Yeah. Monologues and jokes, mostly. Some songs, too."

"You write songs?"

"I do, yeah. Raps."

"Cool."

"I do this one in a Speedo about baby seals and date rape. Jungle drums and fake pubes bursting out the sides and everything. I can beat-box, too."

Picturing the Loach rapping in a Speedo with bursting pubes was an alarming image.

"Yeah, I got a lot of ideas," he continued. "I think I might do that copyright thing."

For the first time, although fleetingly, I recognized something naive and boyish about the Loach that I would qualify as genuine, innocent charm.

"That *Opie's Half-time* ain't a bad story, bro," the Loach added, clawing at his groin area. "I mean, I don't know *all* those big words, but I get the gist of what you're, like, tryin' to say and stuff. There were times when I was actually entertained."

Instead of correcting his bastardization of my title, I let it go. I simply said, "Cool." It was strange. I think this was the first real conversation the Loach and I had ever had. At some point I even told him I'd like to come and see one of his stand-up performances.

Perhaps this was a sign of better times to come between us? I have heard it said that friendship does at times spring from the most unlikely sources.

When we were finished talking, I continued smoothing out my crumpled pages.

And then I put them in the freezer, as I had for the past eight months.

A New Neighbor and a Welcome Letter

ONE AFTERNOON IN MID-JANUARY, after returning from the corner deli, I saw a man with no legs climbing the stairs ahead of me. He was bald and wore weight-lifter's gloves. His tattooed triceps bulged out impressively as he ascended the stairs on his fists.

When he reached the third floor he keyed into the Tins' apartment and closed the door behind him. For some reason I associated him with John Anderson-Allensworth. It wasn't that far-fetched, considering the numerous surreal tectonic permutations that existed in our building.

I knocked on the door of unit three, and moments later my new neighbor opened the door.

"What?" he said, annoyed. His voice was deep and harsh. He was now housed on a reinforced, padded plywood square with casters. The room behind him was as dark and mysterious as it had been before. Bert Tin's Pert Plus art had run down the wall a bit.

"Is Tim around?" I asked.

"Who?"

"Tim Tin."

"Don't know him."

"He lived here with his family. He had a wife and son."

"They went fishing," the man said.

I said, "Like, ice fishing?"

"Like fishing for fish food," he replied obliquely.

"Oh," I said.

He possessed many facial piercings and wore dark eyeliner. His bald head featured a thumbprint-size raised birthmark at the top of his crown. He was an anatomically reduced, Hercules-armed Goth freak. Down the center of his right forearm, one of his tattoos read BUILD YOUR OWN PRISON AND LIVE IN IT. He had somehow changed his shirt, and in white letters his sleeveless black-hooded sweatshirt said A THOUSAND REASONS TO. I assumed the prepositional cliffhanger was featured on his back and that it most likely had something to do with medieval pain.

His diminutive stature made the Tins' apartment seem enormous.

I had a strange impulse to depress the raised birthmark at the top of his skull.

"Do you know if the Tins are coming back?" I asked.

To which Legless Goth Man replied, "Not in the foreseeable future." He really punched the F's in *foreseeable future*.

Then he said, "Taste your exit," and slammed the door in my face.

The faux brass knocker broke my nose and I stood there tasting my exit for several minutes. Its primary flavor was equal parts blood, mucus, and the gunmetal of unit three's door.

Using the wall for balance, I held my face and bled into my hands. Why were these things happening to me?

When my head started to feel too heavy for my shoulders I slid down the wall and sat on the floor.

I wanted to knock on the door again and take umbrage with Legless Goth Man, but my sympathies for his handicap seemed to undercut that notion and so instead I remained in a seated position and cried a lot.

For several minutes I could faintly hear his caster-board squealing across the room.

Two days later, after a long, sleepless night of trying to ignore the small earthquake of pain in the middle of my face, I emerged from my room to discover the Loach and our new neighbor from unit three doing cocaine in the living room. The Loach had my bathroom mirror upturned on his lap and Legless Goth Man was snorting a line through what appeared to be a cut fast-food straw.

I had designs on a glass of water to wash down the aspirin I had thus far resisted due to my chronically sensitive stomach. When my bedroom door closed behind me they both turned and stared. One of the living room windows was wide open and the apartment was freezing. The Loach was bare-chested and the sleeves of his snowmobile suit were dangling at his sides. For a moment it looked like something sexual was going on, as Legless Goth Man's slick white skull was positioned fellatio-like over the Loach's lap, his raised birthmark an odd punctuation mark dangling at the end of a very strange sentence.

After a breathless pause, they broke into a chorus of screeching laughter that no doubt had to do with the lopsided, distended potato that was now my nose.

"Door taster!" Legless Goth Man cried, twisting a little on his caster-board.

I touched my nostrils self-consciously, sending a tremor of pain through my face. I almost retched and their laughter hit another impossible octave.

After the screeching subsided the Loach introduced us.

Legless Goth Man's name was Lars and he apparently had something to do with the Loach's old comedy troupe, The Screaming Ninja Clown Brigade.

I briefly wondered if the Avenue A Christmas-tree thieves were affiliated with this organization.

"Lars was sort of our GM," the Loach explained.

"Yeah, until Packer's girl let me eat her pussy in the green room," Lars scoffed. "What a fuckin' monkey on that one!"

"Monkey muncher!" the Loach screamed.

"Monkey muncher!" Lars the Legless Goth Man screamed, a vein throbbing near his eye.

"MONKEY MUNCHER MONKEY MUNCHER MONKEY MUNCHER!" they screeched in unison.

My nose throbbed and my eyes watered and after I decided against the glass of water I closed myself in my room and downed the aspirin dry.

For several minutes they continued chanting and screec
brilliant alliterative phrase in a way that seemed appro
brigade of screaming ninja clowns.

On the final Monday of January, I received a long letter from the Owl.
It was passionately written with various expiring pens and multicolored ink. It had been at least two months since his departure and I was
so thrilled to hear from him that I almost tore the envelope in half trying to get to the letter.

> *DEAR HOMON,*
> *Greetings from the road.*
> *When I close my eyes at night I see only the many variations of*
> *asphalt and painted yellow lines.*
> *There is no radio, so I've been living with my own thoughts for*
> *weeks now. They are disturbing and fractured, Homon. Thoughts*
> *that involve arson and other manifestations of hatred for*
> *corporate America. I duct-taped three U.S. mailboxes thus far,*
> *and this is just the tip of a very toxic iceberg. I'm not sure what*
> *the duct tape actually prevents as it is easily removable, but it*
> *feels right, and with each strip I gain clarity.*
> *I have investigated the many uses of bleach and other*
> *household cleaning products. I have come very close to buying an*
> *inordinate amount of illegal fireworks from the backs of random*
> *semis and shady-looking Winnebagos, but the MBA candidate in*
> *me—that sluttish fuckhead coward that I abhor—is preoccupied*
> *with maintaining fiscal solvency.*
> *There are times when I find myself reciting state capitals just*
> *to distract the anarchist that is also in me. I do them*
> *alphabetically, and I sing their names into the frosty glare of*
> *oncoming headlights.*
> *Augusta, Austin, Albany, Annapolis, and Atlanta. Boston,*
> *Boise, Bismarck, and Baton Rouge. Carson City, Charleston,*

Cheyenne, Columbus, Columbia, and Concord. Denver, Des Moines, and Dover. Frankfort. Harrisburg, Hartford, Helena, and Honolulu. Indianapolis. Jackson, Jefferson City, and Juneau. Lansing, Lincoln, and Little Rock. Madison, Montgomery, and Montpelier. Nashville. Oklahoma City and Olympia. Phoenix, Pierre, and Providence. Raleigh and Richmond. Salem, Salt Lake City, Santa Fe, St. Paul, and Springfield. Tallahassee, Trenton, and even Topeka—capital of my hated Kansas.

I sing the cities, and I imagine the various municipal buildings and their civic-hero statues and small walking parks with maple trees and birds.

After I wrested myself from the jowls of the Lincoln Tunnel I headed directly west. Don't worry, Homon, even though I was technically in a VW bus heading west, I did not stop in Kansas, I promise. I had short-lived plans to hit Idaho. Big timber. Glacial lakes. Communing with elk and deer. I read somewhere that your personal freedoms are protected with great ferocity in Idaho. I have no idea what my personal freedoms are at this point, as I spent too much of my youth watching television and wanting to buy things out of department-store catalogs. I thought the elevation of Idaho would be somehow purifying.

The nosebleeds and thinner air.

But I never made it to Idaho, Homon. In short, it was a romantic and stupid notion and my ass started to get really cramped.

A few days after my departure I fought off a cluster of headaches that had me paranoid about monoxide seepage. I spent seventy-two hours driving with the windows down. It snowed and rained in the bus, Homon. My traveling partners were the colder elements. Frost and rain and fog and sleet and all sizes and consistencies of snow. There have been entire seasons in the passenger's seat.

Driving through Pennsylvania was a dark and lonely experience. Allentown, Bethlehem, Harrisburg, Hershey. Towns folded into the hills like books in a blanket. And dead deer all over the shoulders. Their thoughtless, solemn faces. The way animals become meat on the interstates. It's another kind of fast food. I believe there is a secret custodian who scrapes death off the shoulders of our great highways with a giant spatula. I had to stop counting these unfortunate animals after sixteen because I feared my own delight in such morbidity.

Some municipal guerrilla sect bored these endless, Kubrickian tunnels right through the Allegheny Mountains. Before you enter there are signs that read PLEASE REMOVE SUNGLASSES. *Someone is watching the activity in your eyes, Homon. Retinal control. Encoding the rods and cones. Big Brother. Uncle Sam. Smokey the Bear. Magic Johnson.*

Cameras are everywhere, Homon, and I am carrying around a can of black spray paint to undo whatever surveillance systems I might come across during my travels.

These tunnels I speak of are covered in white tiles and lit with hanging fluorescent trays. Halfway through one of them— somewhere near this town called Breezewood—the bus started making weird constipated noises and I feared total ingestion, the tunnel seizing my vessel and engulfing us like some Roald Dahl nightmare.

The truck stops are where the real America is, Homon. Salad bars and video arcades. Fast-food chains next to public bathrooms with shower stalls. Don't get Irish Spring in your cheeseburger. I counted thirty-seven different kinds of beef jerky. I have been keeping a log. I understand the philosophy of jerky, Homon. There is a pattern to the flavors, and I think this helps people.

Truckers and their titanic stomachs. Dirty children with Popsicle stains on their faces. Indigents that give way to tragic dental disorders. The incontinent. The afflicted. Armed women in corduroy suits. Security guards on psychoactive medication. People without transportation just randomly there as if the rest stops imagined them. And all the teenagers smoking like their lives depend on it.

It's weird, Homon; certain white Americans walk through the world wearing shower caps. What does this say about the state of shampoo in a modern, free-market democracy?

The mechanic at the Marathon station in Akron fixed the monoxide problem and showed me how to seal a radiator by frying a raw egg on it. He was whole-hog Christian and talked about John the Baptist like he might walk into the garage at any minute. The fried-egg trick got me all the way to Joliet, Illinois (I-80), where I replaced the radiator, abandoned my Pacific Northwest idea, and instead headed south to Champaign.

Wrote two songs about nothing in particular at a Holiday Inn where there was a recent suicide. Yellow chalk lines outlining the dead body. A web of police tape all over the second floor. The hotel continued renting rooms. I guess during a recession we all forge ahead, right?

The death was a confirmed suicide. A mixture of kitchen cleanser and Coca-Cola mainlined into the carotid artery. Apparently there were bizarre chemical reactions and the corpse flailed a lot and foamed out the ears. The girl was twenty-three and worked as a cashier at the local Econo Foods.

People needing to erase themselves has been on my mind a lot. I'm like government cheese. Put me in a sandwich and I am digested and later transformed into fecal lumps. I am floating waste in a sewage system. I travel under cities and arrive at the water-cleaning plant. I am purified with chlorination. I am swilled through a kitchen faucet and mixed with colloidal Kool-Aid and drunk by putty-skinned children with a desire to solve electronic video-game systems.

What is a human history, anyway, Homon? A collection of debt and minor achievements? Little League trophies and scuffed baseballs? An old tackle box? A closet full of clothes? Can our time here transcend our capitalistic instincts and the need to consume? I'm so lofty and above the rest of everything else I feel like floating. I am Balloon Man! Without television could we live like certain indigenous peoples? Without magazines would beauty be measured by the same polystyrene standard? Would people create a telekinetic language and grow closer to our animal brothers?

I am currently experiencing a kind of glugging in my small intestine. I will be right back . . .

So now I'm back. It's dark out there, Homon. The trees whisper a lost history to each other. Nocturnal birds of prey fly invisibly. The air is brutally cold and my breath smokes out automotively. The moon looks like a shriveled oyster. That might be a Tom Waits lyric. If it's not, it should be.

I walked around the bus a few times and the glugging went away.

Despite the obvious eerie conditions at the Holiday Inn in Champaign I slept like a baby that night and gorged myself on the continental breakfast the following morning. At the cereal bin a man with bicycle reflectors pinned to his hat sold me a dozen asthma inhalants for three bucks and I've been sucking away at them nonstop. Now that I can breathe I need as much air as possible.

Been eating lots of fast food. If you are what you eat, then I am a soggy double Quarter Pounder with cheese and an orange Fanta because that's what I have been putting inside me. Nutrition is overrated, Homon. I find the whole fitness enterprise to be useless and hedonistic.

Cholesterol will free you.

Fat will make you great.

So the guitar has changed my life.

There was my life before the guitar, and now there is my life with the guitar. Everything preceding our union was a time of darkness. I was a thoughtless fish person swimming underwater in a murky, bottomless lake.

But now there is light and my fin-hands are no longer destined to grope the mossy rocks.

My fingertips hurt from the strings, but the calluses are coming.

I need to talk about Kansas.

As you know, something about my state of birth haunts me to the bone, Homon. Nothing traumatic so much as its simplicity.

The state capital is Topeka.

Its chief resources are cattle, wheat, sorghum, soybeans, hogs, and corn.

The blossom is the sunflower, or Helianthus annuus.

The bird, the western meadowlark.

The tree, the cottonwood.

It was admitted as a state on January 29, 1861.

The Kansas song is "Home on the Range," and I sometimes sing the first verse while pounding my fist into the meat of my right thigh. "Oh give me a home, where the buffalo roam, where the deer and the antelope play." I want to change "play" to "pray," and I wonder if this is somehow illegal or unpatriotic.

I now have a lavender bruise on my thigh that reminds me of all that I am and all that I am trying to escape.

And there are the tiny things from my youth. Like the banana seat on my old Schwinn, how I patched it with Six Million Dollar Man trading-card stickers. And lighting my G.I. Joe paratrooper on fire and throwing him off the roof of my cousin's house in Overland Park and yelling "Go, burning man! Go, burning man!" The smell of wet Nerf. The intoxicating free fall of annihilating toys. The puppet government of paper routes. These things just about do me in, Homon. So I'm writing about them. I have emerged from the lake with my fish hands and I'm putting it down in multicolored ink and chronicling all of this in a purple spiral notebook that I have reinforced with the same silver duct tape that I am using to seal the mailboxes. It's all connected, and I feel my life gaining mass in new ways. I'm composing a mosaic of lyrics that I will pull from to construct my songs. The phrasing comes to me in fits. It's more about the musicality of the words than the meaning.

I'm not keeping very good time on the Fender yet, but the open chords are ringing better and better. D, A, G. C, G, E-minor. The open-F is a thorny enterprise. It requires pressing two strings with one finger. That might take months to figure out. The intricacies are infinite. Each finger has its own brain, and I accept this arrangement.

I never thought I had something to sing about, Homon, but my throat has opened and I do. Things like chrome napkin dispensers. And the multiplicity of telephone poles. The things forgotten in parking lots. Abandoned drive-in movies. Root beer stains on half-demolished screens.

The water towers we used to make fun of are holy to me now. And all those people traveling around in the backs of pickup trucks are geniuses.

The roads in our country are a great circulatory system, and the bus is simply a bit of protein floating through its bloodstream.

I am a wandering triglyceride.

I am a lipid.

A lipid with a beard.

I found a twin mattress in a Dumpster in Indiana. I treated it with several cans of disinfectant and I sleep on it in the back of the bus.

I stopped trimming my beard and I sleep in my coat. Hygiene means nothing to me now. I urinate into a three-liter plastic bottle. I defecate under trees like a yak.

For weeks the Fender was my only friend. I held her all night. I found comfort in her curves. Forbearance in her long, smooth neck. Sympathy in steel strings. Happiness in her hole.

But I must admit that I miss so many things, Homon. Not New York, but further back. Before all the post-KU wanderlusting. Way deep down. Like the hot chocolate at the ice rink. And those snow sleds with the two runners—how you could get hurt on them. And Magilla Gorilla . . .

Jesus, I'm crying all over this letter . . .

I think at some point I forgot how to feel and this will be the subject of my next song. The human's conversion to his automaton self. Wires replacing veins. Valvoline blood. Duracell organs. A carburetor for a heart.

I'm learning my first bar chord—a B-minor—that I'm figuring into a D-A-G progression. Following the A, the B-minor subverts the expectation of another major chord and yields a sweet-sad melancholy.

Music is math and calculus will free you.

A guy at a rest stop in Clarksville told me dipping your fingers in Anbesol numbs the sting out of them. He was spending the weekend ice fishing on Lake Barkley and his face alone made me want to write a novel in song form about a man who falls in love with people on Greyhound buses.

I'm not interested in playing leads, Homon. Just squeezing chords hard and playing them well and keeping time. As soon as I learn how to bar I'd like to get percussive, but that's a ways off.

Highway 57 to 24.

I do the road numbers in my head to take up space. There are reasons for enumerating the places where we travel, but I haven't sorted out any viability for this.

It's been a punishing winter, Homon. The windchill makes me cry. Literally bullies the tears out of my body. Lots of forlorn-looking farmland and poorly painted motels. Fields of hardened black soil climbing into the horizon. I saw a cat frozen to the side of a tree. I tried to sketch it but my hands were too cold.

Champaign led to Nashville, where I ate my first regular meal at a diner near Vanderbilt University. I got into a shouting match with some erudite pipe-smoking undergrad tweed boy about The Sheltering Sky. *He kept calling Bowles's masterpiece a fucking science-fiction novel. I informed him that Bowles wrote stories about* psychological terror *and* otherness, *not* science fucking fiction! *Then he threw half of his Monte Cristo sandwich at me and started quoting Philip K. Dick or something. I had an impulse to put the twit in a full nelson but I opted for eating his sandwich half instead and then headed back to the bus. I'd like to think that I am beyond those kinds of altercations now.*

I am a peace-loving brother and the chicks dig this, I assure you, young laddy.

My beard is growing and I own the fact that I have an obvious, slightly pretentious need for people to perceive me as being wiser and stranger than I am.

After Nashville I was going to head into Faulkner's Deep South, but I took the wrong exit (65 North, instead of 40 East), and after a few hundred miles of jersey blocks and asshole-ish semis I wound up in D.C., where I parked the bus in some pay-by-the-hour garage near Union Station and boarded a commuter train whose last stop was some small antebellum town in West Virginia. I have no idea why I did that, Homon. Just some weird need to not know where a particular day might take me. The bus got old for a minute and I needed a new perspective. A new viewfinder, if you will.

Once we got past the city limits there was a brutal poverty that I witnessed from the window of that commuter train, Homon. The misfortune of railroad property. Nine-foot houses that lean and buckle. Four-story tenements and half-burnt two-family homes and boarded-up shacks that are so low they look more suited to the penning of chickens. Domesticated garages and their tethered dogs not barking but watching with a kind of bitterness, as though their lust for velocity—the need to run and chase and fuck—has been somehow stolen from them by the fleeting trains they abhor. Arthritic porches that have seemingly transformed into the gutters of all things once domestic that turn irreversibly to junk. Crooked refrigerators. Saddle-backed sofas and kicked-in TVs and half-built bikes. It's as if the houses themselves have marshaled this banishment of failed assets. The random vacant lot choked with weeds and strange sea-like half-trees and a '72 Cutlass on blocks that has been ruthlessly picked clean of its parts with the industry of ants or vultures. At these stops the train doors opened and closed a little faster, as if to quarantine a pestilence. Then the indigence starts to fade and the protective forests emerge, as if some great Appalachian giant had walked along the train tracks and whistled a curse that forever stunted these homes from their suburban aspirations. The giant whistles until he reaches the edge of the timberline, where he sleeps with the forest creatures and keeps sentry for the Southeastern poverty line.

We were delayed for an hour where two children had been killed trying to race a train head-on before it entered the covered bridge. It was the previous commuter train and the local officials were still investigating the horrible scene. The two sisters, eleven and thirteen, were killed instantly, their bodies blown to pollen faster than thought.

Apparently, racing the train is a rite of passage in these parts. During the delay I looked out my window and saw the parents of the little girls speaking to the policemen. They'd left their house open and I could see clear through their cluttered living room and into the kitchen, where they had left the refrigerator open. I took note of a very white gallon of milk and a box of Count Chocula cereal. Count Chocula in the fridge, yes.

While speaking to the cops the parents seemed more relieved than anything else. I imagine that poverty will eventually turn your children into pets and other animated burdens.

They eventually let the other commuter train continue on its route and I made it to the end of the line an hour or so later. Then I turned around and headed back to D.C.

After I got the bus out of the garage I headed farther south, feeling a need to understand those people I'd watched from the train window—to commune with them or buy things out of their stores or something. I wound up in Boone, North Carolina, where I've been parked for the past few weeks.

Boone is a college town in the Appalachian Mountains with lots of head shops and antique stores and little coffee joints that have homemade cinnamon rolls and shit like that.

Last week I met the most beautiful woman I've ever seen in my life. Her name is Holy, I bullshit you not. She's an exchange student studying anthropology at Appalachian State University. She's from Madagascar and she has almond-shaped eyes. I mean, you hear about almond-shaped eyes, but you've never seen almond-shaped eyes like these eyes, Homon. Her last name is like

twenty-seven letters and I can't even get my mouth to come close
to uttering its beautiful music. She grew up on the shores of the
Mozambique Channel, where her father repaired fishing boats.
We met at this indie-rock record shop near where I'm parking the
bus. I've already written three songs about her. She calls me
"Mister Owl" in a very French-sounding accent. The songs pretty
much deal with Holy and the natural elements. Holy in the snow.
Holy in the water. Holy making air. Here's a sample of some
lyrics:

> *Holy in the snow*
> *where will she go*
> *mill the flour on the dough*
> *Christmas cookies, Christmas pie*
> *don't rescind the lie*
> *the Owl was born, the Owl will die*

> *or*

> *Red Rover, Red Rover*
> *send Holy right over*
> *there's some hay in the maker*
> *and an owl in the clover*

Holy still lives in campus housing but she's been staying with
me in the bus for the past few days. She's only nineteen, Homon,
but I fear this not. We have an electric blanket plugged into an
outlet from the record store. We also have a hot pot and plenty of
Dinty Moore products to keep us fed well.

There is love on the bus, Homon. Not since New Mexico has
the warmth of another's body felt so real. I am alive again. I am
resisting my automaton nemesis self. I will fight the Valvoline
bloodstream, the carburetor heart.

Homon, my advice to you would be to quit your job and finish
your novel. Your work will take a leap when you deprive yourself

of comfort and resources. Your novel should be everything, all-consuming, your sustenance, your bedevilment.

I left my laptop computer in my closet. It's under a bag of business clothes. I realize that you are a Luddite and don't partake in the narcotic trappings of technology, but for god's sake use my laptop! It's faster than that electric shrimp boat that you were passing off as your typewriter, and with the laptop there's a way to save your work on disk. So take it, as I no longer have any use for it.

The guitar has opened my eyes and my heart.

I have just decided in this very moment that my singer/songwriter enterprise is going to be called Jorge's Washing Machine. I will paint this on the bus and have a Dinty Moore feast.

The corporate system is a spiritual slaughterhouse and fluorescent lighting turns you into a rat in a very deadening maze.

I'd love for you to write back but I am currently a man without an address. Perhaps this is my fate.

I'll leave you with another non-Holy thing that I've started:

The madness of gypsum slats
these, those, and thats
re-elect the Cat in the Hat
Could Scatman Crothers really scat?

Stay away from that westbound bus, Homon!
The Port Authority Bus Terminal is not part of our vocabulary.
I will not return to Kansas and you will not return to Iowa.
We swear this on the eyes of our periwinkle souls.

Your friend always,
GLENWOOD "THE OWL" LEDBETTER

I folded the letter and put it back in its envelope. Then I found a thumbtack on the floor below my desk and stuck it to the wall because things of this magnitude should be hung like banners.

I imagined the Owl and his undergraduate love from Madagascar. Happy and freezing in his VW bus, layers of thermal underwear, his black beard accruing mass, his bloody fingers, the occasional screech of guitar strings. Holy lying across his chest, her soft, brown, Indian Ocean–bathed breasts spilling down his meaty flanks, her accented English finding its way into his songs.

The Swan Dream

THE LATE-JANUARY DARKNESS was like balancing a heavy book on my head.

One night when I couldn't get any work done, I fell asleep at my desk and dreamed that Basha had given birth to a swan. It was snowing and we were in Tompkins Square Park and there were no bulldozers or backhoes and the trees were silver with ice. Basha was sitting on a park bench across from me, breast-feeding our baby swan. I thought I knew her but maybe I didn't. Maybe her eyes were different. Behind her children were ice-skating on the frozen basketball courts and trying to catch snowflakes in their mouths.

I was so proud that we could produce such a beautiful thing.

When I reached out to Basha and my suckling child, my dream arms were suddenly as heavy as iron and our swan hissed at me and bared its black, asp-like tongue.

Chocolate Milk

ON FEBRUARY 1 BASHA DECIDED to have an abortion.

I had saved up four weeks' worth of unemployment pay and promptly set up an appointment for the following Monday at the unnamed private clinic on the Upper East Side. It was a Tuesday, and earlier that morning I had fielded a call from the New York City Unemployment Office inquiring about the status of my current job search. I made up a few leads, cited three or four fictional references (including one John Anderson-Allensworth), and quickly got off the phone.

It was well below freezing, and seemingly overnight the city decided to initiate an aggressive road-construction campaign. The First Avenue pavement had been torn up and the blocks between Seventh and Eleventh streets had been transformed into what looked like a bombed-out gully of scored and striated concrete. Two blocks south, men in thick canvas coats were shoveling smoldering asphalt out of dump trucks and the smell of tar was so thick it almost inspired hunger. The steam rose off the street and evaporated east across St. Mark's Place like fugitive ghosts.

"It's like Poland," Basha observed as we turned away from the scarred moon surface of First Avenue.

We had originally planned to take the M15 Bus up to Sixty-sixth Street and walk west to Second Avenue, but instead we caught a cab on Avenue A. Despite my poverty, under the circumstances I figured being driven to the unnamed clinic was an acceptable luxury.

The ride was melancholic to say the least. Basha stared out the window, seemingly lost in her own thoughts. When I offered my hand she clutched it so fiercely I initially mistook the pressure for a displaced act of retribution for being in this situation at all, but moments later I realized she was simply petrified.

Our cab crossed Fourteenth Street at the southernmost edge of Stuyvesant Town and headed west. Due to the First Avenue construction, traffic was gridlocked, and between the sounds of woofing choppers and the discordant fifths and sevenths of blaring car horns the noise was almost maddening. Basha took her hand back and pulled both sides of her knit hat over her ears.

I told her I loved her and she nodded.

"Yes," she said. "Love."

At Twenty-third Street an antique sports car with gull-wing doors collided with a moving truck and traffic had to be diverted west. Between Second and Third avenues the congestion was even more unbearable. Drivers were standing outside of their cars, leaning on their horns, and screaming foreign and domestic obscenities toward the impossible destinations of intersections only hundreds of feet away.

When we finally wended around the Grand Central Station bypass and reached Forty-ninth Street we hit yet another gridlock, so we paid our cabbie, got out, and walked the rest of the way.

The apathetic majesty of the large Fifth Avenue buildings and their tailored canopies bordered on cruelty. The costumed doormen stood at their posts with an air of immortality. Peering past them into the lobbies, I noted that the winter seemed to have little effect on these monoliths. The chandeliers floating in amber light, the multicolored floral arrangements, and the far-off brass elevator banks were like an impenetrable fantasy that might take thousands of years to gain access to. It was as if Fifth Avenue real estate had been supernaturally pardoned from the realities of New York City's brutal Februaries. I even had the strange sensation that it was suddenly ten or fifteen degrees warmer than it actually was. Perhaps the colder seasons didn't exist here? Even the trees looked silvery and robust compared to the trembling, anemic maples and cottonwoods on my block.

We walked east at Fiftieth Street and headed toward Third Avenue.

I had a strange impulse to carry Basha piggyback, but when I offered the ride she simply shook her head and kept walking.

"Come on," I said. "Let me carry you."

But Basha shook her head again and continued on, a few steps ahead of me.

The cold air bit at my hands and I drove them into the pockets of my Dockers, where I had secreted the $660 in cash (the clinic wouldn't take a check or a credit card). I had gotten up early that morning and counted and recounted the money at the kitchen counter. When I was finally convinced of the amount, I'd folded the wad in half and secured it with a rubber band before driving the knot into my left pocket. What started as a simple arrangement of twenty-dollar bills had begun to feel like the millstone that would pull me under a mountain of ground grain. I couldn't help but resent the ramen noodles, catsupy pasta, and other two-dollar deli fare that would surely become my diet for the next several weeks.

When we reached Third Avenue, Basha suddenly turned and hugged me. For the briefest moment I thought she was going to execute a two-point takedown and I nearly assumed a junior-varsity wrestling stance, but when her weight went slack and I could feel the warmth of her body radiating through our winter coats it became pretty clear that she simply needed comfort. I imagine it was confusing, embracing the nemesis defiler of her womb like that. Perhaps I had already lost my status as the man she loved, and that day I was simply a live body whose heat was all she needed?

Pedestrians ogled us curiously. I suppose from a certain angle it might have looked like I was squeezing the breath out of Basha, as I, too, was holding on for dear life. Through her knit hat I could detect the faint scent of Polly Parker's french fries.

When we broke from the hug we turned north on Third Avenue and pressed on like hikers in high altitude.

Again Basha stayed a few paces ahead of me.

During the seventeen blocks north Basha stopped in three different delis, where she bought several bags of Japanese gummy candy and a half dozen or so pints of chocolate milk. I reminded her that she had strict instructions not to eat before the procedure and she said that she knew; the treats were for later. It was obvious that she was having second thoughts.

"We don't have to do this," I told her outside the Korean deli on the corner of Fifty-eighth and Third, confiscating her third plastic bag of sweets.

Under her knit hat, her green eyes caught the February sky in such a way that it made me want to sit on a fire hydrant, so that's what I did. I sat down with her three bags of sweets and six chocolate milks while she stared off in some indecipherable direction. Our breath curled above us.

"We can turn around," I said.

When I heard the words come out of my mouth I felt sick to my stomach. To this day I can't be certain as to whether I was more afraid of the abortion or of the possibility of getting back in a cab and heading home.

"We go to clinic," Basha said, pulling me off the fire hydrant.

Approaching the corner of Second Avenue and Sixty-sixth Street was like trying to breathe inside a zipped sleeping bag. While my feet suddenly felt impossibly heavy, Basha appeared to be rendered weightless by the anxiety—emboldened. Her stride lengthened and she held her head higher. She seemed as though she were about to get in line for a roller coaster.

To get to the clinic we had to take an elevator to the basement of perhaps the most nondescript building I have ever seen in Manhattan. Substituting for a doorman was a rather anorectic ficus tree whose rubbery fruit looked as poisonous as it did synthetic. As we boarded the elevator I had a strange impulse to apologize to the tree and although I envisioned myself bowing my head and genuflecting altar boy–style at the base of its imitation clay pot, I resisted the urge when Basha again clutched my hand as she had in the cab.

"I love you," I said again, and she nodded.

"Love, yes," she said again.

The unnamed clinic's bare, minimally designed waiting area resembled that of a dentist's office. Outside of a small, vinyl caduceus centered on the wall, there was no discernible medical paraphernalia; only blank white walls and slightly perforated gypsum ceiling tiles. A pair of spleen-colored, uncomfortable-looking sofas flanked either side of a large block coffee table that was covered with a smattering of magazines. There was no TV or any other form of electronic entertainment; just the magazines and a few standing lamps whose yellowish tungsten light softened the room that I'd envisioned as being harsh and unforgiving with fluorescence. It appeared that Basha was the only scheduled patient.

It was ten-thirty in the morning.

Behind a reception cutout, a heavyset woman in her forties confirmed our appointment and I pulled the knot of money out of my pants and handed it to her. She carefully counted the bills and returned the rubber band, which Basha then took and doubled around her wrist for reasons I will never understand. The whole transaction had an air of Vegas shorthand to it; I half-expected a deck of cards to materialize. It was obvious that the receptionist was well versed in the counting and clearing of currency.

Moments later, a nurse came through a door and greeted us. I remember neither her features nor her voice. She might have been a faceless scarecrow being puppeteered with fishing line. Basha and I started toward the door but The Nurse Who I Can't Remember stopped me with an outstretched hand, saying, "Only Ms. Kieslowski."

Basha and I exchanged a look, and then she nodded her approval.

"Have a seat in the waiting area," the receptionist said kindly. I turned to her, and then she and The Nurse Who I Can't Remember shared a look, and then the next thing I knew, Basha had disappeared through the clinic door.

I turned back to the receptionist, feeling a little abandoned, looking for some good old-fashioned succor.

I opened my mouth but nothing came out.

The receptionist said, "Twenty, twenty-five minutes. You might want to take your coat off."

I nodded and took a seat in the waiting area.

The sofas were actually much more comfortable than they appeared to be.

In a men's health magazine whose cover boasted a thirtyish male with damp, bulging abs and a hairdo that resembled black Astroturf, I tried to read an article about planning a day around my "body clock," but got annoyed when the fitness journalist suggested that spending more time in the sun would help to improve my mental and physical outlook. The last sunny day I could remember was sometime back in the fall, when the drifts of leaves covering the cobblestone square in front of St. Mark's Church had a strange gilded quality. Since then it had been mostly gray skies, or the occasional curdled-milk cloud cover. I came to the conclusion that journalists who write for men's fitness magazines must spend a lot of time reclining in the sun on chaise longues and tossed the magazine back on the coffee table. I resisted the urge to sample the other offerings, as I figured there were no doubt pro-choice pamphlets folded in with the periodicals. The last thing I needed was to feel good about being at the clinic.

I eventually removed my corduroy coat and started to pace and claw at my arms. It's perhaps an indication of my mental state that I chose a short-sleeved shirt on such a cold day. I had also forgotten to put on socks, and I was suddenly aware of how much my feet were sweating.

There was a circular cafeteria clock over the receptionist's cutout, and I must have glanced at it twenty-five times during my ten minutes' worth of pacing. The sweeping second hand seemed to be moving at an impossibly slow velocity.

The receptionist looked up from her paperwork and said, "Don't worry, she's fine."

It suddenly dawned on me that the woman before me resembled the portrait of Dolley Madison that loomed over a pair of antique Shaker rocking chairs in my parents' living room. My mother had always been impressed by Mrs. Madison's pre–First Lady life, when she'd served as the White House hostess for the widowed Thomas Jefferson.

"How long do you think she's been in there?" I asked the receptionist.

"Maybe ten minutes."

"That's it?"

"I'm afraid so," she answered. "Feel free to pace as much as you'd like."

It was ridiculous, really—me marching back and forth like that. We were *not* having a baby and I was acting like I was moments away from hearing the sound of a wailing infant.

"Do they sedate her?" I asked.

"I think sometimes they do," the receptionist answered, examining a cuticle.

"I just hope she's okay," I said.

"They usually give her something to take after the procedure."

"For the pain?"

"Just something to help her relax."

My hands were shaking, so I hid them behind my back.

The receptionist looked at me for a moment and said, "What happened to your nose?"

"Oh," I said, touching it gently. "I sort of ran into a door."

She said, "Ouch. Is it broken?"

"I don't know," I answered. "It might be."

"Well, you look tired."

Then the receptionist matter-of-factly returned to her administrative duties, as though we had been discussing additions and deletions to her current grocery list.

I paced a bit and then for some asinine reason I said, "We should have used a condom."

After I said that the receptionist turned to me with one of the blankest faces I have ever seen. I stood very still for a moment. My nose suddenly felt too heavy for my face, and I was keenly aware of how badly I was slumping.

"But we didn't," I continued, "because it just seemed okay."

The receptionist nodded a few times and then she licked a postage stamp and affixed it to the upper-right-hand corner of a business envelope.

That's when Basha came through the door to the waiting room. She was barefoot and wearing a white hospital smock patterned with small blue dots. Her winter coat was balled in her arms and she was holding it in a way that made it seem incredibly valuable. She looked dazed and a little sad.

"Hey," I said.

"Hello," she said back.

The receptionist stopped licking stamps and stood up in a manner suggesting there was a course of action to be followed that might involve seizing the patient. She was much taller than I would have guessed.

"I wish to deport," Basha said. Her eyelids seemed frozen open.

Then The Nurse Who I Can't Remember appeared behind Basha, saying, "We already started the procedure, honey."

"I wish to deport," Basha said again, with exactly the same intonation, staring directly at me. Then she said something in Polish that sounded like *tree clubs in disposal.*

The Nurse Who I Can't Remember put her hand on Basha's shoulder and Basha stepped away from her. Then the receptionist came out from behind her cutout and I made a quick calculation of her body type and distribution of muscle mass in case of grappling. The full nelson was always a surefire schoolyard move, so I zeroed in on her neck-shoulder region.

Everyone froze for a moment.

I had the strange sensation that the clock above the receptionist's cutout might start laughing.

"So let's go," I said to Basha. "Where are your shoes?"

"I do not wish to keep them," Basha replied.

"Sir," said The Nurse Who I Can't Remember, "it could be a threat to her health."

"Ms. Kieslowski has to go back in," the receptionist said, ever so kind, but Basha had grabbed my hand and we were out the door and into the elevator so quickly it was as if we'd thought ourselves there.

The elevator doors closed and we stood in the hermetically sealed silence without pressing a button. Basha was breathing heavy and I was breathing heavy and our breath was hot and smelled of toothpaste. Basha then began snapping the $660 rubber band that she had doubled around her wrist. It snapped four or five times, and then it broke and fell to the floor.

"We should get your shoes," I said, but Basha just shook her head. She didn't blink or change her expression; she just kept shaking her head. Her eyes were downcast now, almost shameful. I helped her into her coat, after a fair amount of bullying to wrest it from her arms. I draped it over her shoulders and kissed her on the cheek. Her face was icy.

"I think we should get your shoes," I said again. "It's pretty cold out."

But Basha had finally pushed the button and we were ascending toward the lobby. I studied the inspector's log for a moment, not thinking about the broken rubber band on the floor of the elevator and not thinking about the iciness in Basha's cheek and not thinking about my trembling hands.

When I looked back down, Basha was on her hands and knees, picking up the soft, mollusk-like pieces of her placenta from the elevator floor. It came out without a sound. I wanted to kneel as well but my legs were locked.

Amid the strange mass of bilious, violet-colored fluid and other nameless bits of tissue I'd like to believe that I saw the tiny, blind eyes of the fetus, but in reality I was transfixed by the look on Basha's face, which was one of profound concentration. She worked on the elevator floor with an almost pleasant, prayerful determination, as if she were gathering raspberries for an important Sunday pie.

When the elevator finally reached the lobby, the doors parted and through the glass entrance at the end of the long hallway I could see southbound traffic sluicing down Second Avenue. While Basha continued to work on the floor, I pressed and held the OPEN button, keeping the elevator doors parted.

Basha rolled everything into the hem of her hospital gown while I helped button her into her peacoat. Her underwear was sopping and fluid was running down the insides of her white, trembling legs. Fortunately, the oversize peacoat was long enough to conceal most of this.

From a door to the stairwell, the nurse who had urged us to stay suddenly appeared. Her mouth was moving and she was saying things in a loud, alarmed manner, but all I wanted to do was get out of that place. When we passed her I lowered my shoulder and nudged her out of the way.

Outside, the wind had kicked up and the traffic rushed by indifferently. The nurse walked very closely behind us, pleading. I wanted to turn and stiff-arm her into traffic, but I wouldn't let go of Basha, who wound up walking two blocks of winter streets barefoot and with her arms buttoned inside her coat, cradling our baby's remains. I felt myself starting to panic and I had no idea what to do, so I decided to get us back downtown.

On the corner of Sixty-sixth Street and Second Avenue Basha vomited into a garbage can while I held her around the waist with one arm and hailed a cab with the other. The nurse continued shouting at me but her voice had the quality of a vacuum cleaner now. When the cab finally pulled away, I felt as if I had escaped a horrible fate.

The ride back downtown was surprisingly fast. The gridlock of an hour before had dispersed and our cab caught a series of green lights that had us in the East Village in less than ten minutes.

Despite the terrible sight we must have been on that Upper East Side street corner, I was grateful for so many things. I was grateful that I had been there with Basha while she vomited, curling her dark damp hair behind her ears. And I was grateful to have experienced that feeling of strange, euphoric paralysis in the taxicab on our way uptown. And, of course, I felt shamefully lucky that I wouldn't have to be a father.

And somewhere near the ether of that gratitude hovered a tiny spot of misanthropy, an almost infinitesimal pinprick that in a short number of weeks would metastasize into a black planet of hatred for all things.

The Bowery

WE SPENT THE NIGHT at a cheap hotel in the Bowery where the pillows smelled like mothballs and cigarettes.

Basha refused to check herself into Beth Israel and at the suggestion of returning to her parents' apartment in Stuyvesant Town, she grabbed my right biceps so fiercely that she left tiny fingernail serrations.

There was no way I was going to take her back to my place with the possibility of encountering the Loach cavorting with Lars.

The hotel was fifty-five dollars for the night and our room was anything but luxurious. The lone view was of a forlorn, debris-addled courtyard that featured a large rotting ash tree whose shadow trembled on the window like an enormous hag's hand. The king-size, mule-backed bed boasted a dictionary-thin mattress, and when I turned down the comforter I was greeted by a citrus-and-ammonia smell of cheap disinfectant that was obviously masking other, less desirable odors.

Furniture-wise, in addition to the bed there was a small bureau whose only working drawer contained a miniature Bible; a cigarette burn–plagued bedside table on which sat a push-button phone with a mouthpiece that smelled like tortilla chips left in an ashtray; and an imitation brass sconce that had been screw-gunned into the center of the warped headboard, which was itself mysteriously affixed to the wall. The fireproof carpeting was colorless and mottled with stains. The bathroom was small and surprisingly clean, and it came well equipped with a strange plethora of multicolored towels stacked on top of the toilet tank. Somewhere there was a perpetual, faint buzzing noise that sounded like a cow lowing in a distant field. When I called the front desk to complain, the woman who'd checked us in (I still remember her Halloween eyeliner and scarlet, fly-away hair) said it was the pipes and suggested that we turn on the television.

After I helped Basha out of her smock and peacoat, I filled the tub with warm water and bathed her. She sat in front of the faucet with her knees drawn up to her breasts. A sharp metallic odor rose from between her legs and reminded me of the smell of recently cleaned engine parts under the hood of my father's prized '66 Buick Skylark. I washed her back and shoulders while her torso trembled slightly. The knobs of her spine seemed to pearl with tension. Eventually she surrendered to the weight of my hand and was able to relax a bit.

Within minutes the bathwater had changed to the color of a pale Bordeaux and I realized that Basha was still bleeding pretty steadily. I told her I was going to call the hospital and she screamed at me not to. I was shocked by the volume of her voice. I couldn't believe the amount of noise she could make, considering her condition. I said okay and calmed her and helped her stand and finished washing her with the detachable shower nozzle while she steadied herself using my shoulders.

After bathing her, I ran downstairs and bought a box of maxi pads at Munchies Deli, where I felt transparent and small-hearted. I was sure that the other patrons knew my dreadful business. Behind the cash register an old Korean man with mustard-yellow skin made change quickly and wouldn't look me in the eye. For a moment I worried that by collaborating on an abortion I had somehow forfeited the privilege of simple social interactions with all future cashiers and customer-service workers. I feared I would be shunned in delis, gas stations, fast-food restaurants, and shopping malls all across America.

In terms of trying to identify what had actually happened at the clinic, to this day, either through some sort of blank spot in my memory or the convenient, necessary ether of denial, I waver between referring to the event as an abortion and calling it a miscarriage. I still have no idea whether the nurse or any other medical professional gave Basha anything that might have brought the pregnancy to an end.

What I do know is that what happened in that clinic elevator was the worst thing I've ever experienced. It was like losing an important, weight-bearing bone, and I knew I would spend the rest of my life trying to figure out how to walk the streets without it.

When I returned to the hotel room Basha affixed a maxi pad to her panties and I helped her change into a pair of cotton sweats that I'd fetched from my apartment before the cab dropped us at the hotel. The hooded jersey boasted my college's insignia, with CRUSADERS below it, embossed in gold and purple block letters. Dwarfed by the sweat suit, Basha seemed like a junior high school student fighting through her first wave of menstrual cramps. The abdominal pain caused her to fidget and sweat incessantly.

Terrified of some sort of infection, I several times raised the possibility of calling the paramedics, but Basha held firm in her refusal to seek medical help. In retrospect I realize that she was probably more concerned with immigration officials than stainless steel gurneys or scary health professionals.

In Basha's delirium, she clung to my arms and started talking about where we might someday spend the rest of our lives.

"Should we perhaps erect a cozy homestead in New York City?" she asked.

"Sure," I answered. "I can't imagine living anywhere else."

"But to raise childrens here would be exceedingly difficult, no?"

"It could be hard, yes. It's actually much cheaper in the Midwest," I offered.

"Where there are very many cows and sheeps."

Her breathing was shallow and rapid.

"In some places," I concurred.

"Are there very many cows and sheeps in your hometown?"

"Not directly in my hometown, no. But there are nearby."

"What is the name of your hometown?" she asked.

"Dubuque."

"Dubuque," she echoed. "What American state possesses Dubuque?"

"It's in Iowa," I said, inhaling the hot smell of her hair, wishing I could take on more of her pain.

"Dubuque, Iowa, sounds very enchanting."

I said, "I wish it was."

Basha squeezed my arm and said, "Foretell to me about your hometown with the pigs and the sheeps nearby."

So I told her all about Dubuque, Iowa, and what it was like growing up there with its rolling hills and its cliffs overlooking the Mississippi and the surprisingly competitive basketball at Asbury Park and the Saturday-night cruise, where hundreds of families pile into their antique Chevys and drive west to Maquoketa, every car in the convoy listening to the same classic-rock station. I told her about the dog track that I used to sneak into on the weekends and the beauty of greyhounds when they surge out of their kennels in pursuit of the artificial thighbone baited at the end of the squealing pace pole and the fishfly seasons that refrain as often as presidential elections and the dark, Victorian lobby of the Julian Inn, where I kissed a girl for the first time and the fecund smell of the riverbanks in August and the weeks I had spent in Clinton detasseling corn for six dollars an hour and Timmerman's Supper Club, where I bussed tables for two summers. I suddenly realized that I was far less embarrassed to talk about my hometown than I had been just months earlier. The Midwest suddenly seemed like a place of simplicity and beauty, not the backward, culturally retarded Norman Rockwell painting I had fled some months before.

Hell, I was even proud.

Basha fought sleep and offered a few phrases of fevered Polish. I dabbed at the sheen on her forehead with a damp washcloth.

"Do you very much miss Dubuque, Iowa?" she asked, suddenly speaking English again.

"Sometimes I do," I answered, surprised by the sentiment in my voice. "Do you miss Lublin?"

"No," she said. "There are very few cows and sheeps in Lublin. My Uncle Staszek raised his boyhood in the Carpathian Mountains in the village of Wislok Wielki, where very many cows reside. There are an exuberant sum of peasants and it is very poor there. Uncle Staszek used to speak of pulling milk from the cow's breast and putting it into a glass with honey and drinking it."

"Where is your Uncle Staszek now?"

"He resides in Lublin with my cousin Albert. He is very old but rises every morning to sell Levi's five-oh-one blue jeans and Snickers candy bars in the metropolitan square."

I imagined Basha's post-socialist Poland, the streets teeming with Levi's and Snickers bars, and I thought about the possibility of us actually finding each other in this world separated by oceans, and for a moment I sentimentally fell prey to my literary worship of books by Ernest Hemingway, F. Scott Fitzgerald, Theodore Dreiser, and Edith Wharton, those novels in which love is everything—even maddening, doomed love—and it gave me a false sense of hope to think that I had become like a character in a piece of epic fiction.

"I wish to travel to Dubuque with you someday," Basha said, her voice rich with fatigue.

"Sure," I said, continuing to dab at her gluey forehead. "Maybe when you start to feel better we can rent a car and drive there."

"I would like this very much," Basha said, her back alternately convulsing and going slack.

We tried watching TV for a while; the afternoon soap-opera actors seemed to only further spoil an already somber mood, so we opted for Nickelodeon instead.

Turned away from me, Basha eventually fell asleep in a tightly coiled fetal position. Her body was tense, and even through my Crusaders sweatshirt I could feel the chill on her back. I worried again about infection. I thought about the end of *A Farewell to Arms* and fought a panic attack.

I eventually turned back to the TV.

At some point I found myself crying through an episode of Yogi's *Laugh Olympics*. Yogi and Booboo's team lost in the tug-of-war to a team of their foes headed by Snaggletooth and a famous, vaguely incestuous-looking Marvel Comics superhero couple. I thought this was incredibly unfair to Yogi and Booboo, and I couldn't hold back anymore. Before the next Hanna-Barbera offering began I seized the remote and turned off the television.

The pipes continued to moan and it felt like their mysterious distant droning was controlling my thoughts. Evening crept into the room like an exhausted thief as the window light turned gray and indifferent.

While Basha slept a light snow fell. She was curled in her fetal position for most of the night, making double fists at her abdomen.

For dinner I ate a bag of gummy peaches and drank one of Basha's chocolate milks. I eventually took off my pants and got under the covers with her, my eyes burning, my temples throbbing, my head heavy with confusion.

I woke up in the middle of the night with a throbbing headache. Basha was in the bathroom, sitting on the floor, a blue towel bunched between her legs. Next to her on the sink was the maxi pad, sopping and bloated.

"Are you okay?" I asked.

"It is very much," she said, proffering the towel, a large splotch of blood soaking through.

At the letters of my Crusader sweatshirt was a long oval of sweat. For the next hour or so, Basha comforted me as if I were the one who'd had the terrible thing happen to my body.

The mouse of shame that had been my liver or some other hepatic organ was starting to crawl through my small intestine, surely headed for my stomach, and then my throat. In the face of weakness perhaps all of our necessary parts threaten to turn into rodents and scurry out of our bodies, the heart—a future rat, no doubt—being the toughest vital organ to transform and the last to exit.

Eventually the bleeding slowed. Basha affixed another maxi pad to her underwear and I helped her back to bed. A thin, persistent snow continued to fall across the window of our hotel room. The light outside was a murky cobalt and the shadow of the tree in the courtyard trembled rheumatically on the window.

Back in bed I told Basha I loved her again. She nodded and gently squeezed my hand.

"Love, yes," she said.

In the morning Basha drank three pints of chocolate milk and then threw it all up in the toilet. I begged her again to go to the hospital, but she insisted that she would improve on her own.

I went out for twenty minutes or so and brought back a soy-burger meal from Dojo on St. Mark's Place, telling myself this was the beginning of many years together. Despite our history being forged by a bit of sadness, I looked forward to growing old with Basha.

I took the stairs two at a time, excited to eat and return to my nursing duties. I discovered that for the first time in months my knee felt almost completely normal. I found it strange how diminishing body pain is so easily taken for granted. At the landing to our floor I bore down on my left knee with all my weight, defying my nine-month-old limp once and for all. Still there was no pain. I was ready to play ball and get back into shape.

When I opened the door to our room Basha was gone.

She'd left the remains from the clinic on the bathroom floor, swaddled in her outpatient smock.

I ran up and down St. Mark's Place and the Bowery looking for any sign of her. People stared at me and moved aside. Desperation will clear a way for you, I can tell you that.

I flailed my arms and kicked things.

A garbage can went tumbling.

A cop approached me.

I picked up the garbage can.

"Everything okay?" he asked. He was a few years older than I and impeccably shaved.

"I'm fine," I said.

"What's the problem?" he asked.

"No problem," I answered. "I just sort of lost someone."

"People lose people every day," he said.

His remark was neither here nor there, so I told him what I thought of it.

"Your platitude sucks," I said.

"My what?" he asked sharply, his arms tensed.

"Nothing," I answered.

The space between us was suddenly charged and I was aware of my own body odor.

"You got a place to get to?" the cop asked, genuinely pissed now.

"Yes," I said.

"Well, then get to it."

Back in the hotel room I sat very still for an hour.

I counted to fifty several times.

Then I changed positions and sat and counted some more.

On the wall next to the window I noticed a painting of a small child walking along a riverbank with a full-grown bear. This painting hadn't been in the room before, and I worried that someone was playing a trick on me. Or perhaps I was in the wrong room? Even though their backs were facing me, I thought the child and the bear seemed happy.

I stood in front of the painting for a long moment and then tried to turn it over but it was bolted to the wall.

Then I heard the distant buzzing sound again.

Was it coming from inside my head? I wondered.

At some point do we all get our own personalized vacuum cleaner?

Eventually, I grabbed the phone and called every emergency room in Manhattan.

In a strange, previously untapped soprano I yelled at several hospital operators and generally made an ass of myself.

Basha Kieslowski had not been admitted anywhere.

I came home to a message on the answering machine from Alexa. Judy Klooszch had been asking after my novel. Numbed by all that had happened, I found that I couldn't have cared less if I ever published anything for the rest of my life.

In the kitchen I came upon a dead mouse paralyzed in a glue trap that I had placed next to our plastic garbage receptacle some months before. It had died facedown, suffocating in the epoxy. One of its forelegs was twisted, and I was moved by the desperate effort it had obviously made to free itself.

I tried to calculate how many days it had been there, but as I counted backward the numbers stopped making sense in my head.

I cried for the mouse and didn't get off the floor for several hours.

A Visit

BY FEBRUARY 24, FIRST AVENUE had been thoroughly recovered with fresh asphalt, and the smell of hot tar cut through the cold air as potently as the stink of smoked trout. Men hanging off the back of a slow-moving pickup truck sprayed yellow dashes onto the blackened street with a hydraulic paint gun.

On the corner of First Avenue and Tenth Street a guy I'd noticed at the full courts at Tompkins Square Park was shilling cocaine, using his bedroom whisper on everyone who walked by. He was maybe twenty-three and one of the better all-around players in the park. I'd had no idea he was a drug dealer.

When he saw me he said, "What's up, player? You still ballin'?" He blew into his fists and then wedged his bare hands into the pockets of his puffy red coat.

"I've been injured," I said, feeling somehow honored that he didn't try to push anything on me.

"Back?"

"Knee."

"You get it scoped?"

"No. But it's almost healed."

"Don't get that joint scoped unless you have to," he said. "Aaight?"

"I'm not planning to."

"Cool. See you back out on the courts, then."

"Hopefully," I said, turning south on First Avenue.

At Polly Parker's they said Basha had mysteriously stopped showing up for work and they hadn't seen or heard from her in over three weeks.

The manager asked me to have her give him a call if I ran into her. I took his number and left mine, requesting the same of him.

In Tompkins Square Park, bulldozers and backhoes hewed at the asphalt like they were starved creatures from some other planet who wanted to ingest the neighborhood. The noise was almost deafening, and as people waited at Avenue A bus stops and walked in and out of cafés, their hands covered their ears. Saigon and his shopping-cart duck seemed unfazed by the noise. He just looked at the construction site as if he were beholding some great hidden truth.

I noticed an increase in the pit-bull population, both puppies and older dogs. It was as if they were taking over the East Village as aggressively as Mayor Dinkins's park demolitionists. Soon these dogs would be walking their former human masters and owning and operating the real estate from Houston Street to the fringes of Stuyvesant Town.

I sat in Leshko's for several hours, eating a plate of pancakes, drinking coffee, and staring out the window, employing a stakeout strategy. I figured if I remained in one place long enough I'd have a good chance of spotting Basha.

To pass the time I feigned reading a thick novel by a young literary star who'd garnered a six-figure advance. It was about a murder and was set at an elite private college in a remote town in the Northeast. The film rights had been sold while the book was still in galleys and the novelist was no doubt basking in luxury somewhere. I couldn't read even two sentences without looking out the window.

The waitress continued pouring me coffee.

"Everything okay?" she asked. Her face radiated kindness, but that didn't help me much.

I nodded and continued to pretend to read the 947-page novel.

I thought about getting a six-figure advance and all that I could do with that kind of money. I imagined myself wearing reflecting sunglasses, driving a European sports car, and growing a lot of chest hair.

Three hours passed like this, with Basha failing to materialize.

In fact, the passersby were almost painfully her opposites: mostly cops, nonrioting, prolifically bearded homeless men, and more pit bulls. Eventually I had to leave, as Leshko's coffee induced borderline incontinence and I didn't trust the restaurant's graffiti-plagued, marshy facilities.

After some twenty-two days of not hearing from Basha, I decided to finally call the Kieslowski home. For two days straight I called at least twice every hour. In the past there had always been an answering machine with Basha's voice narrating a greeting in slow, deliberate English, but now there was nothing.

Finally, on the morning of the third day, a man with a thick Polish accent who I assumed to be her father answered. His voice was a gravelly, exhausted baritone. I imagined him with wild, Einsteinian eyebrows, an unkempt mustache, and bulging forearms. I couldn't muster a greeting.

"Hello?" he said.

During the ensuing pause I felt like a capsized canoe slowly sinking in the middle of a lake, and after an onslaught of infuriated, exclamatory Polish I hung up and stupidly, impulsively punched the useless imitation-brass thermostat next to our front door, bloodying my knuckles.

I even went so far as to call Sherman Furl, the author of *Boots, Bats, and Sticks*. I knew it was a long shot, but when it came to Basha's acquaintances I didn't have much else to go on. Sherman was listed in the phone book at an address on Bank Street. I imagined Basha convalescing at his West Village apartment, Sherman writing a lead role for her in his new off-off-Broadway play. When I got his answering machine his nasally speaking voice annoyed me so much that I didn't leave a message.

I spent a whole day walking up and down First Avenue, hoping to catch a glimpse of Basha. I popped my head into Laundromats, florists, delis, cafés, guitar shops, palm readers' shops, hardware stores, sushi joints, bars and lounges, thrift stores, record shops, used bookstores, the McDonald's at Seventh Street, an apothecary's, a cobbler's, a used-furniture store, Indian restaurants, Italian restaurants, Ukrainian restaurants, Cuban Asian restaurants, and any other nameless storefront I happened upon.

I combed both sides of the avenue, from Houston to Fourteenth Street.

I scoured every open doorway.

Any woman with a navy peacoat and dark hair took on for me an almost lifesaving, mythical stature.

I didn't even realize I had forgotten to wear my corduroy coat until I caught a glimpse of myself in the display window of the Italian bakery on Eleventh Street. I was, in fact, sporting a pitifully stained short-sleeved white T-shirt, and my hair was standing out in about five different directions. I looked horribly thin and puffy-eyed. Among the carefully arranged cannolis and profiteroles I looked like the ghost of some forlorn homeless kid who'd died with a bad case of bedhead; either that or an insomniac, hormonally imbalanced version of Amelia Earhart. My mouth was as dead as an ax wound.

Why would Basha want to be with *that* freak? I thought.

On Sixth Street between First and A, I spotted a woman I was so certain was Basha that I grabbed her by the arm and spun her around, for which I nearly got slashed in the face with a key. The woman was practically forty and had severe acne scars and reptilian slits for eyes.

"I'm sorry," I said. "I thought you were someone else."

She turned and walked away, shaking her head and cursing under her breath.

Eventually, I mustered the courage I had in reserve and headed to Stuyvesant Town.

The Kieslowskis' building was in the southeast sector of Stuyvesant Town. Dirty rags of snow intermittently marked the balding mange of yellowish-gray lawns, on which a collection of flotsam whipped about in strange, seemingly choreographed mini-cyclones.

A few homeless men stood in mysterious rectangles of sunlight, motionless, somehow looking arranged, their heads hooded, their fists clenched. Perhaps this was a small group of the homeless who had been evicted from Tompkins Square Park that previous May? I imagined the rest of the exiled scattered about Manhattan, searching for little rectangles of sunlight to stand in.

The entrance to Basha's building had been wedged open with cigarette butts, so I was able to avoid having to use the surveillance phone to dial up and thus risk rejection at ground level. I wanted to confront Basha melodramatically, face-to-face, while looking into her eyes.

I went up to the seventh floor. I was relieved to find the elevator unoccupied; this gave me an opportunity to check my voice.

"Where the hell have you been for the past three weeks?" I growled at my blurry reflection in the brushed stainless steel doors. "I thought we loved each other!"

My voice was deep from lack of speaking.

My beard was mossy and looked barely postpubescent, like a jumbled collection of half-grown spider legs.

My eyes could have been a pair of stuffed and swollen anuses.

Over the fiberglass window of the elevator inspector's log, in black Sharpie ink, someone had written:

The World Is Designed to Destroy You!
Get off the Grid!
Shark Man Bites Cock!

There was a phone number scrawled beneath the graffiti. I had no idea what the three statements were supposed to inspire in the elevator's occupants. If one called the number, would a conversation take place? If so, would it be conducted by the author, or would it simply be a recorded message? What sort of advice might one gain from such a paranoid, apocalyptic message? Or was the three-line proclamation simply an urban poem?

After a moment I realized that I was once again staring at an elevator inspector's log. This brief reminder of the abortion clinic almost made me retch. I vowed to stay away from elevators for the time being. I would take the stairs back down, from Basha's, and as often as possible after my visit.

Behind the Kieslowskis' door I could hear the sound of a TV competing with a vacuum cleaner. I imagined Basha lying on the sofa, sipping chicken broth and watching a soap opera while her mother cleaned the house. The possibility of Basha's daytime-television nonchalance coupled with her dismissal of my nursing skills made me feel slightly bitter.

I knocked on the door.

Moments later, the vacuum cleaner ceased, a few chains and deadbolts were manipulated, and the door was opened.

Mrs. Kieslowski was a short, dark-haired woman with enormous, venous hands and icy-white skin. In her late forties, she was as beautiful as her daughter, but her eyes—green like Basha's—were tired. She wore what appeared to be a blue housekeeper's uniform. I found it odd that she was wearing this while cleaning her own apartment.

"Hello," she said. Her Polish accent was thick and luxurious.

"Is Basha here?"

"No," she said quickly.

Over Mrs. Kieslowski's shoulder I could see that the apartment was impeccably clean. She had been vacuuming a large, multipatterned area rug. The wine-colored sofa and matching Barcalounger were upholstered with thick plastic. In the center of a coffee table sat a crystal dish filled with wrapped butterscotch candies. The TV was indeed tuned to a soap opera, but there was no evidence that anyone besides Mrs. Kieslowski was watching it.

Wound tightly around her knuckles was a black rosary, most of which was hidden in her fist.

"Do you know where she is?" I asked.

"Who are you?" she asked.

"A friend," I said.

She studied me for a moment and said, "Are you this boy?"

The space between us seemed to take on a strange, religious quality. It was as if we were in some dislocated urban sacristy, and I was returning the sacred vestments to their proper positions and she was the supervising sexton.

"What boy?" I asked.

"This boy for to give her a baby," Mrs. Kieslowski said.

"Yes," I said. "I guess that's me."

I didn't see the slap coming. I just remember staring into her tired green eyes, feeling very much like an ashamed altar boy, somehow trying to summon forgiveness. Then there was the sting, like being blindsided by a ball on the playground.

The door was closed in my face, and its many chains and locks employed. Moments later, the sound of the vacuum cleaner resumed.

I stood in the hall and considered my options, which were slim at best. For a second I thought I might kick down the door and start demanding answers, but I didn't trust my karate skills and I feared another several months of knee pain.

So I knocked again.

A few seconds later the vacuum cleaner stopped again and the series of locks was undone. This time when she opened the door she was holding a hammer, which I found to be more surreal than threatening.

"I love your daughter, Mrs. Kieslowski," I heard myself saying. "I'm really sorry about what happened. I can't undo it. I wouldn't even know how to."

As we stood there the hammer seemed to take on a telekinetic prescience. "I haven't slept in three days," I added dramatically. "I just want to speak to her."

"Basha travel back to Poland with her papa," Mrs. Kieslowski said, still clutching the hammer. Her brow was furrowed. Her pupils seemed to contract with a contained fury. I noticed that the rosary was no longer wound around her fist.

"When did they leave?" I asked.

"This morning."

"Oh," I said. "Is there any way I could maybe call her in Poland?"

"No," Mrs. Kieslowski answered.

"Why not?" I asked.

"Because."

She pronounced it *becoz*, and the intonation was not a warm one.

"Is she coming back soon?" I asked.

"No," she repeated, with the exact same intonation.

And then she closed the door again.

And then the series of locks.

And then the vacuum cleaner.

I knocked one more time but there was no answer.

My cheek still stung from the slap, and when I got home and looked in the bathroom mirror I could make out little indentations where the prayer beads had bitten into my flesh.

Spring

THREE WEEKS WENT BY.

And then four.

Early March was even colder than February had been.

The pit bulls marched about the streets and the naked trees outside my window trembled so much at times that I thought I could hear them groaning.

I continued to collect unemployment.

I spent less time in my bedroom and found myself sleeping on the sofa more often.

I stopped showering and let my beard grow.

I developed armpit smells that could be compared to various bad potluck meat dishes.

I tried to befriend a mouse that mocked me with its courage.

One day I woke to realize that I hadn't seen the Loach in over two weeks. His sudden absence was like a spell of wicked rain subsiding. The apartment seemed to absorb sunlight in a new way. I checked the sofa and saw that his crumpled brown paper bag was missing, as was his *Wolverine* comic book.

He never returned, and I spent $115 changing the locks.

I ate tuna out of the can and stopped changing my clothes.

On March 23 I called Alexa and explained the fate of *Opie's Half-life.*

"You lost your *novel?*" she cried.

"It was stolen," I lied.

"Judy's been practically begging for it."

"I'm sorry," I said.

"Well, you have to find it!"

"Not possible." And I hung up, never to speak to her again.

Two days later I sold the Owl's laptop computer to a used electronics store on Canal Street for two hundred dollars and a large box of books to the Strand so I could pay the Con Ed bill; nothing rare or beloved, just the titles I had accumulated during my days at the publishing house. Paying for the new locks took a pretty big bite out of my unemployment budget. I would make two more trips to the Strand: one to stock up on nonperishables and one to cover a phone bill that included several international calls to Poland, during which I'd tried to get information on Kieslowskis in Lublin. It turned out that there were twenty-seven listings, and my inability to understand Polish left me feeling frustrated and inept.

The advent of spring brought to life the various aromas of the East Village like the thick, sudden smell of manure drifting across a windswept, recently fertilized Iowa field. But instead of cow shit and nitrogen there was the reek of pigeon death, putrefied pods of garbage, bus exhaust, ammoniac waves of urine, and the all-too-familiar, sickly sweet stench of human feces.

Tompkins Square Park had evolved from demolition to construction site and was now becoming home to a new breed of machines as the backhoes and bulldozers were replaced by larger, more powerful earthmovers, hydraulic dump trucks full of steaming asphalt, and rotund, perpetually spinning cement rigs that heaved their guts into the recesses of new foundations. This machinery was grinding out what would eventually become the new epicenter of the East Village.

On the southwest corner of my block, scaffolding had been erected to protect pedestrians from falling debris as trios of men employed a series of ropes and window-washing boxes to rappel up and down the front of St. Nicholas Carpatho-Russian Orthodox Church, restoring its century-old façade. That spring there seemed to be a perpetual symphony of jackhammers, sandblasting, and honking traffic.

On the St. Nicholas Carpatho's announcement board the following message had been arranged in white pushpin letters:

To Belittle Others
Is to Be Little Yourself

On Avenue A, a black homeless woman named Hot Dog was walking around with her head on fire. She would apply Noxzema skin cream to the singed, nappy ends of her Afro and ignite a three-inch-high blue flame that would burn for entire blocks at a time. She seemed to enjoy the shock and awe she inspired in others.

"Hot Dog, yer feckin' hair's on fire!" an Irish homeless man with tattooed eyelids told her as she passed him on Avenue A.

"No it ain't," Hot Dog replied. "That's just my mind makin ennigy!"

I started counting the black gobs of gum marking the sidewalks. The East Village walkways were like a graveyard of distended punctuation. Perhaps the streets themselves were a kind of grammatical purgatory where the periods, quotation marks, commas, colons, and semicolons from all the forgotten manuscripts and unpublished novels met their fate?

When I got into the thousands I stopped counting and started making strange bull's-eye noises instead. This asinine behavior numbed my lips, fatigued my cheeks, and inspired confused looks from passersby, so I eventually abandoned that as well. But the non-biodegradable black spots would haunt me for a long time.

On the corner of Tenth Street and Avenue B a middle-aged woman with Halloween hair used a bullhorn to announce to the rest of the neighborhood that there was an artist in the West Village who was sculpting unpoliced dogshit into the face of a Democratic presidential hopeful.

Apparently the likeness was uncanny.

The hair was perfect, she said.

The consensus was that the nose was miraculously similar.

"WE MUST VOTE FOR THIS CANDIDATE!" she cried hoarsely through her bullhorn. "WE MUST!"

New businesses were moving into the storefronts along Avenue A. There was a bridal-gown designer next to a fledgling burrito shop. A sushi restaurant next to a vegetarian anarchist café.

A fresh platoon of Connecticut teens could be seen clustered on the pavement in front of Lina's Deli, feigning homelessness in their army fatigues, flaunting their facial piercings and inoculated dogs.

"Got any change?" they'd say, bemused by their smelly little adventure.

"Help feed my dog?" they'd almost laugh to all who passed them.

I put into effect a fierce spare-change moratorium against these poseurs and started to bitterly resent them the day I realized that the condition of my clothes was slightly worse than that of theirs.

It rained a lot in April and I spent most of my time pacing back and forth in the apartment. In my room I made piles of things and stared at them and then made other piles with those original piles. I stacked the books that I hadn't yet sold to the Strand into little foot-high gravestones and mourned the author I would never be. This bit of grief mingled with the now ubiquitous, almost intestinal Basha ache and I wound up eventually transferring my clothes to the closet in the Owl's room, closing the door, and dramatically vowing to never enter my old bedroom again.

Practically speaking, I figured it wasn't wise to spend a third of my life in a space haunted by both love and a novel that was lost to the freezer of a broken refrigerator.

The books I'd left stacked in the room would serve as a kind of literary mausoleum and I imagined that someday, when I was older, I would sentimentally open the door and breathe in the sweet-stale air of grief and perhaps experience the slow, dull quivering of wisdom.

When I did sleep, infrequently and fitfully, I did so on the sofa. Lying in the former bed of my nemesis felt appropriate. This, too, would make me stronger. Deep within the cushions, the subtle, lingering smell of the Loach was as certain as the smell of the Mississippi River in August. And breathing him in felt somehow essential to my survival. After all, when it comes to overcoming spiritual contamination, one must ingest the toxin in small doses if one is to succeed in developing a true resistance. The vaccine cannot be born without a thorough understanding of the original bacillus.

I tried living in Feick's room for a few days, but I couldn't sleep because the scent of eucalyptus drifting from the Russian and Turkish bathhouse started to taint my dreams. I vowed to never patronize the bathhouse because its odor only reminded me of my failure to stay connected to my lost brother. Whenever I walked past it I would do so with disdain.

I tried to live in the Owl's room for a few days, too, but I was convinced that something was wrong with the floor, as several of the wooden parquet tiles had loosed themselves and the original floorboards were seemingly willing their way back to prominence. I swear I saw the nails rising as if they were being beckoned by an eerie prewar presence.

While the April showers turned the streets to glycerin I amused myself by recording the traffic of mice. There were scores of them, and one in particular would stop and stare at me almost mockingly, as if it might break into song. I was sure I was being ridiculed. Whenever I spotted a mouse, I would launch items I found between the couch cushions—loose change, ballpoint pens, and a bent spoon—across the living room, grenade-like.

In this same spirit of aerial assault, one morning I woke up and without even the slightest premeditation threw my replacement Smith Corona daisy wheel electric typewriter into the courtyard. When it hit it made a sound like the detonation of shoulder pads at the line of scrimmage.

For a fleeting moment I thought about pitching myself out of Feick's window as an encore, but I imagined the act yielding results that were more bitterly amusing than tragic, so instead of a botched suicide attempt I opted to go into the bathroom and sit on the toilet seat and make strange grunting sounds.

I had about a month and a half left of unemployment, so I decided to pardon my own death. After all, when it comes to choosing between living and dying, the security of economic solvency is always a practical, persuasive argument.

———

Using black ink on a yellow legal pad, I wrote a letter to myself from Basha. In the letter she told me she missed me and effusively proclaimed her love.

"Love, yes," she wrote several times.

She also wrote about the ocean that separated us and how she'd carved our initials into several trees in the various forests of Poland. She chronicled the beauty of Lublin and raved about the effects of her country's new free-market economy.

She also wrote about a production of *The Seagull* in which she had been cast in the role of the confused wannabe actress Nina Mihailovna Zaretchny. Rehearsals were going "exceedingly fortuitously," she wrote, and she wondered if I had ever read this "masterful Chekhovian drama." She went on to state that I would make an "exuberant and tragic" Konstantin Gavrilovitch Treplev and that being in rehearsals every day made her "effervescently contemplate" me always.

In closing she wrote that she was sorry she had had to leave New York City and would someday return to her "valiant secret librarian man."

I wrote the letter from Basha left-handed and mailed it to myself from the post office on Fourteenth Street between First Avenue and Avenue A. I couldn't wait to receive it, and for two solid nights I dreamed of the soothing, healing effects it would have on me.

When the letter arrived I opened it with the tip of a ballpoint pen and read it over and over, crying myself silly, clutching the yellow pages to my chest.

On May 1 a flat manila envelope was slid under the front door. The envelope contained a typewritten letter in a barely discernible legalese informing me that the building, which had been taken over by the bank due to the previous owner's inability to pay the mortgage, had been sold to a Japanese businesswoman named Yuka Logan. Ms. Logan, the new landlord, would be contacting me shortly about either vacating the premises or staying on as a tenant.

The market value of my unit was listed as thirty-five hundred dollars per month. The figure itself made my stomach contort into a small iron fist. As was indicated by the excellent paper stock and impressive stationery design, the letter had been drafted by a high-powered attorney, and I called the listed number to check its authenticity.

When a highly articulate legal secretary answered the phone at the the triple-surnamed law firm, I hung up and returned to the bathroom, where I again sat on the toilet seat in the dark for a while.

Three days before my twenty-fourth birthday, I received a brief letter from the Owl, dated June 7. It was scrawled on the back of a take-out menu from a Chinese restaurant in Ashland, Oregon, and it read:

> *DEAR HOMON,*
> *Three weeks ago Holy and I got married in Las Vegas.*
> *She's pregnant and I can't wait to be a father.*
> *Still traveling around in the van.*
> *I have stories.*
> *Love is a beautiful thing.*
> *We will be in NYC for a few days in July and we would love you to meet your godchild. We haven't come up with any names yet, but yours is one we are considering, my friend.*
> *More to follow soon.*
> *Yours,*
> *GLENWOOD*

Block Party

ON THE SECOND SATURDAY OF JUNE, there was a block party thrown below my window. There was an aluminum trailer stage on which a reggae band performed for three hours straight.

I watched the proceedings from the perch of my fire escape. Several of the small private businesses in the neighborhood brought their merchandise to the street and were shilling their wares from large folding tables. The trees, thick with leaves now, seemed to sway to the reggae music. I flirted with the idea of setting up a table and selling the remainder of my book collection, but I couldn't bring myself to do it.

Toward the east end of the block I spotted Feick walking hand in hand with a young Asian man. They stopped at a table of homemade jewelry and briefly handled a turquoise belt buckle. The reggae music pulsated as people milled about Tenth Street eating Polish sausages, soft pretzels, and lemon sorbet.

I used the fire escape to descend to the street. The rhythm section of the reggae band collaborated with me on this superhuman feat, and when the last segment of my building's ladder rolled down and I let go of the final rung and my feet met the street there was an ovation from the crowd that actually made me feel proud.

I made my way through the throngs of people, keeping my eye on Feick's white-blond head. He and his friend had moved away from the jewelry table and were now buying Italian ices from an elderly black man at the helm of a small refrigerated truck.

I tapped Feick on the shoulder just as he handed the man money for his Italian ice.

He turned. I saw that he looked healthy and happy, that his eyes were clear and alert.

"Hey," I said.

He said, "Hey. I was just on my way to see you. It's your birthday, right?"

"It is," I said.

There was an awkward moment that felt something like falling off a bike in front of a group of younger kids at the bus stop.

My brother's hair was long and wavy. He hadn't shaved, and there was the faintest hint of red in his beard.

"This is Ronnie," Feick said, introducing me to his new friend.

Ronnie and I exchanged hellos and then the elderly black man gave Feick his change.

"We were gonna go sit in the park and watch the bulldozers," Feick said. "Ronnie knows the guy who's doing all the ironwork. You wanna join us?"

"Sure," I said.

"He's a really cool guy," Ronnie said. "They just started putting in some of the new park benches, so it's sort of a privilege to get to watch."

Ronnie was smaller than Feick and had perhaps the most symmetrically perfect face I have ever seen. It turned out that he was a former member of the Marquette University diving team and was currently performing a late-night show at a theater in Chelsea with an all-Asian improv comedy troupe.

"I'd love to tag along," I said.

Overcome with sentiment, I hugged Feick.

I'm almost certain that I hugged him too hard and held on a little longer than an older brother might under normal circumstances.

Then I hugged Ronnie, too, who actually reciprocated and patted me on the back.

I hadn't been so happy to see someone in a long time.

Feick bought me a raspberry Italian ice and I ate it with a miniature tongue depressor. As we headed toward the hurricane fencing that was blocking off the Avenue B entrance to Tompkins Square Park, the breeze suddenly smelled strangely of urine and wet cherry blossoms.

Tenth Street was still damp from the early morning rain and the sun shone brightly on the tops of the trees.

"So, happy birthday," Feick said as we ducked under the makeshift fence.

"Thanks," I said.

He told me I looked thin and I nodded.

Backhoes, bulldozers, and other unmanned earthmovers sat idle throughout the park. I saw not a single homeless person—only a few NYPD squad cars roving about here and there.

My visit with my brother and his new friend was brief, but it felt good to reconnect. While the three of us ate our Italian ices, I told Feick that I was going to move back home and he nodded gravely and although he didn't let on I'm almost certain he was embarrassed for me.

Shortly after that we said our farewells and I walked back through the street fair and climbed the stairs to my apartment.

Three days later I boarded a westbound bus at Port Authority. As the Owl had reported during our Thanksgiving meal, the walls of the lower-level Greyhound terminal were plagued with a sea of orange tile that seemed to radiate a dull, mocking indifference.

My bus would arrive in Dubuque approximately one day and fifteen minutes later.

I had $172 dollars to my name, and I spent $135 on the bus ticket. I traveled with a duffel bag and another small suitcase containing a few toiletries and *The Alexandria Quartet*, which the Owl had left behind for me some months before.

I left in the refrigerator my unfinished novel about acute knee pain and the end of the world.

Acknowledgments

The author would like to thank David Halpern at The Robbins Office, the Camargo Foundation in Cassis, France, where the book was birthed, and Denise Oswald at Farrar, Straus and Giroux, whose dedication to seeing it through has been an inspiration.